FREE BOOK OFFER

**Get the companion novella
in the *Destiny* series FREE.**

Sign up for my no-spam newsletter
and get *BREACH*.

**Details can be found at the end of
*FIRST LAW OF ATTRITION***

FIRST LAW OF ATTRITION

BRONWYN LEROUX

Don't crush it! Carefully, I manipulate the controls guiding my airpliers, watching on screen as the camera in the tip of the pliers brings the microscopic gear into view. With minuscule adjustments, I angle the airpliers to grip the precious gear without damaging it, then ease it from the workspace to the waiting robotic hand.

While nanites can repair most injuries, even reattach severed limbs with a 99.23743% success rate, they can't recreate them. At least, not yet. Limbs devoured by feral creatures (supposedly roaming the tunnels under our city), lost to explosions, or obliterated by other accidents equal a body which can't be made whole again.

It's my job to change that. When Cygnus (Cirrian Conglomerate's Director, and my benefactor and boss) assigned this current project, he requested I invent something linking a robotic limb to the patient's residual neural tissue. My answer? These tiny intelligent gears. Once inserted and activated, fiberoptic tendrils unfurl, seeking the body's nerves, then smart-connecting to transmit signals between robotic limb and brain. Voilà! Integration facilitating movement.

I purse my lips in concentration as I maneuver the gear for placement. Almost there. Then Director Cygnus (as I'm allowed to call him) will use his vast power to arrange a visit with my family. Maybe even work his magic to wrangle a call with the one I haven't spoken to in over a decade.

"Chiara!"

I startle so violently I drop the gear. It tumbles onto the workspace, and my gaze dashes after it, worried it will disappear. Only when I'm sure it's settled on the workbench, safe, where I can reach it again, do I turn and glare at Sarissa. "What?"

Sarissa grimaces, the action highlighting perfectly accented cherry-red lips. "Sorry."

My best friend looks so contrite I have to smile. "You're forgiven." I wag a finger at her. "But only because I didn't lose my gear. What's so important you had to interrupt?"

"The director wants to see you."

The director. Much as he has a soft spot for me, he's still the single most powerful man on the planet—and not someone to trifle with. Also, someone who seldom asks for me mid-project. Have I done something wrong?

Dread leadens my bone marrow, turning my legs into gelatinous goo. My hands shake so much they knock over a nearby sample tray. I fumble for a rag, dabbing at the spilled liquids, the action an excuse for time to compose myself.

Being the friend she has become, Sarissa would recognize my trepidation if I looked at her. Evidently, she doesn't need eye contact to know how I feel. She places a hand on my arm and gives an encouraging smile. "You'll be fine. He's not going to eat you."

"Are you sure? I've heard his teeth are pretty sharp."

Sarissa giggles. "Come on! You know he'd never use them on you."

I wince. "So you say, but whenever he asks for me, it's like being summoned to the headmaster's office at the academy."

"Aw, it's not that bad. You know you're not in trouble. You've done so well on this project!"

Still, I can't shake the feeling this visit isn't a good thing. "Do you know what he wants?"

"No. Only that you've been summoned. So you'd better get moving."

Sarissa makes a shooing motion, and I tug my hands free of my gloves, then, reconsidering, put them back on. If I have to shake his hand—perish the thought—at least he won't know mine is sweating. A wild grin escapes. Small victories.

Not removing the rest of my lab gear, I scurry to the elevator assigned to whisk the censured to the director's office. If he asks, I'll tell him I didn't want to keep him waiting because I was removing my PPE. In truth, it's a shield. Although my specialized lab coat won't make me less apprehensive, I'll have more confidence if I'm wearing it.

Why can't Director Cygnus just leave me to play in my sandpit? I'm in my element there. After all, not every girl gets a fully stocked lab and unlimited resources to work with. But no, he had to interrupt! And when I was so close...

The elevator dings, and I step inside, tapping the button for the top floor of CC headquarters. Deliberately, I link my fingers in front of my stomach so I don't fidget. What could Director Cygnus possibly want with me today?

An eternity seems to have passed since the day he swooped in and rescued my family. Saved us from our broken world. Traumatic as that day—and those that followed—were, it's all in the past. While that awful day meant separation from my family, every action was for our benefit. Our lives are so much better now. All thanks to Director Cygnus.

Because of him, my family have opportunities they never could've dreamed of, and I have my lab (and a stellar underlying education) to invent to my heart's content. I'm proud to say my inventions have played no small part in healing our world.

And I'm back to wondering what the director wants. Is it a new task for my R&D labs, or something to do with me, specifically?

The elevator glides to a stop. It's time. My breaths are shallow as I exit and approach the woman anchored behind a desk squatting directly in front of the director's door.

"Mask!" she snaps.

I fumble it off. Hag Lady inspects my face, then gives a single nod to the door behind her. "He's expecting you."

Incapable of speech, I round the desk, wishing I had stopped to take a sip of water before getting into the elevator. Too late now. The black-garbed guards flanking the door observe as I raise a shaky hand to knock.

"Come!"

The command comes: imperious, cold, demanding. So like him. Or rather, how he behaves with other people. Reminding myself my fear is unfounded, I nevertheless stiffen my spine and lift my chin as I enter his sanctuary. A lamb to the slaughter. I stifle the urge to giggle. Where is my head at today?

Upon entering the room, I halt just inside the doorway, slapping my right hand palm down over left hand palm up, keeping my elbows elevated and straight out to the side. Then I slide my hands apart until my fingers catch at the ends, curling them up into a squashed delta symbol and drawing my hands together again. "All for one and work for all!"

"Chiara! So good to see you." Voice significantly warmer than when he bade me enter, Director Cygnus lounges behind his enormous hewn wood desk, rocking back in his (yes, real leather!) executive chair as greets me. Intense hazel eyes follow me into the room, but he makes no move to rise, so no handshake required. *Small mercies!*

"Thank you, Director. Likewise."

His laugh is jovial, but I never know how he manages it, considering his thin lips barely stretch enough to reveal his perfect teeth. "I am pleased to hear it. How is your project coming along?"

For a fraction of a second, I tense again. Did I miss a deadline? No, impossible. Even though I'm known for losing myself in my projects, it took only one failed deadline to make a point of setting several alarms, so I never repeated the error. Director Cygnus isn't very nice when I've vexed him. "On schedule, thank you, Director. I'm close. It's a matter of fine-tuning the link now. I should have a functional prototype soon."

Cygnus beams and claps his hands. The sharp, unexpected sound tenses my muscles as I repress the urge to jump. "Excellent! How do you feel knowing you will improve the lives of countless citizens?"

I relax, taking in his evident excitement, basking in his approval. I allow the smile I've repressed to surface. "Incredible! Thank you, Director Cygnus, for the opportunity to help these people. I can't wait to see the wonder on the first person's face when they use their new interactive limb!"

Glittering eyes study me. Did he notice my earlier apprehension? I hope not because it irks him when I'm afraid. The director has told me repeatedly I have nothing to worry about from him. Or is he just taking in my tumbled dark hair (a mess, since I haven't been home in days), the dark circles under my topaz eyes, or my waifish frame?

Uncomfortable under the director's continued scrutiny, I subdue the shiver as sweat trickles down my spine, surreptitiously moderating my breathing until a modicum of calm returns. "May I go, Director?"

With an audible huff, Cygnus rises from his chair and stalks around his desk toward me. I try not to cringe. Remaining where I am takes all my willpower. At only five foot five, it's difficult not to feel inadequate with him looming over me.

When he stops before reaching me, my breathing stutters back to normal. He perches on the corner of his desk. Not that it diminishes him. As if reading my thoughts, he says, "Sit, Chiara."

Wooden legs dump my body into the chair behind me. He hovers over me, his six-foot-one height seeming more than it is.

"I want you to assign your current project to someone else."

"What? I mean... pardon? But... I... my family—" The words stammer out before I can stop them. Before I remember who I'm talking to. Director Cygnus may be gracious where I'm concerned, but how many times do I have to remind myself he's still the director?

Cygnus waves an impatient hand. "Yes, yes, I've pulled some strings so you can still celebrate your achievement with your family. In fact, I've even managed to set up that meeting tomorrow."

Stunned, my mouth opens and closes, but no words emerge. This has never happened before. As Director Cygnus has often apologized for, rearranging my family's (equally hectic) schedules so they can spare time from their own dreams to meet with me is nearly impossible. If we all want to be our best, we should focus on finishing current tasks before rewarding ourselves for partial ones. As a result, I never get to see my family until I finish a project. Successfully. Why, then, would Cygnus allow me to see them now, with the project incomplete?

My brain races until I realize he's waiting. How could I forget? "Thank you, Director Cygnus. You are most generous."

The words stick. While Director Cygnus may be charitable towards me, this is out of character. There must be another reason. Has something happened to someone in my family? My thoughts arrow to the one missing member. The one I regret never saying goodbye to. Is there news?

Cygnus's face gives no hint of an answer. Instead, he ignores the thanks he typically adores and presses on. "I have a new project for you."

An answer. Not the one I was hoping for, but an explanation. To warrant such an unprecedented move on his part, this new assignment is either incredibly important or time-sensitive. Curiosity jabs me. "Certainly, Director. What do you need me to do?"

"Create a cold fusion energy source."

I blink, mouth gaping wide. I know, I know, I shouldn't be swallowing flies in front of Director Cygnus. But did he just say, "cold fusion energy source?" Clearing my throat doesn't quell the squeakiness when I speak. I don't care. "Excuse me, Director?"

His mouth thins into obscurity, displeasure creasing deep grooves into the corners. "You heard. A cold fusion energy source. I know I don't need to explain the concept to you."

I'm having trouble breathing. Someone has shoved a gigantic ball into my throat, blocking my airways. My lungs want to explode. How can he give me a project which seemingly defies the laws of physics? More importantly, if I can't do what the director asks, how can I keep my family safe?

2

Unable to breathe, I shove my head between my knees. I'm more worried about living than caring what the director gleans from my display. At least with my head down low, I can think without the additional burden of concealing my emotions. I wouldn't want to annoy Director Cygnus further.

But why didn't he block this impossible assignment from the Board as he has in the past? Kill it before it reached me? He's always taken care to ensure they never ask more of me than I'm capable of. It's integral to our relationship. Because, for as long as I've been under his care, we've had an understanding. Provided I churn out the inventions Director Cygnus assigns to his satisfaction, he makes sure my family continues receiving the benefits keeping them on the same societal tier as me. Benefits, without which, they would soon drop to the lowest tier. Or worse, disappear.

Yes, I've heard the rumors. Those who don't feed the voracious conglomerate machine vanish without a trace. No one knows where. And while my compassionate Director Cygnus would never subject me to that, his Board would have no such compunction. For them, it's all business. Whatever, or whoever, doesn't improve the bottom line goes. In a world of limited resources, our clean air, pure water, and ample food all come at a price. Is Director Cygnus powerful enough to protect my family if I can't deliver?

Cygnus's hand on my shoulder is little comfort. I know he means well, but his touch is unsettling. Sufficiently so to shake me from my pathetic response. One can never, ever show weakness to Cygnus McQueen, no matter how much you may mean to him.

Mortified, I bolt upright, the action knocking Cygnus's hand away. I barely register the simultaneous relief and fear as I scramble to pull myself together.

Cygnus's face is unadulterated concern. "Chiara, are you alright?"

I swallow. *Pull it together! They're just rumors!* "Yes, thank you, Director. I didn't have enough lunch. Just a small dizzy spell. You know how I get when my sugar's low."

A frown mars his handsome face. With skin bronzed by daily swims in the outrageously lavish amount of water squandered on his swimming pool, his perfect Roman nose, gilded hazel eyes, and temple-streaked dark hair, his overall appearance is golden. A presentation most find irresistible. Unfortunately, I'm not one of them.

Cygnus tuts. "Chiara, you know better."

"Yes, Director Cygnus. I'm sorry."

With a sigh, Cygnus leans back over his table and activates his intercom. "Julia, have the cafeteria bring food. For Chiara."

There's a brief pause before she replies. "Yes, Sir. For Chiara, Sir."

I would protest I couldn't eat right now, but that would only stir the pot of his anger. Best not to provoke him. "Thank you, Director Cygnus."

Cygnus studies me. "You know how important it is that you eat regularly. Why did you skimp on lunch?"

Flustered, I wave a hand and shrug. "I was too excited about finishing my project."

Another tut. "Yes, well now, we can't have that, can we?"

For a dreadful moment, I think he's going to cancel the visit with my family. It's how he shows he cares for me, reminding me to eat as I should so I remain healthy. I rush to answer. "No, Director, we can't. I'll exercise more discipline." I hold my breath. *Did it work?*

But he ignores my reply. His mind is elsewhere. Voice quiet, he asks, "Who brought your lunch today?"

Terror clamps my throat again. If I tell him, they'll suffer. They don't get the same courtesies I do. I pretend panic. Not that difficult. "I don't know, Director Cygnus. I'm sorry. I wasn't paying attention."

Cygnus steeples his fingers, then raises them to just under his chin, his eyes distant. Thinking man pose. "Yes, well, *they* should have been." Shaking his head, he drops his still-clasped hands to his lap, then focuses on me again. "I know this seems an insurmountable task, Chiara. But I've given you other assignments in the past which, on the surface, appeared impossible. You conquered them all. Why should this be any different?"

I want to scream. *Because all the other projects you gave me weren't things people spent centuries failing at!* But anger will accomplish nothing. Needing time, I ask the question I know he craves hearing. "Why would you like me to do this?"

I've never understood his reasons for requiring such a banal question. I already know he's the best director we could ask for. How much he does to improve our lives. Or could it be to remind me how much *I* should appreciate *him*? While I'm grateful for everything he's done for my family and me, I can't possibly think of him as anything other than a surrogate father. If that. *Ew*! The mental image I just conjured is disgusting. (And seriously, Chiara?) I glance at Cygnus, wondering if he noticed my grimace, but his eyes are distant again.

"We need a cold fusion energy source for several reasons. Foremost, our planet must remain healed from the fuels that previously polluted it. You're well aware how toxic the air became because of those fuels and how that toxic air led to the virus that wiped out billions. However, now that we've cleaned the air, population numbers are rising again."

"I'm sorry, Director, I'm not seeing the correlation."

"An increasing population means a greater demand for power. With our raw materials dwindling, it's only a matter of time before we are forced to resort to fossil fuels again. An action that can only result in history repeating itself."

"So… your proposed clean energy means the virus won't return?"

"Not only the virus, but the starvation accompanying it."

My brain scrambles. "I don't understand. Didn't the food carriage system and greenhouses I invented—" His eyes flash, the only warning he's taking offense at my audacity to take credit for his assignments. "My pardon. The projects commissioned at your request—didn't they improve nutritional quality and speed up plant growth so we could abolish hunger?"

The director's sigh makes me feel like an imbecile. I rebuff annoyance, wanting an answer.

Cygnus's stare is meaningful. "What do you think allows those greenhouses to run?"

"Oh." The word is small as I finally understand. "They need power."

When Cygnus nods and smiles, I fear he may lean forward and pat my shoulder again. Thankfully, he doesn't because me squirming away wouldn't have helped me make my point. A point I must convey. "Thank you, Director, for helping me understand. I appreciate your concern for the people. We are fortunate to have someone as forward-thinking as you at the helm of the conglomerate. And thank you for the wonderfully interesting projects you assign me. You know how I love inventing things. However, I confess, I sincerely doubt my ability to bring this cold fusion project to fruition."

The smile vanishes, the sharp angles on Cygnus's face becoming as unyielding as obsidian. "Need I remind you what happens when you defy the Board?"

I gasp, my breathing forsaking me again. My hands claw at the arms of my chair. He wouldn't let them do that! But his steely glare tells me he wouldn't have a choice. No matter how much he may want to, he could not intervene. So much for my attempt at making him understand. With difficulty, I gulp air, easing the ache in my lungs.

When I have the strength to speak, I concede. "No, Director, you need not remind me. I will do as you ask." Even as the words leave my mouth, I'm dying inside. As my family soon might be if I fail.

"Go home and think about it."

The director's command is as unusual as it is a dismissal. I rise, turning to go.

"Did you forget something?"

I pause, sparing a second to compose myself before turning back. Repeating my earlier actions when I entered the room, I conclude with the customary slogan. "All for one and work for all!"

Cygnus nods and waves his hand, a formal eviction as his eyes return to his work.

Exercising supreme willpower, I resist the urge to flee. With measured steps, I make it to the elevator, tapping the button to whisk me to a safer place. Then I wait, numb and staring mindlessly at the floor.

3

The elevator dings, and I jump, then scuttle inside as soon as the doors split wide enough. I want to sink back against the far wall, collapse onto the floor. But what if someone sees? I must keep it together, just a little while longer.

Only when I reach the sanctuary of the lab floor and tumble out do I crumble. Darting through the aisles between the workbenches to my office, I rush inside, keeping my back to the door as I struggle for air. It takes long minutes before I've restored my lungs sufficiently.

"How did it go?"

I whirl, startled by Sarissa's question and her sudden appearance in the doorway. Then I'm momentarily flummoxed when I realize I don't know how to answer. *Oh, you know. My family is going to die a horrible death, and I'll be to blame because I couldn't deliver on an impossible project.* Sure, that'll fly. While Sarissa may be my best (only) friend, there are still some secrets I've yet to share with her. I shrug.

Sarissa studies my face. "That bad, huh?"

I rally, reminding myself she's a tier eight. She can't learn the whole truth. But part of it won't hurt, and it'll stop her pursuing this line of questioning. "The director is giving my project to someone else."

Sarissa's warm chocolate eyes, with their enviable lashes, round to match the *O* of her startling cherry-red mouth. "What? He can't! You've worked so hard on it." Sarissa slaps her hands onto her hips, leaning forward. "Do you want me to speak to him?"

As the daughter of two prominent members of Cygnus's Board, Sarissa has limited protection. But I would never want her in the director's crosshairs because of me.

With a shake of my head, I wave away her offer. "Thank you, but the director's right. I'm far enough along on the project for someone else to complete it."

A quirk of those perfectly plucked eyebrows. "Really? You're just going to hand it over?"

Suddenly, it's all too much. I'm suffocating in my PPE. Unbearably hot in the silly suit. My pulse races, and my head hurts. Worse, the thought of standing here and lying to Sarissa for a second longer is intolerable.

"Well, he gave me the afternoon off. Said I should go home and think about it. So, I'm leaving." I yank at the ties, stripping off my PPE. My relief increases with each piece that falls to the floor.

Sarissa gapes. Not because I'm leaving, but because it's unlike me to blow her off. I don't even resort to that when dodging her attempts to drag me to the nightclubs she frequents.

I place a placating hand on Sarissa's arm. "Sorry, I need rest. You know how many hours I've invested, especially this past week. Some downtime will do me good. I don't want to look like a ghoul when I see my family tomorrow."

Pleasure suffuses Sarissa's face. "You do?" Then she crinkles her nose. "I mean, get to see your family, not look like a ghoul."

A small smile teases my lips. She knows how much my family mean to me. "I do."

Sarissa squeezes my hand. "Then you'd better get home and catch up on your beauty sleep. Want me to come over and do your face in the morning?"

This time, my smile is more heartfelt. "No, I think I've got it."

"You sure? You still don't quite have the knack of—"

I give her a playful shove. "Stop fussing. My makeup may not be as perfect as yours, but it's only improved since you started coaching me."

Laughing, Sarissa shakes her head. "Well, if you change your mind, you know where to reach me."

I tap the comm link under the skin behind my right ear. "I sure do." Across the massive expanse of the lab floor, I spot the Serenity Sentry hurrying toward me, food tray in hand. The stuffy SerSent looks pompous in his imperious olive uniform, its shiny silver buttons bouncing as he trots along. Time to go.

As I dash for the elevator, I toss parting comments to Sarissa over my shoulder. "Don't stay out partying too late tonight. I need you sharp tomorrow, so you can help me draw up a list of suitable candidates to 'hand' the project over to."

Sarissa's face souring at my pun is the last thing I glimpse as I make my escape. In seconds, I'm free of the gleaming chrome-and-glass monstrosity dominating the skyline, marking CC's HQ. No coincidence it's located in Cirrian, the city named after the almighty conglomerate which controls the world.

I jog through the park surrounding the headquarters to the light rail, my ride home. Waiting for the trundle, I realize this is another piece of technology requiring power. Can't Cygnus dump all the tech?

Laughter bursts free (lucked out! No one around to witness my descent into madness!), thinking of a world cast back to the Stone Age. That would be quite something. Especially considering technology gave CC the power to seize the world. Whoever thought one little tech security company would expand into a multinational conglomerate with the resources to topple economies and sink governments?

With a whoosh of air, the trundle glides into the station, disrupting my thoughts. Hissing, it settles on the maglev tracks, and the doors slide open. People may call it the trundle, but it's no slouch zipping around the city.

I hurry inside and find a seat before the thrust accompanying the train's departure throws me off balance. As I drop into the hard plastic, I wince, wishing there were other options for travel, options where the conglomerate's provisions didn't limit my travel choices. Cygnus and his Board use helivates: personal flyers, like jumbo drones with quarter-circle-shaped passenger domes perched on rectangular frames supporting the skids below. Long running rails span the lengths between dome and skid frame, extending well beyond the edges, and bear the four massive propellers, shooting the helivate to its destination.

Now, if I had a helivate, I could go where I wanted. I sigh, thinking of the series of commands my life is. Live in this sector, eat now, work on this project, ride the trundle, shop only in these areas.

Stop it, Chiara! I'm succumbing to the POMs (poor-old-me's) because I'm tired. I do genuinely love my work (what's not to love when I get to invent all day, every day?), and I'm thankful for my incredible life. Even the nimble trundle. As I stare out of the window, I dimly recall a time when the only option was my own two feet. I turn away from the memory. Those times were so difficult. Do I even want to remember them?

Fear threatens to paralyze me once more as my mind drifts back to my family. I can't let them down! They depend on me for their wellbeing. If I fail to fulfill Cygnus's request, they will pay the price. Like they did that one awful occasion when I dared defy the Board in my youth, because I didn't know any better. Because I didn't know the conglomerate didn't tolerate childish tantrums. It was a terrible object lesson. Because of me, my family was left without a protector, and without a protector, my family were helpless.

Not for the first time, my heart contracts, hurting. I desperately want to see my father again. He left that fateful day and never returned. If only I'd said goodbye. If only I'd given him a hug and kiss when I had the chance. If only he hadn't gone away…

I'm convinced if my father had been there, he would never have allowed Cygnus to separate me from my family. Why *did* Cygnus do that? What made him single me out? I still have no answer. And he's still Cygnus. The only difference now is his suits are more expensive —and he wields more power.

Since the dreadful day when he isolated me from my family and placed me under his personal care, so much has changed. From my early years sequestered in the secluded halls of the academy until now, I've gained multiple doctorates, become the head of CC's R&D labs, helped create a world infinitely different from the one I was born into, and secured the education my siblings will need if they're to compete in this tiered society. An awful lot to be thankful to one man for.

While I still mourn the separation from my family, I accept Director Cygnus's point. Limiting their potential because I want their time would be selfish of me. At least he's kind enough to insist they make the time to see me when I finish projects so we can celebrate.

But now Director Cygnus has demanded a project I can't possibly complete. *No, he's allowed the Board to sneak one past him.* What if this was always where my relationship with Cygnus was headed?

Appalled, I'm stunned it's taken me so long to reach this realization. Then again, while I can decipher complex chemical and mathematical formulas with ease, reading people and situations has never been my forte. I wilt in my chair, crushed by the blow. But my mind races. Life can't continue this way. Something must change. I just have to be the right kind of "smart" to come up with a solution.

4

This resolution grants a measure of peace, and my gaze finally absorbs the beauty on the other side of the window. A lush park speeds by, the water spraying in its fountains transformed into shimmering rainbows by the sun.

Seconds later, we slide into the dappled shadows of a small glade. The sturdy trunks stand sentinel over scattered berry bushes, banked potato rows, stringy pepper plants, and curly parsley greens crowding the spaces between.

We hurtle back into full sunlight and round a corner. In the distance, a waterfall cascades down the side of the cliff, hemming the western edge of our city. Then it's gone as apartment buildings rise on either side of me, their lower levels stuffed with the malls Sarissa loves shopping in. Bright windows shiny with merchandise slip past in a blur of color and light.

Before I've had time to prepare, my body jerks forward as the trundle slows for my stop. I rise as the doors open, then race out, eager to get home.

Sudden weariness dogs every step as I trudge the two blocks to my building. Finally, my body is succumbing to the extended hours spent in the lab. The lack of sleep. Also, that empty pit in my stomach is telling me it's been too long since I've eaten.

I'm sagging by the time I reach the ornately etched glass doors announcing the mezzanine level of my building. The doors discern my approach and swish open, welcoming me, and I stumble inside. My eyes slip to the bustling lower levels as I shuffle down the concourse to a tiny foyer allowing residents access to the apartments above.

As my hand clasps the brass handle of the foyer door, the sensors within register I'm a legitimate resident, and the lock clicks open. Ensconced in the tiny foyer, I sink forward for the retinal scan. My second biometric accepted, the elevator door opposite the entrance yawns open.

Not registering the trip up to the lower mid-levels, I have eyes only for the door to my apartment as the elevator sighs away. I slog the last few feet, then pass my wrist over the scanner to open the door. Home.

Or rather, a space that's all mine, but not a home. Homes are filled with life and family and laughter. Deep longing fills me as I think of my family. Then sheer joy surges up and drowns the sorrow. *I see them tomorrow!*

No, the clinical lines marking out the utilitarian cabinets on the walls of the small white and stainless steel kitchen will *not* get me down. Not tonight. Nor will the conglomerate-provided furnishings dampen my excitement, even though they're another stark reminder of all the space lacks. Their ultramodern style is absent of personality and, by extension, warmth.

Besides, I could change this if I wanted. Al-Li knows I can afford to buy better furniture. Another way Director Cygnus has taken care of me. My salary as head of CC's R&D labs is obscene. Not to mention the insane bonuses I receive when I complete a project. Neither matter since the only reward I want is time with my family.

Despite my desire to cling to the elation suffusing me only seconds before, sudden loneliness overwhelms me. Abruptly, the furniture rankles, a reminder of what my life is. Spartan, functional, unemotional. The thought elicits a weary sigh. Enough of the POMs. Food, a hot shower, and bed. I'll only be able to think clearly, make decent plans, once I've dealt with those. I wish I could skip straight to bed, but if I don't eat, I'll wake in the night. The last thing I need right now is a disturbed sleep.

Opening my magic refrigerator (it restocks itself!), I scan the rows of prepackaged food. The glut of options sparks a memory, something the director said. How is starvation still possible? Even if the population has increased, the greenhouses I designed speed up food production exponentially. Plus, the carriage system I invented allows us to add nutrients to improve our food's nutritional quality, further reducing consumption. A food shortage is inconceivable.

I work the math in my head but still can't fathom a solution. Unless the population has increased a thousandfold (unlikely in the five years since I created the carriage system), things don't add up. But my head is hurting again. And I'm dithering, as I'm prone to when I'm this exhausted.

With a sigh, I coax myself into action, selecting a roast beef and vegetable meal and sliding the pre-packaged food into the blitz. Five seconds later, the food is perfectly hot. Using quick jabs of my fingertips, I flick the heated food tray onto an empty plate.

Exhausted, I sink onto the (offensive) couch and call up my recording of *Casablanca*. Its exorbitant price tag was worth every cent. I take guilty pleasure watching something the conglomerate-run channels would never ordinarily screen. A fitting reward I treat myself to when I finish a project.

I settle in as the familiar first scene launches and tuck into my dinner, suddenly ravenous. The food vanishes before my stomach registers I've fed it, and for a moment, I debate a second meal. But that would be too much, and I have no desire for the "snacks" I'm provided with. (Aren't snacks supposed to be unhealthy and crave-worthy?) Dessert, on the other hand...

That's the last thing I remember thinking before I doze off. I rouse to find the closing credits rolling. With a yawn, I shut the entertainment system down and bumble off to bed.

I wake the next morning, starving and itching for a shower. A quick check of the time confirms I can eat at home today, so I pop my favorite protein bowl in the blitz and guzzle it while reading a thriller Sarissa recommended. Can't say it's holding my attention, though. The spy is skulking about, trying to gather information, and I'm just not in the mood. I need to get clean.

As I stand under the jets pummeling my body from every angle, I savor the scalding water stinging my skin. I still marvel every day at the ability to take a shower, let alone the miracle of heated water.

Before Cygnus entered our lives, my mother used to scrub us down once a week with a dirty, damp sponge. Water was that scarce back then. A nagging thirst permeates every memory of those long-gone childhood days. I doubt I'll ever forget the intense desire to drink something or the inability to satiate that need.

Clean air to breathe. Food for the taking. And water enough for showers. Cygnus truly has made the world a better place. Although his swimming pool is still an excess. Especially given its size. What does one person need so much water for? If you want to get your exercise by swimming, use a training tank like everyone else.

Sarissa says it's Cygnus's way of demonstrating how special he is. Granted, it does set him apart. And I have to admit, he can only do things like arrange meetings with my family because he's so special.

Excitement fizzes. My family! I see them soon! It's been months since we last met. How much will my younger siblings have changed? I notice their changes the most, probably because they're growing. Unlike my mother, who seems to shrink. Is this simply the effect of her younger children getting taller or time taking its toll on her? She's getting older, and I'm not around to help her.

I shove the miserable thought aside and stop thinking, focusing on the water, letting it slough my cares away. When I feel refreshed, I toggle the switch, and the water becomes heated air, blasting across my body and driving the water droplets away. When the nozzles sense my skin is dry, they pepper it with a soothing lotion.

Stepping from the stall, I rub the lotion in, the delicious French pear fragrance a heady balm easing me into the day ahead. Mood remarkably restored, I run a comb through my mass of chestnut hair, almost too much for my head, and viciously knotted after extended hours in the lab over the past week where I forgot to brush it.

Once I've tamed the tangle, I turn to leave and catch sight of my petite body in the full-length mirror on the opposite wall. I'm slouching again. An old habit from years of wanting to go unnoticed. Also, not the image "Director Cygnus" wants me to present.

Perish what he wants! Has he known all this time what I only just realized? And *Director Cygnus?* I snort. What a joke! How could someone who claims to care for me do this to my family?

In a blur, memories rush back, reminding me of all he *has* done, leading to a single, startling conclusion: Cygnus really *does* believe I can build this cold fusion energy source. Otherwise, he never would've asked. He doesn't want to put my family in jeopardy any more than I do.

Although surprised by this realization (will the man's faith in me never cease?), it doesn't erase my own doubt, either about my ability to build the machine or the potential consequences for my family if I don't succeed. There's more than one solution here, though. Resolute, I straighten and square my shoulders, then march out of the bathroom, mulling possibilities.

I don my usual "uniform," the one Sarissa can't abide: a t-shirt, flannel overshirt, and jeans (yes, the designer kind Sarissa made me buy!). Then I hurry out of the bedroom. My eyes graze the living room wall clock, and I curse. I spent longer in the shower than I intended.

Quickly grabbing an apple (delicious things!), I snatch up my purse and race out of my building. Only when I'm stepping onto the trundle do I remember I forgot to put makeup on. So much for all those hours Sarissa spent teaching me. My family won't care (sooo excited!), but Sarissa won't be impressed.

The thought makes me grin. I'll just tell her I need her skills—in a speed session. That'll make her day. And mine, because she can erase those dark rings under my eyes like no one else.

Scampering into CC headquarters with a scant half hour to spare, I dash to the labs. Sarissa should already be there. As my personal assistant, her first daily task is to brief me on my schedule. Besides, she'll want to see me before the visit with my family—if only to check how well I dolled myself up!

I'm not disappointed. Her welcoming smile turns upside down as she notices the lack of cosmetics. Before she says anything, I sidle into her office. "Don't you look gorgeous, as always! Good morning! I hope you have your war paint with you."

She blinks, then laughs. "Oh, I get it! You want me to do your face?"

With a nod, I take a seat. "There was no point in me handling it. You'd just want to fix it when I got here, so have at it. I'm all yours for the next," I glance at the clock, "twenty minutes. Think you can make me look half as pretty as you?"

A giggle is her only answer as she gets to work. I need something to take my mind off the imminent visit. "What did you do last night?"

Sarissa shares snippets about the new club she tried, not sounding overly enthused. What a relief. If she doesn't like the club, it's one less place she'll try to drag me off to. Sarissa prattles on, and I listen with half an ear.

"Stop squirming."

The admonishment makes me realize I've been fidgeting as the clock ticks ever nearer to the appointed time. I'm abruptly over the entire process. "Are you almost finished?"

With a flourish, Sarissa leans back and pulls a mirror from her bulky purse. I stare at the person reflected back at me, so totally unlike my usual unadorned visage.

Sarissa's talents have highlighted the steel-gray rimming my topaz-blue eyes, turning them into huge, tranquil pools hinting at deep water. The peach tint glossing my lips makes them look as juicy as the fruit. While she's covered the dark smudges under my eyes, I'm relieved Sarissa left the rest of my porcelain skin without foundation

—probably only because excitement already flushes my cheeks a delicate pink.

"So?"

"I'm stunned. Spectacular job as always." I bounce up and hug her. "Thanks!"

Pleasure radiates from her. But Sarissa holds the hug for a second longer than necessary. I want to pull back, eager to see my family, yet something tells me she desperately needs this hug today.

When Sarissa releases me, I draw away and study her face, noticing the hints of exhaustion under the makeup. Then I realize how unusual it was for her to have been so ambivalent about a new club. "Hmm, I think more happened last night than you mentioned?"

Sarissa's face falls. "I'm sorry. I didn't mean to throw a dampener on your day." She sniffs, then waves anxious hands in the air. "Go, go, you're going to be late!"

I don't budge. "Are you going to tell me about it?"

Distress now marks every tense line of her body. "Yes, yes. But not now. You must go." This time, she actually pushes me, nudging me out of her office.

Alarm bells jangle. I don't know that I've ever seen Sarissa this agitated before. "Sarissa, what's wrong?"

Dashing a hand under her eye—is she catching a tear?—she almost shouts. "Not now! Later! Go, see your family." Then noticing my devastation, she adds, "Please. It's nothing. Just ignore it for now. I don't want to spoil your visit."

Troubled, but knowing how stubborn she can be, I nod. "Fine. But as soon as I get back, we're having a chat."

Sarissa nods, pushing me all the way out of her office, then closing her door. I stare at it. Panic squirms. A snake trapped in a pit. What happened?

A hand touches my arm. I jerk, startled, and turn to find a SerSent at my elbow. "Your family is here. Follow me."

Consternation over Sarissa wars with excitement over the impending visit. But I can't be thinking about Sarissa when I see my family. I can't focus on anything except them. Every moment with them is precious, not something I should squander.

With considerable effort, I steel myself and cram my concern for Sarissa into a box way too small for the problem, I trail the SerSent to my waiting family.

5

As we approach the room holding those I love, I attempt a few deep breaths to calm a heart beating so frantically blood pounds against my skin with each pulse. Trying to rub the throbbing discomfort away, I wait for the SerSent while he passes his wrist over the access lock.

With a soft click, the door opens, and I brush past, not caring if I bowl the SerSent over barreling into the room. The elated faces waiting for me are the catalyst for tears, streaming down my cheeks. I try to hug them all at once (I know that never works), but it's the quickest way of touching everyone. To verify they're real, truly there.

My mom allows a few seconds before extricating herself from the complex bundle of arms, her cheeks also soaked with tears. Her hair is even grayer, her face more lined than ever.

Releasing the others, I take her into my arms. "Hey, Mom. It's wonderful to see you."

She says nothing, just nods. Our shared emotional distress is too great for either of us to talk. Then Mom releases me, gently wiping a finger under my right eye. "Can't let you spoil that perfect face."

I'm blank for a second. Then I realize she's referring to the mascara, which must've run with my tears. Laughing, I swipe at the same spot on the other side. "Sarissa wouldn't be thrilled if I spoiled her work."

"How is she?"

My mom's question obliterates the time we've been apart. As I reply, I tug Xanin, my oldest sibling, into my arms. There's no doubt we're related. Same heart-shaped face, same upturned nose, same mass of riotous dark hair, but his eyes are dark coffee, and his tattoos contrast with my unmarked skin. Younger than me by eighteen months, he's been taller for about as long.

Xanin's grin as we exchange hugs is a delightful change from his usually sullen expression. One revealing how young he still is, despite his height.

"How tall are you now?" I step back and fully extend an arm, barely skimming the top of his head. Last time, I could reach the same spot with ease.

Xanin chuckles. "Tall enough to look older than you."

A laugh burbles out, and I slap his arm, unsurprised by the bulky muscle my hand encounters. "Nothing new. People always thought you were older because I'm so petite. But now, these shoulders," I whistle appreciatively, stretching my arms wide to touch either end, "those are impressive! You're turning into a bit of a beast."

A faint blush warms his cheeks, and his expression turns sheepish. "Thanks."

"Been working on them?"

"Don't you know it." Xanin smiles, but this time, it doesn't reach his eyes.

Cursing myself inwardly for my mistake, I try a different tack. "Have you been equally diligent with your education?"

The scowl doesn't disappoint. "Aw, Chiara, did you have to go there?"

My mother laughs and clips the side of his head. "I told you she'd ask."

That only deepens the scowl. But he gets points for answering. "I'm working on it. Gangly Ivan still reigns. I doubt I'll ever be first."

Laughing, I squeeze his hand. "You'll get there. Just keep at it."

A pair of weedy arms wends their way between us. "I'm going to be as tall as Xan, and look, my muscles are growing!"

I drop to my haunches and gently squeeze the tiny bulge in Frankie's wiry little upper arm. At twelve, he's showing no signs of a growth spurt yet. "Wow! Those are huge!"

An impish grin darts across his face. "I've been training. Xan's been teaching me."

"Yes, but we don't use the big boys yet, do we?" Xanin notices my confusion and gestures at Frankie. "Tell Chiara about the big boys."

Frankie slides onto my lap, little arms curling around my neck as he explains "the big boys," the hefty weight plates the older kids use. I'm too distracted by the sweet smell of my baby brother to pay attention. More so when gorgeous raven-haired, ice-eyed Octavia slides up next to us and tries to perch on the leg Frankie isn't using.

I slip an arm around her waist and pull her in, tucking her against my body. Tall and willowy, her height, like Xanin's, comes from my father. I take after my mother, who is even shorter than I am.

I smile at Tavi, and she grins back. With all the moody, privileged teenagers I had to deal with at the academy, I can honestly say Tavi's the happiest fourteen-year-old I've ever met. A shadow scuds across my thoughts again. I know the reason for her bliss.

Xanin is their protector. He's taken the place of my father, a role he was always too young to assume, but one he foisted on himself in my absence. If only Cygnus had allowed us to all attend the same academy. Then I could've shared the burden—because Xanin would never have allowed me to shoulder it alone.

For the umpteenth time, I wonder why Cygnus separated me from my family. And what happened to our father on that day? I don't want to ask, but I can't help myself. "Any news?"

The crestfallen faces are answer enough. Swallowing the disappointment, I cradle my two youngest siblings in even closer. The physical contact eases some of our anguish.

My mother rests a hand on my shoulder. Her pale blue eyes are worn, but her smile is warm, displaying the dimples we share. "No news is good news."

I wish I could agree. It's been eleven years since any of us heard from my father. He's on a mission in space, one the director told my mom would keep him from us for at least fifteen years. Cygnus said the distance prohibits communication with us, but I've seen those old movies. The ones I have the money to buy. The conglomerate would never send people so far away without the ability to send information back.

My secret fear, the one I haven't shared with my mom and siblings, stems from what else those old movies showed: how easy it was for things to go horribly wrong. While I'm well aware this is real life and not a movie, what if we haven't heard from my dad because he was a casualty of the mission?

The day my dad left home and never came back is a hazy memory. I remember only two things distinctly: never having the chance to say goodbye (why didn't he wake me before he left?), and the chaos afterwards when Cygnus arrived, then separated me from my remaining loved ones.

The depressing thoughts have me reaching for more cheerful memories. "Tavi, can you still catch a ball?"

Tavi grins. "That's a random thought! Of course I can. Why do you ask?"

"Remember the red ball we used to play with for hours?"

Tavi sobers. "How could I forget? I loved that ball. Dad brought it home for us." Before the void where our father belongs consumes the space, she smiles, pride on her face. "It was the only ball in our entire neighborhood."

I nod, remembering, then glance at Xanin. "Remember how we rented it out so we could get extra food?"

"I do."

My heart pinches at the memory. Not for the ball rental, but for what Cygnus did to my family the one time I rebelled. "At least we don't have to worry about being hungry anymore."

A stilted silence follows my comment, and I flounder, unsure of the reason or what to say. As usual, my mother steps in to rescue me. "Tell us your news. What success are we celebrating?"

By now, I should know. As much as I yearn for their news, their desire for mine is equally strong. Over the years, I've learned to gloss over the scientific details because, when I talk about my work, I get lost in it. And lose my audience after the first few sentences. As a result, my family get the basics—enough to understand the gist of my projects without overwhelming them with specifics. I explain my last project helped those who'd lost limbs.

Frankie squirms, locks of golden-brown hair sliding over one another, prompting me to finger-comb them back into place. "What's a limb?"

I pause, wondering if I should've perhaps excluded him from this conversation. Then again, he must've seen people without limbs. I'm told there are plenty. "A limb is another word for someone's arms or legs. Our hands and feet are pentadactyl limbs, meaning they're limbs with five digits."

"Pen-ta-dac-tyl." Frankie sounds the word out.

"That's right!" I squeeze him, enjoying his soft, cuddly body curled against mine.

"How do people lose their limbs?"

The little furrow on his brow has me hiding a smile when I realize he's imagining people removing a limb and leaving it somewhere. I search for an age-appropriate answer.

"Sometimes people have accidents. When they do, they might hurt, say, their leg really badly. So badly that they can't use it again. Then we say they lost their leg." Frankie scowls. "They didn't really misplace their leg—they lost the use of it. Understand?"

Solemn cobalt eyes meet mine as the frown disappears. "That's very sad."

"It is."

"I'm glad you can help them." Frankie's arms twist around my neck again.

I duck my head, tucking my nose into the sweetness of his neck. Such a precious boy. Suddenly aware of time slipping by, I blow a raspberry onto the tender skin.

Frankie shrieks with laughter and jumps off my lap, running away.

Smiling, I turn laughing eyes on Tavi. She giggles and leaps out of reach. "Oh no, you don't!"

"What, you're too old for me to play with?" I jump up and chase her around the room.

Raucous laughter fills the tiny space as Xanin joins in, he and I pursuing our two younger siblings. I've missed doing this with him. I've missed *him*. My partner-in-crime.

Before Tavi arrived, it was just the two of us. Then Mom was so busy with Tavi, it only cemented our bond. By the time Frank Jr. arrived (Junior to recognize my father, Francois, who insisted on a less elaborate name), Xanin and I were inseparable.

Xanin is the sibling I've missed the most. In the years we've been apart, he's slipped a little further away with each visit. A loss I grieve every time I see him. Especially when I perceive what he's turning himself into so he can protect my mother and younger siblings.

Frankie squeals as I make a grab for him and miss. He was just a baby when Cygnus stole our time together. So this wild running around, a version of tag, is what Frankie expects in these limited family meetings. The only connection we've been able to form over the past decade.

As we race past my mother, I spare her a glance, soothed by her smile. She's enjoying watching us as much as we're enjoying chasing each other.

A loud bong stops us in our tracks. The warning gong. We only have five minutes left. I want to scream, yell it's not fair. But that would just upset them. I must make the most of these precious moments.

I snag Frankie and tuck him in close. Not as easy as it once was, but still possible. Landing kisses all over his face, he wriggles in my embrace. Then he's free and running for my mom.

Tavi doesn't wait for me to catch her. She runs into my arms, hands sliding around my waist as she hugs me tight. I feel the silent sobs and know she's not letting them loose for the same reason as me. The realization only makes it more difficult to keep my own at bay.

Determined, I manage. Then it's Mom's turn. She hangs on to me like she's afraid she may never see me again. I don't blame her. If I don't succeed, her fears may be realized. I hug her fiercely, then pull back, my perfect mask in place. "I love you, Mom."

"I love you too," she whispers, touching my face, then stroking my hair. Her quivering lower lip is the only sign of her contained inner turmoil. "Go, make us proud!"

The sob is a lump in my throat as I nod, incapable of words. I turn to Xanin, the last one as always. He pulls me into his powerful arms, stern resolution his only expression.

"Look after yourself. Live to fight another day." Xanin's voice is a growl, too soft for anyone but me to hear.

"I will. You too. And thanks!" He pulls back and looks at me, a question on his face. I lean closer and whisper, "For taking care of them."

Xanin's smile is grim. "Always. As long as I have breath."

The door clangs open, and armored arms tear me away from my family. But I don't scream. It would only make everyone fall apart. As I'm dragged away, my eyes drink my family in, trying to absorb every feature, remember every detail with my eidetic memory. Xanin's scowl. My mother's arm reaching toward me. Tavi holding Frankie's shoulders, tears shimmering in her eyes. Frankie's little balled fists.

Then we're out of the room, and the door snaps shut, taking them from me. The barriers I held so tightly crash open, releasing the floodgates. I'm a puddle, easily hauled away by the SerSents. Like a piece of trash. They toss me into a nearby empty room, the door slamming behind them. Then only my wracking sobs keep me company.

6

I take the full fifteen minutes Cygnus permits composing myself. By the time the SerSents reappear, my eyes are so swollen, they feel like they'll pop out of my head. With no mirror, I can't tell how I look. I guess it's hideous because the first stop the SerSents insist on is a nearby bathroom.

"Fix your face," one snaps.

Without a word, I enter and head for the mirrors. *Astatine!* Mascara runs black trails down my cheeks, the patches of skin between more porcelain than usual. I look like something out of a horror movie.

As I wash away the evidence of my tears, I remember why I never bothered with makeup before. It's too easy for people to see I've been crying.

Once my usual countenance is somewhat restored, I exit the bathroom, the two SerSents flanking me as they escort me back to the labs. Insultingly, they don't leave after depositing me in my office. Sending a heated glare their way, I use my intercom to request Sarissa join me in my office.

I would prefer she didn't see me this way, but the idiots aren't giving me a choice. Sarissa flounces in, takes one look at my face, and

32

then glowers at the SerSents. She drops her folders and rushes over to wrap her arms around me.

The comfort makes the waterworks start up again. I swallow the tears, desperate to push Sarissa away. I don't want someone else getting too close to me. Another person Cygnus could separate me from. But it feels so heavenly to have her support, I don't relinquish it, instead drawing solace from the embrace.

When she eventually releases me, Sarissa studies my face. "Feeling better?"

I nod, still doubting my voice.

Sarissa must understand because, with another venomous glance at the two goons (can't they take a hint?), she returns to her side of the desk and retrieves the pile of dumped folders. She extracts her copies (manila folders), then slides my (colored) pile toward me before taking a seat and opening the first file. "Let's start with your schedule, shall we?"

I drag my pile closer. The first folder has Sarissa's customary, perfectly laid-out day's schedule. Good old-fashioned print on paper. I have no idea why she still likes things analog. Lifting a stylus from the tray on my desk, I toy with it as Sarissa proceeds.

"Right, we can check off your early morning meeting."

I notice how carefully she avoids mention of my family. What a rock star! After crossing off the first bullet point on her list, Sarissa moves on.

"This morning, we'll take stock of your current project. If time allows, we'll catalog any requisitions for items you think the new incumbent may need to complete it. After lunch, we can go through the personnel files of the prospects you—"

The rest of her sentence is lost as the goons exit the room. My sigh makes Sarissa break off and glance at me. Following my gaze, she turns, then adds her sigh to mine. "I thought they'd never leave!"

"You and me both. How about we skip out for a while and visit the mall for lunch?"

Sarissa gapes, shock widening those lovely milk-chocolate eyes. "Really?"

"Yes, really. I'd like a day where I'm not on a schedule."

Sarissa fiddles with the files on her lap. She opens her mouth, then closes it again. A frown mars the perfection of her face.

I sigh a second time. "What?"

Her lips twist left and right as she debates with herself. Then, with a quick indrawn breath, she decides. "If you're sure you can still get through all your work for today, I suppose it would be alright?"

Her sentence ends on a question, and I hear what she isn't saying. She knows as well as me: if I don't do the director's bidding, there will be consequences. Unpleasant ones. No matter that I'm a favored child. "Sarissa, without this excursion to the mall and a lunch with you, there's no way I could do any work. Let alone slay this massive pile before the day is done."

Relief relaxes her features. Then her sweet, heart-shaped mouth curves into a wicked smile. "Do we get to do some shopping whilst we're there? Maybe I can get rid of that tacky t-shirt you love so much!"

I glance down at the offending clothing, then feel a twinge of regret when I realize how old it is. I've probably worn it most of the days Sarissa's known me. With good reason. My mother brought it to a family meeting around the same time I met Sarissa. I shrug. "You can lead a horse to water..."

Sarissa laughs. "We'll see about that!" Tossing her folders onto my desk, she offers a hand. "Shall we?"

"We shall."

Giggling, we hustle down the corridors between the workbenches to the bank of elevators. One whisks us downstairs, and as soon as the doors open, we tear across the lobby to the glorious sunshine waiting outside.

The mall is only two blocks beyond the massive park surrounding CC HQ. We walk the short distance, taking our time and soaking in the sun. It's a blissful two hours of forgetting my woes as we waltz in and out of stores in search of Sarissa's perfect shirt for me.

When she finds it, she insists I wear it. Immediately. I admit, the pretty blouse boosts my spirits more than I thought it would. Perhaps because every time I catch sight of my reflection now, the reminder of my family isn't in my face anymore. We spend another hour eating a leisurely lunch in the food court, me telling Sarissa about the visit with my loved ones.

By the time we get back to work, I'm feeling more like myself. The dull ache is still there, but the sharp bite of anguish is gone. True to my promise, I throw myself into my tasks with a passion born of the desire to drown myself in them.

Work is my refuge. A place I escape my worries and cares. Where the wonders of science eclipse all else. By the time the day is officially over, we've ticked every box on Sarissa's list.

With a cheery grin, Sarissa winks at me as she readies to leave for the evening. "Want to party with me tonight?"

"Nice try, but no, thanks. I need to dig into my new project."

Sarissa gives me a curious glance. "You never told me what it was."

"No, I didn't, nor do I plan on detaining you by telling you now either. Go, enjoy your evening. I have to research a few things before I can give you any direction on what I might need you to dig up for me."

"If you're sure?"

"I am. Get out of here! I'll see you tomorrow." She turns to leave. "And, Sarissa?"

"Yes?"

"Thanks for today."

Her smile is gentle, warm. "You're welcome."

Then Sarissa's gone, and I'm alone. Time to start my next project if I'm to have any hope of seeing my family again before they age out on me.

7

The SerSent slaps a tray down, jarring me from my thoughts.

"Director McQueen sends his regards."

Resisting a sigh, I wave the SerSent away. "Thank you." He doesn't leave. (Annoying gnat!) Forced to look up from my research, I glare at him. "What?" The SerSent ogles the food. I glance at it, then realize what a lavish spread it is. "Would you like it?"

"Uh, no, ma'am, thank you. But Director Cygnus wanted to know what you thought of it?"

How am I supposed to make progress with interruptions? I'm bending my plastic stylus to an alarming degree. Any second now, I'll snap it in two. I grit my teeth, but with deliberate care, I place the stylus in its tray on my desk. Sometimes, I wish Director Cygnus didn't care so much.

"Tell him I appreciate the gesture and send sincere thanks."

"You're not going to eat?"

I sigh. He's obviously not going away until I've tasted it. I shove a forkful of the steaming food into my mouth. "Delicious! Satisfied?"

Tim (for timid—of course I don't know his real name!) fidgets a little. "If it's that good, can you at least finish so I can tell him you ate it all?"

I roll my eyes, wishing Cygnus didn't know about my hypoglycemia. Since the food is rather yummy, I take another bite. But my work can't wait. Popping a pair of headphones in, I order the video I was watching to continue playing on my wall screen. Then I pick up the food tray and spin my chair around so I'm facing the wall. As I submerge myself in my research once more, the food slides down, unnoticed. I register neither finishing the meal nor Tim removing the empty tray, and himself, from my office.

The elusive idea of perpetual energy is a never-ending vortex. While Cygnus requested a "cold fusion energy source," he meant a machine generating more energy than it consumes. If only.

Nuclear energy in all its forms harnesses the power of atoms. Either by splitting one atom into two (fission) or combining—fusing—two atoms into one (fusion). Whoever said it was easier to break things than build them could just as easily have applied their sentiment here.

Because while there has been much success with fission (yes, those toxic nuclear power reactors, not to mention atomic bombs) fusion is another story. True, the sun and stars are natural examples of fusion, but I shudder when I think of how man tried to emulate them and came up with the hydrogen bomb. A horrific portrayal of one major problem associated with fusion: the inability to control the reaction in a contained space.

If this wasn't enough, I'm now compounding the problem. Fusion and fission both create their enormous amounts of energy because of the extreme heat and pressure under which the reactions occur. So how am I supposed to recreate the fusion effect if I'm eliminating one of these critical elements? Yes, that's right. I'm attempting *cold* fusion, which means achieving that excessive energy output without the insane temperature input.

I pore over the countless articles detailing projects others have attempted—and failed—trying to build such a device.

No matter what they named their device, they had the same objectives: clean, abundant power, no radioactive waste, and only cheap, abundant fuels to trigger the process.

The early failures, then claims of success by others who then couldn't replicate their alleged successes led to alternate terms, all created to distance themselves from the negative connotations associated with the taboo "cold fusion."

I gloss over the terminology and related acronyms: LENR (Low Energy Nuclear Reactions), CANR (Chemically Assisted Nuclear Reactions), LANR (Lattice Assisted Nuclear Reactions) and CMNS (Condensed Matter Nuclear Science).

Finally, I delve into the most advanced approaches last in development: the magnetic confinement found in toroid designs and inertial confinement of laser designs. Fascinating!

By the time I finish reading, I don't care to know how late it is. I'm beyond weary and still sleep-deprived from my last project. It's time to call it a day. Allow my mind to work on the problem subconsciously. I leave a note for Sarissa to tell her I'll be in late tomorrow and gather my things.

Dragging my bones home takes all my waning strength. Only when I'm about to open the doors of my building and notice a bedraggled girl, obviously drunk, stumbling to her own home, do I remember Sarissa's odd behavior this morning.

I meant to question her after I'd seen my family, but I was so engrossed in my own woes, and so eager to allow Sarissa to pluck me from them, I neglected her needs. Some friend I am!

Annoyed with myself, I enter my building and trek down the corridor to the resident's foyer. The mall's ground floor below is as empty as I am. Drained of any and all life.

By the time I finally ease into my apartment, I'm spent. My purse and briefcase clatter as I drop them just inside the door, not caring if I spill their contents or not. I stumble the last few feet to my bed and collapse onto it, face down. The world crashes as sleep claims me.

When I finally wake, sun streams through my windows undimmed by the privacy window films preventing peeping Toms from spying on me. Blearily, I focus on the time. I'm awake in an instant. Almost noon! When I told Sarissa I'd be late, this isn't what I meant. I leap out of bed, fly through a shower, throw on some clothes, and grab a breakfast-to-go from my magic fridge.

As I scoop up my purse and briefcase, I'm thankful now their contents didn't scatter. I dash out of my building and jog to the trundle. Then wonder why I bothered when I have to wait five minutes for it to arrive.

Still irritated, I find a seat, only to tear my finger open on a jagged piece of metal sticking out from its underside. *Astatine!* Could this day have started worse? Hastily plucking my Nanogo from my purse, I'm not fast enough. A drop of blood falls onto my shirt. Really? Now I'll have to clean that too before I get to the labs! Muttering, I spray the Nanogo on the open wound, then watch, fascinated as the blood congeals, and the skin closes over, leaving no sign of the injury. Nanogo isn't called the magic cure-all nanite spray for nothing. If only it could heal more than superficially. Why didn't they make it so it could cure my hypoglycemia?

· With a sigh, I remember I should eat. I munch on my breakfast, absorbing the views outside while the trundle zips me to work. I calm as I take in the passing panorama, part of my morning ritual to get my brain into gear. Focusing on the wonder and beauty of nature gives me a sense of space, of freedom.

Somehow, this tricks my brain into thinking it's free too, not an organ confined to my head. The tiny fantasy kickstarts my mind into focusing on the science I'm attempting to unravel. Just like that, I'm back on task, my miraculous brain firing on all cylinders, and attacking problems presented by the project. By the time the elevator delivers me to the labs, my brain is fully engaged. I hurry to my office, already considering an angle I want to explore.

I spot Sarissa exiting my office. Although striking as always, today her appearance jars. A little too much pizazz, like she's trying too hard. A month ago I wouldn't have noticed. But since she began teaching me the fine art of applying flawless makeup, I've learned when it's too little or too much.

Today is definitely the latter, a mistake Sarissa would never normally make. The thought halts my approach. Something niggles, something I was supposed to remember. The memory flares, uncomfortable as I dredge it from the depths. Plastering a smile onto my face, I stride to Sarissa's office and tap on the doorframe. "Morning!"

Startled eyes gaze back at me before her mask snaps back into place. "You mean afternoon!"

Her attempt at levity falls flat. I know the moment she realizes I've caught her out. Sarissa's face crumples. "Don't look at me like that! I know what you're going to ask."

I slip into her office and close the door, putting my things down and folding my arms. "So tell me."

"It was nothing, really!"

"If it was nothing, you wouldn't be trying to hide it. Now spill!"

She rolls her eyes theatrically, but her shoulders droop. "It was just a guy."

I stand straighter, body taut. "He didn't hurt you, did he?"

Sarissa gives an odd laugh. "No, not in the way you think."

I wait, knowing she'll cave if I give it enough time.

"Fine! It's just... he just—" Sarissa breaks off, her eyes glazing as she searches for words.

Words I doubt the truth of.

"I met him at that new club. You know how it goes—small talk, some dancing, some drinking. I thought he was decent. Then he said something nasty."

True, except for the last sentence. "What did he say?"

Anger flashes in Sarissa's eyes. "Does it matter?"

It's her turn to give me the silent treatment, to wait me out. I'll have to find another way to get her to reveal her secret. Perhaps a shopping spree? Ugh, perish the thought! But she's always way more relaxed when she's buying things. My mind drifts to the mall in her building, the one I loathe. The one she loves. Do they have to make the clothes there so expensive? Honestly, I can't tell the difference between their clothes and the ones in less expensive stores, although Sarissa assures me it's significant.

Sarissa is glaring at me. Why? I'm convinced the reason for it is important. There was something I should've pursued, but I can't remember now. "Sorry, what were we talking about?" Sarissa wears an odd expression. "What?"

A sigh, then Sarissa waves her hand. "Nothing. Should we go over your schedule for today?"

Mutely, I nod, sinking into the chair opposite hers. She talks (waack, waack, waack), but I can't focus. There was something... something I was going to ask.

"Chiara!"

The sharp accusation in Sarissa's voice slices through my thoughts. Blinking, I sit up in my chair. "Yes?"

"Did you hear a word I said?"

Chagrined, I shake my head. "Sorry, I was thinking about something else."

"The new project? Are you going to tell me about it?"

Absently, I pick up a stylus from her desk. My fingers fiddle with the metal clip as I consider the project. "It's a doozy." Sarissa says nothing, but her eyes follow my movements with the stylus. Concern plays across her face. Too much makeup! Why did she slather it on today?

It's been almost two years since we first met. She walked into my office, a vision of beauty and elegance. Impeccable makeup played up her Asian ancestry, highlighting her dark eyes and incredible cheekbones. Her straight black hair, drawn into a braid, ran halfway down the back of the tailored lavender suit gracing her lithe body. My newly assigned PA to go with my newly assigned position as head of this R&D lab.

She'd been a little intimidating. Then she'd grinned, and it broke the spell. Since then, Sarissa's educated me in things I would never ordinarily have been interested in. Things to teach me how to fit into my new role. A world where clothes and makeup and designer purses play a part. Where the way you walk and talk and dress can open doors otherwise firmly shut. Where all our dressing up and shopping and hours spent getting to know one another led to a friendship I could never have dreamed of. Because no one else ever wanted to be my friend before Sarissa.

Ah! That was it! "Want to get out and go do some shopping?"

Sarissa gapes. "What? Again? It's the middle of the day!"

Good point. I don't know why I suggested it, just that it was important. "Your mall?"

As I'd hoped, Sarissa stops asking questions and leaps to her feet, eyes bright and smile wide. "Sign me up already!"

8

Giggling in hushed tones (who knew that was possible?), Sarissa and I make our escape, skipping through the park to the trundle as soon as we're free of the monstrous CC building. A trundle pulls in just as we reach the platform, and we hop on.

It will take only a few minutes to reach the posh area where Sarissa lives, a sector I'm not allowed without her. The short distance is a perk of her tier. The higher your status, the closer your building to CC HQ. Sarissa's parents, being Board members, live in a building adjacent to CC HQ, so no need for them to catch the trundle. Not that they would. They have a helivate. I frown.

Sarissa notices. "What's wrong?"

"Your parents live right next to where they work, so how come they have a helivate?"

Sarissa gnaws on her bottom lip.

I understand in an instant. "Oh, it's a tier thing."

Quick to place a hand on my arm, Sarissa winces. "I'm sorry. I didn't mean to make it one."

Glum, I shake my head. "You didn't. I did, by asking a question before thinking."

"You shouldn't have to apologize. Just because you did, how about I buy you a really nice dress today?"

Ridiculous as the offer is, my mind spins instead to what Sarissa calls "a really nice dress." A scrap of sparkly fabric barely covering the essential bits. Nothing like the perfectly tailored suits she wears to work. But she looks so excited at the prospect (and wasn't I supposed to be encouraging her to shop today?) that I don't have the heart to decline.

"Sure."

Sarissa squeals with delight, clapping her hands and drawing the attention of the other passengers. Oblivious to their stares, she prattles on. "Something you can wear when we next go clubbing together."

I hide my dismay. What did I get myself into? Regardless, I allow myself to be dragged out of the trundle at the next stop, Sarissa bubbling enthusiasm over me.

We've been trolling the mall for nearly three hours, and Sarissa's worn my legs down to stumps by the time she tugs me into a tiny boutique. *Il Mio Cuore* is tucked away in a discreet corner of the mall. A glance at the first price tag explains why. With prices like those, remaining hidden was a deliberate move on their part, where only the most exclusive clientele could find them.

I'm about to tell Sarissa we should leave when I spot a midnight-blue dress at the far end of the store. Shot through with silver thread, it shimmers as the light catches it. Best of all, it's a *whole* dress (not flimsy pieces tacked together), with more than enough fabric to suit my comfort level yet still skimpy enough so Sarissa won't reject it outright.

I turn, looking for Sarissa, but she's already stuffed her nose into another section. Not wanting to bother her, (she's humming!), I stroll over to the dress. Up close, it's even better than I thought. When I search for an assistant, I find one less than two feet away. "Hello. Could you please tell me if you have this dress in my size?"

"We don't serve zeeches here."

Stung by both her tone and the scathing glare, I frown. "I'm sorry, have I done something to offend you?"

"You offend me just breathing. How did you even get in here, Zeech?"

"I brought her."

Sarissa's tone is frigid, her scowl enough to freeze the assistant, who obviously recognizes her.

"Miss Kasumi! How lovely to see you again."

"Get this dress in my friend's size." The assistant's eyes bulge. "Now!"

Frazzled, the assistant hurries to obey. In undertones, I ask, "Why did she call me a zeech? What does it mean?"

Sarissa tucks my arm into hers and pats it. "Never mind her. She's just an ignorant ass. Now this," Sarissa stops patting to finger the fabric of the blue dress, "this is perfect! Come on, let's get to the dressing room. I can't wait to see it on you!"

While still unsettled by the surly assistant, I allow myself to be swept along by Sarissa's excitement. When I put the dress on, it doesn't disappoint. Sarissa's jubilation is contagious.

"We'll take it," Sarissa tells the assistant, not even bothering to check the price.

I tried to find it, but the tag was notably absent. Deliberately removed by the assistant, or is this just common practice for the dresses not on the boutique's floor? No, I don't want to know the cost. I amble over to another section as Sarissa pays for my dress and her own purchases. How did she find six things in the time it took me to find one?

"It doesn't matter who your friends are. You're still a filthy zeech!" Hissed words, but there's no mistaking who said them.

I whirl, searching for the assistant, but can't find her. Probably best she stays hidden (behind a clothes rack?) because although I'd love to call her out on her behavior, I hate confrontation. However, she has confirmed something. The word is definitely derogatory.

Tired of this store and its (ignorant-ass) people, I stomp to the doors to wait for Sarissa, but she's finished paying and meets me there almost simultaneously. She takes one look at my face and frowns. "I thought you'd be happy you found a dress."

"I am. Thrilled, actually. It means we can finally grab some food. I missed lunch, and I'm starving!"

"And?"

I force a smile. "And nothing. Thank you so much for my dress. I love it!"

Still debating pressing the issue, Sarissa must change her mind. "My pleasure! Now I just have to convince you to come clubbing with me so you can wear it."

My grin is honest this time. "Just how do you plan to do that?"

"Oh, I have a few ideas."

We leave the accursed store, chuckling, and make our way down to the food court. But the closer we get, the more aware I am of… "eyes" on me. Covertly, I sneak a glance at a passing couple. Yes. They're looking at me with the same contempt as the assistant. I can't fathom the reason for this behavior. I've never noticed it before.

By the time we reach the food court, I've lost my appetite. "I'm not hungry anymore. Can we just leave, please?"

Sarissa's frown is back. "I knew I should've asked you earlier. What's the matter?"

"Nothing. It's not important."

Not to be dismissed this time, Sarissa grabs my hand, earnest, warm brown eyes seeking mine. "It is. To me. Tell me."

A huff of air escapes, enough to lift the tendril of hair floating near my eyebrow. I know she won't let it go. "While you were paying, that horrid assistant snuck up somewhere close and whispered the same thing again."

"What did she say exactly?" Sarissa's face shows no emotion, but her knuckles on the hand gripping the shopping bag are white.

"She said no matter who my friends are, I'm still a filthy zeech."

Sarissa's curse has me raising my eyebrows at her. Then I giggle. Who would've ever thought perfect Sarissa could lose it like that?

But my laughter doesn't erase the anger from her face. "She doesn't know it yet, but she's just been fired."

Shaken, I grab the hand Sarissa just dropped. "No, you can't do that."

Sarissa's eyes are hard. "I can, and I will."

I've never seen Sarissa like this. Yes, we've been friends for just on two years now, but our time together outside the lab is limited. And when we do hang out, it's usually shopping or doing makeup or, on the rare occasion, clubbing. As a result, most of our conversations center on these areas. We've seldom discussed family or anything deep. Part of the reason she doesn't know about my family "situation." How well do I really know her? Aren't theories meant to be tested?

"Sarissa, please, that seems a little extreme. You know what could happen to her if she loses her job." (Or is the slur terrible enough to warrant this action?) The thought raises the same question. "You never told me what zeech meant."

Only because I'm watching Sarissa so closely do I notice the fear sparking in her eyes. In the space of a blink, it's gone again. What was that about?

With a sigh, Sarissa explains. "It's just a word people use here. The snobs in these stores think people from other sectors are below them. They view them as leeches, living off the lifeblood of the upper tiers. So that's what they call them."

Too pat. Like Sarissa thought about how to answer this between the incident in the store and now. Why? But another question slips out my mouth instead. "But why zeech and not just leech?"

There's no mistaking Sarissa's alarm this time. She steals quick glances at the surrounding people, before offering an (unbelievable) offhand shrug. "I don't know. Why is the sky blue? Perhaps they substitute 'z' because it's the last, and lowest, letter in the alphabet." Another furtive glance. "Chiara, can we just drop this? Please?"

Not sure it's the right decision, I cave. Only because I can see how panicked Sarissa is.

Sarissa nods at the nearby food stores and offers a wan smile. "Come on, let's eat. We'll both feel better after some food. Or a milkshake if you still don't feel up to eating? You know you shouldn't let your sugar get too low."

While this is flawed thinking (half a banana would be better for me), my blood sugar is just fine today, and I can't resist the offer of a milkshake. My kryptonite. (Odd expression since Krypton is color-less, tasteless, and odorless. Must research that!) "Only if it has loads of chocolate."

Sarissa beams. "Lots of chocolate in a milkshake it is, then." Tucking my arm into hers once more, we set off toward the ice cream store.

I'm polishing off the last of my milkshake when I feel the stares again. This time, I ignore them. Who cares what they think? Sarissa certainly doesn't, and it only makes me appreciate her more.

There are only thirty-one minutes left until clock-off time when we finally make it back to the lab, having spent another hour wandering the stores at Sarissa's mall. Entering my office, I carefully hang the precious dress on the hook behind my door. Wouldn't want to damage something that probably cost more than someone's annual wage. I dismiss the gloomy thought and plop down in my chair.

Sarissa settles in opposite me, eyes inquisitive. "So, are you ready to tell me more about the new project yet—I mean, other than that it's a doozy?"

I pout. So much for a relaxed afternoon. "The director ordered me to create a cold fusion energy source."

"Well, that's exciting, right?"

I pick up a stylus and run it through my hair, relishing the soothing effect. "It would be if it were possible and not some fantasy of science fiction."

Sarissa laughs. "You've said that before, but every time, you've pulled off the impossible."

The phrase grates, a reminder, almost to the word, of what the director said. I study Sarissa. Eyes too bright. And that astatine-forsaken makeup! (Didn't I already think that once today?) "What's with all the war paint?"

"What?" Sarissa blinks, fingers subconsciously drifting up to her face.

"Come on! You know your hand was too heavy today. Didn't your mirror speak to you?"

I don't expect her to whip out her compact and study her face. But she does, inspecting her makeup before replying. "Hmm, I did go a little overboard, didn't I? Too much partying last night and not enough time this morning. Tell me more about your project."

Bells ring strident alarms in my head. Since when did Sarissa not leave enough time for transcendence? But mention of the looming project shoves further thoughts of it from my mind.

"Honestly, Sarissa, I don't know how I'm going to do this. It's like the holy grail of inventions—or one of them! A machine making more energy than it uses goes against the fundamental laws of science." I don't bother explaining the first law of thermodynamics.

"But you can find a way, right?"

I snort. "Yeah, right! I just have to wave my wand and poof! I've divined a way to bring two hydrogen protons close enough for them to fuse. Oh, don't forget, it must be nuclear fusion, not a chemical reaction, or it won't generate the exponential energy required." I snap my fingers. "And, oh, yes! Do that without using excessive heat." I've lost her. I blow out a sigh. "Never mind."

Sarissa's smile is gentle, probably the singular thing that drew me to her initially. "Chiara, you know I don't pretend to understand what you do. But I do know how smart you are. If anyone can do this, it's you."

Her belief in me isn't entirely unfounded. At the dreaded parties the director demands I attend, my IQ is a frequent topic of conversation. One guest even dared suggest my intelligence is the result of being born to parents afflicted by the toxins polluting our world back then. That the specific combination of my parents' genetics led to a kid with a super brain. But that's pure speculation. There's no foundation for it because neither he nor any of the others who agreed would have any way of knowing my parents' genetic makeup.

Backing off my rabbit trail, I strive to keep that lovely smile on Sarissa's face. For some reason I can't remember, I know she needs support today. "Thanks, friend. I appreciate your confidence. I'll do my best to live up to it."

9

To say the next weeks are grueling is an understatement. The more I explore the cold fusion attempts made by those who preceded me, the more frustrated I become. Even with the industrial advances in magnetism and lasers, I'm still stymied in my search for viable options for a functional machine.

But today is a new day. I had a decent sleep last night—so amazing I overslept and had no time to even snag my customary breakfast-to-go, let alone wrinkle-free clothes—and I'm feeling atypically optimistic. Perhaps today is the day I'll find an answer. Or at least the hint of one.

Ready for work, I touch my data cube, and my holoscreen flares to life. I browse the folders Sarissa compiled and sent to my PC in our first week working on this assignment. Each holds countless files, all the information Sarissa could glean about each project. The comprehensive folders include not only detailed specs for the projects, but information on the researchers, their other work, funding, press releases, publications, and any minutia she thought might be relevant.

Unable to ignore the obvious (the pile of unopened folders is now smaller than the pile I've moved into the "processed" folder), I resolve not to let the dwindling pile cow me. I won't give up. Besides, it's not like I have a choice. I *must* find a solution.

Tapping the first unopened folder, the files stream onto my screen. Instead of processing each file in the folder sequentially as I have been, impatience spurs me to open the file with the project details first.

Ah, yes, the scientist who helped develop a unique "bubble chamber" particle detector, something he later used in a muon-facilitated fusion experiment. My hunt for information I might've missed on my initial forays into the project reveals nothing new. His experiment ended the same way as all the others—in failure—when they recognized two major shortcomings. The half-life of muons meant they decayed too quickly to facilitate the number of fusion reactions required, and the astronomical energy needed to produce these muons meant energy output would never exceed input.

Agitated, I skip the rest of the files in the folder and flick it aside as incomplete, slapping the screen to open the next project. Again, I focus on the project details and ignore the other files. In this project, the researchers claimed they could transform hydrogen into helium by nuclear catalysis (where palladium atomized under pressure and at room temperature absorbed the hydrogen)—a claim they later retracted. *Even more useless than the first folder!*

The following folder is equally worthless, (fusing hydrogen into helium in an electrolytic cell with a palladium electrode), as are the next few detailing experiments using heavy water. Desperation hounds me, and I tap folders and flip through information at an increasing pace, skimming the information ever faster.

I'm almost hyperventilating by the time my shaky hand taps the last folder. Breath held, I access the project details. I need less than five minutes to conclude this is the least promising option.

"Aargh!" The screech is feral, but does little to improve my morale. Frustration boiling over into physical manifestation, I swipe an arm across my desk. The resounding crash of items hitting the floor is satisfying. But it only feeds my hunger to act. To do *something*.

I dash onto the lab floor, eyes wild as they dart back and forth, seeking something capable of taking a beating. My gaze lands on the containment room, lit up as it is, a beacon beckoning in a distant corner of the lab.

As I barrel toward it, Sarissa exits her office. She must've heard the commotion. The thought spikes hysteria, and my legs pump faster, eager to reach the containment room before Sarissa—or anyone else—can stop me.

I charge into the room, breathing hard, more because of rage and vexation than because I'm unfit. Snatching up a heavy, long-handled metal clamp, I smash the unit—and just about knock myself out as the metal bounces off the unbreakable glass, narrowly missing my face.

Somewhere, my brain registers the glass is not the place to hit. Not nearly satisfying enough. My gaze flies around the room and lands on the metal vent pipe. I slam the clamp into the pipe, and a gratifying clang tickles my ears. The sound is so liberating I hit the vent again. And again. And again. My fervor matches my increasing satisfaction. Like years of fury are finally free for me to unleash on the pipe.

A body blow knocks me to the ground. Frantic, I claw for more of that satiation, that rewarding thwack of the clamp, the delicious clang. My addled mind takes a moment to realize a SerSent is lying on top of me. I blink at him, unsure what he's doing. He must've slammed me to the floor.

His face is coolly assessing. "Are you done?"

Dazed, I stare up at him. When I catch sight of the vent pipe over his shoulder, my anger drains away, and my mouth pops open. Smashed to smithereens, part of the pipe now hangs at an angle, completely disconnected from the containment unit. Worse, the venting mechanism appears damaged. Did *I* do *that*?

Stunned, I try rising, but the SerSent is still pinning me down. "Let go of me!"

"Are you going to do something stupid?"

I shake my head, too spent to speak. The SerSent backs off, and I stand, unsure where to look. I now understand the phrase, "having the wind knocked out of your sails." In more ways than one. Not only did the SerSent's impact knock the breath clear out of me, but realizing what I've done is even more devastating.

I never knew I had blind ferocity in me. It must be blind because what sane person would do that?

A hand on my shoulder startles me. Sarissa's brown eyes watch me, wary, appraising. I'm immediately defensive. "Are you going to ask if I've lost it too?"

Her face remains grave. "What happened?"

"I... I don't know. Honestly, I just lost it. I can't even begin to explain." For a second, I think I have things under control. Then the solitary tear slides out. "What's happening to me?"

I'm thankful for the way Sarissa shields me from my curious coworkers as she eases me from the containment room and guides me back to my office. Gently depositing me in my chair, she leaves me to shut the door and close the window blinds. When she faces me again, she's gnawing on her lip.

My shoulders sag. "You don't have to say anything. I know how bad this is."

Sarissa's stare is frank, and she pauses before she answers. "Do you really?"

The way she says it shoots prickly shivers across my skin. Like there's something more to my momentary loss of sanity. "What are you saying?"

With a quick shake of her head, Sarissa looks away. When she replies, I can't see her face. "Nothing." After a second, she shakes her head again. "Just that word of this will get back to the director. And—"

I interrupt, unwilling to hear more. "Stop! You don't have to say it." Abruptly, it's all too much again. I hunch over, tucking my face into arms folded on my desk as I give in to sobs. *How could I have lost it so spectacularly? I never do that! What's happening to me?* Hands shaking, I lift my head and push my hair back. The world is spinning out of control.

The door bangs open, and I bolt out of my chair. Eyes wide, I stare at the two SerSents standing there. Confusion becomes comprehension when I see the food tray one SerSent holds.

The other SerSent barks at me. "When last did you eat?"

Duh! My sugar levels are off. As I try to gather my thoughts enough to remember, I stammer, "I, uh, um, this morning?"

Then I remember I missed breakfast. My cheeks flame. Should I admit as much? Cygnus already gave me one "warning." But misery bowls me over. Does it really matter? Eventually, even he won't be able to prevent something unthinkable happening to my family.

My voice croaks. "Um, to be honest, I forgot breakfast this morning."

The gruff SerSent's irritation (I'll call him Yappy) is impossible to miss as he gestures for the other man to hand over the food. I stare at it. The last thing I want to do is eat. But I know they won't leave until I do.

With the autonomous actions borne of years of repetition, my hands ferry the food to my mouth. It tastes like ash. I swallow, not bothering to chew properly, almost gagging on every mouthful but desperate to be rid of them. When I've eaten, I snatch up the orange juice and chug it, slamming the glass down.

Some of my anger has returned, and I don't bother hiding my resentment as I ask, "Satisfied?"

Yappy glares right back. However, he chooses not to growl again, and indicates the other man should retrieve the tray. Wordlessly, they leave my office. My tension eases.

Stifled giggles draw my attention. Red in the face from her attempts at suppressing her laughter, Sarissa sputters. "I thought he was going to implode!"

Suddenly, I'm laughing too. We lurk in my office, fresh giggles erupting every few minutes as one of us sets the other off again. I don't know how much time passes before we laugh ourselves out.

On a huge indrawn breath, I accept it's time to deal with the consequences of my actions. Or at least two of them. The third, which I have no doubt is coming, is one I'd rather avoid. Forever, if possible.

Because Sarissa applied her expertise and cosmetically covered all signs of my earlier meltdown, I don't shrink from the stares following me, striding onto the lab floor with confidence. I march to the middle of the room and face my coworkers.

"May I have your attention, please?" While I give it a second, it's superfluous considering every eye in the room is already riveted on me. "I apologize for my outburst. I didn't mean to scare you. As you know, we are sometimes under tremendous pressure to finish a task."

A few scattered nods, some muttered agreement.

"This time, I lost it before I'd even really begun. But that's not when we should lose control, is it?"

Scattered laughter encourages me.

"As immensely satisfying as it was to hit that poor pipe, I daresay neither the pipe nor the vent feel the same way."

"Although, occasionally, we'd sure like to *vent* the same way too!"

I can't tell who spoke, but general laughter follows. Anxiety leaks out of the faces before me. "That may be, but if you don't want to lose it like I did, I encourage you to take your breaks and eat your meals."

Surprised applause ripples across the room. I have to smile.

Nothing like your boss telling you to take breaks. Let's hope it doesn't come back and bite me in the butt. "Carry on."

With that, I turn to the next task. The muted conversations surfacing across the room buoy my spirits… until I enter the containment room, boggling anew at the damage I wrought. I must have applied some serious force. The absurdity of the situation strikes me again, and I can't decide between laughing and crying.

Grudgingly, I accept Director Cygnus might have been right. I should be more diligent about eating in a timely manner. My gaze drops to my hands. The shaking has stopped, and, with a start, I realize how much better I feel overall.

"Sarissa?" My friend is at my side in an instant. She'd been tailing my progress from my office, but I hadn't realized she was so close. "Can you make a note to check on me at mealtimes? I can't afford to do something like this again."

Relief floods her gorgeous eyes, more luminescent today with the shades of gold brushed across her eyelids. "Yes, I'll do that."

But as she strides past me to gawk at my handiwork, something else flickers in those eyes. Anger? Annoyance? I must be imagining things because when she turns to face me, there's no trace of anything except a question. "What should I do about the containment unit?"

I grimace. "Fill out a requisition."

Sarissa pulls a matching face, her sentiment echoing my own.

Unexpected requisitions draw the director's attention. Not my preference, but we can't get merely anyone to repair this. Besides, I console myself, word of my little "episode" will no doubt trickle back to Cygnus. He has a way of getting information he shouldn't have. Part of what has made him such an excellent director.

"Please verify the mechanic has both the clearance to access this lab and the skill to ensure he sets the seals properly." I shudder, thinking what could happen if the seals are faulty. While electronics and micro-mechanics fall in my realm of expertise, macro-mechanics are another beast altogether and something I'd rather leave to those qualified in the subject.

"Sure. Anything else?"

"No, I think I've done enough for today." My smile is grim. Without me voicing the words, her expression tells me she's thinking the same thing. *What will the director say and, worse, do about this outburst?*

I skulk back to my office, avoiding my coworkers this time. One wrong word and someone might set me off again. Unlikely because I feel measurably calmer than I did twenty-seven minutes ago, but best not to take any chances.

Astounded, I stand in my office doorway, surveying the mess on the floor. *Wow, excellent job!* Nothing left on my desk. With a groan, I trudge over to pick things up. I check my data cube first, worried I might've damaged it, which would entail another unnecessary requisition. Another chance to vex Director Cygnus. Much as he has taken care of me, he never lets certain things slide. Waste is one. However, the cube's virtually indestructible. The wireless connection hooks the cube up to my holoscreen on the first attempt. Just to be sure, I check, and yes, no files missing. Everything's intact.

Relieved, I transfer the other items from the floor to my desk. I'm crawling under the front of my desk, my lovely derriere facing the door, when there's a tentative knock. Startled, I jump. My head jerks up, banging into the underside of my desk. Muttering and rubbing my head, I back out and turn so I'm sitting on the floor.

I meant to use that position to rise and stand, but I'm literally floored. Al-Li and all her alloys! What did I do to deserve *him?* A drool-worthy hunk decorates my doorframe, a grin on his handsome face. "If that's how you treat your furniture, let alone your head, I'm dying to see what you did to the containment unit."

His deep voice is as easy on the ears as his looks are on the eyes. With a whoosh, air leaves my body. "You're the mechanic?" My voice is annoyingly squeaky.

"Well, there's a vote of confidence if I ever heard one!"

I pray Sarissa's foundation is hiding my cheeks flushing crimson as I try to stand. But the massage ball, usually on my desk, finds its way under my hand. I crash back down onto my elbows, wincing at the sharp pain. "Ow!"

"Careful, now." Handsome leaps forward. His hand slides under my arm as he helps me up.

Impossible not to notice the strength in his supporting grip. My brain casts about, still trying to reconcile this cute guy with someone meeting the arduous requirements for the containment room repair. My lips are paralyzed, useless at forming words but nonetheless flopping around.

Sudden concern replaces the humor in those incredible gray eyes, sun shimmering off dull steel. "Are you okay?"

Pull yourself together! "Yes, fine, thank you." I tuck a wayward strand of hair behind my ear, running into the stylus poking out from the mass. I must look a sight. For lack of something to say or do (because Al-Li knows, I only want to ogle the man!), I extend a hand. "I'm Chiara."

His devilish grin gives me pause. *Can he read my mind?* The thought is mortifying.

"Deran." He shakes my offered hand. "Do you always greet people so formally?"

Now I *know* he's laughing at me. Those full lips are curved in a generous smile, emphasizing his strong jawline. My eyes run up that jawline to wavy, auburn hair, shorn on the sides but longer on top. The wayward spikes only add to his rakish appeal.

Discombobulated, I turn away, hobbling around my desk as I fight for composure. Time spent not looking at him gives my brain space. *He's the mechanic. Send him to the containment room.* I turn, but the moment my eyes meet his, the words abandon me. Traitors! Deran gives another dashing smile. *Could you please stop doing that?*

"Since it seems you won't answer my question, how about showing me what you want me to fix?"

His question? What question? The worry returns to his face, so I square my shoulders, rising to my full five-foot-five glory. "Yes, this way."

As I pass him on the way out of my office, his height dwarfs me. Must be over six foot. About the same height as Cygnus. That thought sobers me right up. Or maybe not, looking at the handsomest guy I've ever laid eyes on.

All the way to the containment room, I berate myself. I will not act like a giddy schoolgirl—or how I think she would act. I will behave with the decorum befitting my position. I will talk to him like a normal human being.

Having bolstered myself sufficiently by the time we get there (and deciding it would be advisable to not look at him when speaking), I keep my eyes on the containment unit and show him the sad state of the vent pipe and mechanism.

I'm unprepared for the laughter rumbling out behind me. Deep and sonorous, the warm sound wraps around me like a fluffy blanket. *Girl, what is wrong with you? Get a grip!*

"*You* did *that?*"

His incredulity is irrationally offensive. "Is that so difficult to believe?"

More laughter. "You're just so little. How did a tiny pint like you do so much damage?"

Anger beats down the humiliation of my actions. I let the rage rise, knowing it will allow me to face this boy and at least ease some coherent words out.

Whirling, I glare at him, a thrill of delight fluttering through me at his bewildered expression. "Just because I'm short doesn't mean I can't pack a punch."

The grin is back as he raises his hands. "I surrender."

His retort plucks a reluctant smile from me. "Good. Now get to work. Please." I'm almost out the door, desperate to escape, when I remember he might need materials. "Is there anything you require?" A gleam in his eyes. My brain goes haywire again, and I quickly avert my gaze to the floor. "I mean, do you need my assistant to requisition any supplies for you?"

"Thanks, I'm good for now. I need to assess things first. Then I'll let you know."

His voice is so quiet I must look at him to catch the words. Does he look… contrite? Flustered, I wave a hand as I turn and leave. "Carry on then."

I scuttle back to my office, closing the door behind me, then leaning back against the cool steel. *What was that?* My heart sends my pulse skittering again as a knock sounds.

For a moment, I'm frozen. Then I leap away from the door like it could burn me. A second later, the lever goes down, and Sarissa enters.

My hand goes to my chest, and I wheeze out air. "Oh, it's you!" I flop onto my chair, unable to stand for a second longer.

Sarissa giggles. "Yes, he's yummy, isn't he? What's his name? Is he the mechanic?" She shimmies into my office, closing the door again before plopping into the seat opposite me. "Well?"

Hysterical laughter jabbers out. I can't take much more today. "Yes, he's the mechanic. Can you believe it?"

"I can't! They usually send that old dowdy fellow—um, Jack? John?"

"Jason," I supply. "And he's not old, he's ancient!" A snort from Sarissa. Then I sigh. "Yeah, they really upended things with this new guy."

"New guy? You didn't get his name?"

I replay the recent conversation. "Deran."

"Hmm, I like it! Strong name for a strong man."

Another wild cackle hiccups out. "If you say so."

This time, Sarissa's eyes sparkle. "You would know. Did your hand linger on his arm a tad longer than it should've when he helped you up from the floor?"

"You saw my first attempt at getting up?"

Sarissa hoots. "Funniest thing I've watched in a while. You made my day."

I cover my face with my hands. "Did I make a total idiot of myself?"

"Sorry to say it, but you did."

At that, we break into peals of laughter. I don't care if it's hysteria. Releasing all the pent-up tension feels sublime.

Eventually, I wipe my eyes. "This must be one of the strangest days I've ever had!"

"I agree!" After a moment, Sarissa asks, "Why do you think they sent Deran instead of dowdy dude?"

I shrug, not bothered. As long as Deran can do the work. "Maybe Jason was busy on something else?"

Sarissa nods, but her eyes have that faraway look again.

"Why do *you* think they sent him?"

The thoughtfulness evaporates, pollen dispersed by a breeze, replaced by a mischievous grin. "I think they sent him to mess with you."

"What? Why would you say that?" Then I blush. "Oh."

Sarissa gives a satisfied smile, nodding her head like a Cheshire Cat. "Since you've made my day, how about something to eat?"

I glance back at the containment unit. "Ugh, I couldn't. Besides, what if Deran has questions?"

"He can call you, can't he? Or are you keeping your eye candy in sight?"

If I was close enough, I would've swatted her. As it is, I chuckle. "Okay, okay, let's get out. But not for something to eat!"

"Milkshakes then?"

She knows my weaknesses too well. "Fine. But small ones!"

Grinning, Sarissa picks up my purse, holding it out to me. "Shall we?"

11

After milkshakes with Sarissa, I can't settle. Whether it's the excess sugar or the wild day, something has me on edge. I spend a restless few hours trying to work, but my brain jumps about like heated kernels of corn, and I can almost feel the pops, surveying the half-read folders on my PC.

Unable to sit for a second longer, I rise and pace. My office is too cramped. I stride onto the lab floor, my feet taking me to the containment room. When I'm standing in the doorway, watching Deran methodically catalog the pieces, I wonder what I'm doing here.

Deran glances at me, a question in his eyes. Those gorgeous gray eyes… no! Be professional! "How are the repairs coming along?"

"Fine. I should have a list of requisitions soon."

I nod, then turn before I can embarrass myself further. I march back to my office, but before I get there, Tandize stops me. Older than Sarissa and I, she's still significantly younger than the rest of my coworkers, who have all been in the lab for decades. While she's relatively new, she shows promise—when she stops to think about things. "Chiara, which report am I supposed to use for these results?"

Proving my point! Her question is as irrelevant as it's annoying. "Did you get the submission sheet for reports when you joined us?"

Tandize frowns. Then her face brightens as she snaps her fingers. "Oh! You mean this?" She scratches around on her desk.

It's my turn to frown as I survey the jumble of papers, books, knickknacks, and... crumbs? "Tandize, you know I approve of eating, but really? The mess?"

She blushes and tries to brush the crumbs off her desk.

"No, not onto the floor!"

Frozen, Tandize stares at me, eyes wide.

Inwardly, I cringe. My tone was sharper than I intended, but I have no time for trivialities. "Get organized. Find that submission sheet. *Read* it! If you still have questions, ask your group leader. But before you do, get a brush and pan and clean. The last thing we need are insects crawling around in the lab."

Bewildered by this fresh outburst, but resolute in my decision not to back down, I attempt a smile to soften the blow. My face probably resembles a squished monkey's. "Come on, sweetheart, you can do better than this."

Her smile is slow, but it finally breaks through. "Yes, I guess I can."

It's about all I can do not to grab both her arms and shake her until her teeth rattle. What sort of response is that to give your boss? Either you can, or you can't, and if you can't, you have no business being here.

The vehemence of my thoughts prompts me to turn and leave. Curious glances follow me as I stomp back to my office. Thankfully, no one else dares stop me.

Still irritated, I try not to slam the door shut. *Could this day get any worse?* A second later, I curse myself for asking when Sarissa enters, her face ashen. I know what she's going to say before she voices it. "The Director?"

Gloom dampens those usually cheerful features as Sarissa nods.

I sigh. "I'm on my way."

It could simply be my frame of mind, but as I clomp to the elevator, I spot the way Tandize cringes when one of the SerSents passes her desk. Is she afraid of him?

My focus should be on my upcoming meeting, so I lower my gaze.

For the first time, I notice the shoes of some of my coworkers. More shocking is the state they're in. Some of their shoes even have holes in the soles! Most look like they've seen a century of use.

Their shoes plague me for the duration of the brief trip up to Cygnus's office. A plight I set aside the moment I see Hag Lady. Her severe bun holds her hair as restrictively as always, making the scowl on her face more menacing.

"He's waiting!"

Fine, and hello to you too. I dare not say the words out loud. Instead, I head for the door, mentally checking my mask of serenity is in place.

Before I even raise my hand to knock, the door flies open. Startled, my mask slips a fraction, and I step back. The director stands there, holding the door for me. "Well? Are you coming in?"

I'm so taken aback I need a moment to reply. "Yes, Director. Thank you, Director."

As I pass Cygnus on the way into his office, I swear I can feel the craters his eyes burn into my back. Standing taller, I cross the short distance to the place where I usually wait in front of his desk, keeping my back to him when I get there. Maybe this will discourage the dreaded handshake.

No such luck. Cygnus stops right next to me, then takes my hand in both of his, using the gesture to turn me to face him. I fight the urge to rip my hand free, pouring all my energy into keeping my face impassive. Still, those soft, fleshy hands crawling over mine are nearly impossible to ignore. As is his proximity. (Is this why I had those wayward thoughts the last time I was here in his office?)

I keep my gaze glued to the ground, avoiding those probing hazel eyes. Regret, then revulsion, fills me a second later when Cygnus tucks a hand under my chin and lifts my gaze. Now I fight to keep my mask in place, every fiber of my being straining against knocking those abhorrent hands away. *Stop it! You're imagining things and only likely to inflame matters if you keep this up!* I breathe, striving for calm.

"Chiara, Chiara, Chiara! What happened down there today?"

I blink, his kindly tone not what I was expecting. But I'll take it.

"My apologies, Director. I have no excuse. I should've exercised more control."

"But *why*, Chiara?"

I allow my shoulders to slump as I provide the carefully planned answer I came up with after realizing what I'd done. "The project seemed impossible in that moment."

"In that moment?"

Relieved he took the bait, I press on. "Yes, Director. But hitting that pipe helped me realize the problem wasn't insurmountable because those actions sparked the idea for a new mesh framework to bombard the atoms against. If I can rework the composition of the mesh and alter the toroid—"

"Yes, yes, it gave you an idea."

"It did, Director." My exultation at how well my subterfuge worked manifests to Cygnus as "delight" I found a solution. Cygnus loathes it when I talk science. Even though some of what I said was nonsense, it was enough for him to release me (though no happy dance yet!) and stalk around to his side of the desk.

He sits, then steeples his fingers under his chin. "Chiara, while I am pleased you had a breakthrough, you still haven't answered the question, have you?"

My heart jolts. *I didn't fool him for a second.* I pretend confusion. "Pardon, Director?"

"Come, Chiara. We've known each other too long to play these games. I know you understand."

With trepidation, I finally admit to what he already knows. "Yes, Director. I would not normally act so irrationally. My blood sugar levels were clearly off."

Cygnus sighs, content with my admission, then leans back in his chair. But his eyes never lose their intensity. "Are you going to make a habit of skipping meals?"

There it is. No matter how much I hoped he wouldn't hear I had missed breakfast, all information has a way of flowing back to him. "No, Director." I could explain it was an oversight caused by a lack of sleep, leading me to waking up late and not having enough time to eat, but Director Cygnus isn't interested in excuses.

"I'm pleased to hear you won't. Because if I have to call you in here again to discuss this… well, you'll force me to take action. You know how I hate doing that. I'd rather you make time to take care of yourself adequately."

Cygnus's concern bolsters my ability to provide a suitably humble reply. "Yes, Director, thank you for your kindness. You'll be pleased to know that after this morning's incident, I've already set safeguards in place to ensure no repeat performances."

Cygnus studies me for so long I wonder if he intends responding. I do my best not to squirm. As I stare back at him, a revelation about knocks me over. He's searching for something, something specific, something I don't know to hide and can't be careful of!

"What are your impressions of the new mechanic?"

The irrational change in topic floors me. And in that infinite sliver of time where my mind scrambles, my mask slips the teensiest fraction. The satisfaction lighting Cygnus's eyes is impossible to miss. Somehow, I gave him an answer. But what was the question?

Disturbed as I am by the thought, I hide my misgivings under my surprise. No point shoving it back under my mask. He's already glimpsed it. "The mechanic, Director? Um, well, uh, he's only just started working on the machine. I can provide an accurate assessment once he's completed the work."

Even to my own ears, my answer is underwhelming. But this was the last thing I expected. Figuring out *why* he asked will have to wait for a more opportune time. Alongside that other, more disturbing, question he sought an answer to so intently.

"Very well. You may go."

Stunned for the second time in as many minutes, I nod. "Thank you, Director." With the usual accompanying actions, I spit the infuriating words. "All for one and work for all." Barely waiting for his returned sentiment, I withdraw before he changes his mind. Or realizes I never went through the motions when I entered his office.

12

I forbid myself from thinking as I ride the elevator back down. Too many realizations and too much information in too little time. Difficult as it is with all the thoughts shrieking for attention, one more strident than the rest, I hold them captive all the way across the lab floor until I'm safely ensconced in my office. Then I turn my chair so my back is to the door and give them free rein.

With a deep breath, I close my eyes and lean back as I calm myself, focusing on letting the core issues come to me. In my mind, the questions rise and fall like sentences on a tide until the most pressing finally find their way to the crests of successive waves.

First, how could I have forgotten Cygnus's customary greeting when I entered his office? Will there be repercussions? No, Cygnus would've dealt with them then and there. Or did he not dole out justice because he was too focused on something else?

No, no, more of that topic later. I can no longer drown out the most vociferous thought. The way Cygnus always seems to know everything. There's only one rational explanation. Cameras recording our every action in CC HQ. Is this how the SerSents knew to bring me food after my meltdown this morning?

The revelation makes me sick to my stomach. Unable to deal with it, I let the next wave crash over me. This was the second meeting with Cygnus in less than a month. Typically, months pass between our meetings. Was my outburst the sole reason?

I think not because another factor looms large. Cygnus's manner was… disturbing today. He was looking for something. An answer to that question I still can't fathom. What, exactly, was he looking for?

Carefully, I replay the entire meeting in my mind. When I review things this way, he obviously meant to unsettle me from the outset. From opening the door for me, to his question about Deran, then his summary dismissal, he sought a response.

What responses had I given? I analyze my reactions. Surprise every time. Surprise I couldn't *hide or temper* each time. And let's not forget about my drastic faux pas forgetting to greet him properly.

Okay (deal with it—it happened), so what did my behavior tell him? What question was he really asking? I consider the problem for nearly half an hour, but come up empty. On the surface, my surprise is nothing unusual. But Cygnus gained knowledge from it, and therein lies the problem. What did he discover?

Over the years, I've learned to adapt to Director Cygnus's variable moods. But today was something else. Could it pertain to my current project? I cast my mind back, thinking about previous projects and looking for any indication he's behaved this way before.

My first project, assigned when I'd barely been at the academy three months, was a compound allowing heating element filaments to operate for longer periods of time. Director Cygnus said constant filament burnouts meant people couldn't stay warm, and he couldn't have a population complaining they were cold. Although a simple project, it still took me the better part of a year to complete, working on it as I was in between classes.

This was followed by the chemical inhibitor aimed at discouraging plants from growing in all directions and following a single trained path instead. Cygnus said this would let the botanists grow plants vertically, increasing food production without requiring more space. Fewer people would go hungry.

After this project, and some others, came the mandate for tiny transmitters, designed to travel down wiring paths and send images back so supervisors could detect and correct problems in manufacturing and power plants before malfunctions occurred. I was quite proud of those little creations—they ensured the machines needed to sustain life continued running without interruption.

Other projects followed, each more complex than the last, like he was testing my limits. Then came the order for a new coating on the synthetic chips used in our comm links. I remember the difficulty that one posed, and my finger touches the spot behind my right ear where my implant resides. The coating reduced allergic reactions when the chip encountered human tissue. Almost impossible, but I managed it.

Only to be confronted by the greenhouse project. The project where I dared defy the conglomerate—and where my family paid the price. A price I pray will never be exacted from them again. The object lesson where the Board used my family to demonstrate what would happen if I didn't deliver. If Director Cygnus hadn't stepped in...

Bitter thoughts drive me to my feet. As I pace the confines of my office, more projects sift through my mind. The replay, as always, allows me to see things from another angle. It's only now I understand at last.

I stumble to a halt, the realization a gut punch felling me. My knees crash down, but pain is a distant cry. I cover my mouth with my hands, stifling the scream tearing free. Horror rakes talons down my skin, leaving bloody trenches. *No! It can't be! Please, no!*

But I can't escape the truth. Today is not the first time I've felt Cygnus was hiding something. In all those meetings where he imposed assignments and told me the Board's reasoning, he had that pitying look. Like he knew something I didn't. And I finally think I know what. An answer I cannot bear to look at. A revelation I want more than anything to *not* be true.

There are alternate applications for every single thing I've invented. What if the reasons I was given were never real? Did the Board always intend using my work for something else?

The thought bites. I can't believe I was duped all this time! I run blindly from my office, streaking down the narrow paths between lab benches to the elevator. Rattled, I stab at the button, then realize I can't wait. I slap the stairwell door open and dash down the stairs until I reach the gym floor.

Battering the door open, I sprint along the corridor to the reception area, frantically waving my arm over the access pad. The machine beeps, and the bar lifts, not fast enough because I hit my hip on it as I dash through. Though I grunt at the bruising contact, I don't stop.

In seconds, I'm in the locker room, flinging the door to my unit open the moment the chip in my wrist gives me access. I strip out of my lab gear, snatch up the workout clothes in my locker, and toss them on. I take only the most essential amount of time to tie my shoes.

Then I'm in the gym, hopping on the treadmill, pumping up the pace. My feet pound the rubber track, thumping, the sound not nearly loud enough to muffle my thoughts.

No, no, no! It can't be! Was I so desperate to believe I could be a savior to the tormented masses I closed myself off to the reality of my situation? After a ruthless five minutes, the panic recedes as my feet beat the track. The regular rhythm and familiar exercise calms me as nothing else does.

With the more composed perspective, my brain functions again. Instead of beating against a cage, a bird trapped, unable to find its way free, the door opens, and my mind soars free.

If Director Cygnus knew they were lying to me, why didn't he tell me? *Duh! Because he's probably under duress similar to my own; his every move monitored and controlled by the Board.* So, what would the Board have to gain? No, wrong question. Obviously, the other applications for my inventions could've made them richer than sin. But they have too much money already. What is the conglomerate's core desire?

Double duh! Power! I almost trip, catching myself against the rails on either side of the track to avert a disaster. I stand, feet on either side of the track, frozen. *Yes, they could definitely have used my inventions to gain an advantage.*

But if so… Rage boils, pumping over the edge of the pot. On its own, running won't suffice today. I snap the treadmill's power off and bound over to the punching bag hanging in one corner. While I would love to beat the stuffing out of it without pause, I must protect my hands.

Shoddy though the wrappings are, they'll do. I bounce up and take my fury out on an inanimate object. The thought elicits a berserk little laugh.

It breaks free, and I stop punching, looking around to see who heard. Thankfully, no one. I set to work, pummeling the bag until I feel better, working up a good sweat in the process and numbing my mind to further agonizing thoughts.

When I'm breathing so hard I think I might pass out, I stop for a drink of water. Time enough for a quick round of push-ups, pull-ups, and sit-ups. Then a spin around the circuit should do it.

By the time I finish, I'm so exhausted I can't even think. Perfect. Exactly what I was aiming for. I stagger back to the locker room, toss my sweaty clothes into my designated hamper, and step into the shower.

Hot water rains down on me, easing the ache in my trembling muscles. More than an hour later, I finally exit the gym, absolutely drained. I limp back to the lab, bumping into Sarissa as I exit the elevator into the lab.

"Good workout?"

"Yes."

My following groan draws a concerned glance. "You didn't overdo it, did you?"

"Nope, you know me. Have to work through those problems. Get a handle on them." I pump my fist for emphasis.

Sarissa watches the beads of perspiration still forming on my face. "I don't know how you can stand to be so active."

"You probably get as much of a workout on that dance floor every night."

A giggle. "I suppose I do. Did you eat yet?"

With a start, I realize it's almost dinnertime. I glance around the lab and notice it's dark. Most people have already left. "Did Deran give you a list of supplies to requisition?"

"He did. And you're avoiding the question."

I blink, processing the preceding conversation. "Oh, sorry. I wasn't trying to avoid it. It just didn't register—"

"Because you haven't eaten," Sarissa interrupts. Then, sounding a little less accusatory, she adds, "You asked me to remind you about meals."

I take her hand in mine. "Yes, thank you, I did. I'll call for dinner now."

"I have a better idea." The glint in Sarissa's eyes warns me. "Why don't we go home and get you into that gorgeous dress I bought you? Then we can grab dinner together before we go clubbing?"

"Aw, Sarissa, you know how I feel about the clubs."

"But you haven't worn your dress yet! Don't make me regret buying it for you."

I could point out I didn't have a choice, but that's not the issue here.

Using her hands to cover mine, Sarissa pulls me toward her. "Come on! Please? I know it was a rough day. Perhaps a change of scenery will help." She hesitates. "You know I don't understand all the science stuff, but perhaps you can talk at me over dinner, and that will help?"

More like give her more time to convince me about the club. Not that she needs to. When Sarissa mentioned the change of scenery, I identified with that. I'm tired of being cooped up here. Worn out by the constant thoughts and fears. "Okay."

"Okay?" Wild delight in her eyes, a smile spreads across her face. "Really? You'll come clubbing too?"

"Yes. Now let's get out of here before I change my mind."

13

Two hours later, I'm wondering what insanity made me agree. The club's pounding music is giving me a headache, and the dazzling swathes of psychedelic lights raking the room make it worse. Did they have to put those astatine-forsaken rolling lights on the walls *and* ceiling?

Blearily, I scan for Sarissa on the dance floors: several of them and stacked at varying heights. How do they stay aloft? I peer up at the underside of one floor, but the pulsing light makes it impossible to discern anything.

"Thinking science again, Geek Girl?" Horton plops down next to me, sliding an arm behind me along the faux-leather bench seat we share.

I scoot away from him, his sweaty body against mine repugnant. His leer follows me, and my desperation to find Sarissa increases. I'm beyond exhausted. I need to leave. Why did Horton have to end up with me in Sarissa's absence?

Ever since I did some freelance work for Horton, he's thought he has some kind of right to me. More so after he mentioned it to some of his cohorts and they added to my freelance work. Although I'm grateful for the work that kept me occupied over long, lonely weekends when I was between projects and the untraceable chards they paid me with (no cash to trace with chip cards), I owe him nothing. Besides, he and his cronies aren't the only people I've done outside work for. "What if I am?"

Horton snorts derisive laughter, tapping the side of my head with none-too-gentle jabs. "Always thinking, always scheming, aren't you?"

"You know she is. How else will she raise her tier?"

Karina plops down on the other side of me, sandwiching me between them. Panic rises because I know what's coming.

Cool, assessing eyes study me as Karina drums long, pointy nails on the table. "Do you know how far you have to go to rise even one tier?"

"I don't think she does." Horton slithers closer again, that arm curling around my shoulders. The rank odor of his stale sweat and cheap alcohol swamps me.

"Horton, get off!" I shove both the hand caressing my shoulder and the hand on my bare thigh away. Then I bump a hip against Karina. "Excuse me, I need to get out."

A soft chuckle. "No, you don't. You don't understand the system, do you?" Karina raises a lazy hand, beckoning to one of the nearby servers who scurries over. "Get us another... why, Chiara, is that orange juice?"

My cheeks heat. Does she have to be such a... no, no name-calling! My mother raised me better than that. In the little time she had, anyway. And why do I feel the need to apologize for not drinking? After the workout I had today, it's the logical choice. "Unlike you, Karina, I don't need alcohol to enjoy myself."

Horton's guffaw echoes over the thumping music. "That would be classic if it were true. But Chiara, your face is pinched enough to outdo a prune! You wouldn't know how to have fun if you tried. Why don't you let me show you?"

This time Karina laughs, the sound shrill and spiteful. "Yes, Chiara, let us help you." Glaring at the poor server still waiting for her order, she barks, "Bring the lady a Titteraba."

I have no idea what that is. Only that it's the name of a penal colony, so it doesn't bode well. Desperate, I shove Karina a little harder, smirking when I succeed in moving her. (If only I could've knocked her off her perch and onto the floor, but a girl's got to take what she can get, right?)

As Karina debates fighting me or giving way, I remember this is another reason I hate coming to these places with Sarissa. Because of how they make me feel—like an interloper. Which, of course, I am. Maybe not to Sarissa because, for whatever reason, I can do no wrong in her eyes. But it's obvious her friends don't share her sentiment.

Karina must realize I won't back down because she huffs and slides out, allowing me to exit the booth. "You'll crawl back soon enough."

Horton's raucous laughter drowns anything else she might say as I struggle through the crush of people on the dance floor. I must get out! I'm beyond caring about finding Sarissa to tell her I'm leaving when I bump into her. Or rather, she stumbles into me.

"Chiara! There you are! Come dance with me." Her words are so slurred, I struggle to understand. She winds her arms around my neck, pulling me in as her body sways to the music, sinuous and sensual.

Uncomfortable, I wriggle away. Sarissa's drunk. Really, I have to deal with this too? "I'm going home."

"Aw, but why? We just got here. Come on, stay a little longer. Dance with me."

As she moves, her dress slips off one shoulder, exposing a dangerous amount of cleavage. I hook the strap back up. "Perhaps we've had enough partying for one night. Why don't I take you home?"

Sarissa's pout only makes her more beautiful. "Don't be a party pooper. What's wrong?"

I'm surprised she can even tell something's bothering me, but a response slips out before I can censor it. "Your friends. They don't like me very much."

"Aw, don't worry about them. They're just jealous." Sarissa loops her arms over my neck again, drawing me close and whispering in my ear. "They wish they could invent things like you do. Then they could help Cygnus and become his darlings too."

I freeze. "Pardon?"

Sarissa titters. "Don't you know your inventions are the only reason for Cygnus's meteoric rise through the ranks?"

Abruptly, I'm overheating. There's not enough air. Out! I must get out! I stagger away from Sarissa, ignoring her pleas to come back. Pushing blindly through the crowd, I bump and bash and beat my way to the exit. Then I'm free. Outside in the cool night, and sucking in air.

My mind reels. Did Sarissa really mean it? Or was the alcohol giving rise to wild speculation? Did the Board really appoint Cygnus as Director because of my inventions? As I shuffle back to the trundle, I ponder Sarissa's words. It's possible technology, or rather technological innovation (CC's kryptonite), made Cygnus director. But was his rise solely my doing?

When he liberated our family so we could "be all we could be," he was just another officer in charge of another group of people. Now he's the director of the conglomerate. The only tier ten in our society. Yes, it's quite possible I'm the reason for his rise. Or at least partly.

But I don't care to consider the depth of truth in Sarissa's flippant comment. The realization is too painful. I'm worn out, beyond the capacity for rational thought. Wearily, I hop onto the trundle, riding it home and collapsing into bed, waking the next morning with a still-fuzzy head. Too fuzzy for my morning trundle ritual, so when I reach work, my mind is still stuck on the bomb Sarissa dropped last night.

Sarissa is waiting with my coffee and schedule when I reach my office. I stop and stare, unable to assimilate the transformation. Eyes clear, perfectly made-up face and sleek, upswept hair, paired with a crisp, tailored navy suit that screams, "All business." Huffing out air, I toss both arms up in disbelief. "How can you look so put together after last night? I swear, I didn't drink a drop, but it sure doesn't feel that way!"

With a laugh, Sarissa hands me my coffee. "I'm used to it. Shall we get started?"

I sip my coffee before responding, observing Sarissa's perkiness. How does she do it?

Who am I kidding? The coffee and errant thoughts are only delaying the inevitable. I'd love to ignore Sarissa's comment because the last thing I want is to sour things between us first thing in the morning. But I don't have that luxury.

"Are my inventions really the reason Cygnus is the director?"

Sarissa fumbles the folders, and they fall to the floor, spilling paper everywhere. She drops to her knees and starts collecting the mess, but I didn't miss the panic in her eyes. If she thinks she can use her actions to avoid answering, she's wrong. I'm about to press the issue when she rises, a fixed smile on her face. "Why ever would you say that?"

"Because you told me that last night."

Now fear and confusion cloud those lovely brown eyes. Was she too drunk to remember telling me?

"No, I didn't. Maybe that's what you heard, but that's not what I said."

The way Sarissa sneaks a glance out my door and then around my room spikes echoing fear through my own body as I remember my concerns about cameras in CC HQ. Abruptly, I'm as anxious as she is to drop the subject. "Yes, I'm sorry. You're no doubt correct."

Although I expect relief from Sarissa (and there is some), there's more... fear? Suspicion? I can't quite work it out before it's gone and she's taking a seat, handing me my folders, and carrying on as if the whole surreal conversation never happened.

Once she leaves my office, though, Sarissa avoids me for the rest of the day, reinforcing my belief in her claim. But reconciling this truth with my caring Director Cygnus is difficult. Is it possible he's just been using me all this time? I refuse to believe it. After everything he's done for our family, it's unlikely. Besides, isn't he entitled to a little good fortune returning to him considering how much he's helped us?

But my mind remains troubled. I make no progress during the day despite a visit to the gym to clear my head and several attempts at picking up the nebulous thread that's my work. Late that afternoon, too restless to sit for another second, I march onto the lab floor and pace up the first aisle, inspecting the various projects my coworkers are engaged in.

For the most part, their projects are independent of mine and almost all are requisitioned by the Board. Although occasionally, I enlist their help with sections of my own project (where they have the skill to handle it) or assign them something I've had an idea for and which the Board (via Cygnus) has approved. Whatever the task, as head of this lab, I must oversee their work. The fun (and interesting) part of this job I enjoy, because Al-Li knows, I hate the assignment part. Deciding which person or group is best suited to a new project is wholly disagreeable.

By the time I reach the last aisle, having dealt with all the questions asked, calm has returned. Finally! More because I know what I must do to set my mind at ease. Something I should've done yesterday. I leave the lab floor, late enough my coworkers are already packing up for the day and settle back at my desk, picking up my digital notepad.

I almost drop it in surprise again when Sarissa pops her head into my office. "I'm off. This is your reminder to eat, as you requested."

"Yes, I'll eat." She waits, and I sigh, pressing the comm link behind my ear and ordering the meal. "Satisfied?"

Sarissa blows a kiss, then hurries away to catch the elevator while it still lingers on our floor. Or to avoid more awkward questions from me?

My eyes return to my digital notepad, still clutched in my hand. No time like the present. Indifferent as to order, I list the (Cygnus-approved) projects the Board assigned me on one half of the pad, then use the other half to match alternative uses for each. I'm careful *not* to save my work. Paranoid as I now am about those invisible eyes, who knows if they monitor what I save? I glance at the first few projects that came to mind immediately:

- Reflective paint to keep buildings cool > shielding strong enough to hide military installations from infrared scans.
- Tiny transmitters > can travel along any wires, not just those in industrial machinery. Used to spy on people?

- Comm link coating > suitable for coating anything to avoid a reaction with human tissue; what other things are in our bodies?
- Greenhouse project > my special designer glass is strong enough for a cage; a glass cage that could serve as a prison? (*Really, Chiara? Who uses glass prisons?*)

Mortified at how easily these first few came to mind, I continue. The list grows. When it overflows the screen, I set the stylus down. With deliberate care, I swipe across the screen, deleting all I've written before leaning back in my chair and considering that list. That insanely *long* list.

Perhaps I went a little crazy. Whoever would use my inventions in those more outlandish ways would've had to make significant modifications. Even if they *could* alter them or simply used my inventions as they were but for another purpose, what could I do? Confront Cygnus? Demand to know what the Board was really after?

Mirthless laughter snips the air. If Cygnus hasn't told me the truth thus far (assuming he even knows all of it), what makes me think he'll tell me now? No, I have to be canny. If he has been playing games with me, I have to get with the program. Be better at those games than he is. Figure out what he does, and doesn't, really know.

I smile, afforded some comfort by the thought. I'm virtually unbeatable when I put my mind to things. Then again, I am going up against Cygnus. A formidable opponent at any time, let alone when his position is on the line. Possibly even his life, if the Board has the same hold over him as they do over me. But if all I think might be true is, then I'm about to become his fiercest opponent. Let's just hope I'm smart enough (and strong enough) to dominate the challenge—and my family won't be caught in the crossfire.

14

With a sigh, I rise. It's time to go home. I spot the food tray on my desk, the gravy congealed, vegetables glued to the plate, and salad a soggy mess. No way. I'll eat when I get home. I dump the meal in the nearest incinerator, then leave the empty plates on my desk.

Despite not planning on staying late, my list took longer than I thought. It's hours past midnight by the time I gather my things, switch off the lab lights, and make my solitary way out of the building.

As I plod to the trundle, I seek solace in the only important thing: my recent actions haven't resulted in consequences for my family. But I can't continue taking such risks. Another outburst, another careless conversation or any hint I'm questioning Cygnus, and the outcome for them could be vastly different.

When the trundle arrives, I'm shocked to find it crowded with people. In fact, it's so full I struggle to find a seat. Although, as I fight the lurch of the trundle propelling itself toward the next stop, I'm even more astounded by the suspicious glances I receive.

Unnerved, I check I'm not still wearing my lab coat. My hand goes to my hair, but no, I combed it out, and I don't have one or more styluses stuck in it. Maybe I have something on my face. No, I didn't eat, so... Coming up empty, I slink into a seat near the back and slide down, hoping the chair in front will hide me from prying eyes.

Regrettably, it doesn't shield me from the person next to me or those across the aisle. They shrink away, as if I'm going to infect them or something. I feel only marginally better when they treat the next person who steps on the trundle the same way.

This man, stepping onto the trundle, provides insight. He and I are the only ones with briefcases. I drop my gaze again. The shoes of my fellow travelers are in the same dire state as those of my coworkers. Unable to help myself, I glance at the clothes worn by the lady next to me. Threadbare and thin enough to be mistaken for rags. My own clothes are luxurious by comparison. Decent quality and thick enough to still keep me warm despite the cool night air. Surreptitiously, I peek at Briefcase Man. His clothes are as respectable as mine.

The lady next to me shifts, and I feel the heat of her glare. Not wanting a confrontation, my eyes swivel downward again. How have I never noticed the state of some people's clothes before? Are my coworkers' clothes in the same state as their shoes, but I can't tell because their lab coats hide it?

The trundle jerks to a stop, and I realize it's mine. No other passengers have disembarked in all this time. Meaning all these people live further from CC HQ than I do—their tiers are lower. Could explain the clothes. Catching sight of the hostile glances directed my way, I exit hurriedly, then scuttle down the road to my apartment, liberated on the empty streets. However, my respite is short-lived. Stepping into my building is like entering an unknown world.

Instead of the glittering lights and bustling shoppers, the dark maw of the lower-level gapes at me. Worse, like cockroaches scattering from the sun, I hear skittering feet as people scamper to hide in the deeper shadows.

Curious, I stop and squint into the dark corners, trying to make out shapes. "Hello?" Soft shuffles, feet shifting on the marble floors, but no reply. "Hello? Who is down there?" More silence. "If you don't show yourselves, I'll call the SerSents."

This time, a man of indeterminate age steps into the small pool of light cast by a lantern in the food court. "Our apologies for disturbing you, ma'am. We're the cleaning crew. Please, don't call the SerSents."

His words don't have as much of an impact as his attire. Why am I so obsessed with clothes tonight—and what on earth is the man wearing? Scraps of fabric stitched together into a large, shapeless coat. Even worse than the clothes worn by the lady on the trundle. "What's your name?"

"Sam, ma'am. Please, don't concern yourself with us." Sam's eyes dart around, as though he's expecting a platoon of SerSents to storm through the door. He picks at the fraying hem around the sleeve of his coat, licking cracked lips, shifting from foot to foot.

"Sam, am I making you nervous?"

His head bobs. "Yes, ma'am. You're not supposed to see us. Could you please go?"

What is he talking about? "Sam, who is 'us?' And why am I not supposed to see you?"

The foot bobbing picks up. "'We' being the cleaning crew, ma'am. We must remain invisible."

An incredulous snort (very unladylike!) huffs out. "Really? You expect me to believe you're cleaning this building when droids exist?"

"It's the truth, ma'am. Droids are too expensive to use anywhere except secure locations."

His explanation floors me. How have I never known this? Is this what he meant when he said they had to remain invisible? No, no, that can't be right! "Sam, back up! You mean to say humans clean all buildings?"

"Not all buildings, ma'am. Just those where security levels aren't high." More shuffling and nervous glances as Sam's agitation rises. "Please, ma'am, if you could just be on your way and forget you ever saw us? We'd be much obliged."

I gawk, unsure whether to be outraged or offended. But the man's eyes roll around so much now they're almost falling out of his head, scanning for that hidden threat.

"Alright, Sam." I raise my hands to soothe him. "I'm going. Just one last question?"

"Yes, ma'am?"

"Would you like a new coat?"

I didn't expect his stunned expression. It's followed by suspicion, then terror. "No, ma'am. I do alright, thank you."

I strain to catch the last words as Sam backs into the shadows again. Then he's gone, swallowed by the dark.

***

The next morning, I'm back to the grind, my usual morning trundle routine already providing ideas for the machine by the time I reach the lab. I forget to ask Sarissa about the cleaners as she takes me through my schedule for the day. After she tells me Deran (lots of winking and leering on her part!) will be around later to finish repairing the containment unit, I dismiss her and settle down to science. I tap the first folder I was too impatient to deal with thoroughly before and begin reading.

"I brought you some lunch."

I jump, almost stabbing myself in the eye with the pointy end of the stylus I was fiddling with. Sarissa stands on the other side of my desk, two food trays in hand. I didn't even hear her enter. Hmm, a peace offering after avoiding me yesterday? Smiling, I stretch, extending my arms over my head. A quick check of the time confirms I've lost the morning. "Thanks. Are you joining me?"

"If that won't disturb you?"

"No, I need a break." I do a few more stretches, working out the kinks in my neck and shoulders before sliding my tray closer. Only then do I notice the color. Blue. *Ugh!* I glance at Sarissa and catch the frown marring her features. Best to get this over with. "Yes, my turn."

"Oh, Chiara! I'm so sorry! I about bit the head off the lady at the cafeteria when she said you could only have blue trays. When did it change?"

"I'm not sure. I didn't notice when I ate last night—too tired or too dark, but the fact of the matter stared me in the face this morning when I opened my refrigerator."

Like me, Sarissa also had green trays once upon a time. Then, one day, hers were suddenly blue. Her obvious devastation at the change made me hesitate about asking the reason for it. But my curiosity got the better of me, and two days later, I capitulated.

Lips curling with obvious disdain, Sarissa explained that as we aged, our metabolisms slowed. Since Cygnus was all about "taking care of the population," our food accommodated our aging. While the meals remained more or less the same, they modified the nutrients added to prevent us from gaining excess weight.

Later, Sarissa became obsessed with weighing herself when her tray color changed again, going from blue to yellow and then, a few months later, orange. Blows she struggled to overcome. Is still struggling to overcome. I've seen the envy in her eyes as I pick out my green trays. *Picked out.*

Sarissa shivers. "Isn't it weird how the food just changes like that?"

Now that Sarissa mentions it, I wonder how it's done. "Do you think people sneak into your apartment to change things out, or do you think they have some sort of conveyor with a back entrance to your refrigerator?"

The surprised bark of laughter from Sarissa is unexpected. "I think your inventive mind is running away with you. I doubt there are any conveyors or back doors. More likely gnomes that slip in and change things out."

My turn to chuckle. "You mean I'm not wrong about my refrigerator being magical?"

We collapse into hysterics, fueled more by the desire to escape the depressing aspects of the change than genuine mirth.

When we finally quiet, Sarissa is about to tuck into her food but then she slides me an enquiring glance. "So, any new discoveries?"

Thankful for the change in topic, I shrug. "Perhaps. It's too early to tell. What's your news?"

We fill the next thirty minutes with idle chitchat, Sarissa going on about a new restaurant that we "simply have to try" and her clothing dilemma for an upcoming party hosted by her parents.

The only knowledge I have of her parents is what little I've gleaned in the few times I've met them as Board representatives at Cygnus's dreaded parties. Sarissa rarely mentions them, but when she does, it's always with a sense of duty. I've often mused whether there's any love in the relationship or merely a series of obligations she must fulfill.

Since discussing them upsets her, I allow her to prattle on about her dress choices, oohing and aahing when she shows me pictures. Am I a terrible friend because I'm relieved when Deran pokes his head into my office? "Sounds like the party's in here."

An idiotic grin finds its way onto my face, the sight of his cheeky smile scattering coherent thoughts. Sarissa, still with her back to him, rolls her eyes at me before turning in her chair. "Hi, Deran."

The greeting spurs me to supply my own. It also reminds me why he's here. "I believe we have all the supplies you requisitioned. Sarissa?"

"We do." Sarissa rises. To my eternal envy, I can't spot a single crumb or speck of food on her impeccable gray business suit. "If you'll follow me?"

She leaves, Deran in tow, and I'm left sitting alone in my office. Well, not totally alone. I watch Deran's easy stride, those long legs, and sigh. Maybe next time I'll be less addled. Turning back to the file I was working on, I dive in.

Over the next days, I keep returning to two specific projects. I'm sure I'm not seeing something. It's like grasping smoke: the moment I reach out to grab it, it splinters into wisps, eluding capture. And precisely like smoke hinting at a fire, I'm convinced the prospect of further developments lurks inside these two project folders.

However, I just can't seem to draw the lines leading me to the desired conclusion, revealing the blaze burning beneath. Increasingly, my brain feels fettered. Able to stretch only so far before an unseen chain yanks it back. Like a broken choke in a long-ago automobile restricting the flow of air, I can't seem to find the lever to release my mind.

So I plug away at the problem. Through a tedious process of elimination, I narrow the files in each folder down to a paper a researcher wrote in the one project and a tangential product the researcher worked on in the other.

This done, I realize both options have a problem. Some of the macro-mechanics are beyond my technical abilities. I need a specialist. With a touch of the button on my intercom, I ask Sarissa to call engineering and request a consultation.

When they send Deran, I can't say I'm surprised, but really? Couldn't they have sent Jason so I could at least remember my questions? Instead, Deran graces my office doorway early the next afternoon. At least he doesn't find me with my butt facing him. He didn't even have to knock. I had been staring into the nothingness above my desk, using my mind palace to think through a problem, when he appeared. A vision.

I snort at the thought, then wish I could take it back when Deran's eyebrows quirk upward. "Nothing, sorry! It's just me and my silly imagination."

"You won't tell me what that imagination conjured to bring that smile to your face?"

My smile? Had I smiled? "No, not today, not ever."

Deran laughs. I've missed the sound, even though I've only heard it once before. But the laugh brings the same warm fuzziness as last time. *Stop it!* "Um..." For the life of me, I can't remember why he's here.

"You wanted a consult?" Deran prompts.

"Oh, yes, thank you! Won't you sit?"

Deran folds himself into the chair opposite, and I hastily avert my gaze to my holoscreen. The sight of his hunky frame squeezing into that too-small chair sends my mind down paths best left unexplored. For now, anyway.

With a flick of my wrist, I cast the schematics (wretched antiquated 2-D images) from one project onto the wall behind my chair.

This way, I can show him the bits I have questions on without looking at him.

"Perhaps you can help me make sense of this—" I begin, before launching into what I think the colliding beam fusion reactor does and how. I'm doing fine, in the flow of things, when I realize he's standing next to me. Startled, my eyes fly to his. Contact with those gray eyes wipes all thoughts from my head.

Dastardly eyes crinkling around the edges, he directs my attention back to the screen, pointing at a piece on the diagram, drawing my gaze back there. "You were talking about this particle accelerator design."

Voice a little strangled, I'm soon back on track. Until his hand accidentally brushes against mine as he reaches for another part of the image. I freeze, mentally and physically.

Deran takes it in stride, either not noticing or pretending not to. His arm continues forward in a smooth motion, touching the static target we were discussing and explaining how using it to replace one of the colliding beams won't affect flow rates and is thus unlikely to result in increased fusion.

He studies the options I've lined up at the bottom of the screen before selecting a different particle accelerator design and putting it on the main screen. "Now, if we tweak this design, here and here," Deran indicates the two places, "I believe we can improve acceleration by up to fifty percent."

I raise my eyebrows. "And you just came up with that number off the top of your head?"

Another devastating grin. "No, I worked it out. Don't tell me you couldn't do it in your head if you knew how."

Rising to the challenge, I lift my chin. "Try me. After all, I should verify your calculations."

Eyes flashing with humor (how does the silver there do that?) Deran explains the formulas. Fortunately, they're complicated enough I'm forced to focus on them and not those mesmerizing eyes. "So, the 'd' value for displacement needs to be at a maximum, right?"

"Correct."

I consider the variables, then plug them into the formulas Deran gave me, changing the variables to account for alternate possibilities and coming up with a range of solutions. "Huh! 49.8372% on the top end. I suppose I'll grant your fifty percent claim."

"Gee, thanks!" Deran's voice is dry, but that amused smile says more than it should.

"You're ridiculously good at that."

"Leering at you?"

Stumped, I don't remember what I meant.

Deran takes pity on me. "Sorry, couldn't resist. No, don't worry, I know you meant the mental arithmetic. Thanks. I've always had a knack for it."

"I'd say more than a knack. You did the calculations faster than I did."

Laughter now. That soothing blanket. "You sound put out."

"I am. I'm not used to anyone being better than me at math."

"Never mind, I'm sure now that you understand the formulas, my superiority will soon be a thing of the past."

I ignore the indulgent grin by turning my attention back to the particle accelerator design we were considering. "So you think this is the one we should use?"

"I do."

Once we've exhausted my remaining questions on this type of reactor, I replace the data with that for magnetic fusion energy reactors. Deran is far more animated about these, explaining how the construction of the drum containing the bulk plasma can be modified to increase the chances of the ions colliding.

I'm so engrossed in his explanation, I step forward without thinking and trip over my own feet.

Grinning, Deran catches me and helps me regain my balance. "Should we wrap you in cotton balls?"

Flustered, by the strength in his grip again, the unexpected tingle where his hands held me and my own embarrassment, I can't find words.

"Maybe not then? Or we could use the cotton balls in the reactor. Do you think that would work?"

I blink at him for a second before realizing he's joking. A startled giggle slips out. "I don't think the cotton balls would do too well in the plasma."

Deran rubs his chin thoughtfully. "You don't think so? Well, we could try a different plasma, one with a lower density. I mean for the ions, not the cotton balls." Just like that, he's back to our interrupted discussion of options we could consider for this type of reactor.

Somehow, I bumble through, and by the time Deran leaves, I have a better understanding of what I'm looking at. I'm also acutely aware of how considerate he was. Every time I faltered, acted like I've never seen a boy before, he steered the conversation back to the machine. Back to my comfort zone. Something else I could lose myself in.

Deran isn't yet out of sight before Sarissa slips back in. "You did much better. Only lost track of what you were nine times."

The laughter is a release. "You were counting?"

"Of course! What else would a P.A. be doing instead of sticking around to help her boss?"

"You mean ogle the guy!"

Sarissa giggles. "That too! Could he help?"

"Yes. He must be talented to have reached such proficiency at his age."

"At his age?" Another eye roll from Sarissa. "You make him sound ancient. You do know he's only three years older than you?"

A laugh sneaks out. "And you only know this because you had to confirm he was older than you? So now you know he is, what are you planning to do about it?"

Sarissa pretends to pick at the berry-colored polish on a perfectly manicured nail. "Oh, I don't plan to do anything with him." She levels her gaze at me. "I was rather hoping you might."

Something between a snort and a laugh escapes. "Sarissa!"

"What? He's cute. And I can see you like him. Come on, admit it. You know you like him, you know you want him." She delivers the last sentence in a singsong voice, reminding me of some old movie I once watched.

I hurl my massage ball at her. "Out!"

Chortling, she catches it, then tosses it back before waltzing out of my office.

I stare at my screen again, aware I have an enormous smile on my face. I'm just not sure of the real reason. Nor do I care to dwell on it.

15

After Deran's explanations, it was a matter of sitting down and grinding through options. It took serious work and long days, but I'm almost giddy with delight when I come up with not one, but *three* potential solutions. The first two are significantly more promising, so I'll focus on them. Hopefully, one will succeed. If neither does, I can explore the third as a last resort. Although I really hope I won't have to go there because it has more obstacles than the first two.

I call Sarissa to my office. She appears seconds later. "Yes?"

"I need to talk at you for a few minutes."

Grinning, Sarissa sinks into the chair opposite me. "Sure. Although, you know Deran's probably more likely to understand what you're saying."

"You know why I didn't ask him."

Sarissa chuckles. "I do. But it would've been fun watching you try."

I throw my massage ball at her and she almost misses catching it she's laughing so much. "Would've served you right if it had hit you." But I can't hide my grin. While talking at Sarissa helps me clarify ideas, the reverse would've been true if I had to do this with Deran. "Although, I am getting better at talking to him, right?"

Sarissa only grins. "I'm here. Talk away."

"Okay, I've come up with two options. First, I'll try reproducing the contamination in the original Cluster Impact Fusion experiment."

"Wait, what? Contamination?"

My turn to chuckle. "At least you're listening. Most days, you just zone out."

"I do, but contamination? How will that help?"

"A contaminant is the reason that team saw a fusion reaction. When they used a magnetic filter to eliminate it, they couldn't recreate their results. So I propose adding more of the contaminant, or variations thereof, to see if I can reproduce their accidental fusion effect."

Sarissa huffs. "That doesn't sound safe. This *is* nuclear energy we're talking about."

"Wow! You're really into this today."

With a toss of her hair, Sarissa touches her face. "I like this face. I'd hate to lose it."

"You won't. Adding the contaminant is perfectly safe. It's just means coating the wire mesh with different chemical combinations. If those don't work, I can experiment with meshes made from some new metal alloys they didn't have back then. Since accelerators have also advanced, I don't anticipate any problems."

"Okay, you've lost me."

"Never mind, you don't need to understand the accelerator issues. Suffice to say that was prototype number one. Prototype number two is a version of magnetic confinement, using field-reversed configuration."

"Field-reversed configuration? Really. Chiara?"

I laugh at her scowl. "It's just the name for a type of plasma device. Basically, I'll use magnetic fields to confine the fusion fuel in plasma form. The real problem is containing the plasma at sufficient densities for an extended period."

"And how will you overcome that, genius?"

"Let's hope I can! I'll arrange the magnetic fields in various ways and hopefully hit on the right combination."

Sarissa waits for more, but when she realizes I'm finished, she relaxes visibly. "Okay, that wasn't so bad. Did you get it clear in your head?"

"I did, thanks!"

"So, what's next?"

My turn to pull a face. "Requisitions."

A groan from Sarissa. "Really? How many?"

"Plenty, and they all have to be signed by the director."

Another groan. "You do know that will alert him to your progress?"

"Regrettably so." I can already see his smirk as he says he told me so—that I could do it. Pull the rabbit out of the hat. When I notice Sarissa's raised eyebrow, I elaborate. "These requisitions are coming far earlier in the process than they usually do. Normally, when I requisition materials, they're all I'll need to complete the work. This time, they're what I'll need to *start* the work. I'll have to add a rather explicit caveat that these materials could yield no results since neither prototype may be viable in the end."

"Oh, I can see how that might be a problem. Perhaps we should get started then. Do you have a list?"

I hand it over, wondering how much explaining Cygnus will require.

When the requisitions return with a mere request for a report, but no command to meet with Cygnus, I'm ecstatic. On the flip side, a meeting with Cygnus could've allowed me to temper his expectations.

In lieu of the meeting (yes!), I provide the report, making it painstakingly obvious I require these materials for testing prototypes —not the real machine.

I explain (do I really have to repeat myself several times?) the theories are still in their infancy, and it may be a significant amount of time before I hit on a solution to the ultimate end goal.

Whatever I may have thought, I don't expect the requisitions to come back approved without further inquiries. Nor do I expect the accompanying note from Cygnus—the real shocker!

The note congratulates me on the "step forward" (does he understand this is only the beginning?) and states he's set up a meeting with my family for the next day: "Your reward for two prototypes with the potential to liberate our world."

Ecstatic I get to see my family again, my eyes snag on the last three words. Why mention this? Our world's already been liberated. Life is so much better than when I was a kid. Those childhood memories are faint, but now and then, one comes back to haunt me. The near-constant thirst. The burning sensation in nose and throat on a particularly toxic air day. The creative solutions Xanin and I constantly hunted for to secure more food.

Now, we have clean air, running water, and magic refrigerators. The only thing left to want is a family by my side instead of isolated from me. That thought jerks me back to reality, and I do a happy dance. *I get to see my family! Tomorrow morning!*

The rest of the afternoon passes in a blur. For once, I head home at the same time as my coworkers. Sarissa invites me to that new restaurant for dinner, but I beg off, telling her I need the downtime. In reality, the thought of food, let alone forcing it down when I'm so excited, is far from appealing.

I manage a milkshake before bed (who doesn't love chocolate and milk?) and count that as dinner. In the morning, I swallow a few mouthfuls of yogurt. My stomach won't tolerate more, so once I've settled on the trundle for my ride to work, I set an alarm to remind me to eat as soon as I've seen my family. I don't want another meltdown.

This time, I don't make the mistake of heading to my office. Instead, I wait in the lobby, knowing the SerSents will find me here. (Yes, those unseen eyes!) When they collect me, I skip along as they lead me upstairs, their security chips granting admission to levels even I can't access.

As we walk down the final corridor to the door at its end, the door I know my family waits behind, I wonder again where they stay when not in that room. It must be elsewhere because the rest of this level is empty. The open doors to most of the rooms reveal vacant meeting spaces, just like the one my family and I see each other in. But where do they *live?*

The thought nags as the SerSent waves his arm across the access panel. Then all questions evaporate the moment my family's beloved faces are revealed. I dash inside, gathering my family close, wishing my arms were longer. Despite this, we laugh and hug and cry and manage that touch.

When we finally pull apart and I start on the individual round of hugs, Tavi's pale face shocks me a little. I study her. "Are you okay?" While her head bobs, her eyes remain empty. Alarmed, I touch her cheek. "What's wrong? Are you sick?"

Tavi pulls back, and I'm more than a little upset by her withdrawal. But not as upset as I am by the thought Cygnus might not be taking care of them as he promised.

Before I can say anything, my mother pulls me into a hug. With her ear pressed tight to mine, she whispers, "That time—just cramps. Leave her be."

Sorrow weaves a strangling cage around my heart. Tavi is growing up, and I'm not there to share it. Not there to whisper secrets at night. Not there to share sisterly experiences. Veering from the depressing thoughts so I don't come undone, I drown myself in my mother's hug.

Is it my imagination, or does she hold me longer than usual? When she finally releases me, I smile at her, noticing again how much she has aged in the last few years. Another unhappy thought.

Brushing it aside, I swing Frankie into my arms. His squeal of delight is pure music to my ears. I hug him close, savoring the sweet small boy smell of him. Then Xanin puts his brawny arms around us both, and I relax into the familiar touch.

The sense of the comfortable brings another ache. I glance at my mother. "I probably shouldn't ask, but have you heard from Dad?"

Her eyes slide away as she shakes her head. Avoiding my eyes could mean many things, but everything else accompanying the action jars me. Her shoulders droop, her mouth compresses into a tight line, her fists ball. I pull free of Xanin and set Frankie down, still watching my mother. Her stance is unwavering, almost like she's holding the pose, holding her breath. "Mom?"

My mother's micro-movements give her away. How she tries to

stand taller, the way she pastes on a cheerful expression, an almost inaudible sigh before she lifts her eyes to find mine. "No, we haven't heard from your father. Don't you think we'd tell you if we had? Or that we wouldn't bring him to see you?"

I catch the slight hitch in her voice, the words spoken too calmly. Uneasiness stirs within me. It's like she's already given up on my dad. As though she thinks it's unlikely we'll ever see him again. The obvious non-answer is the most glaring statement.

Meanwhile, Frankie tries to pull Tavi into a game with the ball she brought. A red ball. But I can't think on the significance of that toy now. Or was that the point of bringing the ball? My mind skips back to news of my dad.

I drag my mother aside, all too aware of Xanin's keen dark eyes following us. Has he always looked so tired? I keep my voice low. "Did something happen to Dad, and you haven't told us?"

My mother waves a weary hand in front of her face, like she's trying to shoo a troublesome fly. *I am not an annoying bug! I'm your daughter! Tell me!* "No, no news. But don't we always say no news is good news?" Her eyes are jaded, her voice bleak. How have I never seen her this way before?

The thought is disconcerting. I flick a questioning gaze Xanin's way. Movements barely perceptible, Xanin nods toward the ceiling. My eyes follow the path he indicated, finding the tiny, dull red dot, almost invisible in the dark recesses where walls meet ceiling.

I don't need an explanation. But the revelation is shocking enough I want to break something. Preferably Cygnus's head, were I able to storm into his office and demand an explanation. If only I had the courage.

Almost unable to believe I've never noticed the camera before (where has my head been? How could I have missed so many things?), I slide a comforting arm around my mother's shoulders. I lean in close, hoping my voice won't carry. "You are serious about the no news, right?"

My mother nods, her arm clamping over my forearm, her grip

tight. We stay huddled together for an eternity, drawing strength from each other.

While we're standing like this, I catch Tavi scratching her arm. I think nothing of it until her sleeve rides up ever so slightly, revealing red, flaky skin. With jerky movements (I want to be sick!), I remove my mom's arm and march over to Tavi. She stands her ground, her chin lifting defiantly.

Snatching Tavi's wrist before she can dart away, I yank up her sleeve. The skin is raw, blistered, and inflamed to her elbow. I yank up the other sleeve and find the same thing. Distraught, I hold Tavi's arms out to my mother, yelling, "What is this?"

My mother's eyes are huge, her lips quivering. She looks like a trapped animal. Xanin steps forward, but then the door crashes open. I stand rooted, gaping, as SerSents swarm the room.

Before I can react, they've herded my screaming family away, shoving them from the room. The door clangs shut behind the last SerSent, my family's cries still ringing in my ears as I'm left alone in the vacant space.

16

Devastated, I stand there. My life just shattered into a million glass shards, poking and pricking and piercing every part of me. While my body is immobilized, wracked with pain, my mind races.

The thoughts swirl, a kaleidoscope of disjointed images and numbing realizations. My family is not being cared for. Cygnus is not keeping his promise. There's more to my dad's disappearance than my family can say. And how, oh how, did I never notice the cameras? What secret did they think my family might divulge to need surveillance?

I remain frozen, some part of me aware this is the best way I can react. Because I still sense those hidden eyes. Watching, waiting, measuring. As long as that red dot remains lit, I am not free to express my true emotions. Somehow, I know these will work against me. I just can't quite figure out how right now.

My brain slips, the images careening past one another again. What on earth happened to Tavi's arms? And why didn't they apply Nanogo? Unbidden, the red ball floats across my mind's eye, and I want to cry. Did Tavi bring the ball so we could replay some childhood memory? Or was there a deeper meaning, something about Dad?

The kaleidoscope twists yet again, and I see the way Xanin pointed out the camera. In the time we've been apart, he's become so observant. What has or hasn't he seen in me when I didn't even realize he was paying attention?

And Frankie! Beyond caring what I may reveal, I let the tears flow. Tears are acceptable, aren't they? We didn't even get to play tag today. His shrill wails as the SerSents dragged him from the room still assault my ears. Resonate with the fury on Xanin's face as he separated Frankie from the SerSent and tucked his little brother into his shoulder.

Most appalling though is my mother's total lack of reaction. I close my eyes against the memory of the way her eyes went blank the second the SerSents stormed into the room, her ensuing meek, submissive compliance. Like every inch of caring has been squeezed from her, leaving a dry, empty husk.

Click! Another shift. The kaleidoscope breaks apart, falls away. Instead of mental images, I find a SerSent in front of me, face obscured by a riot mask. Round black discs instead of eyes, hard molded plastic mask rendering his features generic. A stun stick sparks in his hand, ready for trouble.

"Let's go!" He (or she? Blasted voice modulators!) points at the open door with his stick.

I force my feet to move, sure if I could see his face I would find surprise there. Shock that I'm doing what he asks with no coercion. Maybe even suspicion at my docile behavior.

Who gives a flying fig? They took away the only thing I care about. Almost an afterthought, I ponder Cygnus's reasons for granting this meeting. Was it to be deliberately cruel? Prove his power?

No, I did nothing to disappoint him. Unless... My stomach curdles, remembering my outburst from weeks back. That can't be it either. Cygnus is usually swift to dispense discipline.

My brain wades through the quagmire. If only I could think faster. I traipse after the SerSent, thoughts rolling like a ship lost at sea. I'm delivered into the tiny room I usually have for my "recovery" time.

The SerSent leaves, and I'm alone again. I don't weep. Or scream.

Or break every single piece of furniture. Much as that would scratch a gigantic itch, it's not the solution. Instead, a glacial calm descends, the frigid water beneath offering a deep lake I can submerge myself in. I accept the offer.

Closing my eyes, I sink to the very bottom of that imaginary lake, focusing on the cool water covering me, the soothing waters lapping around me. In that space, my mind settles. The images stop crashing together like flying bricks. As the bricks fall to the ground, I pick them up, one by one.

The first brick, the largest, is my family. Cygnus promised he would take care of them. Clearly, he hasn't. Evidently, they aren't important enough for him to make them a priority. A memory slams into me, reminding me of what made them his priority once before. My one and only attempt at daring rebellion.

Even now, the memory hurts. But staggering me, forcing me to crumple into the solitary chair the room offers, is the accompanying realization as those awful days spring to stark life. Scenes that have eluded my infallible memory for years replay the traumatic events. I can only attribute their recall to shock. A greater stressor today than that which forged the original PTSD obscuring the memories.

Up until a few minutes ago, I believed the Board were responsible for every punishment inflicted on my family. But the truth is indisputable now. Sick to my stomach, I somehow manage to keep the rising bile back, thankful I've eaten so little over the past hours.

Why, oh why, did I never give credence to that small voice inside me? The one that told me something was wrong, warned me all was not as it seemed. But no, instead I insisted it couldn't be Cygnus. There was no way my kind, caring, compassionate Director Cygnus was the one pulling the strings.

How wrong I was! As I play the memories back, hazy at first, but gaining definition, it's painfully clear. *Cygnus*, not the Board, is at the center of all those memories. Those looks he sent my way I interpreted as pitying? Contempt—pure and simple. How have I misread him for so long?

Still, I must be sure. Fighting nausea, I allow the replay of those horrific days. An "object lesson" Cygnus said, to show how others would feel if I didn't finish the greenhouse project. How the hunger of thousands would be on me—and the real face of that terrible hunger. There's no doubt. Cygnus stood right there in front of me and gave the orders to stuff my family into that tiny windowless cell, a room so small they had to take turns lying on the floor because they couldn't all rest at the same time. A cramped airless room with its harsh fluorescent lighting showing all too clearly the shine of tears on Frankie's face when he begged for food.

I allow the knife to sink deeper, twist a little more. Confined as I was in another room, tied to a metal chair with my head braced and my eyes clamped open, I couldn't even avert my gaze from the wall screen playing out the scene in vivid detail. I could do nothing except watch as Cygnus starved my family. *Cygnus!* Not the Board. *Their* punishment for *my* act of defiance.

Light-headedness assails me and I realize I haven't breathed for I don't know how long. Ragged breaths shudder as I force air in and out of my lungs. But there's no denying the ugly truth now, or forgetting Frankie and Tavi's moans and pleas for food as hunger gnawed at them. The stoic resolve on Xanin's face when he comforted them while my mother huddled in a corner and wept.

Oh yes, Cygnus knew exactly what he was doing. I capitulated long before they were truly hungry. But this "warning" came with an explicit threat. Should Cygnus have to repeat the reminder, he would ensure my family learned the true meaning of starvation before he fed them the next time, regardless of any early surrender on my part. How could I ever forget he was the one responsible? Scarier, how did I think he had stepped in to save them "from what the Board were doing to them?"

I have no answers. Yet, one thing remains unchanged. Any subsequent time I considered crossing him, the blurred memory of that solitary incident bludgeoned me into obeisance. The worst to happen since has been Cygnus withholding scheduled family visits when I haven't made progress on my inventions quickly enough.

However, replaying these incidents, I witness Cygnus's implied threats that my family's suffering was increasing for every hour I tarried in making headway. A sudden realization shoots ripples through the lake, disrupting the calm waters. Is it possible my family have been mistreated all this time? That when there were no pending visits, they were abandoned or, more distressing, abused?

My mom and sister are so thin. Even Frankie. I had written his skinny arms off to his age. But what if that's not the truth? Xanin's brooding eyes and sullen moods aren't those of the boy I grew up with. Were all these signs indications of something deeper, something I should've seen before?

Unlike Tavi's arm. I could hardly miss that. Granted, it was fortuitous I looked at her when I did, that her sleeve slid up. But replaying the scene, this time I detect the glint in Tavi's eyes when she scratched her skin. Almost like she was daring me to notice.

Wincing at the pain scratching those blisters must've caused, I tell myself I'm making things up. Who would want to live with that pain? This returns me to the abandonment theory. That my family are left to fend for themselves in the times between our visits.

Is it possible when Cygnus ordered this meeting, there wasn't time to heal Tavi's arms? No, the Nanogo could've repaired the damage overnight.

Which raises an additional question: did Tavi deliberately hide the injuries so I would see them? Surely not! Xanin would've told her about the cameras. But her empty eyes come back to haunt me. Like Mom's.

The lake water suddenly isn't so pleasant anymore. It gushes over me, chilling me to my core. Did my family come to this meeting resigned to punishment if Tavi revealed her blistered skin?

The red ball bounces back into view. A coincidence or another message? The ball my father brought us. My father!

I pick up another brick from the sandy floor of the lake. The question of what really happened to my dad. I fight the mists that want to roll in and obscure the memory, letting the water wash the moment clean.

It's early morning when I wake. Hungry and thirsty as usual. In the kitchen, I find my rations already laid out at my place on the table. So Dad's already left for the day. I didn't get to say goodbye. But I'm more interested in my food than missing him. He'll come home later like he always does.

Except he doesn't. Instead, the monitors invade, swaddled in their black beetle suits. Kevlar exoskeletons protect their bodies, air filters a ridged thorax between the suit and the giant convex eye of the onyx shields hiding their faces. They swarm our home, crawling through every room, snatching up each family member.

We're forced into the front room, where people insulated in white suits jab needles into our arms, arms pinned down by the monitors. My blood flows into the tube at the other end of the needle, and I cry for my mother.

Xanin, next to me, stretches out the hand the monitor isn't pinning down and clasps my hand as the ghost exchanges one tube for another. By the time the ghosts remove the needle, I feel faint and more than a little sick.

That's when *he* enters the room. The man in the suit, Cygnus. Disgust turns his lips down as he studies us. Then the monitors drag my mother outside. Xanin and I scream, but the beetles won't release us. Their claws burrow into our arms, pincers pinching and not letting go.

Cygnus follows the monitors who dragged Mom outside. From my place in the front room, I have a direct line out the door to where he stands, talking to my distraught mother. I stop screaming, straining to hear. But all I can hear are Frankie's squalls as my mother cradles her baby in her arms. Tavi has pressed herself in so close to my mother's side, I almost can't separate her from my mom.

I cringe when Cygnus looks from my mother to me and back again. They continue speaking, with more glances directed my way. Then Cygnus signals the beetles. They carry us outside, a tide that won't be denied.

My mother shrieks and stretches her arms toward me, but she's hauled away by two monitors. Shoved into an armored personnel carrier. Then they yank Xanin free of my grip, tossing him and Tavi into the APC with Mom. I make to follow, but my feet are pulled out from under me as I'm lifted off the ground. I'm left dangling at the end of a monitor's arm.

"Just where do you think you're going?"

Cygnus's quiet voice beside me is terrifying. I can't speak. Not that Cygnus wanted an answer. I'm frantic when I'm carried not to the armored vehicle holding my family, but to a different APC. One the director arrived in. The monitor stuffs me into a chair, secures my harness, and steps back just before the doors close, sealing me off from everyone I know and love.

My vision blurs, tears flooding any images I might otherwise have captured. But my mother's tears and wails...

In this quiet lake, with the brick in my hand, for the first time, I consider those cries may not have been for us. Did Cygnus tell my mother my father was dead?

A sob chokes free. Is this a burden my mother has borne alone for all these years? A lie she could never reveal for fear of what Cygnus might do, either to me or her other children? Because I have no doubt Cygnus would've made threats. Abhorrent as the thought is, he no doubt backed it up with some despicable action. I know how he behaves with people who aren't me. No, I've just deluded myself all this time. The way he treats me is worse.

I cower from what he might've done and direct my thoughts to my father instead. Deep down, I've always suspected I'm the reason my father is no longer with us. Nothing in the memory I've dredged up reveals why I feel this way, but when I consider how my family always dodged questions about my father, how they finally admitted he was working "off continent" and it would be decades before he came back, how the statement suddenly became "off planet" when I pointed out this shouldn't stop us from speaking to him on comms… it all makes me doubt everything about my father's disappearance that day.

Abruptly, I realize why I may have always felt I was responsible for his absence. What if Cygnus told my mother my father wasn't dead, but detained until they handed me over?

No, no, no, that doesn't make any sense. I rub my fingers against my temple, the headache unbearable as the pain forces the water back.

In an instant, I'm ejected from my tranquil lake, the very real pounding in my head no match for the fist thumping against the door.

"Time's up! I'm coming in to get you. Stand back."

17

The march back to the lab is uneventful. Although the SerSent walks behind me, riot mask gone but stun stick still in hand, I think he knows there's no need for even that. But he takes no chances, escorting me back to the lab floor, then waiting at the elevator for another SerSent to fall in next to him before he tucks the stun stick back into its holster.

My only explanation for this strange behavior is Cygnus doesn't want my coworkers seeing me for the prisoner I am. Yes, another realization that hits home. When we reach my office, I enter without giving the SerSents a second look. I cross to my chair and take a seat, swiveling around after flipping my screen onto the wall behind my desk.

With my back to the door, I pretend to process the files waiting for me. But all I'm doing is flipping pages, tapping folders, moving them around. As I keep up the pretense, my mind churns.

I've always thought Cygnus was my boss. Always thought he was the one in charge. But maybe I have it back to front. Am I his boss? I think about why I'm in the labs—why I'm *here* specifically.

From the time Cygnus kidnapped me (let's call it what it is), a series of events led to this moment. First, those harrowing few weeks where I felt like a lab rat. Poked and prodded and made to take endless tests. Subjected to lateral thinking challenges. Forced to answer endless questions.

Then the academy. The snotty kids who all looked down on me. Until I put them in their places by trouncing them in every test. How I was encouraged to keep pushing myself, keep getting to the next level regardless of what grade my age dictated I should be in.

All those brief years where the focus was science. Endless science —in all its forms allowing me to graduate with several doctorates at age fourteen. Unheard of, they said. But they never did their research. There have been others like me over the centuries. We're just a select few.

I recall entering my very own lab for the first time after graduation. The year of projects before they made me head of the R&D labs —much to the chagrin of several senior coworkers who'd spent decades pursuing the coveted position. Cygnus assuaging my anxiety by telling me if they couldn't do what I could, they didn't deserve my position. How resources and projects were thrown at me, things I could submerge myself in.

Every moment from the time the director took me until now, I've been kept in seclusion. Lulled into a false sense of security by the unlimited resources of the conglomerate and the indulgence of every whim for any invention I dreamed of. Shiny toys to keep me distracted from the actual truth.

If my inventions really were the catalyst for Cygnus becoming director, doesn't that make me the one in charge of him—of his destiny?

I smirk. What a shock it would be if I just didn't turn up to work one day. Would that worry Cygnus? But my smirk falls away when I remember what he would do. The reason I've never failed to follow protocol. I've always done my work on the condition Cygnus supported and cared for my family.

My fingers cease their endless movement, the file I was scrolling through stuck mid-page. I stifle a gasp. I never demanded or requested that quid pro quo. How could I? I was six years old when Cygnus absconded with me. I would never have thought to make that request then.

Pretending I need to write something down, I turn and grab my tablet, relieved to find the SerSents no longer there. Two less people to report I had some sort of epiphany. I swivel around again, keeping my back to the door and my head down, ostensibly to work on the tablet on my lap.

But I seethe, try to release the tension building inside of me like a pressure cooker. This has all been Cygnus, all along. He made me think this "agreement" was my idea. In reality, the way he treated my family when my actions displeased him deceived me into thinking I'd requested their preferential treatment if I cooperated. *But I never did!*

The more I think about it, the more I realize Cygnus just retaliated on my family when I didn't do as he asked. All this time, Cygnus has been driving this lie of, "I'll do what you want so you keep my family safe." Is that why he always looks so smug when he mentions them?

Cygnus's betrayal burns hotter than thermite. I clench my fists to keep from leaping up and smashing every item in my office, nails gouging deep enough to draw blood. I can't draw attention, can't let them know I've had this realization. Another one. So many things I've never seen before. The pain shooting along my jaw makes me pause long enough to unclench it consciously. I know one thing for certain: Cygnus will pay for his betrayal.

Restless, I rise, knowing I won't be able to work. The alarm I set this morning to remind me to eat beeps, and I bat it away. I can't possibly tolerate food now. Instead, I head to the gym for release, pushing all the questions aside. CC HQ is not the place to ponder these things, a place where unseen eyes lurk. I don't want any inadvertent reactions caught on hidden cameras. Especially now I know they're watching for something I can't fathom. I must behave as normally as possible.

Allowing myself the luxury of enjoying the exercise for once instead of using it as a means to punch through a problem, I take my time, not pushing myself. I meander through my routines, squandering a full two hours, then spend another hour on a leisurely shower and lunch in the cafeteria before finally wending my way back to my office.

It's already early afternoon, so I should make it look like I'm doing some work. The easiest way would be spending time in Sarissa's office. She's sure to have something to natter on about. A little more time I can fritter away, edging me closer to home. A place where I can think and plan and plot. Absorb all I've learned today.

But Sarissa's office is dark. With a frown, I flip the light back on. I peer behind Sarissa's desk and find her purse gone. Her jacket is missing from the hook on the door too.

"Sarissa never came back after lunch."

I turn and find Tandize behind me. "Oh?"

Shadows mask Tandize's eyes. "A SerSent came and collected her stuff."

"Why would they do that?"

"Maybe something happened to someone in her family?"

Tandize's reply is more a question than a statement, but more obvious is the fear she barely conceals. "Tandize, why are you so afraid of the SerSents?"

Stiffening, Tandize tosses her head. "I am not."

The lie is unconvincing. Before I can question her further, she walks away, throwing a parting comment over her shoulder. "I just thought you might want to know she probably won't be back today."

I yell after her, "Well, did she say anything before she left to go on lunch?"

"Not to me."

If Tandize adds more, it's lost in the corridors between the lab benches. I stare after her retreating form, scowling. Something was so wrong about that entire conversation. Like Tandize was trying to give me a message without using the actual words.

Unsettled, I return to my office. I have to get past this paranoia. I can't be suspicious of *everything* here. Just because Cygnus has lied to me for years doesn't mean a boogeyman lurks in every corner.

Still, I'm worried about Sarissa. I touch my comm link and order the call. I listen, worry intensifying as the call goes unanswered. Perhaps it was her parents. Maybe they've summoned Sarissa to one of those events she has to attend as their daughter. The answer could be as simple as Sarissa leaving for lunch, then… not being able to get back in because her security pass was in her purse.

That's a joke of a lie! The last time we had to show our security passes was never. The chips in our arms are all the access we need. I tap my comm link, trying Sarissa for a second time. Still no answer. What if something happened to her? Visions of Sarissa lying injured or hurt somewhere fill my mind.

Unable to let it go, I collect my things, turn off the lights in my office, and leave the lab, telling everyone I'll see them on Monday. I hustle to the trundle, riding the short distance to Sarissa's elite area, trepidation a hand around my throat. I'm not allowed in this sector, but I have to verify Sarissa's okay. It takes less than a minute from the trundle to the foyer of her building.

I stab the buzzer. No reply. I stab it again and again, fear and concern ramping up with each attempt. After five minutes, I give up. Either Sarissa isn't home, or she's not taking calls or visits. I tell myself she is *not* lying unconscious on the floor of her apartment.

Then I crumble. She's my only friend. What if she is, and I don't attempt accessing her apartment, and then something unthinkable happens? With a deep breath, I press the button marked "Security."

Two SerSents from Sarissa's building appear almost instantaneously, looking me up and down. "Wrist," one bites out. I'll call him Sharky.

I offer my arm, and he wands me.

Sharky glares. "You're in the wrong area. You do not have clearance for this building. You don't even have clearance for this sector."

Sucking my cheeks to hold back the retort I would dearly love to unleash, I strive for calm. "Sarissa Kasumi is my friend. She lives in 25A. Please verify that."

Whether it's mention of Sarissa's last name or her floor level (almost at the very top of her building, indicating her level of importance), Sharky hops to it. While he verifies the information, I study the second SerSent. More senior.

"Who did you say you were?" This time, Sharky's tone is more circumspect.

"Chiara Baschet. Sarissa is my friend and coworker."

"I see," Sharky says.

Clearly, he doesn't. I rush on, desperate to explain, for them to understand the urgency of the situation. "Sarissa left for lunch but never returned. I've tried calling her, but she's not answering. It's not like her to leave work and not tell anyone. I thought she might be sick, so I came to check on her."

Sharky frowns. "You know we can't let you in."

I swipe a frustrated hand through the air. "I know. But can you at least just go up and check if she's in her apartment? If she's okay?"

Pressing a hand over his ear, Senior turns away. He nods a few times and murmurs in a voice too low to catch the words, then faces us again. "Miss Baschet, Miss Kasumi is in her apartment. She is unwell and not accepting guests."

The hard glitter in the man's eyes is unnerving. Does he think I'll try to barge my way in? I almost laugh at the thought of my slight frame going up against his bulk. About to smile, I crush it when Senior takes a step toward me, hand going to his stun stick.

My hands go up as I step back. "Please, I don't want trouble. I just needed to be sure nothing had happened to her. But if you say Sarissa's sick, I don't have to worry she's banged her head and is bleeding all over the floor with no one to help her."

Senior only glowers at me, saying nothing.

"Okay, I'm leaving. Could you at least ask her to please call me?"

Senior's voice lowers an octave. "We are not messengers. Leave her a message, and I'm sure she will call you when she's feeling better."

Aware I've outstayed my welcome, I back away before turning and exiting Sarissa's building. I'm on the street, walking to the trundle before I allow myself to run that conversation back. I have no doubt something was off in the way Senior said "better." But what, I have no clue.

More fatigued than I've been in days, I decide it's time to head home. At least there, I can process all this without having to worry about people spying on me.

18

I don't hear from Sarissa for the entire weekend. Although this causes insane worry, it also helps me cope with my family's plight because my mind is on something else. Funny how forgetting one problem is easier when faced with another, more immediate one. Besides, no matter how mistaken my belief, I think I can do more about Sarissa's situation than my loved ones'.

Unable to sleep on Saturday night, I remember the cleaners lurking in the bowels of my building when no one else is around. For lack of something better to do and wanting something, anything, to make me feel better, I gather clothes and bundle them into a large trash bag.

I ride the elevator down to the mezzanine floor, stepping out to a dark world. Although I peer into the shadows, I can't see anyone. "Sam?" No reply, but a faint rustling. "Sam, I know you and the others are here." No acknowledgement.

Then I remember how much my presence scared him. How all he wanted was for me to leave so he wouldn't be caught with me. Appalled by my lack of forethought, I realize it would be best if I leave. But not before I've dropped this off.

"Sam, I know you can hear me, and I'm going so you won't get into trouble. But I'm leaving some things here at the elevator. I hope you can use them." I'm about to get back into the elevator when I think of something else. "And I hope you're not offended."

While I wait a few seconds for a response, none comes. With a sigh, I allow the elevator doors to close and head back up to my apartment. Well, that was a bust. I pray the rustling I heard was the cleaners and not my imagination. It would a terrible miscalculation on my part if they've already cleaned and gone home, then got into trouble for a stray trash bag left lying in the middle of the floor.

By the time Monday rolls around, I'm about climbing the wall. Lack of both food and sleep from a weekend spent fretting has not put me in the best mood. I race through my morning routine, taking a breakfast-to-go but leaving it untouched as the trundle ferries me to work.

As I enter CC HQ, I modify my run to a fast walk, eager to get to the lab but leery of raising any red flags, hoping Sarissa will be there. But when the elevator dings open, her office is still dark, even from this distance. I tap my comm link to verify the time, then gnaw on my lip. It's past the hour Sarissa would normally be here.

I take a slow walk to my office, peering down every corridor of lab benches, checking Sarissa isn't just hanging out, chatting with someone. By the time I reach my destination, I'm sick with anxiety. I fight the nausea. Sarissa is renowned for coming in late on Mondays—especially if it was an intense weekend partying.

But an hour ticks by and no Sarissa. I rise, about to leave work and visit her apartment again, when my comm link beeps. Finally! "Sarissa! Where have you been? Why didn't you call me back? Do you know how worried—" The rest of the tirade dies on my lips as she comes into focus on the comm link screen.

I've never seen Sarissa looking so… washed out. Her face is devoid of both color and makeup, her gorgeous hair lackluster and limp. Dark circles ring vacant eyes. She can't even scrounge up a smile for me.

"Hey! Sorry to say this, but you look dreadful!"

Even this comment doesn't merit a grin. Instead, Sarissa stares at me, like she's trying to remember who I am or even why she called. Her eyes roll to the side, then drift back before finally finding some focus. "Hey, Chiara."

"How sick are you?"

The question must prompt some thought because Sarissa blinks, then offers a tepid smile. "Sick. Caught some nasty bug."

Shockingly, she bursts into hysterical cackling. The hairs on my arms stand on end. Then I notice the room behind her. It's not her apartment. "Sarissa, where are you?"

Again, that blank stare slides across her face. Her head almost rolls off her neck as she twists it, surveying the room. Then her attention snaps back, like someone who's having their picture taken and the photographer calls for attention. Disconcerting is an understatement.

Sarissa's eyes move left to right. Then she gives a goofy grin. "Oh yeah! I'm in a med bay."

"A med bay? Why?" Even as I ask, I'm searching for the equipment I'd expect there. I find none. Instead, bare gray walls fill the space. No window. If Sarissa were sick, wouldn't she at least be in a bed, not on a... stool? What is she even sitting on? "Sarissa, where are you? I'm coming to visit."

"No!" The single word is sharp, emphatic. On some level, Sarissa must realize her error because she attempts another crooked smile. "Isolation unit. Told you, nasty bug." While she holds back the insane laughter this time, the hysteria in her voice is obvious.

I don't know that I believe her. "Even in an isolation unit, they'll at least let me visit you."

Sarissa's eyes are panicked, darting around the room again. They settle on something behind the lens of her comm link's camera. "Um, I'll be going..." She pauses, squinting like the light is too bright. Then her face clears. "I'm going to stay with my parents for a bit. They have the facilities to take care of me."

Her parents? Sarissa barely tolerates them. I'm not buying it. "Sarissa, let me handle it. Come stay with me. There's no need to go to your parents."

This time, Sarissa's voice slurs. "No, told you. I'm going to my parents."

"But—"

"Chiara, got to go. Not feeling great. Look, just called to say don't expect me back at work any time soon."

I open my mouth to say something, but Sarissa waves an unsteady hand. I shrink back. Her usually manicured nails are a mess, deep red berry lacquer ending in jagged ends. Fear spikes. "Sarissa, tell me where you are! I'm coming to see you."

"No, must go." And the feed cuts out.

I stare at the space where my comm link screen showed Sarissa's face only a second before. Am I totally losing it? Seeing demons in every shadow, I pace. My stomach growls.

Food is fuel, I remind myself. And lack of fuel, especially with how I've eaten over the weekend, is likely to cause more trouble than it's worth. I decide against calling for a food tray in favor of a walk in the fresh air outside to the nearby mall and its food court. I tell my coworkers I'll be out for a bit and leave without further explanation.

As I exit the lab, I catch Tandize's worried expression out of the corner of my eye, but I'm beyond adding to the burdens I'm already bearing. I slip into the elevator, eager to get outside, into the sunshine.

Leaving CC HQ is like escaping a prison. I shouldn't feel trapped, but today, I do. For the most part, I've spent many blissful hours in the labs. Science is "my thing," and I love it, despite the circumstances I might have practiced it under. But I'm so cut up by the events of the past few days, seeing the bright side right now is difficult.

I take my time, ambling to the mall, making frequent stops to take in the scenery, running my fingers through the water in the nearby fountain, smelling the sweet frangipanis blooming along the sidewalks leading into the mall. Simply stunning! Their heady fragrance cheers me, and as I enter the mall, I decide I deserve a milkshake.

The large chocolate malt is the first thing I order, and as I suck on the soothing comfort food, I automatically get in line for Chinese food. Only when I'm selecting my color-coded options do I realize this is what I would've eaten (green instead of blue too—ugh!) had Sarissa been with me.

That single thought is all it takes for the tears to roll. I check out at the auto-teller, thankful there isn't a human operator, or she might've decided to call some sort of therapist.

I choose not to sit in the food court where Sarissa and I would normally hang out. Instead, I take the food and my now almost-finished milkshake to the shaded patio on the far side of the mall. Sitting down next to the tranquil pond with its koi fish, red-lacquered Japanese lanterns, and Asian-styled bridges, a measure of calm returns.

I ignore the food as much as I can, considering I have to eat it, watching the fish, the water trickling over the stone sculpture, the couple strolling over the bridge. Over an hour later, I finally decide it's time to go back to work.

Admittedly, the food has made me feel infinitely better. I'm not so shaky anymore, and my emotions have settled. Why did I risk not eating the entire weekend? Who knows when I might've gone off pop with my sugar levels off! Or what the result could've been for my family.

Even that thought doesn't cause the usual dismay. Maybe it's the fresh air and sunshine, the quiet down time, or (more likely) the brunch, but I suddenly feel more energized than I have in days. My walk back to CC HQ is brisk, and when I march back into the lab, my brain is already attacking the chemical compounds I want to test on the various metal meshes.

For the rest of the day, I lose myself in science, working late into the night, and then continuing the pattern for another few days. I refine considerations for the first two of the three possible proto-types, deciding what alloys to use with which meshes, the most effi-cient hole size for the mesh, other contaminants I could use to reproduce or, possibly, amplify the fusion effect, the arrangement of the magnetic fields, the shape for the plasma containment unit to maximize efficacy, and more. The options are numerous and complex, and every time I think I've reached their end, I imagine another combination I could explore, one that might be even better. When I next surface, I only know it's Sunday because the cleaning bots sweep through the empty workbenches. I've had no weekend to speak of.

With a deep sigh, I recognize I need a break, no matter how much I'd prefer to *not* think about the other things bothering me. I stand and stretch. A yawn slips out. Then, two seconds later, another yawn escapes.

Home time. A decent sleep in my bed instead of the office couch will be heavenly. Besides, while the cleaning bots make a racket, the noise doesn't bother me as much as them bumping against me until I move so they can get under my chair and desk. Far too disruptive to have to keep standing, then sitting, then finding my place again.

I switch off my PC, gather my things, and depart. If the cleaners weren't androids, I might've said something to them. As it is, their little machine brains run on, telling them where to clean and what areas to leave untouched.

I make the trip home, my mind numb. Honestly, I don't even remember the walk to my apartment or the biometric tests necessary to get into my apartment. All I'm aware of is the bed abruptly looming large in front of me. I flop onto it, and sleep swallows me.

19

When I wake, it's to the horrid sensation of drool sliding out my mouth onto an already wet pillow. I lurch up and rub a hand across my mouth. *Ugh, I should not have slept in that position.* My neck has a crick, and my one arm prickles with pins and needles as blood flow returns.

My feet slap the floor, but I remain seated on the edge of the bed as I take stock. Sun? Just streaking the sky indigo and bronze. Dawn. Day? That takes a moment. Monday. Time? I tap my comm link. Early enough I could sleep for another hour.

Tempted to flop back down for more rest, I rise and pad to the bathroom instead. Much as the idea of extra Zs is appealing, it never works for me. I step into the shower, and preheated water sprays me, tiny stinging droplets pummeling my skin and waking my brain.

All the worries I've worked so hard to bury for the last week resurface with a vengeance. I groan. *No, no, no. Not now. Just let me have five more minutes of peace before I have to face the ordeals of the real world.* But the thoughts nag, relentlessly chasing each other through my head.

When faced with unpleasant topics, as I am now, I employ a trick I've perfected where I narrow all thought processes to the single track of concentrating on my current project. While the worry doesn't completely recede, it's swamped enough to be a distant vexation.

Thinking about my work, I realize I've made progress this past week. Another two or three days, and I could start building the prototypes with all my initial hypotheses almost complete. The thought returns a little bounce to my step.

Still, the trip to work is tedious. Despite the trundle's speed, I feel like it isn't moving fast enough. This is what happens when you try to run away from your problems. They simply pursue you until you slow down enough to acknowledge them.

Adamant my irrational fears remain buried, I drink in the scenery, focusing on chemical formulas and mathematical equations. The chemical compounds found in the passing plants. *(One oligosaccharide is α-L-Fucp-(1→3)-[α-D-Galp-(1→4)]-α-D-Glcp-(1→3)-α-D-GalpOAll. General Formula_Cn+1(H2o)n.. Structure Formula..C12'H22'O11. Another is...)* Math equations *(flow rate Q equals Av)* allowing me to calculate how much water cascades over the edge of the cliff every second in that glorious waterfall marking our western border.

Another thing that's always bothered me. No matter how often I do them, my calculations for the volume of water provide an outlandishly large answer. If that amount were in fact tumbling over the cliff, water would flood the valley.

I always mean to check the actual width of the waterfall, its height, depth, and rate of water flow so I can correct my estimates, but never remember by the time I get to work. And who wants to check things on the 'net while riding a speeding bullet? Just the thought is enough for motion sickness to twinge. Setting aside my food, I begin another calculation.

Once I start playing these "games," it seems mere seconds before the trundle delivers me to my stop. On the walk to the office, I keep my mind similarly occupied with numbers and elements. When I enter my office and find Sarissa sitting there, waiting for me, it's a shock.

"You're back!" I drop everything and run to her, flinging my arms around her shoulders. She stiffens, and I immediately let her go. "Sorry, are you still hurting?"

Sarissa smiles, but her eyes are flat, lifeless. "Yeah. Sore all over." She rubs a hand down her arm. The bruising on her hand is obvious.

"Your hand! What happened?"

Tucking it into the crook of her arm, Sarissa shrugs. "Oh, you know, IV meds. That's where they inserted the tube."

"The nanites haven't repaired the bruising yet?"

Sarissa glances at her hand, then shakes her head. "Evidently not." Then she looks up at me, the first authentic smile gracing her face. The smile that drew me to her when we first met. "Enough about me. I'm all better. What's new around here?"

There's that word again, only obvious because she delivered it in the same strange tone. *Better.* Better from what? The fact both she and Senior used the same word, let alone delivered it in the same eerie tone, raises goosebumps on my flesh.

"Are you really? Better, I mean? What was the bug?"

Sarissa rolls her eyes. "I can't remember. You know me and scientific names. Who cares! What did I miss? Anything happening with you and Deran?" She lifts her eyebrows suggestively, wiggling them up and down.

I want to laugh, but it comes out as a squeak when I remember Sarissa's nails. My gaze flies down to the visible hand, resting on her hip. Perfect manicure, but a bold, turquoise polish. Not a color I've ever seen Sarissa wear. Doubting my sanity, I replay our bizarre call from a week ago. No, I'm not imagining things. There was definitely damage there.

"I see you fixed your nails."

Sarissa glances down, a vaguely mystified expression on her face. "Yes. I guess I thought I would try a new color."

She sounds... confused. "Sarissa, do you remember what happened to your manicure?"

A blank stare. "When?"

"The last time we spoke, when you called me to let me know you were sick, your nails were..." I falter, searching for a less alarming way to phrase it. "Well, it looked like you'd tried filing them on a slab of rough concrete."

Laughter trills out, and Sarissa slaps a hand on her thigh. Okay, a little dramatic. But she seems genuinely tickled. "You're kidding, right?"

"No." I sound doubtful. Not because I don't believe what I saw. My memory doesn't play tricks. Because I don't believe Sarissa really is okay.

Then Sarissa's eyes slide past where I'm standing in the doorway. For the briefest second, I glimpse the fear crouching in her eyes. I whirl, expecting to find some deadly threat hurtling toward me. But there's nothing unusual. I turn back. "What?"

"What do you mean, what?"

This time, Sarissa's laugh is hollow. Overly cheerful and so pathetic, even a duck on a broken leg could do better. I suck in a sharp breath as I figure it out.

"Hey, let's grab breakfast! I didn't finish mine on the trundle this morning, and now you're back. We should celebrate." Careful when I grab her unbruised hand, I tug her from my office, not allowing her to wriggle free.

I snatch up my purse on the way out, then all but shove Sarissa down the corridors to the elevator. Her initial resistance ceases the moment she spots a SerSent walking the hallway outside the labs. *I'm right!*

Vindicated, I feel less cruel dragging her out of the building and toward the mall. I only wait for as long as it takes to reach the fountain we pass on the way.

Once there, I pull her off the path and into the bushes on the far side, grunting when Sarissa struggles again. "Stop! I know why you're behaving like this!"

Her eyes go so wide I see the whites of her eyeballs. "You do?" Her voice is a whisper, her face pale under her foundation.

"Yes!" I hiss back. Quick, furtive glances over my shoulder and around the nearby shrubs confirm no one will see or hear us. If we keep our voices low, the water splashing in the fountain should drown out most of our conversation. "You want me to know something's wrong. The director's up to something, isn't he?"

Sarissa looks like she might want to laugh, but then wariness enters her eyes. "What do you think he's up to?"

As quickly as I can, I tell her about the director's duplicity. My misgivings about what really happened to my dad and belief Cygnus is making my family lie to me about it. How, all this time, the director has tricked me into thinking that if I did what he asked, he would look after my family. But he hasn't. Worse, my fear that he's been lying to me since I got here, plying me with science puzzles and lab toys to distract me from the truth.

Everything pours out, not the jumble it was in my mind, but a coherent torrent. As the words stream out, Sarissa's face relaxes, then twitches with repressed laughter. Her reaction makes me listen to what I'm saying. Even to my own ears, my claims sound farfetched. The stream of words peters out.

"Chiara, let me get this straight. You think the director has you here under false pretenses?" She chuckles. "Darling, if you've only just figured that out, you're not as brilliant as I thought you were."

I blink. "What do you mean?"

Sarissa's laugh is brittle. "Aren't we all pawns in his little games?"

"You agree he's playing games, then?"

"Naturally. When has someone ever achieved his position without doing so?"

"But it's my family! Did you hear that part?"

Wrapping an arm around my waist, Sarissa pulls me from our hidden position and leads us back to the path. "I think you're over-reacting."

I can't believe she just said that! "Oh, so you're saying nothing's happened to my dad? That those blisters on Tavi's arms were just my imagination? That the director hasn't been lying to me—he's merely been moving me around like a piece on his board?"

Sarissa sighs. "Okay, there's no arguing with the blisters. But what would the director have to gain by *not* looking after your family? By 'abandoning' them, as you claim? It would only piss you off enough to..."

She trails off, but I finish the sentence for her. "To do something about it." I clench my fists, wanting to knock sense into her. "You think?"

"That isn't what I was going to say."

"Isn't it?" My voice is flint, and I swing free of her arm around my waist, stopping on the path in front of her and getting in her face. "Come on, Sarissa, don't you think I know you well enough for me to guess what you're thinking?"

Sarissa stiffens. "If that were true, you and I would both be in more trouble than you could imagine."

I stare at her, confused, then toss my arms up into the air. "What's that supposed to mean? Are you agreeing with me?"

Sarissa flings her fists downward, a foot stomp accompanying the action. "Argh! Why do you always have to hyper-analyze everything? I just meant people in power play their ridiculous games. I doubt anything has happened to your father. Your sister's behavior is a cry for your attention. As for Cygnus moving you around like a piece on his board..." Sarissa nods, her face distant. "That's actually an excellent way of phrasing it."

Hot, angry tears burn. "I can't believe you're not taking this seriously!"

"And you're making it more than it is. Chill! Life's too short. You should have some fun."

Needing space, I step back, studying Sarissa's face. Cool disinterest. Like this conversation is tiresome and not important enough to merit her undivided attention. Her eyes drift to the displays in the windows of the nearby mall.

How can Sarissa be so callous? She knows how important my family are to me. And she's acting like they're nothing. I suppose I shouldn't expect more from someone who doesn't care for her own relatives. "I've changed my mind. You go on without me. I'm not hungry."

I whirl and head back the way we came before she can speak,

hurrying to work. All the way there, I half expect (and desperately want) to hear Sarissa's call, her footsteps as she runs after me. When I make it back to my desk without her plea, acute disappointment fills the ache where my heart used to be.

Any calm I may have felt when I first arrived this morning, any desire to get on with my project, has evaporated. Only one way to deal with it. I head for the gym.

I've finished my workout and been back at work for nearly an hour before Sarissa exits the elevator and returns to her office. She's been gone nearly three hours. What was she doing?

No, I remind myself, I don't care. Probably drowning her guilt in a shopping spree. I fixedly return my attention to the task at hand. And try not to disintegrate under the hurt throbbing every time I glance at her office.

By mid-afternoon, I can no longer deny my underlying angst. For lack of something better to do, I stroll down to the cafeteria and pick up a sandwich, then plop onto a bench in the eating area. Mechanically, I plow through the food as my mind churns.

Sarissa was supposedly sick. No mistaking the bruise on her hand from an IV or how pale she was when she told me not to expect her back at work. But the way she said *better*. And her fear. How are those related? Are they even related? Then there's the problem of the "nasty bug" nanites can't fix within a day or two. While they can't cure my hypoglycemia, they're quite adept at dealing with viruses and bacteria. What sort of disease could keep Sarissa away from work for a full week? Actually, more, considering there were two weekends as well. Add the nanites' failure to repair that bruise (yes, coming full circle again!), and I know I'm missing something.

Reflecting further, I recall Sarissa's reactions. When I told her I thought Cygnus was up to something, she initially looked like she wanted to laugh. Like she was relieved I... hadn't said something else? Hmm, then her face tightened like she wondered... what? What I *had* figured out? Perhaps that explains why, when I finished telling her all my suspicions, she wanted to laugh again. In fact, she did. Perhaps because I said something unexpected?

All this brings me to the single statement that hasn't left my mind since she said it. The cause of my uneasiness. Sarissa's words echo again. *"That wasn't what I meant."* What *had* she meant?

True, the sentence I finished for her could've been completed in several ways. *It would only piss you off enough to... stop working on projects. Insist my family stays with me. Demand proof of my family's care.* But aren't these all versions of my answer—that I would take action?

My swirling thoughts bash into my headache, a ram battering my skull.

I sink my head into my arms on the table. The only thing I'm sure of is that Sarissa was terrified. So then, when I divulged my suspicions, why didn't she reciprocate and tell me what was scaring her?

In fact, she didn't react at all as I expected. Just agreed with what I said, then blew it off. A sneaky suspicion circles. The more I allow it access, the deeper it sinks its venomous fangs.

What if Sarissa isn't who I think she is? What if she isn't really my friend? Has she been a spy all along? Someone the director placed in my life like everything else—a person who could get close to me so I would confide in them, and they could steer me in whatever direction they were told to? Or could run off and tell Cygnus when I wasn't behaving?

The more I consider the angles, the more foolish I feel. Those times Sarissa took me along to those clubs so I could meet her "friends." They were the ones behaving normally. Shunning me for the tier four I am. How did I ever conclude it was more believable a tier eight would really want to be friends with a tier four? With me? Isn't it more likely she was only pretending to be my friend because it benefitted her?

<h1 style="text-align:center">2 O</h1>

Devastated, I dart out of the cafeteria. I don't even stop to collect my things. Just run out of the building. Leave my office as hollow and emptied out as I am. Sarissa's betrayal incinerates any affection I may have felt for her. Who cares about a stupid project? Besides, with everyone lying to me, isn't it possible something's already happened to my family?

Sapped of emotion and beyond caring, I travel home. But back in my apartment, it just feels like another trap.

I can't get out fast enough. Snatching up my HydroPak (must stay hydrated), I burst through my building's doors into the sunshine outside. I meander aimlessly, letting my feet take me where they will. When Sarissa calls repeatedly, I shut my comm link down. I don't want to talk to her. Or anyone else, for that matter.

I follow the paths to the nearby lake, nursing my wounds. At the lake, I wand an arm over the dispenser to release crumbs, then feed the ducks waddling around. They're so fat they don't need more food, but watching them gorge themselves is oddly satisfying.

Restless, I press on, my feet finding ways to parts I've never been before. Places I'm not supposed to go. Areas falling outside my permissible sectors. I wander, waiting for someone to stop me or for SerSents to accost me. Neither happens.

Somewhere in the vagaries of logic, I register it's getting dark. I should go back. But I don't. When I finally return to my apartment, HydroPak sucked dry and having walked miles, it's hours later. Admittedly, I think most of it was in a circle, but who cares why all the paths seem to curl in on themselves? Just another sign of the convoluted world I live in.

To say my sleep is fitful is generous. I finally give up in the early morning hours, indulging in an extra long shower and a leisurely breakfast before catching the trundle to work. Another thing that never stops in this crazy world.

I'm the first to arrive, a relief, and I go directly to my office, closing and locking the door behind me. I don't know when I reached the decisions I did, other than sometime during the night.

First, I will get these prototypes ironed out. Once that's done, I will demand a visit with my family before I build and test them. Further, I will insist my family come and stay with me permanently. It's unacceptable for us to be kept apart any longer. If the dire lengths Tavi went to are any indication of her desperation for my attention, I can't ignore her.

Head down, I drown myself in the two prototypes I've been focusing on, ignoring Sarissa's knock a few hours later. When she persists, I toss the stylus I'd been dragging through my hair at the door. The soft plink as the stylus makes contact doesn't dissuade her. The knocking continues.

Striding to the door, I yank it open. "What about a closed and locked door doesn't scream 'do not disturb?'"

Sarissa gapes. "Someone got up on the wrong side of bed today."

"Go away. I'm busy." I slam the door on her stunned expression.

Deliberately, I turn my chair so my back is to the door, then pick up another stylus and ease it through my hair again. Enjoying the mild massage, I watch the holographic simulation I just built for the first prototype play out in the space between me and my wall. Not quite right. I remove my stylus from my scalp (why? It was bliss!), and make a few adjustments before running the sim again. Almost there, just another little tweak.

Loud banging on my door makes my hand jerk and accidentally swipe across the area I was working on. I spin, glaring at whoever has the audacity to intrude. The glare barely dims to resentment when I spot the SerSent. For a second time, I fling the door open. Then I see the food tray in his hands.

He shoves the tray toward me. "Miss Kasumi said you needed to eat."

"Did she now?" I snatch the tray, wondering what else Sarissa told him. "You can inform her she's done her duty." And I slam the door again.

I dump the tray on my desk, impatient to determine how much of the change I was working on was destroyed. One peek tells me I should redo the whole section. (Ugh! Can they just leave me *alone?*) There's no telling what that startled swipe might have inadvertently deleted. Since the food does actually smell quite good (I'll never admit that to anyone), I drag the tray closer, using one hand to manipulate the elements I want to change on the holograph, and the other to fork food into my mouth.

Time slips by, unnoticed as I soldier on. Another food tray is delivered, and I only leave my office for bathroom breaks and a vigorous workout to ease some of the tension.

When I switch off my light and curl up on the couch in my office, I don't bother checking the time. It's hideously late—or is it technically early, since it must be early morning? I rub my tired eyes, debating whether I have the energy to get up and apply some Nanogo. Before I reach a decision, I've drifted off.

For days, I keep myself cloistered in my office. I don't know how many, but enough so Sarissa stops knocking in the mornings and no longer tries to pin me down when I dash out to the bathroom or gym or cafeteria.

Despite showering after my workouts, these quick washes are

nothing like the lovely fragrant experiences of my own bathroom (or clean clothes from my dresser), so when I finally emerge from my office, I smell… ripe. But the first two prototypes are done. While my holographic designs are more visual aids than an actual plan of the mechanics required, I know what I want to achieve when building the machines, and the permutations I want to attempt for each. How the machines are constructed will be up to the mech team to figure out. For now, my work is done. It's time to go home, get clean, have a good night's rest, and then request that meeting with Cygnus.

The next morning, when I summon Sarissa into my office, she pops into my doorway, unable to hide her surprise. Or anxiety. "Chiara, I—"

I cut her off. "I need you to set up a meeting with Cygnus for me." She opens her mouth again, but I wave her away. "Go. When it's set, come back and tell me what needs my attention."

Nodding, Sarissa backs out of the room, returning a few minutes later. She hovers in my doorway, fingers fiddling with a button on her suit.

"Well?"

Her head nods so vigorously, it's a wonder it doesn't bob right off. "Yes, yes, I set that up. He's available this afternoon." She bites her lip. "Two o'clock."

"Fine. Now, update me on what my staff have been doing."

Sarissa's rapid blinking tells me she didn't miss my phrasing. I've never called them my staff before, but it's all about business now, right? Isn't that the way the director views things?

Clearing her throat, Sarissa wrings her hands. "Um, can you give me an hour? I wasn't expecting you to want a report. I don't have any files ready."

Eyes cold, I assess her. "Why not? Isn't that your job?"

Sarissa's right hand flutters up and then down again. "Yes. Yes, it is. I'm sorry, I just didn't think you would—"

"No, you didn't think, did you?"

Mortification stamps its ugly mark on Sarissa's face. "Chiara, if you'd just let me explain?"

I don't care for her wheedling tone. "Leave! You have an hour. Don't come back without a full report."

Sarissa scurries out, shoulders shaking. Is she crying? I remind myself I don't care. As long as she gets her work done, there's nothing more between us.

An hour later, Sarissa is back in my office, face flushed, eyes bright. I take perverse satisfaction in her slightly disarrayed hair. For once, she's the disheveled one.

Flustered is the only way to describe her presentation as she rushes through the folders, talking too fast, like this will somehow make up for not doing her job in the first place. I say nothing, savoring her distress. How many times did she laugh at me behind my back?

When she finishes her update, I pass on a few instructions and add some answers to the queries. Thankful my staff have mostly been able to get on without me while I finished my own work, I lean back in my chair, eyeing Sarissa.

"I need a mechanical team. People who can build the prototypes according to my specs. Draw up a requisition so I can get Cygnus to sign it when I see him later today."

Sarissa makes a note, then glances back at me, clearly desperate to spout whatever lies I haven't given her the chance to express since that dreadful day.

I don't take the bait. "You may go."

For a moment, Sarissa remains where she is, struggling between obeying the order and staying to hash things out.

I decide for her, marching out of my office and down to the gym. She won't follow me here, odious as both the thought, and reality, of sweat are to her. Slipping into the locker rooms, I sit on the bench, taking no steps to either switch clothes or exercise.

What I need is time to compose myself. Figure out exactly how I want to approach the subject of demanding something from the director. Because Al-Li knows I don't think on my feet, and just being in the same office as him addles my brain.

When I think I've worked out how to phrase things, I amble down to the mall, avoiding the food court and slipping instead into a little Italian restaurant I've never tried before. It's cozy, with muted lighting and soft conversations adding to the ambience, all overlaid by the delicious aromas of fresh pizza and pasta. *Little Italy* is the perfect name for this place.

Best of all? I don't have to see that awful green tray, even though the mod will be added anyway based on the command from my chip as I wand it across the panel to order my meal. Never mind. I can pretend there aren't colored trays.

The food arrives, and I bide my time eating it, finding my selection more than tasty. In fact, it's the best food I've had in ages. I don't even have to distract myself with the surrounding people to finish every scrap on my plate. With a satisfied sigh, I lean back, then tap the buttons to order coffee. Just enough time to savor a cup. Then I'll head back so I can touch base with my staff before the meeting with Cygnus.

Mellow from the meal, I drift back to the labs, then wend my way down the various corridors, speaking with several staff members. That's where Sarissa finds me. Her expression tells me something's up. "What?"

"The director canceled your meeting. He's been unexpectedly called away to Roxile to deal with a situation there."

Frustrated, I snap. "What situation?"

I can almost feel the gazes of those nearby flying toward me like magnets to metal. *Yes, my tone was sharp. Yes, it is Sarissa I'm talking to. Get over it!*

Sarissa stammers in her uncertainty, both over where she stands with me and because she has no answer. "I don't know. Mrs. Jacobs just called down and said he had to leave."

I scrub a hand over my face. "Did you set up another appointment?"

"No. Mrs. Jacobs wouldn't commit because she doesn't know when he'll be back."

Argh, this really puts a crimp in the matter! When Cygnus leaves the continent, he can be away for months. I'm hoping for days.

Aware of the curious eyes around me, I moderate my tone. "Fine. Keep checking with her to find out when he'll be back. And the moment he is, make sure I'm the first person on his appointment list."

21

I finish the rounds with my staff, then return to my office to address the problem I couldn't in their company.

While I debate not submitting the mech team requisition to delay further work on the project until I've made my demands of Cygnus, I know missing our meeting won't be an acceptable "excuse."

Loathe to accept this, but more aware than ever now how my actions could lead to repercussions for my family, I order Sarissa to submit the request electronically. There's no sensitive information, and a request for a mechanical team is not unusual, so it doesn't fall beyond the boundaries of a requisition I could've reasonably withheld.

I debate approaching Hag Lady (a.k.a. Mrs. Jacobs) to ask Cygnus if he will at least allow me to speak with my family. But it will only tip my hand about how worried I am. How right he is to keep holding them over my head. I need him to believe I will continue working regardless of my family's welfare, so he'll be more amenable to my requests. I don't think about what I'll do if he doesn't agree to my demands.

Rather, I indulge my usual ostrich routine and bury myself in work. When the mechanical team arrives the next morning, the requisition obviously approved, I don't know whether I'm annoyed or alarmed to learn Deran is the team lead. Why did they send him? Is he another spy? Someone sent to replace Sarissa now that she's fallen out of favor?

I can't dwell on it. Worry is like sitting on a rocking chair: you spend energy but go nowhere. Who has time for that? Instead, I resolve to keep things as professional as possible with Deran—or as much as his charm and devastating looks will allow.

With a bracing breath, I approach the mech team waiting for me in the spacious workshop area adjacent to the lab, assigned to me for any projects requiring significant space. Several security measures limit access to the workshop, all of which I've temporarily disabled to allow the mechanical team to bring in their equipment and materials.

As I walk across the echoing floor to where the mechanics stand in a group, I'm surprised to find they're all around Deran's age. Why? Wouldn't an older team have more experience? Or do the team leads get to pick their own team? Worried again, I remind myself Cygnus wouldn't want to hamstring me with engineers who couldn't do the work. No doubt they're more capable than they look.

I focus instead on how clean the space is, how vacant. Just a few short projects ago, I had it stacked to the rafters with equipment. Now it's a blank slate, ready for me to create more magic. And magic it will be if I can pull this one off.

"Hello." Conversations cease as all eyes turn to me. "I'm Chiara Baschet, the project leader. I know Deran. Won't the rest of you please introduce yourselves?"

As they do, I note two women in the team of six, including Deran. It's impossible to ignore the way their eyes never leave Deran. *Drool all over him, why don't you? I'm sure he loves that!*

I shove the sarcastic thought aside and set a cube on the nearby workbench, bringing up the holographic image for the first prototype. Since making sense when I don't look at Deran is easier, I keep my gaze fixed on the projection in front of me. "Right, as I'm sure you're aware, I'm not a mechanical engineer. Hence the need for all of you. So before I begin, please forgive my ignorance in naming things on the holograph or how I envision they will function. I promise, I won't bite if you have the urge to remove my words and replace them with the proper terms instead." A few grins turn to laughter.

While my eyes may not be on Deran, I'm all too aware of him standing next to me as I explain what I'm trying to build. When his hand brushes against mine as he reaches to touch a part of the design he has a question on, a spark runs up my arm. My senses alert to the touch, craving more. It's beyond disconcerting, and I have to ask Deran to repeat his question. Which of course means I look right at him, then feel like an idiot when laughter dances in those gray eyes.

Well, other girls may swoon over you, and yes, I may get tongue-tied, but I refuse to fall for your charm! Determined, I square my shoulders and stand straighter, looking directly at him and daring him to tease some more. His face sobers, and this time, Deran looks away.

The tiny victory bolsters my confidence. But when I walk away an hour later, the mechanics clear on the vision for what I'm trying to build, I debate whether it truly was my victory... or his. While I may have figured out how to speak to Deran without stumbling over my words, is it because I thought I could challenge him, or because he used that same simple technique, directing me back to the science every time I thought I might lose it?

I choose not to let it bother me, vowing to take the victories where I can. There are too many enemies to do otherwise.

While conversations with Deran get easier over the next few days, primarily because his focus is on technical questions rather than on me, conversations with Sarissa deteriorate. She comes into work late more than once in the following days. On the third occasion, when she rolls in close to eleven, I have to give her a written warning. When I hand it to her, she fixes me with a sullen stare.

"Sarissa, I'm not the problem here. It's your all-night clubbing that's getting you into trouble."

"You just don't want me having any fun, Zeech."

I reel back, shocked by her blatant use—on me, no less—of the slur. Much as I'd like to stoop to her level, now is not the time to retaliate. I must get through to Sarissa, or she'll lose her job. Despite no longer being my friend, my confidante, I know what getting fired will do to her.

"Sarissa, that's not true. I endorse enjoying your time outside of this lab. Go out and party all you want. But at least be responsible enough to leave with sufficient time for sleep so you can get to work on the dot."

All I get in return is a hostile nod as Sarissa snatches the written warning and hoofs it back to her office. I watch her retreating form, her resentment reaching across the increasing distance. The closeness we once shared stretches into a gaping chasm. Resigned, I return to my office.

The next day, I'm relieved when Sarissa is punctual. But instead of coming to my office with her usual schedule and folders, she remains in hers, her door closed. Opting out of confronting her first thing in the morning, I continue working.

An hour later, she still hasn't fulfilled her duties. I glance over. Sarissa remains slumped in her chair behind her desk, head against the backrest, staring into space. Time to guilt her into working.

Before I can, Deran knocks at my door. "Do you have a minute?"

I nod, gesturing toward the seat opposite me.

"Can we go back to the workshop? It's something you need to see."

Without a word, I rise, and he indicates I should lead the way. As we walk the short distance to the workshop, him following behind, I cheer myself up by thinking how nicely the first prototype is coming along. Admittedly, I'm impressed, both with Deran's understanding of what I'm trying to achieve and how well he communicates my vision to his team.

Upon entering the workshop, I spot what can only be a holographic drawing (design, sketch?) by a mechanical engineer projected above the nearby workbench. I amble closer, then inspect it, my eyebrows shooting up. Seems someone took my clumsy rendition and converted it into a version the mechanics would understand. Not only is the machine more detailed, but when I touch a piece, the design breaks apart to reveal the individual parts, accompanied by a surprising amount of technical data. It makes for a more efficient way of working because the team probably don't have as many questions now.

"Nice!" I gesture toward the detailed design. "Who did that?"

"I did."

Not for the first time, I doubt our slight age difference. He should be much older with the skill he already demonstrates. Then I smile. Pot and kettle.

"What are you smirking at?"

"Oh, I was just thinking I shouldn't judge someone's ability based on their age." That gorgeous grin flashes, and I hurriedly shift my attention back to the design. "So… you had a question?"

Deran uses the cube I provided the team with on the first day to bring up my (embarrassingly lacking) design. "How essential is it that this pipe here," he shows the one, "is two meters long?"

I mentally replay the simulations. "As long as it's less than 2.783 meters, it will still work."

"Thanks."

"That's all?" I can't keep the surprise out of my voice. If he needed something so simple, why didn't he just bring the cube to my office?

Deran waits until I look at him, grin flashing again before he answers. "No. I needed to show you something on the mesh."

That wicked glint in his eyes, accompanied by a devilish grin, has me wondering if he just lured me here to mess with me. The suspicion grows. The three other male members of the team are watching us, broad grins plastered all over their faces. Did they have a bet about something?

When we reach the mesh, soaking in its chemical bath along the far wall, Deran points to a corner. "I know this mesh was special-ordered for these experiments. Can we cut this one, and the others over there," he points to the other versions stacked nearby, "into circular shapes to fit the chamber?"

Another question he could've asked in my office. Abruptly wary, I nod. "Yes, you can cut the mesh without losing any fingers to the chemicals. Or having the metal on those others shoot blinding sparks." He grimaces at the sarcastic comment, but, losing the battle with my anger, I demand, "Why did I need to come here for questions I could have answered without leaving my desk?"

"If you'd stayed there, I wouldn't have had the pleasure of watching you walk here."

Flabbergasted, I can only stare at him (and tell myself to close my mouth). What do I say to something so… ugh, I don't even know the word!

"I also wouldn't have been able to enjoy all those expressions playing across your face."

That does it! I turn on my heel and stomp out of the workshop. I won't dignify his comments with a response.

22

———

About to dig into work again, I groan. Access to Deran's holographic sketch would be helpful. Design. Drawing. Whatever. But no way am I'm going back there.

I press my intercom's call button. "Sarissa." No response. I wait a few seconds, then try again. When she still doesn't answer, I gaze in that direction, expecting to find her office empty. But she's at her desk, feet up on her table, staring at the wall above the door.

I storm over to her office and fling the door open. "Has your intercom stopped working?"

Sarissa's eyes drift down from the wall to find my face. While her gaze floats around the general area, her eyes are unfocused. A little alarmed, I step into her office.

When Sarissa's hand floats toward the mug on her desk, instinct drives me to snatch it up. I inspect the contents. Golden-brown liquid. Could be tea, but I suspect not. I raise the mug, the sharp whiff of alcohol assaulting me before the mug is even halfway to my nose.

Appalled, I gape at Sarissa. Voice low, I hiss, "You're drinking at work?"

"So what if I am?" Sarissa's words are slurred, and her eyes have lost focus again.

I stand rooted, unsure what to do. No way she could get this drunk on just one mug. Or even in the time she's been here. Then again, I don't know the rate she's been imbibing.

If I report this, as I should, Sarissa will lose her job. May even be demoted to a lower tier. She'd be devastated. Much as I hate what she did, feel the desolation of her betrayal every day, I can't.

Her actions in the weeks since *that* day, at least in part, tell me she does have some regrets. Are my refusals to hear her out making her drink on the job? Perhaps she simply can't face a full day here with me without something to ease the pain?

I snort. Yeah, right! Like she feels any pain. More like she's sorry for herself because she's lost whatever leverage or standing her spying provided.

I can't blame myself for her actions. What others choose to do is on them. Although I may have treated her harshly of late, drinking at work was her choice.

Despite her actions, I can be lenient today. I'll extend grace and hope it doesn't happen again. But how will I get her home? It must've been so simple in bygone days when you could call a "Lyft" or "Uber," mysterious names plucked from conversations I overheard at the academy. Like other mysterious terms I've yet to uncover meanings for.

While I'm strong for my size, I'm nowhere near muscular enough to support Sarissa on my own. Besides, she's five inches taller than me. Who can I ask for help who won't blab? Immediately dismissing my staff, I consider options outside my immediate circle.

Deran comes to mind. But isn't he the enemy? Another spy? I mull the problem. If he is a spy, perhaps he's the best person to help me. This way, if Sarissa has to be reported, I won't have to do it. Cowardly, I know, but I have an ulterior motive.

If Sarissa isn't sanctioned, the kindness Deran has shown me is genuine. Doesn't mean he isn't a spy, but it will tip the scales more in his favor.

Decided, I glance at Sarissa again. Her eyes have returned to that spot on the wall. "Good girl. You just stay here. Don't go anywhere."

Sarissa gives no sign she's even heard me. I close her office blinds before retrieving the incriminating mug. Praying Sarissa will stay put, I leave, shutting the door quietly behind me. A sneaked glance at the nearby lab benches reveals no one's paying attention.

I hustle back to the workshop, dumping the offending liquor along the way in a potted plant. Hopefully, it will survive the abuse. In the workshop, the three men previously stationed near the door have dispersed. Deran sits at the workbench, and when I get close, I find he's updating his... ugh!

"What do you call those drawings?"

Deran's head pops up, a slow smile easing out. "Back for more? I thought I'd scared you away for good."

It takes a moment to remember what he's referring to. I brush the incident aside with an impatient hand. "Not why I'm here, and you didn't answer my question."

Something in my tone must convey my anxiety because the smile falters. He studies me before he answers. "We call them technical drawings. But I don't think that's what's bothering you."

I fidget with the stylus in my hair, second-guessing before resigning myself. "I need help with something... delicate. Can I rely on your discretion?"

Those spectacular gray eyes all seriousness, Deran stands. "You can. What do you need help with?"

"Sarissa, you know, my PA?" Deran nods, and I continue. "Well, it seems she's a little, uh, indisposed."

The confusion on Deran's face clears quickly. "Oh, too much partying last night?"

I'm thankful he was careful to avoid any mention of drinking because if there are eyes in the workshop, or rather, ears, they won't hear I'm not acting on a punishable offense. "Yes. I need help to get her home and into bed." There, that could imply she was just feeling under the weather.

"Give me a sec." Deran disappears behind the bulk of the machine already taking shape.

When he reappears, he's pushing a raw materials cart. I grin. "Why didn't I think of that?"

Deran winks. "You're clearly not as well-versed at dealing with these things as I am."

His statement has me imagining what he gets up to in his spare time. And, before I can stop the thought, with whom. Irritated, I scrub it away, considering the cart instead. With all the back and forth the mech team has been doing bringing materials into the lab, another cart won't be noticed.

I insist Deran take the lead, and his saucy grin tells me he knows why. I follow behind, only stepping in front of him again the moment before we reach Sarissa's office so I can open the door for him. In the blink of an eye, the cart, Deran, and I are all in Sarissa's office.

It's a tight squeeze, but we do our best. Between the time I left and now, Sarissa's passed out, head twisted at an awkward angle against the backrest of her chair. I step forward to help Deran lift her, but he waves me away. "Better if you stand clear."

I do, but note the grimy interior when he opens the lid. The metal floor and sides aren't forgiving either. While apathetic about Sarissa's comfort, it won't do for her to show up with bruises tomorrow. With the way things currently stand between us, she might not use Nanogo to heal the marks to spite me.

"Hold on." I grab the closest thing. Sarissa's coat. A lovely thick woolen one—and expensive because of the natural fiber. Too bad. She can shop for another. I stuff the coat into the cart, creating padding all around. "Okay, good to go."

I step back, then just about trip over myself when Deran lifts Sarissa like she weighs nothing. His overalls, dark blue and the same self-imposed "uniform" he wears to work each day, stretch across his back when he places Sarissa in the cart. What do the muscles beneath that thick fabric look like?

I turn to the door before something in my face gives me away, pretending to check what's going on outside through the small pane of glass.

When the lid of the cart closes, I glance back. "Ready?"

"Yes, but you should leave a few minutes before I do. It'll look less suspicious. I'll meet you by the service elevators on the ground floor."

Service elevators? "I don't know where they are."

"Go through the door to the side of the scanners."

Nodding, I slip out and hurry to the elevator, relieved none of my team (that's a better word than staff, right?) stop me along the way. I reach the service elevators just as Deran exits the one he used. He lifts his chin to another side door I hadn't noticed. "We'll leave that way."

Following his lead, I'm surprised when the door opens onto the back lot of the building. "I don't think I've ever seen this side before."

"More than one new experience for you today then?" There's the trace of that insanely sexy smile, but his voice remains solemn. "Where are we taking her?"

For the first time, I consider the question. When I found Sarissa, all I could focus on was getting her out of HQ before someone else saw her in that state. But I have no clue what to do next.

There really are only two places we can go—her place or mine. Since entering a building I don't know with a somewhat stranger pushing a cart which doesn't belong there may draw unwanted attention, it leaves only one option. "We'll go to my apartment. At least I know how to access the service elevators there, and we won't have any problems getting into the building."

Deran nods but doesn't follow as I make to leave.

"What are you waiting for?"

"Can you watch her for a moment? I think I may know a less conspicuous way of getting her back to your place."

He doesn't wait for an answer, reentering the building and disappearing. I fiddle with the lid of the cart, pretending I have a reason for loitering with it.

Thankfully, no other people appear before Deran returns. I gape at the wheelchair he's pushing. "Where did you get that?"

"From a floor in the building."

"What floor has wheelchairs?"

"Does it matter?"

Clipped vowels have me doing a double-take. Deran's face is

closed and guarded. I bite out a response, irritated he would think I was the one hiding things. "You believe I *want* to know something I shouldn't?"

Saying nothing, Deran transfers Sarissa from the cart to the wheelchair. He drapes her with the accompanying blanket to conceal her face, before running the cart back into the building. By the time he returns, his expression is more neutral, although still wary. What does he have to hide?

23

It's a straight shot from CC HQ to my apartment, and no one stops or asks us questions along the way. As I wave an arm across the panel to access my apartment, I'm shaking. I'm more stressed by this whole situation than I realized.

When Deran wheels Sarissa in after me, he suddenly seems too big, my apartment too small. Crushing the swelling panic, I force a deep, calming breath and point at my bedroom. "Could you please put Sarissa on the bed?"

Without a word, Deran complies, then returns, pushing the empty wheelchair ahead of him. I stare at him, suddenly scrambling for something to say. It wasn't a problem before because a tense vigilance kept us from speaking until now.

The silence looms large between us, and I grope at the first thing that comes to mind. "Um, thanks for your help. I appreciate it."

Looking way more relaxed than he has in the last hour, Deran smiles and leans against the kitchen wall, crossing one long leg over the other. "What now? Are you planning on staying or coming back to work?"

I almost miss the question I'm so busy gawking at the man. A tasty appetizer ready to be sampled. Then I register his words, and reality crashes back down.

I'm a workaholic. I can't *not* go back. That would raise alarms. I realize I'm still staring at Deran, so I rush past him into the bedroom, speaking as I go. "Yes, I'm going back, but before I do, I want to make sure Sarissa's okay. You go on ahead."

"Why would I want to leave already?" There's laughter in his voice.

"Fine, do whatever. I'll be a few minutes." I return to the bedroom and stand in the doorway for a second, absorbing Sarissa's prone form. "Al-Li and Astatine, Sarissa! What were you thinking?" Then, shaking my head, I enter and bustle about, elevating Sarissa's head, rolling her onto her side, removing her shoes and covering her with a blanket. Then I grab the trash can and put it next to the bed. At least if she vomits, she won't choke—and hopefully, she'll find the trash before my carpet or bed.

Passing Deran again as I return to the kitchen to get a glass of water, I can't help but feel his intense male presence tugging at me. I do my best to ignore that pull and hurry back to the bedroom where I place the water on the nightstand. Only thing left to add is a washcloth, so I lift a clean one from the closet and deposit it next to the water.

When I get back to the hall, a flush creeps over my face, as I feel Deran's eyes on me. What is he thinking? Much as I'd dearly like to know, I won't ask. I'll only get that cheeky grin again.

I head down the hall to my front door and open it, glancing back at Deran. "Are you coming?"

With a graceful shove off the wall, he straightens and collects the wheelchair, pushing it out of the apartment ahead of us. As I wand my arm to lock my door, I wonder how I'll make the trip back to CC HQ without making an idiot of myself.

I should've known he'd take care of that. We're barely in the elevator when he asks his first question.

"Ally and Astatine, huh?"

The teasing note in his voice and mischievous glint in his eyes have me rolling my eyes. "Sorry! I didn't think you heard that."

"I did. And now I'm curious. Who's Ally?"

Inwardly, I grin. Is he jealous? "'Ally' is not a person; she's an alloy. An aluminum lithium alloy, to be accurate."

"Oh, I get it. Al-Li!" Deran says, using the letters denoting the symbol for each element. "Why that?"

"No real reason other than it's fun to say."

"You know those alloys are used for constructing spacecrafts?"

"I do. And before you ask again, astatine is thanks to one of my mentors at the academy. He'd use it when he wanted to call someone an ass, but since protocol prohibited it, he'd stress the first part, then tack the rest of the word on like he'd meant to say the whole word all along."

Deran chuckles. "He sounds like quite a character. Where did you go to school?"

A neutral question, easy to reciprocate. "McQueen STEM Academy. You?"

Pewter eyes crinkle at the corners. "I should've guessed—only the best for you. The Academy had some classes I wish my school had offered. I ended up at the Cirrian School of Engineers."

I bite back irritation. "The Academy may be the best school, but you try going to school with stuck-up tier sevens and above." The words are out before I've thought them through. Color heats my cheeks again. "Sorry, I don't mean to offend if you're in those tiers."

Deran's laugh is rich and full. That wonderfully warm blanket. "No, just a humble tier three."

"Oh."

Serious eyes now, silver glinting below the surface. "What made you think my tier was higher?"

"They don't put just anyone in charge of mech teams at HQ. Or grant them the clearance you have."

"I see." Deran nods. "No, those only came through hard work and sheer determination. To make myself as invaluable as possible."

His words ring true, but a deeper truth lurks. A truth I yearn to learn. Hopefully, one day he'll trust me enough to tell me. I register he's asked a question, but I don't know what. "Pardon?"

"I asked if you'd tell me what tier you are?"

I grin. "Guess."

"Aw, Chiara! That's not fair."

"Why? Don't you know it's rude to ask a lady her tier?"

"I thought it was rude to ask a lady her age."

His dry answer elicits giggles, and I relent. "Four." The giggles become laughter at his shocked expression. "Now you know why I never would've guessed your tier."

Rubbing the back of his neck, he shakes his head. "I guess there's no knowing how the powers that be account for things."

"Indeed. So, which classes at the Academy had you drooling?"

Another of those laughs I love the sound of. "Oh, there were many. I think the one I most wanted was Advanced Fluid Dynamics."

"Oh! Professor Cranson's class."

Wide-eyed surprise. I don't think I'll ever tire of the depths of color there.

"You took his class?"

"No, but I heard how amazing it was."

"From one of your friends?"

My laugh is mirthless. "No, Deran, I didn't have friends at the Academy. Those snobs shunned me the moment I arrived. Everything I learned from my fellow students was because I eavesdropped on their conversations." I try to keep the bitterness out of my voice, but it seeps through.

"Oh, Chiara, I'm so sorry. It wasn't a good place for you?"

I shrug. "The academics were amazing. The other aspects, not so much." Deran waits, giving me space to decide if I want to share more. Before I've fully decided, the words tumble out. "I have nothing to compare the Academy to. From the time the director put me in the Academy, until I graduated, it was the only place I knew. They kept me there."

Deran's mouth thins to a sharp line, eyes hardening to steel. "They kept you there? You mean, you were a boarder, but still had exeat time?"

"No, Deran, I mean they confined me there. The director plucked me from my home where breathing was difficult and food and water were scarce and set me in a space where none of those were an issue. By itself, an excellent exchange, except they sequestered me there while they continued cleaning the outside world. When I finally graduated and was allowed outside, I couldn't believe it was the same place."

Deran turns his head so I can't read his expression, but a muscle ticks along his jaw. "The trundle's here."

I'm so startled by the change in subject, it takes me a moment to realize we've reached the station. The trundle sweeps in, gusting air ahead of it, blowing strands of hair across my face. Deran's hand moves that hair off my face, a gesture so unexpected I freeze. Unable to move, I gaze directly into those incredible eyes, moonlight shifting across water. But they reveal nothing of what he's feeling.

"I'm sorry that happened to you."

Deran's words are a whisper. Then he's ushering me onto the trundle, as if the moment we just shared never existed. I'm so confused, I drop into a seat subconsciously, barely registering the pain as I try to gather my scattered thoughts. I'm still working on it when he reaches into a pocket and pulls out a bag.

With a crooked smile, he stretches across the aisle between us. "Maybe this will help. Gummy worm?"

The offer is so absurd I burst out laughing. "Really? You just carry those around with you?"

Deran shoves the bag at me again, a goofy grin on his face. "I do. They help me think. Take one or forever hold your peace. I'm not known to share."

Giggling, I choose one, nibbling on it as we travel ever closer to CC HQ. The food obviates the need for conversation, but it wouldn't have been a burden. He's easy to talk to. And isn't that a shame! If I plan on keeping things professional between us, it would've been easier if he was obnoxious. Then I could've disliked him.

As it is, his increasing appeal makes me almost regret parting ways. We reach the service elevators, and he ushers me into a waiting car but doesn't follow. I raise an eyebrow.

"Probably best if I return this on my own." Deran gestures toward the wheelchair.

I had almost forgotten about it—and the mystery of where it came from. That tension is back in his eyes, and after all he's done to help me, I don't want to antagonize him. "Yes, I understand. Thanks again for your help. I really don't know what I would've done without you today."

When he accepts I won't press him into awkward explanations, the wariness leaves his demeanor. "Lucky for you this isn't my first rodeo."

"Rodeo?" I echo, confused.

"Something they used to say, and do, a long time ago. It just means I've done this before."

"You steal wheelchairs on a regular basis?" Finally, I thought of something witty to say in the moment, then regret it when his eyes shutter again. "Sorry, I didn't mean…" I sigh.

"Never mind. You should probably go, or people may wonder what's keeping the elevator."

His comment makes me realize we've been talking through the open doors for a while now, and yes, that will draw unwanted attention. I nod, not sure what else to say but aware of the subtle dismissal.

I step back into the elevator, allowing the doors to shut fully. As I'm whisked back to the labs, the questions swirl again. The overriding issue remains: can I trust Deran?

When I return to my office, Tandize immediately accosts me. Was the girl just waiting to pounce the moment I stepped off the elevator? Defensive for no reason, I'm careful to moderate my tone. "Yes, what do you need?"

"Where have you been?"

I arch an eyebrow. "Are you my mother?"

Tandize doesn't look the slightest bit put out. "I've been trying to reach you for the last thirty minutes."

"You still haven't told me what you want. If it was that urgent, I expect you would've spat it out by now."

Uneasiness crosses Tandize's face. "I went to ask Sarissa something, but she's not in her office. I can't find her anywhere."

"She went home because she wasn't feeling well." The lie slips out, and I almost can't believe how easily. Then I remember all the years of subtle deception with Cygnus. Perhaps it's bleeding through into other areas of my life.

Of more importance now—why is Tandize here, asking questions the moment I step off the elevator? Did she see enough earlier to put two and two together?

"Oh." Tandize stands still, looking uncertain.

I groan inwardly. This child! "What did you want to ask Sarissa?"

Tandize wrings her hands. "Promise you won't get upset?"

"I can't promise when I don't know what the problem is." This is getting tedious.

"I dropped salt in the chemical bath." Tandize hangs her head, peeking up at me through the curtain of blonde hair falling across her face.

It takes long seconds for me to understand. "The chemical bath in the workshop?" I promise I am trying not to lose it, but my voice is shrill.

Tandize backs up a step. "Yes?"

When her answer comes out more a question than a statement, I clamp my hands together. The urge to box her ears overrides reason, despite understanding she means it more as "What are you going to do to me?" than any confusion about the chemical bath's location.

"Why were you in the workshop?" I keep my voice low, the only way to dampen the rising wrath.

"Koni invited me there for lunch."

"Koni?"

"One of the mechanics. You know, the tall guy with the beard?"

Ah, Takoni. "And why was 'Koni' inviting you into a restricted area for lunch?" Tandize continues sidling away from me. "Stand still!"

Tandize stops, suspended in position, one hand half lifted and one foot still in the air. If I wasn't furious, I might've laughed. "Um, we wanted to have lunch together?"

I can't deal with her. Not now. I'm going to fire her if I continue this conversation. Specifics, I tell myself, just get the specifics. "What type of salt did you drop?"

Her face goes blank, making me wonder why I hired her. Then she obviously remembers there's more than one kind of salt. "Oh, table salt. A bag from the cafeteria."

I bite the inside of my cheek, desperate to let the rage loose. But table salt isn't that serious, and one sachet even less so. Overreacting will ring those wretched alarm bells. The last thing either Deran or I need now are questions or attention focused on where we were or what we were doing. "Am I correct to assume that was what happened about thirty minutes ago, when you started looking for Sarissa?"

"Yes!" Tandize sounds so relieved I asked a question she didn't have to explain. I feel a little sorry for yelling at her. However, she was being irresponsible.

"You know better than to go into restricted areas. Next time, eat your lunch in the cafeteria."

"Yes, Chiara." Voice meek, she remains standing there, still in that daft position.

I'm suddenly overcome by the insane urge to laugh, too weary to fight anymore. But laughing now would not underscore the seriousness of the matter for her. Despite this, I know nothing will stop the maniacal laughter spewing out in a cackle sooner rather than later.

"Go, get on with something productive."

I hurry away, toward the workshop, possibly the best spot to escape the lab and address the issue. Issues, I correct, the first being the hysteria I can't contain. I duck into the nearest restroom and let go—after checking all the stalls are empty.

Five minutes later and less frustrated but drained beyond measure, I splash water onto my face until I feel I can tolerate the few hours remaining before I can return home.

Conversations hush as the mechanics spot me when I walk into the workshop. I don't have to hunt Deran down. He's there with the rest, off to the side with one man in particular. Koni. The moment Deran spots me, he lopes over.

"Chiara, I'm so sorry. I just heard. I apologize. Koni is new and didn't realize he shouldn't bring visitors into the workshop."

I raise an eyebrow. "Really? All the security he has to go through to get in here himself, and he thought it was okay to invite a girl in?"

Deran runs a hand through his hair, making the spikes stand on end. Al-Li! I want to touch those spiky pieces. Run my fingers through them too. Just as well he's more worried about what happened than teasing me.

"Chiara, I know how this looks. But the kid believed it would be alright because the girl works in your lab. He didn't think."

His face is so earnest, I want to take him in my arms and tell him it's okay. *Hell, no, it's not okay!* I take an involuntary step back, then realize I'm trying to put space between us. Keep him out of reach. *All the Al-Li alloys, can this day get any worse?*

Deran is staring at me. Is he wondering what I'm doing?

"Right!" I say, almost stumbling in my eagerness to turn around. "I'll deal with the salt issue." Yet again, I'm rushing away. Why can't this day be over already?

When I reach the bath, I realize I'm not wearing my lab coat. In my urgency to find a safe place to expel that laughter, I forgot to grab one. I stare at the bath, debating just dealing with the problem without proper protection.

But there's nothing for it. Besides, a simple lab coat won't work. To get in the tub and fish the silly paper sachet out, I'll need a suit. I want to curl into a ball and cry. Seriously, what's with all the emotions today?

It's mid-afternoon. I've had nothing to eat all day. Ah, that would be it! I turn and run right into Deran. In my haste, I didn't see him there.

He puts steadying hands on my arms. "Whoa, there!" He studies my face. "Hey, what's wrong?"

Can you stop being so nice? You're going to make me cry. Instead of answering, I brush past Deran and run out of the workshop.

Ultimately, I make Tandize don the suit and climb into the bath to retrieve her silly salt packet. A suitable punishment for her transgression, and one that comes to me as I flee the workshop via the lab for the mall.

Whilst a single pack holds insufficient salt to affect the chemicals, the paper sachet can't remain. Floundering around in the stinky chemical bath hunting for it should remind Tandize not to enter restricted areas next time.

Pausing only long enough to bark out instructions to Tandize, I continue my headlong flight. At last, I'm safely ensconced in the cozy booth at my new favorite Italian restaurant. To say I drown my woes in food wouldn't be inaccurate. But the food is exquisite, and I'm starving, so—justified!

Replete, I lean back, feeling rounder than a tick fat with blood (non-scientists would puke at this thought), and order some coffee. If I spend fifteen minutes drinking this solitary cup, I'll only have to endure another thirty minutes in the lab when I return.

Those thirty minutes feel like thirty hours. The moment I get back, I find out Deran's been looking for me, as has Tandize. I suspect his reason and guess hers when I spot the soggy salt packet on a plate on my desk.

I can't avoid Deran forever, and I need to check the tiny amount of salt or chemicals in the paper haven't irreparably altered the bath's chemical composition, so I wander back to the workshop, excuses in hand.

Deran isn't there (yes!), so I whip out my testing kit and quickly validate the bath. A little off, more likely due to the suit or contaminants Tandize introduced rather than the salt packet itself. I make the adjustments and scamper away before Deran returns.

However, there's no escaping the demands of others. In my absence, a few team members encountered problems with their own assigned projects and have questions I must answer. By the time I finish dealing with those, it's long past the hour to leave.

Hurriedly, I gather my things and propel myself out of the building. I don't care how I look, running to the trundle with briefcase in one hand and purse and jacket in the other. The sheer freedom of the sprint is exhilarating.

Just before the doors close, I leap onto the departing trundle, flinging myself into a seat, breathing hard. I pull out a compact (Sarissa's idea) and note the sparkle in my eyes and flush on my cheeks as I adjust my hair to a more orderly state. At least I don't look as knackered as I feel.

After the trundle delivers me to my stop, I tell myself I should've expected the creeping exhaustion caused by inactivity on the trundle ride as I drag my bones home. When I enter my bedroom, I come to an abrupt halt. I forgot Sarissa was here.

She's still passed out, and from the looks of the untouched trash can, water, and washcloth, she hasn't stirred. I want to shake her awake and order her home, but tell myself I'm only grumpy because I've had no downtime.

Opening a bottle of sparkling apple juice, I sink onto the sofa, only for its unforgiving surface to remind me how uncomfortable it is. With a groan, I rise and return to my bedroom, grab some cushions, and then slog back to scatter them all over the sofa. A marginal improvement.

Obviously enough to afford the relaxation I sought because two hours later I'm still curled up on the sofa when Sarissa stumbles out of my bedroom. Bleary-eyed, she stares at me, clearly confused.

"You were drunk at work today."

"Oh." Still no comprehension.

"I couldn't take you back to your place because I don't have access. Also, I doubt they would've let me enter if they'd seen the state you were in."

"Oh." A flicker of understanding.

"Yeah." I return my attention to my movie.

Sarissa sidles into the space between, blocking my view. "Chiara, I…"

"Don't bother," I reply, not giving her any face time. When she remains where she is, I glare at her. "Do you mind?"

"Oh, sorry."

As she moves aside, she winces, and I figure her head is probably killing her. Excellent! I'm not offering any Nanogo either. She'll have to suffer until she gets home. When Sarissa dawdles, I stab the remote and pause my movie. "What?"

Another wince, this time no doubt at my volume. I'm beyond caring. She caused all the trouble today. I should've reported her and been done with it.

"I'm sorry I came to work drunk."

"Fine, whatever. Don't do it again, or I will report you."

"You… you didn't report me?"

"Sarissa, go home. I don't want to talk to you. You've caused enough grief for one day."

When she doesn't move, I want to scream. I hit play, and the movie resumes. Out of the corner of my eye, I watch her. She's gearing up to say something. Should I let her?

We remain at our impasse for a solid few minutes, me pretending to ignore her, Sarissa starting a few sentences but speaking fewer than three words each time before stopping again. I can't take it anymore.

I push myself up from the sofa and stomp to my front door, tossing it open. "Time for you to leave."

Sarissa blinks back tears, then scurries into the bedroom.

I yell after her. "Your things are still at the office. You'll have to collect them tomorrow."

She reappears, sad and forlorn, standing in the doorway. One look at my face and she wilts further, then shuffles past me and out of my apartment.

When I close the door, the exhaustion I've held at bay all day demands indulgence. I stumble back to my bedroom, toss the blanket Sarissa used onto the floor, and crawl under my covers, finding refuge in sleep.

While enjoying my shower the next morning, Sarissa's desolate expression last night comes to mind. Like she had lost all hope. Not wanting to give her any more reasons to act up at work, I decide if she wants to talk, I'll allow it.

The next few weeks pass in a blur. On several occasions, Sarissa looks like she might want to tell me something again, but every time I give her the opportunity, she flakes. I don't know whether she gives up or if I stop paying attention because the project ramps up its demands, the first prototype nearing completion.

I spend most of my hours in the workshop now. Thanks to the time Deran helped me with Sarissa, I've managed a degree of normalcy in his presence. Whether it was the ease of the conversation on the trundle back to CC HQ that day, or because most of our discussions since center on the project, I can now claim holding a coherent conversation with him is possible.

We fall into a comfortable routine, where I spend a few minutes consulting with Deran each morning about the day's work, before checking in on my own team, then heading back to the workshop for the rest of the day. Fun and games would be an appropriate way to label the time there.

"Chiara, hand me that dogleg reamer, would you?"

I scowl. "Seriously, Koni, you expect me to believe there's a tool with that name?"

Chuckles from the rest of the crew. My scowl deepens.

"Yes. They're right next to the stork beak pliers."

Now I know they're having me on. "Sure. While I'm at it, why don't I find you a hippo wrench too, so you can pull those six-inch nails out my back?"

"No need. The stubby nail eater can take care of that."

They're all laughing so hard now, Silvan actually topples off the barrel he's using as a chair. Even Deran (traitor!) can't keep the grin off his face. He, at least, offers mercy.

"Come on, guys, give her a break. She's the brains of the operation. While she's brilliant at what she does, we can't expect her to know everything." Reaching into the toolbox at his feet, Deran extracts the strangest tool I've ever seen. "The dogleg reamer. Used to smooth burrs, otherwise known as rough edges, off drilled holes so those edges don't act as stress multipliers and cause cracks. Especially important when working with nuclear energy, don't you think?"

Fascinated, I accept the tool and inspect it. "Now I see why it's called a dogleg—looks just like one." I pass the tool to Koni. "I suppose there are also really stork beak pliers and… the nail things?"

Deran lifts each in turn from the toolbox, a wry grin on his face. Impossible to miss, though, is the teasing glint in those silver eyes. "Stork beak pliers and a stubby nail eater auger. Want to learn about more tools?"

Sure I'm missing something when the rest of the team crack up again, I decline, making an excuse for leaving the workshop. I've barely gone two steps when Deran's in front of me, blocking my path. "Aw, come back, Chiara. We won't tease anymore."

I cross my arms. "You mean, not for the next few minutes?"

Deran's laugh is pure delight. "Okay, we promise not to tease for the rest of the day." He turns to his team. "Don't we?"

Vigorous nods, but the grins never leave their faces, making me doubt they'll stick to their agreement. To their credit, they do, albeit because of the occasional reminder from Deran. But the next day they're back to their antics. Needing some space (a girl can only take so much), I wander over to the control panel we've been working on. There has to be a reason the system isn't working.

I touch the nearby cube, and Deran's holographic design pops up. Reaching forward, I touch the outer edge, slowly spinning the design. Breath stirs the hair against my neck, and I whirl around.

Deran's face is all innocence, but the stifled laughter from his team gives him away. I raise an eyebrow. "Really?"

Raising his hands, he offers a sincere smile. "Okay, I repent. I'm sorry." His interest turns to the design. "What are you looking at?"

Carefully, I reach into the image, pulling the design apart, stacking the pieces so they're a little further removed. "This piece, here." I point. "I believe this is the reason the circuit isn't closing."

As he plucks the piece out of the design, Deran's arm brushes against me. The contact is electric, and a shiver runs through me, dazzling enough to not hear Deran's question the first time he asks. "Pardon?"

And his grin is the devil's own again. *He did that on purpose!*

"Earth to Chiara! Hello!" Aware he has my attention, he repeats the question. "I asked which part is faulty?"

When I reach for the 3D piece, determined to answer him this time, Deran abruptly angles it toward me so our hands end up crashing together. Startled again, I can only think to be thankful this is an image and not the actual part—because otherwise I would've dropped it. Fighting for composure, I take a deep breath and hold my hand out. "May I have the piece, please?"

Still grinning, Deran gives it to me. I quickly explain the fault. Deran understands at once, snatching the piece out of the air, then grabbing my hand (*Al-Li! Will he stop doing that?*) and towing me to the control panel.

"Here, hold this so I can see it." Deran passes me the holographic piece, then scoots under the panel.

Scattered, I can't think to do anything except what he asks. In no time at all, he's backing out from under the panel, looking pleased with himself. "Let's try it."

Fully expecting I've solved the problem, I'm unsurprised when the control panel hums—finally! Lights, holoscreens, gauges, and dials come to life. I run a hand over the panel, checking readings. Too absorbed with verifying everything's working as it should now, I don't even notice Deran leave.

Then the day we've been working toward arrives. When Deran messages me one morning to inform me they've finished the last tweaks, I debate delaying testing until Cygnus returns so I can make my demands. But this will apparently be one of his long absences, and I can't justify the expense of the holding pattern.

Besides, I'm desperate for something in my life to work.

Nervous and excited all at once, I shimmy over to the workshop. Deran spots me and ambles over, that lazy smile making my insides do wild cartwheels, leaving me breathless.

Deran rubs his hands together, glee on his face. "Ready to do this?"

I nod, not trusting my voice, and we walk over to the control panel. Sarissa is nowhere in sight. She called in sick today, and I can't help but wonder if she's really sick or just hungover. Either way, now's not the time to think about her or her issues.

I pause before stepping up to the control board. About to place a hand on the switch, a plastic bag crinkles just under my nose. I glance up and find Deran's teasing smile.

"Gummy worm for luck?" He shakes the bag again.

A nervous giggle escapes as I take one. "Thanks!" I lift it in mock salute before biting, unsure whether the chewing motion or sweet flavor helps calm me.

I hear rather than see Deran's team taking their places behind us. They're almost as anxious as I am.

Aloud, I call the checks, and the respective team members confirm the various parts of the machine are ready to run. It's surreal when I receive the last "Yes."

I flip the switch. A slight whooshing sound fills the workshop. Small clusters of heavy water molecules accelerate into the mesh. Why it's called "cluster impact" fusion.

I envision the thousands of molecules impacting the mesh, wondering if the circular shapes Deran cut the mesh into will hold better than the square design I'd originally planned on situating at the chamber's exit. But Deran insisted their welds to keep the mesh in place would hold, despite the improved particle accelerator design we came up with.

For a tense few minutes, the machine runs, every part of every machine piece monitored and recorded. Gauges and dials rise and fall, beeps sound and lights blink... and then the team gives a collective groan when an alarm blares, indicating the mesh just blew out in several places. I switch it off.

Although I knew the chances of success were low on the first attempt, the failure galls. Just as well I went ahead with the test. Time to make adjustments and press on with the next permutation. Hopefully, I'll have it ready before Cygnus returns.

I'm about to leave when I realize how upset the mech team are. Dejected frowns and angry scowls mar their faces. I grimace, tempering my own disappointment.

"This is not a failure. It's only our first attempt and likely to be one of many setbacks on the road to success." My words don't provide the encouragement I'd hoped for. I turn to Deran, shrugging off what I can't help.

His expression wary, he watches me. "You're really not that upset?"

"Oh, I'm upset. Believe me. But that never solved problems. Let's print out these results and get back to work."

25

By the time I hop on the trundle home, I've finally swallowed the bitter pill of failure. Only to regurgitate it when I encounter a family off to spend time in a nearby park.

The boy and his parents are such a tiny unit I can't help hoping they might join more of the boy's siblings there. Something about the thought niggles, but I dismiss it as my thoughts go to my family.

Until now, I've successfully buried myself in work, locking my family into the far recesses of my mind where they are all but inaccessible. But this little group sitting opposite me has smashed those barriers and dredged my family from the depths.

Fierce longing consumes me, accompanied by inevitable trepidation. An urgency to both see the ones I love and verify their welfare overwhelms me. I'm agitated enough to decide I'll pay Hag Lady a visit tomorrow and request a call with Cygnus, beyond caring what message I'll send.

Despite the resolution, anxiety dogs every moment until I stagger into work the next morning. I've had almost no sleep to speak of, and dark smudges underscore my eyes. Too taxing to bother with makeup. I already have enough on my mind.

I stop at my office barely long enough to drop my things off, then hurry to the top floor. Only to discover Hag Lady isn't at her desk. *Argh!* It's the first time I've ever found her missing. No doubt because the director isn't around and she doesn't have to patrol his door like a rabid dog.

Annoyed, I leave a message, then ride the elevator back down to the labs. Before I reach my office, my comm beeps, informing me Hag Lady has returned, and I should stop in now if I want to speak with her.

With repressed irritation, I catch the elevator back up, running through my arguments. When the elevator dings open, I'm as prepared as I can be for her potential questions.

"Good morning, Mrs. Jacobs."

Her greeting is a scowl. "What do you want?"

"May I put in a request to speak with the director?"

"What about?"

"My current project." Not strictly true, but I can build a correlation when I speak with Cygnus.

"What about your project?"

"Mrs. Jacobs, I don't mean to be rude, but do you have the requisite clearance for me to provide specifics?"

Beady eyes glint back. "Girl, you think I attained this position without the highest clearance levels?"

I pretend to fidget. "I apologize. I didn't mean any offense. It's just that I'm precluded from discussing my projects with anyone the director hasn't preapproved in writing. May I request you ask the director to send me that permission so I can provide you with the details?"

This was the part I hoped would be too much effort. Hag Lady strikes me as someone who likes to throw her weight around, but who's also scared enough of the director to not want to bother him unnecessarily. To approach the director twice about the same issue may cross one of her lines.

"I told you I have clearance. Tell me what you want to ask the director." Hag Lady's whiplash tone makes me flinch.

"Again, my sincere apologies, Mrs. Jacobs, but I need that in writing from the director." I want to run and hide. Confrontation is not my thing. But Hag Lady *has* to set up that call with Cygnus. I must speak with my family before I continue with the work he has demanded. For all I know, they're already... well, I just need to make sure for myself they're okay before I press on with the project.

The way Hag Lady inspects me, it's a wonder she doesn't pull out a fork and knife and tuck in. I straighten my already stiff posture, lifting my chin.

"You know," Hag Lady says, tapping a pointy pink fingernail on her polished desk, "I never took you for one to say boo to anyone."

Is that a good thing? Is she coming around?

"If I set up this call with the director, are you going to waste his time?"

Ah, now I get it. Self-preservation. She wants to know *she* won't get into trouble. Unfortunately, I can't promise her anything. In fact, it's more likely she'll get the short end of the stick, but I'm not telling her.

"I'm aware the director is a busy man, and his time is valuable. I can promise I won't take more time than is essential when I speak with him."

Hag Lady studies me, then finally grimaces like I've left a nasty taste in her mouth. "Very well. I'll set up the call. Have your comm link open to accept a direct connection. But if this comes back on me, rest assured, I will find a way for you to feel those repercussions too."

Oh, I don't doubt that. "Thank you, Mrs. Jacobs. I appreciate your assistance."

I don't wait for the dismissal already forming on her lips as I do my best to leave in a stately fashion. But the moment I reach the sanctuary of my office, I collapse into my chair. When I swipe at the perspiration on the back of my neck and above my lips, I find my hands are shaking. But I did it! I wrangled my call out of Hag Lady.

That reminds me. I take a second to set my comm to accept a direct connection. Usually, this is ill-advised because you get all kinds of spam on an open channel.

I can't believe the director communicates this way. Shouldn't he have an encrypted line or something? I make a mental note to confirm the line is secure when we speak, so I don't make a fatal error discussing the project where anyone can hear.

Feeling a little faint, I call for a food tray. I can't go down to the cafeteria, as I have no idea when the call with Cygnus might come through, and I don't want to be in a room with others when it does.

I settle down to work, nibbling the delivered food and studying the results from yesterday's failed experiment. Turns out we had more acceleration than either Deran or I anticipated—the reason the welds didn't hold. The note Deran sent earlier, telling me they're altering the welding compound to resolve the issue, now makes sense. My comm beeps in my ear, and I jump, my heart doubling its beat at the direct connection request. Hesitantly, I open the line, hoping it's not some explicit ad. Cygnus's face on the other end is only a slight improvement. I don't forget to execute the proper protocols before greeting him.

Sitting taller in my chair, I reach for my tablet, holding all my notes pertinent to this conversation. "Good day, Director. Thank you for agreeing to my call."

"I'm hoping you have good news?"

With an inward grimace, I ensure my mask remains in place. "Director, may I speak freely about my work on this line?"

I almost laugh at Cygnus's surprised expression. Does he not know this is a direct connection? I hear someone speaking in the background. Then Cygnus's eyes focus back on me. "The line is secure. Go ahead."

How did he manage that? Not the time! "I regret to inform you our first trial was not a success." You never, ever use the word *failure* when speaking to Cygnus. "The results, however, were enlightening, and I hope to have a second trial in place before week's end."

Cygnus's eyes turn shrewd. "But?"

"Director, you were extremely generous providing the extra unscheduled visit with my family a few weeks back. As I'm sure you are aware, that meeting was terminated before time was up in less than ideal circumstances."

"I am aware."

Clipped tones and an icy glare. I'm glad we aren't in the same room where he can see my balled fists. I fight to keep my mask from slipping, but I'm hanging onto control by my (too short) fingernails. He doesn't even pretend enough concern to offer an apology for the state of Tavi's arms, let alone the way his goons barged in there and dragged my family out. *Cut to the chase!*

"Since that unfortunate end, I must confess my family's welfare has been a mild distraction. If you would permit a brief call with them so I could set my unease aside, I could focus on my work without distractions."

Calling my family "distractions" goes against the grain, but that's how he views them. I wait, searching for any clue how he feels about this request.

His face remains impassive as he studies me. "What can I expect in return if I grant your request?"

How about what I won't do if I find you aren't looking after my family like you said you would, you arrogant jerk! If only I had the courage to say that out loud, but I would forfeit my life, if not my family's, for such impertinence. Fortunately, I planned for his quid pro quo demand.

"I could set a time limit on the prototypes."

His eyebrows rise so much they almost meet his hair. "You could?"

"Yes, Director. I would commit to complete testing on the two prototypes and all their variations within six weeks if you would be kind enough to grant this request." Thanks to repeated calculations, I know I can actually finish in half that time, but he doesn't need to know. All he needs is to *think* he's getting a deal.

"Five weeks," Cygnus snaps.

Dropping the mask a fraction and feigning distress is easy. Except my agitation relates to him approving this request, not the time frame. After faking mental calculations, I finally counter, "Five weeks and two days."

Since Cygnus expects precision from me, I hope this random

number will somehow convince him I'm over a barrel. My accuracy with the time estimations he's requested in the past doesn't hurt.

"Done. But, Chiara?"

"Yes, Director?"

"I don't need to remind you what will happen should you fail."

Repressing my wrath to exhibit mortal fear instead is a fine balancing act. I hope I succeed. "No, Director."

"Very well. Mrs. Jacobs will set up the call. Coordinate with her on details within the next thirty minutes."

"Yes, Director. Thank you, Director."

With the usual drivel constituting the party line, Cygnus ends the call. I'm so wound up I know the only thing to ease the tension is a good, hard run. But I must check in with Hag Lady first.

When the elevator delivers me to her, she's waiting, a piece of paper (really?) in hand. For the second time, she doesn't deign to greet me. "Call this number at precisely three o'clock. Don't be late. You have five minutes for the call."

Rage and bitterness sweep through me in equal measure. Cygnus just *had* to have the last word. Why didn't I think to specify the amount of time I thought would be sufficient? Keeping a tight leash on my emotions, I accept the note. "Thank you, Mrs. Jacobs."

She says nothing, watching me with those beady eyes of hers as I back away, then turn to seek the elevator once more. I swear I feel her gaze boring into me until the elevator doors shut it out.

Memorizing the number, I carefully tuck the paper into a pocket and wait for the elevator to deliver me to the gym. No way I'm wasting time going back to the labs first. I need to vent these emotions *now*! Before I do something rash.

2 6

In a significantly better frame of mind after my workout, I return to the labs energized and set to work with renewed vigor. Whilst I added ample padding to the deadline I gave Cygnus, something might go wrong and cause unforeseen delays.

By lunchtime, I've determined which permutation we'll try next after rerunning our first experiment with the enhanced welds. After giving the specs to Deran, I call for a working lunch, and my team and I traipse down to the cafeteria, where they catch me up on their own projects while we eat.

This was my best solution to both eating and dealing with them in the limited time available to me. If Sarissa were here, she would've filled me in on their activities this morning. Irked anew at her calling in sick again today, I wonder if she's really ill, hungover, or simply decided she wouldn't bother with work today.

Brushing the thought away, I return my attention to the ongoing discussions. We've dealt with most of the business at hand. I sit and listen as I finish my meal, almost untouched since I did most of the talking.

After my last mouthful, I lean back, waiting for a lull in the chatter.

When it comes, I ask if there's anything else. Assured no further matters require my attention, I bid them farewell and head for the workshop. There's just enough time to check if Deran has questions before the call with my family.

He has none, so it's a quick detour. At 2:30, I'm back in my office pacing the floor. The clock drags its way around to 2:59, and I retrieve the piece of paper, laying it flat on my desk. Not that I really need to, because the number is burned into my mind.

At precisely 3 p.m., I make the call. Before one complete ring sounds, my mother answers. Tears stream down my cheeks, even though I told myself I wouldn't cry. "Mom!" I glance behind her, eager to see the faces of my siblings. "Where's everyone else?"

"Chiara, dear, it's just me. They wouldn't allow your brothers and sister to join us. Now," she holds up a hand, "don't get your knickers in a knot. We haven't time to waste. They are all fine."

"If they're all 'fine,' why can't I see them?"

"There's not enough space. This call booth only fits one person."

Call booth? "Mom, what are you talking about? They should all be able to jump on the line with us."

My mother's eyes roam somewhere beyond the camera. Is someone talking to her? Her focus returns a second later, and she offers a tepid smile.

"I'm told you have something called a comm link. We don't have those here yet."

Stunned, I gawk. They don't have comm links? The fact I've never realized this before, never questioned why we could never call one another, wrecks me. How could I miss something so obvious? No, no! That's not the important thing. My mom said something else... "Mom, where are you without access to comm links?"

Suddenly, a face appears, obscuring my mother. I draw back involuntarily, a silly reaction because the person isn't anywhere near me, although I can't help but feel his menace across the distance. His words confirm it. "Miss Baschet, if you insist on asking inappropriate questions, I will end this call."

Aware of time slipping through my fingers faster than water through a sieve, I wave impatiently at him. "Yes, fine, move out of the way."

My words and actions may imply I'm not questioning him, but my mind races. This is worse than I thought. I shelve the chaotic thoughts for now and focus on the critical aspects. "What was wrong with Tavi's arms?"

"She works in the laundries. They changed the detergent the day before we saw you. Her reaction literally manifested on the way to our meeting with you."

A pat answer. While contrived, it also imparts information. "Are you all really okay?"

"We're fine. Same as always."

Her tiny pause confirms my mother's answers are being coerced. While I can only see her face, I don't doubt she's still as thin as ever. The reason for her aging is all too obvious now.

Despite the pulverizing weight of the boulder on my chest, crushing the life out of lungs and heart, I tender a wobbly smile. "Tell me about each of you."

"You first."

At the slight catch in my mother's reply, the boulder reasserts itself. I don't what to believe it, but can it be true? She's asking about my welfare, hoping time will run out before she has to lie to me about theirs?

"Mom, I'm fine. You have no reason to worry about me. Now catch me up on your news."

My mother's querulous breath sighs through the line. "I'm still at home, looking after your siblings. Xanin took first place in class last week. They've moved Tavi from the laundromat to the kitchens because it seems she's allergic to the new detergents. Frankie misses you, but he's found a charming new playmate who keeps him occupied."

Innocuous words, but they hide a world of pain. I almost wish time *was* up. With a quick glance at the timer I set, I find it counting down the last few seconds. I can't breathe. I want the boulder off! Why did I ever think they were living a life of luxury somewhere, able to come and go as they pleased, not required to work? Misery sweeps in, and tacking my mask in place takes every ounce of willpower. The last thing my mother needs is another child to worry about.

"Congratulate Xanin for me. Tell him I always knew he could do it and to keep up the stellar work. Tell Tavi to hang in there, and tell Frankie I'm so happy he's found a new friend." My throat is thick, and the words stick as I force them out. I press on, despite the pain. "And know I love you all."

My mom's eyes overflow, tears tracing shimmering tracks down her gaunt face. "We love you too. Take care of—"

The line goes dead.

I sit at my desk, eyes unfocused, mind reeling. So much information in so little time. I fight to order my thoughts, desperate to gain clarity on all I learned in those brief five minutes. But a headache is coming on, a vicious one that won't back down unless I stop fighting.

Resigned, I close my eyes and lay my head on my desk, making a weak attempt at a few mental notes before the pain does me in completely. This is how Deran finds me. I don't hear his knock and almost jump out of my chair when he speaks.

"Chiara? Are you alright?"

Raising my head, (why is the light so bright?), I decide I must look awful because he rushes inside, eyes wide. "What's wrong?"

Easy enough to supply an honest answer without giving anything away. "Killer headache."

"Have you taken some Nanogo?"

"My supply ran out."

"Can I get some for you?"

"If you wouldn't mind?"

Deran hurries away, and I drop my head back onto my desk. In seconds, he returns, handing over the Nanogo. I take a quick puff, inhaling the nanites as they spray into my mouth. In under five minutes, the headache recedes. I open my eyes to find Deran still hovering. "Thanks."

"Feeling better?"

"Yes. What did you want?"

"I came to tell you we're ready to test the strength of the welds."

"Perfect timing," I mutter, but don't bother explaining when he raises an eyebrow. "Lead the way."

Neither the second, nor third, nor fourth permutations of the first prototype succeed. I keep tweaking the specs, aware this is all part of the process, but wishing we could hit on a solution already—because I've found the motivation I need to finish.

After the dreadful call with my mother, I vowed that *when* I find an answer, Cygnus won't get his precious machine unless he hands my family over. I'll hold my invention hostage until my family are returned to me. The only way to guarantee their care is to have them living with me.

As we plug away at the permutations, my family aren't the only ones on my mind. Sarissa's new and increasing absences are beginning to affect my work, primarily because she's not doing hers. Secretly, I suspect she's coming off benders because when she turns up (on time, of course), she smells like a distillery.

This alone isn't enough cause to issue a warning because technically, she's neither drinking at work nor arriving drunk—or, at least, not that I'm aware of. I'm convinced Sarissa is using Nanogo liberally to facilitate arriving in a functional state. (Is this how she looked so incredible the morning after we last went clubbing?) Although nowadays she must drink to the last second because the Nanogo obviously hasn't had enough time to rid her both of her inebriated state and the alcoholic stink before she gets to work.

Which begs the question: how late is she staying out? Even her expert hand can't hide those raccoon rings circling her eyes. Assuming she's bothering. Because Sarissa isn't only neglecting her makeup. Her suits are increasingly wrinkled, and occasionally, she's arrived at work two days in a row wearing the same clothes. Walk of shame?

While all these details together are disturbing, the most sinister aspect is her behavior. Erratic would be an apt term. Sarissa blows hot and cold, loving me and desperate for reconciliation one minute, then hating me and wanting nothing to do with me the next. Her mood swings from affection to fury, intense enough to have her breaking lab equipment, are still not dismissible offenses. Or not yet, anyway. Even in my distracted state, as is typical when I'm this invested in a project, I can't miss her bizarre behavior.

Eventually, I start watching for signs of drug use (yes, I can fire her for that) when she repeatedly starts standing on a lower level of the building in front of a door marked "Janitorial."

Today is another of those days. Aware Sarissa arrived this morning but finding her absent from her office (why did I think she'd have my schedule?), I go hunting for her. The first place I look is the floor with the mysterious door. I can't figure out what keeps drawing her there.

No surprise to find Sarissa where I expected, staring at the door. Once again, with that blank expression on her face. "Sarissa?" No response, "Sarissa!" A slow blink. "Sarissa!"

Finally, her head turns. Bleary eyes peer at me. "Chiara?"

Her makeup is smudged, like the hand that applied it was unsteady. My gaze sweeps down, spotting mud stains on the bottom edges of her pants. Those were there the last time she wore this dove-gray suit. No longer sharp and smart, but wrinkled and smelling musty. What has she been doing in her work clothes? Gallivanting through the parks at night when the sprinklers are running? No, I remind myself, I am not responsible for her actions. "What are you doing here?"

Confusion fills her face as Sarissa looks around. "I don't know."

Aargh, how long will we play this game? "How long have you been here?"

More furrowing of her brow. "I couldn't say."

"Do you remember leaving your office, walking here?" Another shake of her head. "Do you remember *anything*?"

My tone is a slap to the face. Sarissa snaps awake, hand subconsciously sliding up to tap her comm link. Then her eyes widen. "Oh, sorry! You must be expecting your schedule."

"I most certainly am. Have it on my desk by the time I get back."

Sarissa scurries off, and I belatedly realize I meant to tell her to go home and clean up. Never mind. I'll do that later. After I've settled this matter once and for all. There must be a reason she keeps coming here. Maybe a drug dealer—or her stash—hiding behind the door?

With a cautious hand, I twist the knob. Locked. Unable to drop the matter, I summon maintenance, then stand by as they open the door, anticipating some harrowing answer. I am (thankfully) disappointed. Only mops and brooms and other cleaning supplies.

Satisfied there's nothing more sinister, I head back to my office and find Sarissa waiting with my schedule. One glace at her scrawl tells me all I need to know. "You call this a schedule?"

Sarissa averts her eyes, that sullen pout I hate making her lower lip jut out. "You didn't exactly give me a lot of time."

"What's going on with you?" I lift the paper schedule she gave me (she hasn't lost that penchant) and shake it in her face. "What's with the rambling sentences? Where are your check boxes?"

Somehow, this gets through to her, only to be followed by more slow blinks. Then her eyes swim with tears. "I'm sorry. I'll redo it."

I'm in no mood for her hysteria. Desperate to get rid of her before I cave to her manipulation, I hiss an order. "Go home, get cleaned up, and don't come back until you have your head on straight." Then I march out of my office and leave her to do as she will.

My interest in the room, and Sarissa, wane as the project ramps up. With successive permutations requiring smaller and smaller changes, my presence in the workshop is more essential than ever.

Soon, I spend almost every minute there and forget about Sarissa and her issues. I have no time for them.

Every planned permutation of the first prototype fails, and I'm forced to scrap it. Deran's team clear the workshop of the first machine and return it to a blank slate. A flurry of activity follows as they cart materials in for the second prototype. Fortunately, this one will only take a fraction of the time it took to build the first.

To speed things up further, I oversee much of its progress. Deran doesn't have time to make nice holographic drawings his team can understand. Although, if I'm honest with myself, it has less to do with time (we still have four weeks left) and more to do with how I prefer being here in the workshop, where I can avoid Sarissa and her judgey eyes and volatile behavior.

On Tuesday morning, I walk into work, and my world implodes. The first clue is the stares and hushed whispers following me as I traverse the workbench corridors to my office. The second is the weird SerSent waiting in my office.

I've never seen a SerSent wearing this type of... uniform? Is he an officer? No, there would be at least some consistency across uniforms. This man wears all black, his tight, long-sleeved muscle shirt revealing a body that could break a SteelMax tank. Then I remember where I've seen someone like this. Outside Cygnus's office. Those strange guards on either side of his door.

Fear thrusts its first spike into me. Why is someone who protects Cygnus here in my office? The only thread linking this strange "security" man and Cygnus and me are my family. My legs give way, and I collapse onto my chair. I'm suddenly lightheaded and parched, but I have to know. "Why are you here?"

"Miss Baschet, I regret to inform you..."

The words after "regret" fade, and I don't hear the rest of the sentence. Blinking back tears, I force myself to listen to the words coming out of his mouth.

"... a replacement will be sent."

A replacement? They think they can replace my family? No... No.

There's definitely something wrong with this scenario. "I'm sorry, could you repeat everything you just said?"

To his credit, the man doesn't bat an eyelid, let alone roll his eyes at my pathetic response. "I regret to inform you Miss Sarissa Kasumi has died. Since she was your assistant and the director knows you are on a tight deadline, a replacement will be sent."

Did he just repeat everything verbatim? If only I'd listened the first time. Then his words hit home. My voice cracks. "Sarissa?"

"Yes, ma'am, Sarissa Kasumi."

"When? No, how?"

"Last night, ma'am. She committed suicide."

No apology or sympathy in the delivery. Just facts. His answer rocks me to my core. Sarissa? Suicide? I knew she'd been a little off-kilter the last few weeks, but none of this makes any sense.

"But that's… are you sure?"

"Yes, ma'am. The director wanted you to know."

The man turns to leave. "Wait!" Surely there's something else I should ask? Something more he can tell me? But my brain is fixed in place, a needle at the end of the tracks on an old vinyl record, stuck and making that awful crackling sound.

"Ma'am?"

Stop calling me that! Tell me something of value. But I have nothing. My brain has failed me in the moment, as it typically does. I ask the only thing I can. "If I have more questions, who should I ask?"

For the first time, the man doesn't have a ready reply. His eyes go distant, like he's listening to something. More likely thinking about what he can tell me. Then his eyes sharpen. "Address any concerns or questions on the matter to Mrs. Jacobs, and the director will see you get answers."

This time he doesn't wait, simply turns and marches out with no farewell of any kind. I'm left watching his broad shoulders, winding through the workbench corridors until he disappears into the elevator at the far end. The distance in no way diminishes his stature.

Incapable of moving, of thinking, I remain slumped at my desk. Only when Tandize knocks tentatively on my door do I stir. "Yes?"

"Chiara, what did that… man want?"

Odd she should hesitate over what to call him. My brain must still be rebooting after the shock of the news about Sarissa and can't distinguish between the relevant and the innocuous.

"Don't you think he was a man?" I ask, more as a ploy to avoid giving her the answer she seeks than for any other reason, but Tandize freezes, her face losing color. I file the observation away for later analysis, too numb to process more than simple questions and answers right now. "Never mind."

Tandize remains on the threshold of the door, looking torn between staying and leaving.

The girl is exhausting! "What?"

"Um, you didn't answer my question."

Oh. *Oh!* I'm their boss. I will have to inform my team about Sarissa. The realization hits like a sledgehammer to the gut. Winded, I take a second. "Tandize, please ask everyone to gather in the common room."

With worried backward glances, Tandize scurries away. Through my window, I watch as she assembles the team. Now would be a perfect time to run and hide. But I must do this. There is no one else.

I force myself to my feet, allowing myself time to stop swaying before lurching out the door. Yes, I use the workbenches as support getting to the common room, but by the time I get there, I've found my balance.

Pretending I know what I'm doing (I've never given a death notification before), I take my place at the front of the room, unsurprised when all conversations cease immediately.

This is abnormal enough for everyone to wonder what the commotion is about. No doubt every soul in the lab saw that beast of a man.

Are there men who look like that naturally? Or did he have some sort of enhancements? Either chemical or mechanical, I suppose. Both are possible in this day and age. *Stop dithering!* But where to start?

"Is anyone missing?"

"Jordy's in the restroom," someone calls, and a few nervous titters escape.

I nod, thinking Jordy may be relieved he's not here for this. There's nothing for it but to dive in. "I know most of you saw the strange man who visited me. I'm sorry to have to tell you he brought bad news."

Their reactions are enough to make me pause. One person faints. Many lose all the color in their faces. Two scurry out of the common room, looking ill. I hurriedly raise a hand, hoping to ease their turmoil.

"My apologies, poor word choice! I should've said distressing news."

More nervous fidgeting. What is wrong with them? Have they never had bad news before?

Just blurt it out and put them out of their misery. "I'm sorry to have to tell you that Sarissa is… she died, last night."

Absolute silence follows my announcement. I don't know what I was expecting. Tears? Rage? Despair? I'm unprepared for the relief on many faces. What is wrong with these people? Didn't they just hear me tell them Sarissa is *dead*?

Tandize dares raise her voice in a question. I'm beginning to suspect the others have nominated her as their unofficial spokesperson. "Is that all?"

That does it! "Is that all? A woman is dead, and that's what you ask? What is wrong with you people? Don't you get it?"

Finally, some discomfort, some acknowledgement of the loss. But on only a few faces. I don't know what to make of it. Deciding I'm not personally in the best frame of mind to deal with them and their idiosyncrasies, I leave the room. I have to get out of here!

Craving warmth, I dash outside and hurry to the fountain less than five minutes from CC HQ, relieved to be free of the accursed building. For a few moments, I simply stare at the water cascading down several rock ledges, errant drops catching the sunlight and sparkling. A mesmerizing sight, to be sure, but I need to sit. Eyeing the inviting ledge surrounding the fountain's pool, I take a seat, turning my face up to the sun and closing my eyes.

Glorious heat caresses me, and I soak in the warmth and light. After the abysmal start to the day, I can't help but want something to chase the gloom away. I stay like this for a while, before dropping my head, then trailing my fingers through the water. Normally, a relaxing exercise.

But neither the sun nor water bring peace. Sarissa's death has tainted more than merely the start of the day. I grimace. Maybe it isn't the setting, but the guilt. Because, yes, I'm drowning in it.

How could I not see Sarissa needed me? I mean, I know she was all over the place with her emotions—but was she crying for help? I tell myself I wouldn't have known the first thing about helping Sarissa, but it's a lie. Not abandoning her would've been a start. But, after her betrayal, how could I? On the other hand, shouldn't true friends be able to forgive one another, even for the most heinous of transgressions?

My hand returns to my lap, the pool neglected as my emotions war with one another. Cobalt guilt, crimson anger, ebony sorrow, and coral shame churn together, forming anything but a rainbow. Their combined effect is nebulous, as colorless and formless as I am.

Coming here was a mistake. I have too much time to think. Rising, I jog back to CC HQ, eager to get back to work. My sanctuary. Science, the only thing capable of drowning out everything this miserable world has to offer.

2 8

Away for less than fifteen minutes, I return to find Deran waiting for me, leaning against my office door. A little surprised by the burst of joy the sight of him brings, I wonder at it. Why does his presence make me happy? Despite his charm, isn't he an enemy too? One I said I would maintain a purely professional relationship with?

As a result, my greeting is cold. The effect on Deran is instantaneous. Those eyes, kind and smiling and offering hope a second before, shutter. He stands straighter, and his expression slips into that awful neutrality I'm so accustomed to seeing on the faces of others. No warmth. No connection. No comfort. What did I expect?

I burst into sobs. Mortified, I turn and flee, blindly running for the nearest restroom. Much as I hate for anyone to witness the tears, they're a little hard to hide with snot all over my face and that weird wheezing, hiccupping sound I'm making. Plus, I'm bumping into every sharp corner because I can't see where I'm going. *Ow!*

I skate into the restroom, barely stopping short of skidding into the counter, and snatch up tissue to blow my nose. My sobs sound awful even to me. Do wounded animals even sound so wretched? I decide they must sound worse and try stifling my blubbering, to no avail.

182

The door crashes open, and I dive toward the nearest stall. I only make it halfway inside before I realize who entered. Stepping back out of the stall, I stare. "Deran?"

"Do you always have to run away from me?"

If only you knew! The bitter thought has me dragging my hand through my hair to make myself more presentable. I stop the action, a hysterical laugh tickling the back of my throat. I must look a sight. Then I sigh. I guess it's not for the first time where he's concerned.

Yet, he's still here. Still standing in the doorway, suddenly realizing where he is and debating the wisdom of coming all the way in. I know the moment he decides he doesn't care what people think.

Deran stalks over until he stops right in front of me, defiance streaking those gray eyes.

I raise my chin. "What? You're daring me to run away again?"

"If that's what it takes."

The muscle ticking in his jaw draws my attention, and I stare at it, considering its meaning. Anger. I dare a glance at the rest of his face. Yes, definitely angry.

"What have you got to be angry about?" My voice is a little strangled but audible.

"How do you expect people to help you with your problems if you're always running away from them?"

I gape. Not the comeback I was expecting. As I fumble for a reply, I find my limbs wobbly. In dire need of support, my eyes fly around the room, searching for somewhere to sit. At the same time I realize the toilets are my only option, Deran sweeps me into his arms.

My startled shriek is less than ladylike and more than a little funny. A giggle slips out. I can't believe he just picked me up! And what's with my silly shriek?

Wanting to laugh (what is *wrong* with me?), I beat his broad chest with my hands. "Put me down!"

Ignoring me, Deran strides out of the restroom, still cradling me and aiming for a nearby seating area. I glance around, fearful someone may see, then realize how absurd the thought is. What are they going to think? That he's rescuing me from some dire situation?

No, all they'll see is a man decent enough to offer compassion and consolation where it's needed. I have no clue why that thought calms my rattled nerves, but it does, and I relax into him. He's so warm.

Deran glances down, the tiniest of smiles quirking the corners of his lips. "Ah, now you have me rethinking my strategy."

I blink up at him, tensing. "What?"

He laughs, the sound irrationally another balm. How does he always get to me like this?

Deran follows the laugh with a roguish smile. "Never mind. Forget I said anything. I'll set you down in a chair as soon as I can and won't touch you for a second longer than is necessary."

My cheeks heat. He must think I'm a selfish ingrate. But then why did he laugh? Utterly mystified, I say nothing as he lowers me into a chair. I scoot around, pretending to make myself more comfortable, but it's just an excuse to not speak to him because I'm still fishing for words.

"I only brought you here because you looked like you might need to sit for a while." Deran drags a hand through his hair, restless energy rolling off him in waves.

I note how that hand made those sexy spikes stand on end. *Chiara! Stop it!* The memory of Sarissa's death is the mental slap I need.

As though sensing my change in mood, Deran stops moving. "Look, is there something you need? Tissues? A girl friend?"

A shaky laugh is the best I can manage. "Right now, a therapist wouldn't go amiss." Deran rears back, and I know I've said something wrong. "What?"

"You *are* joking, right?"

Frowning, I ponder his vehemence. "Maybe a little." This talk of therapy reminds me. I slap a hand to my head. "Ugh, I'm so dense! I forgot to tell them."

Deran eyes me like he's wondering what I might do next. I can't blame him. Admittedly, I am acting a little like a loon. I hold up a finger. "Before I scare you off, a few things."

Deran crosses his arms, waiting, but no less suspicious. "This should be interesting."

While he mutters the words, I hear them. No, I can't allow those tantalizing muscular forearms or that grim smile to distract me. What is it with him? Even his grim smile is wildly attractive. *Focus, Chiara!*

I turn my gaze down to the carpet and keep it there. "Well, I guess the first thing I should say is thanks for checking on me. Or should the first thing be an apology for always running out on you?" I wave a hand. "Doesn't matter. As long as you know I'm sincere about both."

I sense, rather than see, him relax somewhat. "Is there more?"

"Yes. I'm not crazy. I haven't seen a therapist since I was, well—" How do I explain the last time was when Cygnus kidnapped me and brought me to a strange place with no one or nothing I loved? "Um, a little kid, so a long time ago."

Deran makes a sound I can't identify, but I hold up a finger again. Best to get it all out.

"Also, what I meant earlier when I said 'I forget to tell them' was the conglomerate offers grief counseling after a loss. As the head of the department, you'd think I'd do a halfway decent job with a death notice."

I'm still frowning at the carpet when his hand takes mine. Startled, my eyes fly up to meet his. Silver reflections on moonlit water. So much life.

Deran's voice is gentle. "Chiara, give yourself a break. You, more than anyone else on your team, suffered the greatest loss. I think you're allowed to forget things when you're in shock and grieving."

Am I? Grieving, that is? I still can't separate the emotions out. They're this horrible tangle of weeds balled around a propeller, no end or beginning in sight, just a mess. I pick at the ball, hoping to at least unravel part of it.

But all I can think about is Deran's warm hand. His presence is all-consuming. Aware I should distance myself from him if I want even a hope of thinking coherently, I set about extracting myself.

When I place my other hand over his, Deran tenses. Solemn gray eyes watch me. "Thank you, for checking on me. I appreciate it. But right now, I should get back and tell my team there is counseling available should they need it." He seems... disappointed? "Could you please inform your people about Sarissa and let them know counseling is available for them too?"

Deran frees his hand from mine, then rises. "I'll do that."

His stiff manner makes it obvious I've missed some social cue, but I can't fix what I can't fathom. I watch Deran walk away, only part of my mind on the problem. No, less than part. Most of my mind focuses on those long legs. I admire the view until he rounds the corner out of sight.

Then my mind shifts. I can literally feel it clicking into top gear, driving me to my feet and sending me back to the common room.

Most of the team are still there, murmurs too soft to hear, even though it must be at least thirty minutes since I left them. Someone sees me and motions, and the others quiet when they notice me too.

"I'm sorry!" The words come out in a rush, and I order myself to speak slower. I'm not up for repeating myself. "I meant to tell you that in situations such as these, the conglomerate provides counseling. Please avail yourselves of it should you feel the need and pass the word on to those who have already left."

"Chiara, can we go home for the day?"

I should've expected the question would come from Tandize. But I also should've thought to offer this. "Of course. I'm sorry. I don't expect you to work after this dreadful news. You're all entitled to two days compassionate leave." Filled with remorse because I didn't think to mention it sooner, I add, "Since that would mean coming in for only one day on Friday, I won't mind if you take that day as leave and only return next week."

They must have been waiting for my announcement because they all move at the same time. In seconds, I'm alone in an empty room.

I should pass the same information along to Deran in case any of his team feel the same way. Not ready to face him in person again just yet, I comm him. "Yes?"

Is it my imagination, or is his voice more than a little clipped? "Um, sorry, another thing I forgot. Could you please tell your team they're entitled to two days compassionate leave?"

Deran nods. "Anything else?"

At a loss for what to make of his behavior, I shrug. "I told my team they needn't come in on Friday either. I suspect most of them will take paid time off and only return next week."

"What about you? Are you taking a few hours?"

I'm on the verge of saying I don't have that luxury, but a few things strike me at once. First, what kind of person wouldn't at least take one day off work if her (former) best friend died? Second, I have time in my projection for Cygnus, so starting the next prototype right away isn't urgent. But third, taking several days off wouldn't reflect well on me if Cygnus heard. Although, fourth, do I want to waste any time when life is so fragile and my family's welfare, even their lives, are at stake? I refuse to consider a scenario where none of the permutations on this second prototype pan out.

"Yes, I'll take time. Not as much as everyone else, but a day at least."

"Fine. You know how to reach me when you return. Just ping me and I'll come in to carry on with the work."

Deran cuts the link. Okay, I'm in the poop box. I don't understand why, but standing here won't help me figure it out. Besides, a more pressing problem just exploded like fireworks in my head.

I abruptly understand what's been bothering me since I found that strange man (guard?) in my office. No, since he told me what happened to Sarissa. The revelation is so vast it fills every available space in my brain. It screeches at me, impossible to ignore.

Sarissa is not the sort of person to commit suicide. Ever. No matter what the circumstances. I have to find out what really happened to her.

29

With the clamorous revelation still shooting sparks through my head, I stumble from the vacant common room back to my office. In the aftermath of the fireworks, a hazy idea forms in the smoke. When its tendrils weave their way into conscious thought, I let the idea play, awed and terrified by its audacity. The more fully the idea comes into focus, the more I can't let it go. Until I know I have to try.

Since everyone else has already left, there's no one to stop me on my own way out of the labs. But I don't head directly home. Instead, I detour to *Lost & Found*, grabbing what I need, then stop in at the lab's supply room and select a few more things before skulking to the workshop.

Relieved to find Deran and his team also long gone, I flip the lights back on. The carts holding the new pieces for the second prototype are strewn across the vast workshop floor. I can only imagine Deran has his reasons for their strange placement.

I scurry from cart to cart, scrounging what I need, and adding the parts to the stash already squirreled away in the backpack pilfered from *Lost & Found*. Hopefully, no one will miss it until Monday.

It's almost lunchtime when I've collected all the available items I think I'll need—and then some. Can't be too careful. Slinking away from CC HQ, I catch the trundle to an electronics store, one I visited with Sarissa when she needed a replacement part for her personal tablet.

Fortunately, they have all the components I still lacked in stock, and I pay for them with one of my untraceable chards before finally going home, backpack bulging.

I'm sweating by the time I dump the heavy pack on my kitchen counter. If I had to worry about drones peering in my windows, I would've closed the curtains. As it is, whatever I do inside my apartment is invisible to those outside, thanks to the privacy window films.

With quick movements, I clear kitchen items from the counter, then carefully transfer the pieces from the pack, setting them out in neat rows. The last time I did a project like this, I was still at the academy.

Thankful for my infallible mind, I find the relevant memory and assemble the pieces as I replay my mental video. Roughly three hours later, the device is up and running, despite the extra time it took for the little tweaks I had to make because everything wasn't exactly compatible. Nothing like cobbling pieces together.

But finally, the gadget's complete. Rising, I stretch, then gaze out the window. Nowhere near dark enough yet. My stomach growls. *Oh yes, food!*

Still stretching muscles tight from hunching over my makeshift workbench for so long, I stroll to the refrigerator and select a meal, popping it into the blitz. My plan is risky—but nothing ventured, nothing gained.

The blitz beeps, and I transfer the steaming food onto a plate before sinking onto the sofa's unyielding planes. For once, I don't mind the discomfort. It's a reminder of the impossible things I'm going to have to do before all this is over. I only hope I can follow through.

I put a movie on, but that's a farce. Too many variables run through my head, demanding attention. I snap the film off, then rise and pace, addressing each sticking point and ignoring the food.

When I'm about as prepared as I think I can be for any eventuality,

I head into my bedroom and change into dark, form-fitting workout attire.

Then I dig out the all-black pantsuit Sarissa made me buy for a costume party. The baggy pants and shirt can be padded and allow me to more or less hide my shape. I grab the balaclava that went with the outfit, then add a gender-neutral floppy hat and wig. Not much I can do about my height other than heels, but they aren't ideal for what I have in mind. Besides, I can't exactly wear fancy shoes with my current workout attire, can I?

Opting for trainers, I toss them on, then stuff the assembled costume pieces into my goodie bag. Right, I'm ready. In the kitchen, I hide the tools littering my counter, then return the small kitchen appliances to their places and take a last glance around the room. On the surface, everything looks as it should. It will have to do.

I slip out of my apartment, then ride the elevator down to the mall. It's the first time I've been here again since I dropped off the bag of clothes for Sam. Unlike that night, the floor bustles with shoppers. With a few hours remaining before the stores close, patrons are making the most of the limited time. All the better for me.

Blending into the crowds, I keep my head down. If not for all my old movies, and the thrillers Sarissa was always recommending, I doubt I would've had any clue about subterfuge. I'm no expert, but at least I hope I'm more adept than not.

Doing my best to lose myself in the crowds so the cameras can't track me, I finally reach my destination—the restrooms. After confirming no one's paying undue attention, I slip into a stall, then change into my costume. While I don't don the balaclava just yet, I add the wig and floppy hat. Then I turn the reversible goodie bag inside out and cram the contents back in. So far, so good.

Pretending to work on my nonexistent makeup, I wait at the mirror for a group of women exiting together. Then I sneak into their midst and creep out with them, keeping my head down to avoid those pesky cameras.

From here, I easily exit the store, then aim for the trundle. For the first time, I'm relieved it requires no fare. I keep my face hidden the whole way, then hop off several stops before CC HQ. Hopefully far enough away they won't check the footage at this stop.

I chose this location for the trees cluttering the area. Simple for someone to get lost in them. And I do. When I think I've moved into their cover sufficiently, I find a tree with a handy shrub beside it. Exchanging my wig for the balaclava, I roll the hat up and tuck it into a pocket before removing my homemade gadget, then stuff the goodie bag under the shrub. Time for the run to CC HQ.

Cool night air fans me as I sprint through the trees, the experience exhilarating. Or perhaps I'm mistaking the adrenaline pumping through my veins for excitement instead of fear. Because the moments of truth, the scariest parts of this whole insane idea, are about to become reality.

Panting, I stop in the shadows of the trees on the far edge of the park surrounding CC HQ. Funny, I never thought about these lush green gardens around the glass-and-chrome building before, with their curving paths and sparkling fountains. They always struck me as simple, beautifying touches. But now I understand.

All this open space between me and my target means anyone watching can easily spot me coming. Not that I expect they're watching for me, specifically, but no doubt they monitor for potential threats.

Vexed I didn't consider this, I lurk in the trees, debating how best to approach without being seen. Or without raising an alarm.

In the end, there's nothing for it. But isn't this why I chose a disguise for my body, hoping it would lead them to think I'm a man instead of a woman and someone a lot heavier?

I tug my balaclava off and put the floppy hat back on, hiding my braided hair under the hat, grimacing because I didn't think to bring a second hat. I hope the hairstyle and color are sufficiently different from my trundle disguise.

After slinking over to a tree closer to the path and out of a direct line of sight from the building, I alter my gait and hobble onto the path. Sweat trickles down my back. Maintaining the painstakingly slow hobble takes more energy than the sprint. No wonder they say stress kills.

Finally, I reach the building's back lot. First test coming up. Before removing my gadget, hidden inside the depths of the voluminous costume, I make sure I'm alone.

Not only am I alone, but whoever installed the cameras placed them on the outside of the building rather than over the access panel (mistake?), so my back and hat hide the gadget as I place it over the access panel.

If someone is watching me on those cameras, let them not wonder why I'm taking so long! Anxious, my eyes never leave the gadget's display. I will the percentage to reach one hundred faster. Then it's done, and a soft hiss sounds as the door clicks open.

Ecstatic, but also a little disbelieving my device actually worked, I remove it and slip inside. Next test. Precisely as my memory told me, there's a door to the side of the service elevators—the ones Deran and I used to spirit Sarissa out of the building. I shuffle over and try the door handle. *Yes! Unlocked!* Now if it only leads where I think it does.

Taking the steps two at a time (they don't have cameras in stair-wells, do they?), I descend into the depths. *Score again!* I'm in the base-ment. I allow a minute to orient myself, never having entered from this side before. But it's basic, a long corridor connecting the service side, where I entered, to the main building on the far end.

I count the doors from that side, finding the one I know won't be locked. Tottering over, I slide inside the room. While I've been careful to keep my head down, my movements decrepit, and the lights off, an overly zealous SerSent might be eyeballing those cameras. Especially since I couldn't hide my approach to the building.

Sprinting to the archaic PC at the back of the room, I tug my gadget out once more. This is the crucial test, the reason for this mad caper. Not only does this forgotten PC have the port allowing a hard-wire connection, it's also on the backend of the mainframe. Hands shaking, I connect my gadget to the computer's port with the leads I brought. Hardwiring is the only way I can access the system without using my chip and revealing my identity.

I discovered this obscure little room in my first week at the labs because I needed a rather unique Teflon beaker absent from the supply room. When I asked where I could find one, someone directed me down here. While bumbling around hunting for the beaker, I noticed the PC. Thinking it too antiquated to still function, I planned to raid it for parts. But the moment I touched the keyboard (who knew they used actual hardware for those?), the screen lit up, and the command prompt blinked.

Smart enough to neither ask questions about the machine directly, nor from only one person, I'd patched together the machine's purpose from several sources. A failsafe in the event of an emergency. I guess this qualifies.

I wait, drumming my fingers on the desk as my gadget hacks its way in. Counting the seconds, I alternate between watching the gadget's display and mentally calculating the time remaining for the hack to finish.

My gadget is faster than I thought. I'm in! Code scrolls down the screen. Okay, a bit rusty on this language. After a few false starts, I find my way around and locate the folder I came here for: *Personnel.*

The subfolders are listed in alphabetical order, but considering the thousands of people CC HQ employs, I'm about to enter a search for "Kasumi" when I spy my name, second from the bottom of the list. Unable to resist, I click on it.

Information rolls onto the screen. Too much to read or absorb in the limited time I have. I flip back to the main folder and check its size. Too large to download the entire thing. My gadget allows me to save information, but not this much.

Selecting my personnel file, I copy it across to my gadget. I'm just entering Sarissa's last name in the search bar when I hear it: the distant clatter of footsteps charging down the steel stairs from the main building. They've found me.

Drat! No time! I should've downloaded Sarissa's file first. But I've lost the opportunity. For now, anyway. Hurriedly, I clear my history, then disconnect the wires between PC and gadget.

A door at the far end of the corridor slams. Unsure whether the SerSents are entering or leaving, I open the door of my room a crack and peek out, watching the closed doors to the other rooms. More bad news. The lights in the corridor are on. No way I can sneak out under cover of shadow. I'll have to make a run for it and hope I'm not caught. My hands sweat at the thought of what capture could mean. Not only for me, but for my family.

A lone SerSent leaves the first room and enters the second. I allow a minute before making a dash for it. I fake a running hobble, hoping my gait is off enough to avoid identification via this technology.

My foot hits the first step leading up to the service entrance, and a door creaks as the SerSent exits the room. I propel myself upward and barrel through the door at the end, half expecting to find another SerSent waiting at the top of the stairs. But the service foyer is empty. I flee.

Outside, I don't bother sticking to the path. Instead, I aim for the closest trees. Why did I think hobbling was such a clever disguise? I keep up the pretense of a pained run as best as I can until I reach the trees' sanctuary.

Screened by foliage, I dare a backward glance. The SerSent is only just exiting the building. So slow! Not one to dismiss small mercies, I abandon all pretense and increase my pace to a manic sprint.

As I hurtle deeper into the trees, I aim for my goodie bag, snatching it up, then hare away. Only when I reach the trees bordering another stop further down the trundle line do I chance a second backward glance. No sign of pursuit.

I remain where I am for a moment, catching my breath and listening intently. Only the night sounds I'd expect. No feet crashing through undergrowth or pounding down the path.

Still cautious, I remove my costume and shove it into the goodie bag. Retrieving my wig, I ensure it's secure before leaving cover, wearing just my workout attire with a t-shirt used to pad the costume thrown over the top. Hopefully, this ensemble is sufficiently different from the workout clothes sans shirt and wig I wore earlier.

A tense few minutes pass as I exit the trees, then wait on the platform for the trundle. Its lights coming down the track bring relief beyond measure.

Before the doors open all the way, I squeeze onboard, huddling in my chair and keeping my face down as I pretend to clean my nails. When we reach the third stop from my usual exit, I hop off again and check the time. Skating just under the deadline. The stores close in twenty minutes. I need twelve to run there.

By the time I arrive, my face shines with sweat, but I can't change that. I hurry inside, glad to see people are still about. Not as many as I hoped, but enough to make my return less obvious than if I'd gone directly to the residents' foyer.

I reverse the process I employed when I left the building, returning myself to myself. This late in the evening, there's hardly any traffic into the restroom, so I settle for leaving with only one other person, staying small and hidden behind her.

I trail her into a store, then try to lose the cameras in the racks of clothes, crawling under a few before rising on the opposite end of the store and walking out. Almost home.

Fifteen minutes later, I'm back in my apartment, shaking worse than a test tube carried in a rack. With the goodie bag, costume, wig, and hat all destroyed in the building's incinerator on my way up, I feel a little more secure. But plenty of cameras had eyes on me tonight. Will I get away with what I did?

If I'm to make tonight count, I should access the single file I retrieved. Mine. I try to moderate my disappointment, doubtful I'll find anything useful. If only I'd been able to get Sarissa's! But perhaps I can pilfer it once I'm back at work. Finding an excuse to go back to the basement storage room will be easy enough. Further, accessing the system a second time should be faster with my gadget already dialed into the PC. The only hindrance is timing. It can't be too soon, or I might raise unwanted alarms.

I console myself with the thought the night wasn't a total loss, then check the hour. Enough time for a shower. Not only will it rejuvenate me, it'll also remove the stink of perspiration, a clear giveaway should any SerSents come knocking.

The luxury of hot water spilling over my skin is enjoyable, so I don't hurry. I savor the pulverizing nozzles massaging my tired muscles, staying under the water until my fingers prune. By the time I pad back into the living room, feeling more human again, almost forty-five minutes have passed.

I retrieve my gadget from its hiding spot behind the loose panel in the back of my kitchen sink closet and return to my bedroom, then hook it up to my tablet using the wired leads.

A wireless connection between the devices, where anyone on the network might see it, would've been too risky. I grin. I never thought I'd count myself fortunate to be one of the few people who has a tablet with ports for connections. A concession granted by Cygnus only because it made my work for him more efficient. Extremely useful now. Nothing like a little payback, no matter how minuscule.

The gadget's display lights up, showing the link is active. I should give my gadget a name, something more descriptive. "Ferret" comes to mind. It's perfect. I access Ferret's storage and open the folder, then blink as I read the first entry on the first file, sure I misread. But it's there, in black and white. Is it accurate?

It's a report filed by an enforcer (beetle) whose name I don't recognize. But with this information, he must've been present that day. Perhaps even under Cygnus's command?

The man's report details the incident precipitating Cygnus's visit to our house on that fateful day—the day that changed my life forever. The first sentence of the report is so outrageous, so unbelievable, I read it again. *Francois Baschet, 31, caught stealing food from the warehouse at Thirty-Second and Main.*

My dad? Stealing? That can't be right. But memories of all those days we went hungry rush to mind. Only the most compelling reason would force my father to stoop to theft. While I still don't want to believe it, deep down, I know there's a remote chance it's possible. Because what father who loves his children would stand by and watch them starve?

Breath hitching, I force myself past this first piece of devastating news and read on.

With stealing a capital offense, Commander Cygnus McQueen ordered a contingent sent to the family's home, where the family could suffer the punishment set forth in Section 12.1, subsection 4 (a).

What does that mean? The reference doesn't even state the code or law it's a part of. I open a new window on my tablet, about to run a search, when I pause. How many people search for law codes? More to the point, how many people search for that exact phrase after someone stole a file referencing it?

I memorize the reference. I'll have to find a way to run the search so they can't trace it back to me. Then I move onto the next paragraph.

Arriving at the Baschet home, all subjects... Subjects? Why use that word?... *were neutralized, and tests were conducted to determine if family members had the E-AMPS gene.*

Is that why they jabbed those needles into our arms? And what's so special about this E-AMPS gene? I've never heard of it. I mull the phrase, but the best I can come up with is something electrically related. After all, amps are the unit of measurement for electricity. And the phrase starts with "e."

All but the mother tested positive. Appropriate measures were taken with the respective subjects. Further information can be found in File 192-2-0001.

Appropriate measures? More confused than ever, I close the report and open file 192-2-0001, hoping for clarification.

During a routine recovery under Section 12.1, subsection 4 (a), the oldest child of Francois and Madeline Baschet, one Chiara Baschet, was noted to have the potential for above-average intelligence. Evidence of this can be found in Exhibit 1, attached at the end of this report.

Eager to learn the reason Cygnus singled me out, I scroll down to the exhibit, then laugh. I'd forgotten about this.

Mom always complained about the pollution-filtered sun not drying our clothes before we had to put them back on after she'd washed them. Tired of donning cold, damp clothes, and wanting to help my mom out, I'd devised a solution.

Foraging the parts I needed took days, most of them dredged from piles of discarded metal pieces next to the factories where our parents worked. Once I had the pieces, building the small wind turbine was all of an afternoon's work.

Although a power source would've been ideal, knowing it didn't exist, I'd built the turbine with carefully arranged gears. Only a small force applied to the crank would spin the dryer line faster than the spinning top my dad had carved for us. My mom loved the dryer! In under an hour, our clothes were dry enough to wear.

This is what caught the director's eye? I delve back in time, trying to remember where the dryer was in relation to the rest of the house. As I dip into the past, my head aches. But the memory comes almost instantaneously. The dryer was likely what the director was looking at when he had my mom dragged outside for his "chat" with her.

I wish I'd never made the wretched thing. But how could I have known it would separate me from my family? Besides, I can do nothing to reverse the past eleven years. They've come and gone. The only thing I can do is make the future better. For all of us.

Time to discover what other truths lurk in my file. When I downloaded it, purely out of curiosity, I never dreamed it would hold answers, let alone answers of such magnitude. The file's already exposed two things plaguing me over the years: what led the director to our doorstep and why he singled me out.

Dare I hope my file holds the truth of what happened to my dad after they "caught" him? Because, knowing Cygnus, not for a moment do I believe this incident was as simple as the report makes the theft sound. Perhaps my dad is in space, but not on some all-important mission. Maybe he's in a prison colony up there. It would explain why we weren't allowed to speak with him. Plus the fifteen-year time frame we were given. Is that the length of the sentence they gave him for stealing?

Desperate for answers, I read on. Regrettably, the next few files are disappointing. They contain information I already know. How the nurse who examined me when I arrived announced I was in a state of shock and needed rest and nourishment before "further testing." The weeks of ensuing tests. Not only for my IQ, confirming I was a genius, but also for countless other things there was no reasonable explanation to test for. Personality, physical health, mental health, and a host of others.

I skip past these reports, impatient to find more of what I don't know. *Hah!* I did not know they placed me in the academy on Cygnus's orders. Or that he commanded I be kept "under his direct supervision." What does that mean? That they sent my report cards to him? While both these tidbits are interesting, they're not the jaw-dropping revelations I'm after.

More files follow, most dealing with my inventions over the years. As I graze through these, a date catches my eye. April twenty-third. Xanin's birthday. The year he would've turned eight.

Like a splotch of squished bug on the trundle's windows, the memory returns, unbidden, unpalatable, impossible to see past. Instead of the expected joyful birthday celebration I'd planned for the meeting Cygnus allowed on birthdays, I'd been forced to attend the extravagant party celebrating Cygnus's rise in status—to director.

Right after I finished work on the greenhouse project. Horror squirms through me, tiny crawling millipede legs setting my nerves on fire.

I race back through the files I just skimmed, noting dates, then running searches for those dates linked with Cygnus's name. Result after condemning result appears. My tablet slips from limp fingers, confirmation a crippling blow. Every time I finished a significant project, they promoted Cygnus.

Sarissa wasn't making things up in a drunken state! So why did she try to hide the truth? Because there's no doubt now. I bet if I ran the search against my appointment calendar, I'd find those loathsome parties at all the same intersections.

Sick to my stomach, I lurch off my bed. Bile rises, the only thing I can throw up considering I haven't eaten all day. The thought of food makes me more nauseous. I stumble into my bathroom and dry heave for a while before staggering to the sink and splashing cold water onto my face, gasping for air.

Minutes pass before I breathe normally again. The nausea's settled too, replaced by inexorable determination. I must know more. Painful as the answers may be, they'll provide insight which could make all the difference. On shaky legs, I shuffle to my bed and retrieve my dropped tablet.

I go all the way back to my arrival at the testing facility—the one Cygnus took me to after separating me from my family. The first place I was ever in other than my home. File 192-2-0002.

This time, I pay attention to the details. Whether I'm familiar with the situations described or not, I comb through every detail. By skipping through on my first go-round, I missed things I might otherwise have guessed at sooner.

Right there in that second file is a therapist's statement, where she recommends Cygnus allow me to see my family if he expects me to make progress. More disturbing is her further recommendation to keep my family alive as a way of ensuring I remain "compliant."

What sort of heartless woman was she? Or did she think she was doing me a kindness, protecting my loved ones but never guessing the circumstances under which Cygnus would do that?

Because, hidden further on in those files, is Cygnus's clear directive to monitor them at all times. Anyone caught facilitating communications between myself and my family outside of his direct orders would be put to death. Even worse, Cygnus instructed the SerSents to ensure my family claimed they were being cared for "by any means necessary."

For the second time, my tablet slips from limp fingers. Does this mean Cygnus hasn't been looking after them? That all this time, they've been... where? In some dark hole?

No, no, Mom said Tavi was working in the laundries—or the kitchen now. And Xanin and Frankie had weights for working out. Frankie has a new friend. The thoughts bring little comfort. While they may not be in isolation (if I even believe that), there's no guarantee they aren't being abused.

I pace, nervous energy pounding through me as I try to settle my concerns, telling myself they must be getting some level of care. Although the lack of any fat on their bones, my mom's premature aging, and Xanin's altered outlook on life haunt me.

For the first time in ages, perhaps ever, I attempt looking at the facts from a purely analytical perspective. Removing the emotion from the equation is a struggle.

Once I get past it, I list the facts I know are true: Cygnus lied about me asking him to take care of my family in exchange for my project work. This work led to his promotions, and while this wasn't a lie per se, I still count it as such, since he never once acknowledged me in any of his speeches at those parties, let alone to my face. Finally, my family has been monitored all this time and coerced into statements about their welfare, making it more likely they'll only be "useful" to him for as long as I'm compliant.

Facts I think I know, but can't confirm: Cygnus may have lied about the true purposes of my inventions (yes, I'm spinning that wheel again). He may also have lied about what happened to my dad after they caught him stealing. (Does my mom know?) Sarissa lied about being my friend. And Deran may be a plant to replace her as the spy in my life.

The conclusions rock me. How have I never figured this out before?

Since arriving in this place, I've felt like my brain has been inhibited somehow. No, I correct myself, not since I first arrived. Only after... I think back. Yes, the first time I experienced the intense headache bringing those cloaking mists was after my one and only act of rebellion.

Are those mists, that pain, why I haven't seen the truth before?

Not sure what to make of the reason for this last epiphany, I stop pacing.

Everything tonight leads to two questions I must answer if I want to know what's really going on. First, where is my family now? Second, more worrisome, what else have they lied to me about?

Lead topics established, I settle down enough to finish reading my files. Some of them make little sense, like the detailed records they keep of what I eat.

I reach the end, finding nothing else. Nothing to prove Sarissa (or Deran, for that matter) were placed in my life to act as spies. No earth-shattering statements about my inventions being used for anything other than Cygnus's stated purpose. Most agonizing, no mention of my family, either directly or indirectly, or any reference to where they might be.

When I switch off my light and try to get some sleep, it's almost two in the morning. Despite the late (early?) hour, sleep eludes me, and I toss and turn. Still restless an hour later, I wonder if the cleaning crew are still at work on the levels far below mine.

It couldn't hurt to check. I'll just take a short walk down there, stretch my legs. Perhaps take some food with as a peace offering in case they got into trouble for the bag of clothes I left on the floor. I stuff almost all the pre-packed meals from my refrigerator into two large trash bags, then stagger under the weight, lugging the food to the elevator before riding it down.

Once again, the mall is quiet, the shadows deep. "Hello?" I know better than to expect a reply, but I wait for one, anyway. "Sam? I wasn't sure if you got into trouble for the clothes I left. My humblest apologies if you did." I feel like an idiot talking to fresh air. "Um, okay, I'm going now. But I brought some food in case you got into trouble as a token of my remorse. If you could at least let me know you're here…" My voice trails off. "Or even if you didn't get into trouble and would like the food?"

The tiniest of scrapes echoes down the corridor. I strain to hear more. Are those hushed whispers?

"Uh, struggling a little here. If you're there, throw some trash at me." While it's all I could think of, I hear a muffled snort as someone suppresses laughter. "Okay, good enough. Sorry again if you were reprimanded. I'm leaving now. The food's here."

I drag the two bags out of the elevator, dumping them in the same place I left the clothes last time, then scurry back behind the doors, not wanting to cause problems for the cleaners again—or for the first time if they didn't get into trouble last time. Whatever. My addled thoughts are a symptom of my exhaustion. When I get home, I should at least try sleeping again.

Seems my little nighttime adventure was all my mind needed to settle. I don't recall getting into bed, but wake to find the sun's rays trickling in through the window films. Bleary-eyed, I rise. Since I have the day off, maybe I'll nap later.

But I feel out of sorts all morning. At midday, I decide exercise will increase my chances of a better night's sleep, and I head outside for a run, chagrined to discover I don't seem to have it in me today.

Listless, I make a halfhearted attempt at pushing further. But when

I come across an ice cream vendor, his little cart stationed next to a park favored by those with young children, I give up.

Settling for a chocolate-coated sugar cone with chocolate ice cream and cookie and fudge crumbles over the top (no judging!), I slurp through the first bit of food I've had in almost two days as I amble home.

This little jumpstart must be what my metabolism needed because I'm ravenous by the time I walk into my apartment. I peruse my options, then choose a favorite meal from my magic refrigerator (yes, I'm ignoring the blue tray), heating it in the blitz before settling in front of my screen.

Between the food, the warm afternoon sun streaming in through the window, and the comfort of a beloved movie, I'm lulled into sleep. I wake stiff and sore late that afternoon and curse the sofa. My reasons for not getting something better seem paltry. Maybe I can bribe myself into allowing the purchase if I'm successful at convincing Cygnus to allow my family to move in with me.

Thankful for my shower, I hop in to restore a little warmth and ease my aching muscles as I consider what I read in my file last night. So much information. Sifting through it, I discover one piece I haven't explored, haven't yet fully figured out. Excitement builds. There may be more clues if I can finagle an answer to this question. I grimace. Why do ideas always come to me in the shower?

Eager to explore options, I race through the rest of my cleaning routine. My mind runs faster. I must know what Section 12.1, subsection 4 (a) refers to. Conjuring a solution requires minimal mental effort. I need to do a little shopping—and not in the stores of my building.

With my chards stashed in my pocket (thank you, freelance jobs!), I catch the trundle to another sector, a place I wouldn't ordinarily visit. But I'm permitted access, so no cause for any unexpected SerSents.

Randomly choosing the first mall I come across, I wander around, pretending I'm browsing. When I find the costume store, I enter, careful to buy more than I need. I pay with my chards, then fake more browsing in other stores before exiting the mall.

Mission accomplished. Next stop, home, to make adjustments to my HydroPak and wait until it gets dark. The two hours twilight takes to fall seem interminable, but finally, it's dark enough outside that any cameras will have difficulty tracking me through the pools of shadow.

Dressed in my accommodating all-black running attire again, I toss the carefully modified and provisioned HydroPak over my shoulders and ride the elevator downstairs. Nothing suspicious here, SerSents. Just someone planning a long run. That's right, look away and focus on someone else.

Even though I haven't yet burned five calories, I'm sweating by the time I exit the resident's foyer. No prizes for guessing why. I hurry outside, then choose the nearest path and start my run, keeping up the pretense.

I sprint to the park I had in mind, seeking those ever-handy trees. When I reach their cover, I'm quick to find a good hiding place. Then I extract the costume concealed in the altered HydroPak and change.

With a grin, I stuff the HydroPak into the stomach portion of the costume so it looks like I have a healthy paunch. I continue through the trees until I reach a mall backing onto these woods. Handy.

The ball cap does an acceptable job obscuring my face. This time, I tuck my hair under a wig of long, straight blonde hair. While I would've preferred a short wig, I have too much hair of my own to cram it under one.

Slinking through the shadows muting a side entrance to the mall, I slip inside. With no time to waste and eager to get this over with, I head directly to the food court. People there always leave what I want lying around.

I've timed it perfectly. The dinner rush is on, and the food court is packed. I sidle up and down the aisles, pretending I'm looking for someone, when in reality, I'm after something. Ah, there's one!

A covert glance confirms no one's paying attention. I swipe the unwatched tablet and drop it into the wide pocket of the costume, walking past like I didn't even notice it was there.

Heart thumping wildly, I amble down another two aisles before throwing my arms in the air, feigning irritation. With luck, anyone watching will buy my failure to find the person I was looking for and leave it at that.

I stomp away from the food court and exit the mall. No point lingering. I have what I need. By way of a circuitous path, I skirt back to the trees on the side of the mall, slipping into their shelter once more.

Once again, I reverse my disguise to the original version, then run through the trees in a path perpendicular to the mall. Twenty minutes later, I reach the smoothie shop I'd planned on. I enter, order a Mango Berry Splash, and ostensibly stare out the window as I wait. When the autobot calls my name, I've assured myself no one's followed me.

I collect my smoothie, then choose a table along the back wall, far from the windows where anyone looking inside might glimpse the information on my screen. My smoothie is deliciously cool against my skin, and I set it on the table before removing my HydroPak and digging into the compartment nestled between my back and the pack.

It will be impossible for anyone to prove the tablet I remove isn't one I brought from home. If I'm ever asked why I didn't log into the store's wireless, I'll say I was reading a file already on my tablet. Plausible enough.

I angle the stolen tablet away from the cameras I scouted, then surreptitiously clip Ferret over the tablet's surface. Whoever owned this device obviously wasn't worried about security because Ferret takes all of two seconds to gain access.

Fingers shaking, I enter Section 12.1, subsection 4 (a) into the search bar. Atypically, it takes a while to process. A message pops up. No results.

Is this good or bad? No, bad, definitely bad! The conglomerate would only hide something if they didn't want the general populace finding it. Worse, have I just put a target on my back running that search? I imagine flashing red lights in some secret SerSent bunker, warning them someone is probing for information barred from the public.

I rise so fast I knock my chair over. It crashes to the floor, and several people eye me over the rims of tablets or smoothies. I raise a hand. "Sorry! Didn't mean to startle anyone."

Hurriedly, I right the chair. Then I toss the tablet into the compartment and sling the HydroPak over my shoulders. I have to get out of here! If I did set off those imagined alarms, SerSents could be here any minute.

As I do my best not to run out of the store, my mind scrambles. My priority is getting rid of the tablet. Being found with it would be incriminating. I dash down a narrow alley between two building, disappointed when I find no disposals.

Hunting one down takes a tense nine minutes and forty-three seconds. Only when the disposal is crunching the tablet into fine dust do I realize the time I spent finding this disposal was beneficial. With the remains of the tablet a decent distance from the smoothie shop, good luck to anyone tracking it way out here.

Careful to stay in the shadows, I make it back to my apartment. I can only hope I've avoided enough cameras for enough time to hide the whole elaborate deception. Question now is… what do I do next?

3 2

The aftermath of the evening's adrenaline-filled antics knocks me out when I crawl into bed. Although, admittedly, the lack of sleep the night before also plays a part.

Either way, I wake late the next morning, alarmed at oversleeping first before remembering I'm still entitled to another day of "compassionate" leave. The mere thought riles me. If CC ever did anything compassionate, I've never seen it firsthand. In a world where people watch their backs while relentlessly stomping on others in their zeal to climb to the next tier, I doubt anyone knows the true meaning of the word.

These pessimistic thoughts negate neither the peace brought by a decent night's sleep, nor my restored energy. Because somewhere between reading my file and this morning, I've resolved two things.

First, nothing will ever change as long as my family are in captivity. It's paramount I get them into my care, either through my ultimatum to Cygnus (politely phrased because I value keeping my head on my shoulders) or by learning where my family are and liberating them myself.

Second, assuming the second option is more likely and I have to take matters into my own hands, I'm not naïve enough to think I can charm people into helping me out of the goodness of their hearts. I'll need money—and chards are the only way the conglomerate can't track it.

With these resolutions in mind and having both a mission and ulterior motive, I head into work. A mission because my lab is the best place I can think of to clone one of my few remaining chards. An ulterior motive because it will look like I'm back to business despite my best friend dying, helping sell the "impossible" deadline idea. At the thought of putting one over on Cygnus for a change, a smile tweaks my lips.

On the trundle, I ponder the challenge ahead of me. I've never needed to procure my own chards before, so not only will I have to reverse-engineer them to figure out how they work, but also make some modifications in the process.

A major drawback of the chards is their inability to be reloaded once their balance is depleted. If I plan on transferring most of my substantial wealth, currently collecting interest in my CC bank account, I'll need rechargeable chards.

Further, I'll have to bypass any balance limits such cards may have —because waltzing around with a suitcase full of the things would surely attract attention.

As to how I'll transfer the funds from my account to the chard, I suspect I can add another routine to Ferret, allowing him to handle the task. But that's another unknown.

My thoughts return to the duplicity of today's mission. Since I'll be in the lab, albeit not working on the cold fusion energy source, all anyone can confirm is my presence there. The purpose is to relay that news back to Cygnus—because word of me losing it a few weeks ago didn't make it back to him in a vacuum. If my family are being monitored, I am too. My paranoia about those hidden eyes doesn't seem so silly now. However, the knowledge gleaned from my stolen file makes me realize I should be more vigilant than ever. While I flirted with escaping those cameras before, now I must get serious about it.

The trundle delivers me to my stop, and I stroll to the office, enjoying the warmth of the early morning sunshine. When I arrive, it's almost a disappointment. Then I remember the work. Time to rise to the challenge.

I settle in my lab, the one assigned to me alone. While most of my team share labs and workbench space, my position as head of the department affords me this privilege. Just one more thing I'm allowed that will ultimately work against Cygnus. At least, if all goes according to plan.

With a soft click, the chard I brought slots into the plate on my workbench. I pull my magnifier closer, then set to work. I'm deep into the microcircuitry of the EMV chip with my specialized software when I remember. The thought is startling enough that I lose my place.

The E-AMPS gene! I have it. If I want to know what it is, all I need do is run a few blood tests. Even though I want to rush off, I can't leave the chard on the workbench where anyone can find it.

Fueled by this new impetus, I find my place again, then work swiftly, mapping out the circuit. I grin when I figure out how it works. Genius in its simplicity. I'm even more delighted because I've also confirmed Ferret can transfer my conglomerate account funds into my crafted chard. I already know how I'll explain that first transfer. Pity it will have to wait a while.

Setting aside my glee, I clone the chip's circuitry, program the laser, and then grab the stash of blank cards I liberated from the supply room. I dash into the machine room attached to my private lab, set the cards up on the laser printer, return to my lab, and start the program.

Since the lab's cards are a quarter of the size of a regular chard, it's unlikely anyone will suspect their true purpose. Also, with their small size, they can remain hidden even when in one's palm. And, because we regularly use these cards in the lab for many purposes, carrying them won't seem unusual. More so because I encrypted the cash portion under a layer presenting the card as something related to the labs on first inspection.

The laser's software program makes quick work of imprinting the microcircuits onto the EMV chips in the blank cards. Once complete, I dart back into the machine room and scoop the finished products into the pocket of my lab coat. Just two more tasks to clean things up.

I shred the original chard, then scrub the custom cash program from my specialized software, satisfied I've left no trace of the deception I just committed here. With this laser system unmonitored because it can generate key cards, I have an added measure of peace. On to the next thing.

Determined, I walk one level down to the biochemistry labs. I'm not sure how I'll explain the actions I plan to take here until my stomach growls, and I remember my hypoglycemia. Perfect.

Drawing my blood is not as barbaric now as it was back when Cygnus and his goons invaded our home. While a DNA test doesn't require a full vial of blood, just a tiny dot, if I'm to carry out my ruse, I must draw the full vial.

I program the machine, then place my arm in the open circular disk, allowing the air cushions inside to guide my arm into position. A soft beep sounds, warning me it's about to shoot the needle into my arm. I wish it wouldn't. The beep only makes me tense up.

Then again, this machine has a precision some human hands lack. I don't feel the needle enter or notice the vials being replaced as it extracts the two I requested. A second beep sounds, indicating it's finished and I can remove my arm.

When I retract my arm, I frown at the bland white bandaid covering the injection site. Would it hurt them to add some cute pictures—or even some color? With a shake of my head, I lift the two vials from the tray next to the machine and amble over to the respective machines.

I drop one vial into the DNA sequencer and the other into a blood glucose analyzer, allowing the machines to extract the blood and dispose of the vials.

While the tests run, I explore the spacious lab, inspecting machines and tinkering with ideas to make this lab more efficient. Then the printer along the far wall comes to life, and I hurry over, eager for the results.

While I'm no geneticist, it's unnecessary because the answer's right there in the *Statement of Results*. Positive for a genetic mutation.

But there's no explanation. All I've done is confirm I have an anomaly. I don't even know if this mutation is a marker for the E-AMPS gene. The results also don't state whether I have a genetic marker for my hypoglycemia. I should've thought of all this before charging down here.

To keep up the charade, I wander over to the blood glucose analyzer and check the results. Normal. Of course I choose a time when nothing will show up. What was I expecting after failing to learn anything relevant from the DNA test?

Deflated, I leave the biochemistry lab, about to head back upstairs when my stomach grumbles again. I really should eat something. I can't remember when last I had food. Not good.

The cafeteria is empty, the lunch crowd having come and gone. I select my meal, then leave the cafeteria, strolling to the park surrounding the building. I eat, paying more attention to the ducks on the small lake than my lunch.

When I know I can't delay further, I return to my office. Bringing up the specs for the second prototype, I check the permutations I hope to run. Time passes unnoticed, and night has fallen when I finally ride the trundle home.

The next morning, I ping Deran on my way into work, leaving a message as promised to let him know I'll be in the office today. But when I join him in the workshop fifty-eight minutes later, I wish I hadn't called.

Before I even reach him, I sense those gray eyes watching me, assessing, analyzing. I tell myself not to make him a villain when I have no concrete evidence. But Sarissa's betrayal lingers, reminding me people may not be what they seem.

Over the next days, as we build the second prototype, then run its first test, that sense of being watched doesn't go away. In fact, it intensifies. I worry my recent escapades have identified me and brought this unwanted attention.

As my paranoia grows, I begin counter-surveillance of my own. If

Deran's going to study my every move, I'll reciprocate. Once I initiate this, it takes less than a day to realize his intentions aren't as shady as I assumed.

While scrutinizing him at length, trying to put a finger on those tiny glimpses providing insight, it becomes obvious. He thinks he knows something I don't and pities me. Are some of those furtive glances an attempt to gauge whether he can trust me enough to tell me what's bothering him?

This knowledge is almost as frightening as it's enlightening. What does he know that I don't? Deranged speculations follow. *They know I copied the file off that old PC. Someone identified me as the person who stole the tablet running a flagged search. My custom chard program went into some cyber trashcan where an overly dedicated SerSent traced it back to me.*

Spiraling down to "them" planning to kill me once "they" have the machine. Or, worse, kill my family because they no longer need them to coerce me into creating the impossible.

With supreme effort, I close the mental faucet spraying its poisonous thoughts. If I want to learn what Deran knows, getting him to trust me enough to tell me is the easiest way. Then I won't have to speculate. I'll have concrete answers.

33

As we run through the permutations on the second prototype, we encounter several problems I hadn't envisioned. I push through, dealing with each in turn, anxiety rising at every step. But it's futile. Every permutation fails.

Despite thinking I would have ample padding in the timeframe, we're down to the wire. Only three weeks away from the deadline I gave Cygnus, an insanely short amount of time to come up with an alternative solution.

More than distressed by the failure of both prototypes, I lock myself in my office and study the data. Neither of these generated more power than they consumed.

I debate making some fundamental alterations to both designs, like using heavy ion beams instead of lasers in the accelerators or changing the shape of the plasma's confinement chamber, but these are radical ideas and totally untested. My only solution in the limited time remaining is to consider that third prototype, the one I initially discarded as too problematic.

This prototype centers on muon-catalyzed fusion. Muons, unstable subatomic particles, allow for a process closest to the idea of cold fusion, whereby little or no heat is required for nuclear fusion, and the opposite of thermonuclear fusion, which requires insanely high temperatures.

Simply put, a muon replaces the lone electron of a hydrogen atom. This reduces the size of the hydrogen atom, meaning the nuclei of two hydrogen atoms can fuse, releasing the desired nuclear energy.

While all this sounds delightful, first, creating muons requires vast amounts of energy. Second, the process is costly. Third, muons are unstable, their short half-life leading to quick decay. Fourth, muons tend to bind to the new alpha particle formed by the nuclear fusion, meaning their catalytic effect ceases.

No, no, no! I can't give up before I even start. I list the problems again, then single out the key problem: energy demand. The cyclotron technology used by the original scientists needed so much power, the final product could never provide energy output exceeding input. I tap my screen to search for the files Sarissa sent me in those first weeks.

Sarissa. The person I failed. As soon as this project ends, if not a spare moment before, I have to sneak back to the basement and grab her file. If mine was so illuminating, it'll be interesting to see what hers reveals.

The folders blinking on my screen remind me they're waiting for a selection. I tap the relevant file. Yes, this is what I remembered. Instead of the cyclotron proton acceleration techniques used initially, later tests switched to pulsed laser-driven muon sources.

With so much progress in laser technology since then, I wonder if today's lasers will fare better than those in this experiment. I dig in and surface some time later, elated to have confirmed so many advances. But not in the industrial sector. In the defense sector. A place I never considered looking when I first analyzed the three options. While overlooking this was remiss of me, I know why—to avoid all the questions Cygnus would want answered before allowing me anywhere near defense technology.

I no longer have that luxury. If I'm to finish within the time frame specified, I need approval for the weaponized lasers. Even if I can only replicate ATHENA (Advanced Tactical High ENergy Asset), one of the first lasers tested for this purpose, then modify it to suit my exact needs, it could swing the balance. More so if I get approval for the newer lasers, because they have made significant advances in spectral beam combining of fiber lasers.

The results inspire me. Enough to be undaunted by the barrage of questions I have to answer (thankfully all in absentia) before Cygnus grants approval. When it comes down mere hours later, I'm shocked. Either Cygnus really wants this energy source, or the matters requiring his attention in Roxile are extremely demanding. If the former (more likely based on his previous actions), this only gives me more leverage to claim my family once I have a functional machine.

Time to draw up plans for Deran and his team. Since most of the original design can be used as is, with a few minor modifications, finishing takes less than two days (okay, and two nights).

Mid-afternoon Thursday, I comm Deran and ask him to come to my office. He must've been in the workshop because before I have time for more than a few stretches, he arrives, leaning against my doorjamb and looking delicious.

Yes, I'm tired, and yes, my resistance is low, and yes, I shouldn't be thinking of him this way. But what's a girl to do? Remembering I wanted to gain his trust so he would tell me what's bothering him, I smile.

It must come out weird because he laughs. "You look like a wolf leering at a person stranded in the woods."

"A wolf?" *Okay, is that good predatory or bad predatory?*

Deran sobers. "Don't worry, I meant nothing negative. Just that you look like you want something."

I do. Two things, but I'll only allow myself one. "Thanks for coming. I have a new design I'd like you and your team to start working on as soon as possible."

Deran's eyebrows shoot up. "You do? That didn't take long."

"Only because I could copy most of the original design, then add a few changes. Here," I throw the design up onto the wall behind my chair, "why don't you come look?"

Already turning my head toward the wall so I don't have to look at that yummy face a second longer (stop it!), I explain what I want.

An hour later, Deran leaves, plans transferred to his tablet. Yet again, I'm impressed by his ability to grasp what I'm after in such a short time.

Not only that, but he also understands the time pressure and has promised to build the machine as quickly as possible. He asked for, and I granted, extra personnel. I trust him to fill the slots, not wanting to micromanage or hinder progress because he has to get my input or approval first.

About falling asleep on my feet, I realize I haven't showered in two days. I haven't even changed. A little worried, I give myself a sniff, relieved to find I'm not stinky. Standing so close while we went through the design wouldn't have been appealing for Deran. Not something I should be worrying about, I remind myself.

Since I should make the most of the time I have while Deran builds the machine, I'm about to head home for that shower when I remember Sarissa's file. Is it too soon after stealing my own to head down there and copy hers? Would it be better if I waited until the weekend, only a day away? But there's no time like the present. Also, starting this new prototype provides an excellent excuse for searching for some obscure item the supply room wouldn't have.

I divert to the gym, finding the narrow space between the end of the lockers and the far wall. A space so small and overlooked I hid Ferret there. As unobtrusively as possible, I slip my gadget out and into an inside pocket of my lab coat.

Then I stop in at the cafeteria on the way down, not wanting to look like I'm hurrying to the basement—and also because I'm starving. I devour the food, blinking when I dip my fork in again and find I've finished. While I'd love more, I should allow what I've already eaten to digest first. And again, no time like the present.

Discarding the disposable elements, I stack the tray, then make for the basement. While I don't hurry, I don't tarry either. I'm a woman on a mission, although not for the reasons anyone watching may guess. At least, I hope not.

When I reach the long corridor between the two sets of staircases, I can't miss the new light fixtures, obnoxious in their brightness. I'm dismayed to find no wall panel to toggle them on and off. Meaning someone in some control room has that power.

The new access panels on each of the doors are the next glaring upgrade since my little incursion. Interestingly, they didn't single out the room I went into. They put locks on all of them. Do the other rooms also have secrets?

As I drift down the corridor, I debate the wisdom of accessing the space. But it would look suspicious, wouldn't it, if I came all the way down here, then went back upstairs without opening any of the doors?

This gives me an idea. Pretending I don't remember which room I'm looking for, I wand my arm across the access panel two doors from my destination. I enter, finding it filled with steel storage boxes. Surely, cardboard would've been cheaper?

I step closer, examining the nearest steel box, and find the tiny keypad restricting entry. Hmm, no clue what the boxes contain since there are just a bunch of numbers on the outside. Numbers in an odd arrangement, separated by three dashes but running sequentially. Unhelpful, because the numbers could relate to anything.

Time to press on. Lingering here would be unwise. I exit the room, then access the next room. Clutter. Junk everywhere. Or at least, that's how it looks at first blush. Lamps, desks, chairs, kitchen appliances, knickknacks, wall décor, and more. Even framed photographs. What in the world?

Just to be sure, I take a quick turn around the room, checking for a PC like the one in the room next door. Nope, not a one here.

Exiting this second misleading room, I keep the smug smile off my face. *No, SerSent, I just needed something and couldn't remember where we kept the old lab supplies.*

I wand my arm over the access to the room I meant to enter all along. This provides my third clue. Instead of stacked items coated with dust, someone has rearranged everything. Shelves fill the space, all the lab supplies neatly positioned and labeled.

Before I reach the far end of the room, hidden by the shelves, I know what I'll find—or rather, what I won't. I round the corner, and my heart sinks. *No! They took it away!* The desk remains, but there's no sign of the antiquated PC I accessed only a few short days ago.

Devastated, I want to stand here and stare at the spot. But I spotted the newly installed cameras. Again, I pretend it was my intention all along to get something from this part of the room (thank you whoever labeled the shelves alphabetically!). I wander down the shelf at the very back of the room until I find the mini Wiley mill.

I've used this once before, when working on the greenhouse project. Although intended primarily for soil and agricultural use, it does a better job of turning the more robust crystals in my lab into dust than our current lab equipment.

Tucking the mill under an arm, I make sure Ferret is still hidden before moving back to the door. I open it to find a SerSent outside. I'm so startled I almost drop the mill.

"Oh!" I fumble at the falling mill, half-relieved and half-annoyed when it evades my clutches. It crashes onto the concrete floor. Thankful the mill provides a reason to bend over and check for damage, I avoid the SerSent's eyes.

The steel casing is undamaged, so I heft the machine and tuck it back under my arm, then rise to meet the SerSent's gaze.

"Sorry, you startled me. Is there something I can help you with?"

Without answering, the SerSent scrutinizes me, eyes probing.

I straighten my back. "I asked if there was something I could help you with?" My voice is cold, emotionless. All the better to hide the tremor that wants to seep through.

"No, be on your way."

The SerSent waves a dismissive arm, and I leave, steps measured. Much as I want to, it wouldn't do to flee. But this isn't my last surprise for the day.

When I arrive back on the lab floor, Tandize is waiting for me, prowling the corridor just outside the elevator.

"Chiara! Where have you been?"

I raise an eyebrow at her tone. But whatever has her rattled troubles her more than my ire. I sigh. "What's happened now?"

Tandize darts a glance back at the main floor of the lab, then checks the corridor to the left and right of the elevator before hissing at me. "What are *they* doing here?"

"They?" I frown, but movement in the lab catches my eye. My breath hitches. It's two of those spooky people who guard Cygnus's office.

As my breathing quickens, I warn myself not to hyperventilate. A panic attack will not serve my purposes. Besides, I reassure myself, the last time they were here it was just to... to tell me Sarissa was dead.

"Here." Suddenly weak, I shove the mill into Tandize's arms before I drop it a second time. I want to lean over, put my head down, allow my breathing to normalize. But I can't.

Feigning a confidence I don't have, I give Tandize an answer. "I don't know why they're here, but this is my lab, and they aren't welcome."

Tandize's eyes go wide and round, terror painting her face. "You can't tell them that!"

"Why not?" I want an answer. I'm tired of being a mushroom, kept in the dark and fed on excrement. These people clearly terrify her more than the SerSents. If the strained faces on the rest of my team are anything to go by, she's not the only one.

Tandize stutters, no complete words making it past her lips. Her face is even whiter now, and I fear she may she faint on me.

"Hey, steady on. I'm here. Do you need to sit?"

Face now a little shiny too, Tandize nods. I try leading her back to her chair at her workbench, but she stiffens, resisting me. Right now, the lab is the last place to ease her concerns. With care, I remove the mill from her stiff fingers and set it on the floor, then drag her into an elevator.

I select the button for the ground floor. If Tandize needs time, I'll garner some for myself too. Fresh air will do us both good—hopefully restore our equilibrium somewhat.

The paths through the massive park surrounding CC HQ are numerous, but I choose the one leading to my favorite fountain. The water tinkling into the pool is soothing, something I hope will ease Tandize's anxiety too.

When we reach the fountain, I gently press Tandize down onto the ledge. Then I perch next to her and wait. Although my body is still, my mind spins.

No way it's a coincidence those weird men—I must find out what they're called—appeared in the lab right after I went into the room which used to hold that old PC. Does this mean I'm in more trouble than I thought? Or dare I hope these men are simply messengers again?

Frightening messengers. If that is their purpose, someone should tell HR to send less intimidating people.

I've all but forgotten Tandize is sitting next to me until she speaks. "Thank you, Chiara. I needed to get out of there."

I nod, waiting. Silence is an excellent motivator.

Tandize glances furtively around the area we're sitting in. Then she leans closer and whispers, "You really don't know who they are?"

"I don't. I don't even know what they're called. Can you tell me?"

Her startled glance, then the way she averts her eyes, implicate her. Before she answers, I know I won't get the truth. "They're, uh, assigned to protect the director and the upper-tier people."

"Uh-huh." I wait, wondering what else she'll divulge, hoping I might glean something useful. When she fidgets, I repeat my question. "What are they called?"

"I don't think they have a name. We just call them upper level security."

The way she answered, with no hesitation, makes me suspect it's a coached reply. I sigh, doubting I'll learn any truths from Tandize. If only one thing is indisputably true today, it's her fear of these "upper level security" people.

I say nothing further, just stare at the fountain, watching the water arcing through the air, the countless droplets gleefully iridescent in the late afternoon sun.

Tandize must realize she's disappointed me because she squirms. I ignore her until, finally, she rises. "We should get back, Chiara."

"Yes, we should."

We return to the office in silence. The closer we get to the labs, the more I sense Tandize's increasing tension. But she had the chance to speak to me, to tell me what bothered her about those people. I can't help her if she won't tell me the truth.

I'm not surprised when Tandize says she'll see me back in the labs, then peels off to the cafeteria. As I continue my solitary march, I steel myself. These people, whoever they are, are only here as messengers— or at least, I try to convince myself of that.

When the elevator doors open, I can't say I'm more prepared for the sight of those strange men again. Are they all men? Do they have women in their ranks?

The moment they spot me, they stalk over. Obviously, I was their target. I'm not sure whether this should alarm me. If it was bad news, like with Sarissa, wouldn't they rather wait for me in my office?

But no, they catch me right in the middle of the lab. Right where everyone can see and hear. At least if they're planning something diabolical, I have witnesses.

"Miss Baschet, please come with us."

Always so formal. Since I have no choice, I follow them back to the elevator. It arrives as we get there, and I wonder if they have a way to make the elevator meet them when and where they want. *No, that's ridiculous!* But I step into the elevator, aware what is and isn't possible in this world is becoming increasingly foreign to me.

When they select the button for the top floor, my eyes feel like they want to pop out of my head. "Why are we going there?" I blurt the words before I think to moderate them.

They don't answer, and my anxiety ramps up. Perhaps Hag Lady told them to come and get me. But why would she want to see me? She loathes us peons. My mind gets stuck, and I can't get past the block. Then the elevator dings, and the doors open.

I'm escorted into Hag Lady's office, but as expected, she doesn't acknowledge me. Instead, she addresses the goons walking on either side of me.

"Send her right in."

If she hadn't gestured toward Cygnus's office, I might've balked. Those words are an eerie reminder of being summoned into the exam rooms for all those tests they subjected me to when I first arrived in… wherever it was Cygnus took me to after kidnapping me.

A little dazed, I allow the goons to usher me into Cygnus's office. I'm about to turn and ask what I'm doing here when Cygnus appears from the bathroom adjoining his office.

I hurry through the expected greeting, my body repeating the actions and spewing the words without conscious thought. He looks like he just stepped off the broadcast studio floor, immaculately groomed in every respect. If I didn't loathe him so much, he might be handsome. Instead, all I see is the calculation in those eyes, the assiduously maintained outward appearance, the thin lines his lips compress into when I disappoint him.

"Director!" The single word is more an exclamation of surprise than a greeting. But he takes it as such.

"Hello, Chiara. How are you today?"

How am I? What is this? He rarely indulges in pleasantries. I check my virtual defenses: yes, my mask is in place, and blinds hide my eyes. A thousand questions scream for attention, one louder than the rest. When did he get back?

"I am well, Director. Thank you for asking. I hope you are too?" *Ugh, the pandering!*

"I am. You've been busy in my absence."

Oh! I'm here because he wants an update. "I have, Director. As mentioned in the communications I sent when requesting the lasers, we've had a few setbacks, but there are some options yet."

Cygnus sits and assumes his (irritating) thinking-man pose. "Can you still meet your deadline?"

Mind scrambling again, I debate whether this is the meeting I was waiting for. The one I requested all those weeks ago. Problem is, I haven't prepared. I can't just babble an ultimatum. Not unless I want some gruesome punishment. Cygnus is studying me, still waiting for an answer.

"Yes, I hope to still meet that deadline, Director." What else can I say? You never move deadlines. Although, if he offers to change them, you accept. Despite knowing you're only digging yourself deeper into debt. Is that what this is?

Cygnus continues inspecting me. *I am not a bug!* Then his hands drop from that hateful pose. He leans forward. Here it comes. "Chiara, I was told you lost your personal assistant. I'm sorry to learn about Sarissa's death."

For a second, I'm too stupefied to speak. Then I stammer, "Thank you, Director." Where in the world is this conversation going?

"Since I'm not without compassion, and because I heard you worked even the day after Sarissa's death, I think we can dispense with that deadline. After all, it was only a call to your family I allowed."

I'm in for it. Dreading the price for this "concession," I rush to correct the "error" he not so subtly pointed out. "Thank you, Director, for permitting that call to my family. I appreciate your compassion."

"Accepted, and I think the work you did after attests to your commitment to keeping the deadline. However, it seems an overly generous bonus, considering my boon was so small."

Yes, I'm definitely in for it. "Director, your boon allowed me to shift my focus back onto my work, where it should've been."

"I'm glad you mentioned as much. Considering your... distress for your family, compounded by Sarissa's death, perhaps a side project will help. Clear your brain a little, right? I've heard you had to scrap two prototypes already."

I'm unsure which statement to address first. Deciding it should be work, I run through my dog-and-pony routine. "Yes, Director. I apologize for the resources wasted on those first two prototypes. At the time, they seemed the most viable options, and—"

"Yes, yes, I understand." Cygnus waves my apology away.

Tingles race up and down my spine. What is more important to him than hearing me beg and plead? My answer comes in the same breath: this "side project."

Whatever it is, I walked into it. I didn't see it coming, and just blundered ahead. I knew he was going to make me pay somehow for removing the deadline. Why didn't I think to wonder what he might want in exchange? Too late now.

"To ensure we don't rush this third prototype, I think you should focus on something else, give the mechanical team time to do a decent job building your machine. Don't they say a change is as good as a holiday?"

I wouldn't know. I've never had a holiday, you greedy, self-centered man! "Yes, Director. Thank you, Director."

Cygnus grins, but it's more menacing than appealing. A hyena eyeing a tasty bit of meat. I see all the dangers of what lies ahead displayed in that smile. The smile he gives when he knows he's getting something he wants—and the person giving it has no choice.

"Well, aren't you going to ask?"

I blink. Oh! "Sorry, Director. Yes, I'd love to hear about the new project—uh, side project."

"You are aware I spent time in Roxile?"

"Yes, Director."

"Part of the reason I was there was to discuss the rising levels of dementia in the world population. The problem is more prevalent than we realized."

"Yes, Director." Still no clue what this has to do with me.

"Unfortunately, evidence suggests this is a lingering result of the toxic air before we cleaned the world. Do you remember that?"

A trick question? "Not really, Director. I remember the air burning my throat when I young. But that was before my time in Cirrian."

"Yes, that burning was because your air was toxic, but the conglomerate has since cleaned the air. All for one and work for all."

I do the usual salute and utter the odious phrase back to him. A second time. *Really?* Abhorrent as it is, I must also add what he expects. "You've been an excellent director, cleaning the air for our people."

The smirk on Cygnus's face makes my skin want to crawl right off my body. I've never been able to interpret that horrid smile. The closest I've come to putting a name to it is smug. What else does he know that I don't?

"Let me explain this side project."

35

I totter back to the lab, dazed. So many things have happened today. I'm reeling. Now this.

I curse the asinine individual who decided I was the perfect candidate to solve this problem. This assignment is not a project for a scientist like me. Perhaps a microbiologist would be better? Or an immunologist? Someone trained to create drugs, whatever those people are called.

But I have my marching orders. Thankfully, Cygnus gave me permission to consult with any person I deemed necessary to aid the cause. Although I've yet to figure out who that might be.

I slip back into my office, barely behind my desk when Deran knocks on my door. His face is troubled, and my flagging spirits drop another notch, immediately suspecting issues with the new prototype. "What's wrong? Did we hit another roadblock?"

Deran waves a dismissive hand. "No, no, everything's going well with building the new machine. I came to check on you."

"Me? Why?"

"Where did those men take you?"

Interesting. He didn't give them a name either. "Those men?"

Deran grimaces. "Yes, the upper level security men."

Unsure how to interpret the grimace, I ponder it for a moment. Deciding the taste of the lie leaves a bitter taste in his mouth, I warm a little, then remind myself this could be a ploy to get me to trust him. Then again, aren't I trying to get *him* to trust *me* so he'll explain his secrets? It's a zero-sum game at this point. I have to take some risks.

"They took me to the director. He has a new project for me."

Deran's eyes widen, more surprised than concerned. "He's taking you off the fusion machine?"

"No, this is just a side project. As the director phrased it, 'a cleansing of the mental palate' and something to allow my brain to kickstart fresh ideas."

Deran wanders into my office (those legs!) and squeezes his (rather delicious) frame into the chair opposite me. "Is this side project something my team and I will need to work on too?"

"No, it's something I feel unqualified for. I'm still stumped why Cygnus assigned this to me."

"Can you tell me what, or is it confidential?"

The teasing glint in his eyes is more appealing than it should be. I want him to trust me enough to share whatever's bothering him. "No, it's not classified. The director asked me to work on a drug to retrain the minds of people affected by a particular ailment."

Deran's smile drops, and he goes so still, you'd think I'd sprayed him with liquid nitrogen. Worse, his face has lost its openness, and his eyes are now guarded.

"What ailment?"

His voice is so low I would've had to strain to hear the words if he hadn't enunciated each like a curse. Foreboding fills me. Undoubtedly, Deran suspects something he disapproves of.

Since I'm not sure what I have to lose, I answer. "I don't know there's a name for it. Cygnus explained this drug would help people whose minds no longer permit them to comply with basic instructions—to correct the clogged neural pathways from past exposure to toxic air."

Quiet fury boils over Deran's face, spilling onto every other part of him. His muscles strain against themselves, cording his neck, pulling on his jaw to bare his teeth, curling his fingers into balled fists. "And you're sure these people have this 'ailment?'"

What a strange question. "No, I only have what Cygnus told me. I intend to confirm it once I receive the trial data."

"Trials?" Deran snorts like the word is offensive. "Sure, you'll get data. But will you be the one at the source, gathering it?"

Bewildered, I shake my head. "No, that's not how it works. And—"

"Chiara, you can't do this."

The statement is so flat, so final, I gape. "You're telling me to disobey the director?"

I glance nervously around my office, then through the window to the lab outside. I really, *really* hope no one is monitoring this conversation.

As though understanding my fears, Deran shakes his head. "No, I'm saying you should inform him this is not your area of expertise and to find someone more appropriate."

I'm confused by his response. He's approaching the whole situation like he has some personal stake. Although what that is, he hasn't said, nor does it appear likely he'll share here or now either.

"Deran, is there a reason you personally don't want me doing this project?"

This time, Deran scans for those unseen eyes and ears before running an agitated hand through his hair, making those spikes stand more on end than usual. "Look, I just don't think you're the right scientist for this task. Also, you're correct. I do have a personal stake in this. If you're working on a side project, then I'm left to deal with the fusion machine on my own."

I want to burst into laughter and explain I can work on multiple projects at a time, but then the tone of his delivery hits. The falseness of it. He lied to me!

My answer is stiff. "Deran, if you think I'm incapable of multitasking, perhaps you're not the right person to head up the mech team."

Deran's eyes blaze, and I understand why he lied. Not to trick me.

To trick those listening to our conversation. But the knowledge comes too late because I've already infuriated him.

"Chiara, if you think I'll just accept you going off and doing this project, you're mistaken. I'll quit."

Wow! No lies in that last sentence. He's that averse to my new assignment. What I don't get is why. "Can you please explain what's really bugging you about it?"

"I already told you."

His bitter tone declares his unwillingness to discuss it further. But how can I deal with the issue if he won't tell me what it is? My anger sparks. "So, let me get this straight. You want me to go back to the director, after I've already accepted this project, and tell him sorry, I can't do it?"

"Yes, that's exactly what I'm telling you."

Again, no wiggle room in his reply. He's adamant. I try a different tack. "Look, Deran, I know you think a second project might divide my attention, but it won't affect your work. If you explain your other concerns, I'll address those too. I'm not trying to sideline you or the fusion project."

Deran's eyes go flat. "For the second time, I already told you my problem. If you can't accept it, then accept my resignation."

Without a backward glance, Deran turns and stomps out of my office. I'm left staring after him. What in the world was that really about? Did he brush me off because he knows I'm being monitored? Or am I being paranoid? Maybe there isn't more to his reaction than my refusal to accept his explanation.

Then his words register. I rise to run after him, but he's out of sight. I hurry over to the workshop, sure I'll find him there. But Koni hasn't seen Deran in the last hour.

Leaving the workshop, I worry my way through the lab (maybe he stopped to talk to one of my team), back to my office (he came to rescind his resignation), and then down to the cafeteria (maybe he was hungry). I don't find him. Should I go down to the ground floor and ask if he's left the building?

No, that would tell anyone who sent him as a spy that he's getting to me. Still, I have to know. Did Deran really resign?

I try to calm down, telling myself that even if he has quit my project, he wouldn't have left CC. I'll still see him. But all this "calming" does is clear the flotsam polluting the waters.

Until this very moment, I hadn't realized how much I'd come to lean on Deran. More appalling, how much I've been enjoying his company. Sure, I was ogling him the whole time, but I thought it was from a distance.

It hasn't been as distant as I thought. His appeal has infiltrated the defenses I believed so impenetrable. I almost can't imagine my daily grind without his smile brightening my day, reassuring me along every step of the project. Without him, what will I do?

The bleak prospect dampens my mood further. Unable to face the thought of work and restless to boot, I head down to the gym and change. Annoyed with myself for flirting with danger, then being surprised when I got burned, I stride over to the treadmill, convinced an extreme workout will clear my mind.

I spend energy frenetically, the tension gradually easing as I run. I'm on the treadmill for twenty minutes before I've liberated my mind sufficiently to think clearly again. Rejuvenated, I sprint on, eager for further release. Bored with the treadmill, I hop onto the circuit, relishing the punishment I dole out to my body as I fine-tune the solutions I've devised. By the time I start my cooldown, my limbs quiver.

Sweaty after the intense workout, I check the time as I angle toward the locker rooms. Too late to remedy the first situation I wanted to address. It's long past the hour Deran would've gone home. But I can address another situation, and I don't have to do it here. It's late enough I can leave and enjoy the luxury of my own bathroom today.

I don't bother switching my clothes again, just nip up to the lab to collect my things, take a spin through the workshop to be sure Deran isn't there (even though I know he won't be), and then exit CC HQ to catch the trundle home.

My spa-like shower further restores my serenity, and when I finally slump onto the couch, I'm ready for a movie. But the hard lines of the couch annoy me more than usual. After the day I've had, I want something more comfortable.

With a huff, I go to my room, where I toss on clothes more presentable than my sweats. Then I plop down on the edge of my bed and haul my gym bag out from under it, retrieving Ferret from his hiding spot in the bag's lining. Time to test the chards I created.

Despite the size difference, I slap Ferret over the top of the first chard and initiate a transfer from my bank account. As expected, Ferret completes the transaction without a hitch. Grinning, I tap his sturdy casing and congratulate him.

Then I carefully tuck Ferret back into his place behind the panel under the sink, before heading out the door. Finding what I'm looking for takes a few stops along the trundle's route, hopping off, exploring, then hopping back on.

The thrift store is tucked away in an insignificant strip mall a few blocks from the main mall most people support. But it has exactly what I'm after. The couch is in near-perfect condition, the padding still thick, the toffee-colored synth leather soft and warm to the touch with no rips marring its supple surface.

I haggle with the store owner until we reach a mutually acceptable sum. Then I wand the chard over the scanner, careful to conceal its size from the vendor. But the man is more interested in his screen, watching for the money coming through. This is the moment of truth. I hold my breath as the transaction processes.

When the computer beeps, I want to break into a happy dance. *Yes! It went through!* I can't keep the grin off my face. I think the store owner is second-guessing our agreed price as he misinterprets my jubilation—but I'm thrilled with my purchase. For more reasons than one. Primarily, I've verified my chards work. Not only that, I've also scored a cushy couch.

With grunted orders and a sour expression, the store owner directs his underlings to carry the couch outside. I follow, then arrange for collection and delivery, waiting next to the couch until the drones arrive.

The longer I wait, the more I sweat. I'm half-expecting SerSents to drag me off, my chards somehow alerting the authorities to their lack of authenticity. I remind myself the drones take time because they're in high demand, despite the exorbitant fees charged to use them. Also, their numbers are limited, something I now understand since they drain our limited energy supply. The reminders do little to quell my fears.

An excruciating eighty-three minutes and forty-two seconds later, the drones buzz down, blades whirring audibly as they hover overhead. Ready to collapse with relief, I send the code verifying I'm the client through my comm link, and they zoom down. The smaller drones shoot bands under the couch, which the larger drones catch and connect to their cargo hooks. The whole pickup takes less than five minutes. Then they soar back into the sky and whiz away, my couch cradled in their mechanical arms.

Exhilarated, I begin my return journey. By the time I get home, the drones are long gone, but the couch waits for me in the secure pickup zone on the roof. Wanding my arm over the access panel, I release the hold and summon the building's droids (how much will this couch cost?) to help me get the furniture into my apartment.

Getting the "old" couch out is problematic for the droids, who end up removing and then replacing my front door to make it work. Honestly, if I didn't know better (yes, I saw Sarissa's apartment and all the furniture she'd bought), I would've thought whoever provided the apartment furnishings didn't want their tenants replacing their things.

But finally, the old is out, and the new is in, and I close the door on the droids as they shunt the hated designer couch away to wherever the owner keeps such things.

With a satisfied smile, I sink into the plush leather, feeling inordinately proud of myself. My first piece of furniture, bought and paid for with my own money. Admittedly, only so I could test my chards and have a reason for the withdrawal, but my first "adult" purchase.

Which reminds me. I retrieve Ferret and use a few keystrokes to hack the bank. I change the description on the withdrawal to the name of a furniture dealer renowned for their expensive inventory.

Satisfied the odd withdrawal amount, the fake transaction name, and my new couch "evidencing" the purchase will confirm I used my bank account and not chards, I relax back into the couch's inviting curves. At last! Time to watch the movie I've been yearning for all evening.

After all my shenanigans, I end up falling asleep in the middle of the movie. I'm pleasantly surprised when I wake the next morning to the sun warming me through the films on my windows, having slept all the way through the night on my new purchase.

I'm even more pleased when I stretch and find no aches or pains. Tickled anew, I run through the morning basics, sans a shower since I took care of that last night. I'm out the door earlier than usual. I won't admit it was so I could hunt Deran down at work and iron things out between us.

But I'm disappointed when I don't find him. His team informs me they haven't seen him. More troubling, no one seems to know if or when he'll be back.

Worried, I return to my office. While Deran's team assured me they could continue without him, I don't want any mistakes. They could prove disastrous, especially with the new task Cygnus has assigned me. I can't oversee things in Deran's absence. Not that I would know what I was doing. I'm many things, but not a mechanical engineer.

I open a comm window and send a message to Hag Lady, asking

for a meeting with Cygnus. If I'm going to tell him running this side project is a bad idea, I'd better get it out of the way.

Message sent, I stare at my screen, debating what to do next. I've accomplished only a single thing (yes, showers are important!) on the list I came up with while running in the gym last night. The message to Hag Lady doesn't really count as declining the project, but at least I've made a start. More than I can say about my hopes of reconciling with Deran.

Until I hear from Hag Lady, I suppose I should at least look like I'm tackling the problem. This way, I'll have tried and failed, and Cygnus will see reason.

I only know time has passed because Tandize knocks on my door and asks if I'd like to join her and the others for lunch. While I accept, it's more because I need to eat than to spend time with my team. Besides, I'm still leery of Tandize after her reluctance to share the truth with me.

Then, halfway through lunch, I realize I'm possibly being biased and decide to run an experiment. Maybe Tandize isn't senior enough to share the information. I turn to Benita, the oldest member of my team and in the labs the longest. As casually as I can, I say, "It was quite something having those upper level security people in the lab yesterday."

Benita shuts down. I shouldn't be startled, but I am. More unsettling, she rises, making an excuse about having to get back to work. I stare after her as she scuttles away, more determined than ever. In five minutes, I've approached three other team members, all with similar results.

No one will discuss the upper level security people. They won't even let me get past my opening sentence. Without fail, they make some excuse to leave without discussing the men. Or men and women, for all I know.

Curiosity satisfied, I lean back in my chair, contemplating the reason.

I feel better about Deran's response. At least he had the grace to grimace about the lie. Where is he? The thought helps me decide my own meal is over. Rising, I bid the others farewell before hurrying back to my office.

As if my thoughts conjured him from the netherworld he's been holed up in since yesterday, I find him sitting in the chair outside my office. My heart skips a beat, and I almost trip over my own feet. Seeing him is heaven.

Serious eyes regard me as I reach him without further mishap. When I do, I stop in front of him, absorbing the quiet storm in those eyes. Turbulent cumulonimbus clouds streaking across a wild gray sky.

"Hello, Chiara."

"Hello, Deran."

His tone turns dry. "I was wondering if I'd have to rescue you from yourself the way you stumbled in. Drinking over lunch, were you?"

I'm so floored by his question, a startled giggle sneaks out. Well, more a cross between a snort and something less ladylike, followed by a nervous giggle. I grin. "For a moment, I thought you were serious!"

The smile breaking across his handsome face has my stomach doing silly little flip-flops. I've missed that smile. Has it only been a day since I last saw it? *Oh dear, I'm in trouble, aren't I?*

"Yes, because you're exactly the sort of person who would."

The warm humor in his voice soothes, and I relax. "Care to come into my parlor?"

Deran raises an eyebrow. "Oh, I don't know. Will the spider eat the fly?"

This time, a full-on belly laugh comes out. Eyes crinkling at the corners, Deran laughs too. Just like that, my world is spinning on its axis again.

We enter my office, and I take a seat, offering him one when he remains standing. But he shakes his head. "No, I need to stand for this. Chiara, I'm sorry about yesterday. I was unreasonable. Please, let me make it up to you. How about a picnic with me tomorrow?"

For a moment, I can only stare. The words have so many undercurrents I don't know which one to isolate first. Then I realize it doesn't matter. He just wants me to get the gist for now.

"That sounds delightful! I'd love a picnic. And yes, apology accepted. But," I raise a finger, "only if you have picalillies on the menu."

Deran guffaws. "Picalillies? Seriously? You eat those disgusting things?"

I sniff, looking down my nose at him. "What's wrong with chocolate-covered popcorn?"

Shaking his head, Deran sputters, "Chiara, it's for kids!"

"So? You eat gummy worms."

More laughter. "Point taken. Fine, I promise I'll find some picalillies and bring them with."

"In that case, I agree. Is there anything you'd like me to bring?"

Deran looks pained. "Now what sort of apology would it be if I expected you to contribute? No, just yourself. I'll message you the time and place."

I nod, aware this is a further way to conceal our destination. It's comforting to confirm I'm not paranoid, that I'm not the only one worrying about those unseen eyes and ears.

"Excellent. See you later, then. I must go check on my team."

With a smile and wave, he saunters out. Yes, I watch every inch of his far-too-attractive frame all the way out of sight. A smile on my face, I turn back to what I was working on.

It drops when I see the message from Hag Lady.

Chiara, The director is unavailable. Send your concerns to me, and I'll pass them on.

The email isn't even signed. Arrogant woman! I bet she'd love to know what I want to talk to Cygnus about. I notice she doesn't say she'll get back to me with a reply. No, if I want to talk to Cygnus, I'll have to engineer a reason for him to contact me. Grimly, I begin working on a solution. And no, I don't bother thanking Hag Lady.

The rest of the afternoon passes quickly, most of it consumed by questions from my team, who have miraculously recovered from their earlier "inability" to talk to me. When I next look, it's way past the end of the workday.

My bidding the team goodnight nudges them on their own way

home. I leave them dribbling out of the lab and hurry over to the workshop to check on the prototype's progress, hoping to catch another glimpse of Deran.

But the workshop is as dark as it is lifeless. Whether it's the black room or the echoing emptiness, a tiny ripple of fear abruptly sends icy waves surging through me. I haven't yet received any comms from Deran about our picnic tomorrow. Did someone figure out we were trying to bypass their monitoring and cart him away to some atrocious fate?

Visions of Deran hauled off by those scary "upper level security" people assail me. Although I try to shut them down, the fear is rampant now. I sprint back to my office. Can I do anything? I consider messaging him, but wouldn't I look needy if he simply hasn't had time to send his own message yet?

Difficult as it is, I resist the urge to comm him, trying to quash my squirrelly fear as I exit the building. The day's dying sun streaks the azure sky, painting the edges of the clouds with gold and rose and lilac. But tonight, my overactive imagination won't allow me to enjoy nature's spectacular display.

I lurch onto the trundle, hunching down in my seat and tucking my hands into the pocket of my jacket. A scrap of paper is tucked into the left pocket.

I didn't put it there. I'm too forgetful. Too many times I've ruined my jackets because I left ink- or chemical-stained sheets in my pockets. I've made it a habit now to keep such things in my hand until I can transfer them to my tablet, or the tray on my desk.

My fingers curl around the paper, wanting to keep it safe. Because the only other person with reason to leave a note there is Deran. Relief courses through me. He hasn't been abducted and subjected to torture. I just misunderstood.

When he said he'd message me, he didn't say how. I was the one who assumed. But if he's using a good, old-fashioned unhackable method for his message, does this mean he doesn't even consider our comm links safe?

That thought is disturbing in the extreme. I mentally run through all the messages with Sarissa—back when she was my friend, at least. How much did I reveal to her, or her handlers, in some of those insanely personal communications?

Aware I'll drive myself into a frenzy again with these thoughts, I stop the deluge. I won't have actual answers until I speak with Deran tomorrow. No reason to work myself up over something that may end up being nothing.

Although I attempt ignoring the panic still swirling like a rip current, it drags me under, and my breathing quickens. But tides and currents remind me of Deran's word choices earlier today when he invited me on the picnic.

With deep breaths, I calm the waters, simultaneously replaying Deran's words in my mind. The first thing he did was apologize for yesterday—but his explanation for being unreasonable indicated he believed neither he nor I were the "unreasonable" ones. And that word...

I call up my dictionary and check the definition. Yes, as I thought. Deran was using the less obvious "beyond the limits of acceptability or fairness" definition. His choice of this word and his tone caught my attention—and it was his way of alerting me to be careful. His sign that all might not be as it seemed.

Then his statement that he wanted to make it up to me. With hindsight, I can see he meant he would explain a lot more than his behavior. Or am I just reading what I want into his words? No, if I was, he would have no reason to invite me on a picnic. An obvious way of telling me we needed to discuss things away from CC HQ.

Most telling of all is his note. While I'm dying to rip it out of my pocket and read it, that would defeat his attempts at keeping the details secret. The note literally burns a hole in my palm as I finger it.

Realizing my hands are sweating and fearing I may smudge his words, I remove my hands from my pockets and stare out the window. But the vistas beyond don't distract me from my thoughts as they usually do. Even the journey home seems tedious today.

Finally, it's my stop, and I leap out, then sprint all the way home. Since this isn't the first time, my behavior won't seem too bizarre.

Then I'm inside my apartment, and I snatch the note from my pocket the moment I've dropped my bag.

Chiara, apologies for the clandestine message. I appreciate you have questions. I will do my best to answer them tomorrow, 10 a.m. at Northsummit Park. ~ Deran.

I reread the message. Okay, time and place are set. Deran better come with his A-game. He said he would answer my questions—but he has no clue how many I have.

37

After spending an inordinate amount of time choosing a pretty turquoise sundress instead of my usual jeans and t-shirt, I leave my apartment and take a circuitous route to the park. If Deran went to such extraordinary lengths with a concealed, handwritten note, doing likewise when heading for our rendezvous seems only prudent.

A little late by the time I finally reach the park, I realize my detours took longer than expected. But I believe I did the best I could with no training in subverting the attempts of others hoping to follow me. Of course, I can't be certain I don't have a tail because I don't even know what to look for besides the obvious.

As I enter the park, I hurry. Deran didn't tell me *where* in the park we'd meet. A problem since Northsummit Park is the biggest recreational space in Cirrian. How will I find him?

I'm about to comm him when I remember his aversion to this method of communication. Now what? I stand at the park entrance, lost, wishing I'd thought to enter the park using the main entrance. Would Deran be expecting me there?

I turn, about to head in that direction, when a hand touches my arm. I whirl, heart stuttering, expecting a SerSent. Instead, Deran's intense gray eyes meet mine. Summer rainclouds shot through with lightning, reflecting the gravity of this meeting.

Then he smiles, and the clouds disappear, the silver in his eyes shining through. The transformation is so startling I drop my eyes to his chest. Only for them to land on his black synth leather jacket, emphasizing broad shoulders, and jeans showing just how long his legs are. I swallow, mouth suddenly dry. Did I forget how attractive he was?

As Deran absorbs my reaction, his mouth curves into a wicked grin. "Hello, Chiara. You look lovely today."

Flustered, I manage a mumbled, "Hi."

Grin fading, Deran's eyes reluctantly leave mine to sweep the immediate area. When he finds (or notices the lack of) whatever he was looking for, his eyes crinkle again. "If you took the precautions I think you did, thank you."

I nod, words forsaking me when he snags my hand in the one not holding the picnic basket. His hand is warm, his grip strong. Through our linked fingers, I feel the steady beat of his heart in his pulse. I want to stay there, simply marveling at how such a tiny amount of contact can bring so much reassurance.

But Deran's towing me along beside him, and there's no time for fascination. Giddy with nerves and excitement, I allow him to lead me where he will. A little breathless, I remember to ask my earlier question. "How did you know I'd use that entrance?"

Deran looks down at me, puzzled. "You're not serious, right?" It takes only a second to realize I am. "Oh. Um..."

Sentence unfinished, his brow furrows. I'm immediately annoyed. Unprepared when I halt, the abrupt movement swings Deran around through our linked hands. I get in his face. "You were the one who invited me on this picnic. Also the one who said he'd answer my questions. Don't start reevaluating what you can and can't tell me."

Deran shakes his head, eager to dispel my anger. "No, it's not like that. I was trying to decide where to start. There's so much you don't know. Also, before I blab, you should understand the risks."

"Really? As if a handwritten note smuggled into one of my pockets didn't signal how serious this is. You don't think if I wasn't scared off by now, I won't be?"

While Deran laughs, the sound is bitter. "Oh, Chiara, you have no idea!"

"So tell me."

With a quick shake of his head, Deran scans the surrounding area. "Not here. Let's get to where we're going first."

I snap my mouth shut at the command in his tone, peeved. I'm not two years old. He doesn't need to put me in my place. Then I realize he may only be taking these precautions for my benefit, and the sting recedes.

The insight also makes me realize how combative I'm being. If my first reaction is to go to war on every new topic he raises, I won't learn much. I should allow him some leeway. Freed by the decision, my blinders fall away. Enough that I want to bolt when I register how close Deran is.

Using our linked fingers, he's drawn me nearer than I would normally allow. His scent teases my heightened senses further. A potent combination of leather and sandalwood, the intoxicating blend is pure male. I sniff again, wanting more.

Deran glances at me. "What are you doing?"

Mortified, I scramble for a reply. But my addled brain fails me. "Nothing," I mutter. I glimpse the smile he tries to hide by turning his head. What must he think of me?

Whatever is on his mind, it's not discouraging. Deran maintains our hectic pace, leading me to a quiet, secluded area bordering the forests surrounding the park. I've never noticed these little hidden indentations before.

Then again, I haven't spent much time here. Northsummit Park is almost all the way across the city, and I seldom venture far from my assigned sectors. Although this park is open to all tiers, it's so distant, it rarely comes to mind as a place to visit.

While Deran pulls a blanket from the basket and spreads it on the grass, I take time to look around. The trees (I don't know their names) form a cozy bower here, the canopy of leaves and walls of living wood providing only a narrow opening back to the rest of the park. If a person didn't know this spot was here, it would be easy to overlook.

The park beyond our private space is wide and open, and a nearby lake glimmers through the trees. Certainly worth exploring further. Making a mental note to use this park for my next long run, I smile when Deran takes my hand and leads me onto the blanket.

My smile turns into a laugh. A bowl of picalillies is positioned prominently in the center of the blanket. "You remembered!"

Deran grins. "I did. I only hope you'll appreciate the lengths I went to hunting them down."

"Oh, I'm sorry!" Since my giggles would signal otherwise, I rein in my mirth. "Were they a hassle?"

Deran shrugs. "Anything worth having is worth spending time on."

Flustered for a second time, I'm not sure what to make of his answer, so I pretend there is no clandestine meaning and hide my sudden uncertainty by pretending to find a comfortable place on the blanket.

Because, of course, now I'm worried Deran invited me here for more romantic reasons. No, "worried" isn't the right word. Romantic reasons would be more than okay with me. Except I'd be disappointed because I thought this picnic was… what?

An apology? A way for him to give me answers? Or a means for me to get to him so I can learn what he's been hiding? The ugly truth of my own potential motives makes me squirm. Why, oh why, didn't I think this through before I agreed to his picnic?

Because the last thing I thought this meeting would be was the prelude to a romance. No, I'm still not being honest with myself. Didn't I want romance?

"What are you thinking?"

Deran's question is so unexpected, I jump. I'd forgotten I wasn't alone. My eyes fly up to find him studying me. "Why did you invite me?"

A little exasperated, Deran runs his fingers through his hair several times. By the time he finally answers, the spikes on top of his head are (adorably) more on end than ever. "Would it be so terrible if I said I had more than just an apology in mind?"

My mind stutters at the revelation. As he watches me with wary eyes, I can almost touch the tension radiating off him. Does he think he might scare me off with this confession? Or is he concerned I might not feel the same way? For once in my life, I understand before I speak how much weight my answer will carry. For this reason, I choose my words carefully.

"No, it wouldn't." I pause, then glance up at him from under my lashes. "Because... is it okay to say I'm on this picnic for ulterior motives too?"

Tension evaporating, he laughs and takes my hand in his. "Have I ever told you I find you refreshingly honest?"

I'm more interested in his hand holding mine than his question. The contact is electric, precluding thoughts of all else for a few dazzling seconds. Then the sensation subsides as my body adjusts to the contact, and I realize he's waiting for an answer.

I grin. "Oh, I don't know about that. I've been subversive a time or two."

Deran's eyes grow serious again, and I wish I hadn't tried flirting since his mind is clearly on other things. "Yes, as I'm sure you've had to be sometimes." Then, seeing the effect his change in demeanor has on me, he nudges the bowl of picalillies closer. "You know, I didn't scour three malls to find these for you to not eat any."

In keeping with his attempt at lightening the mood, I set my questions aside for the time being and dip my free hand into the bowl. "To honor your endeavors, I won't let even one picalilly go to waste." I pop the pieces into my mouth one at a time, savoring each kernel, much to Deran's amusement.

He's still grinning when he releases my hand (did he have to?) so he can tug a thermos from the basket, then two mugs. "Would you like tea to go with those disgusting things?"

"Yes, please!"

Obligingly, he fills a mug, then hands it over before pouring one for himself. We sit next to each other, cross-legged, sipping our tea in companionable silence as we enjoy the sunshine and fresh air. But finally, it's time. I dust my hands together, freeing sugar and salt, then accept the wet washcloth Deran offers.

"You thought of everything, didn't you?"

Sensing my change in mood, Deran sighs. He retrieves a small music player from the basket and places it on the blanket, setting the player a short way from us but turning the volume all the way up. I raise an eyebrow.

Deran flashes that smile I can't resist, and my heart skips faster. Then he leans closer. "You can still hear me, right?"

My eyes widen. "Yes. But how?"

"An audio modifier. It allows sound less than eight feet directly behind the unit to function as normal. Go beyond that range, or in any other direction, and you'll get the full effect of the music instead."

I glance around, understanding his reasons. But we're alone. Still, I whisper. "You've had to use something like this before?"

"No, but considering what I planned to share with you today, I didn't want to take any chances. I built it last night."

My mouth pops open, and I close it, thinking of Ferret. I built him in a less than a day too, didn't I? "Proves my point."

"Which was?"

"You thought of everything."

Deran shakes his head. "Not everything. There are some things I haven't thought of—or, rather, found solutions to." He studies me, expression serious. "You're sure you want to know what I have to tell you?"

I nod, sudden nerves drying my throat despite the tea I just drank.

"You understand once you know these things, your life will change forever? That this information will put you in danger, perhaps mortal danger, and there's no going back once you have it?"

I take a deep breath. "Deran, I've never been more sure of anything in my life. For as long as I can remember, I've felt like something's wrong, but I've never been able to get a handle on it. Every time I've asked questions, I've been shut down." It's my turn to take his hand.

"You're the first person who's ever been willing to share the truth with me. You'll never know how grateful I am."

Deran glances down at our joined hands. "Chiara, do you understand why I invited you on this picnic?"

"So you could apologize and fix things between us?"

"Yes, yes, of course. But also so the cameras—you know there are surveillance cameras in CC HQ, right?"

"I suspected as much." Curiously, he doesn't mention cameras outside CC HQ. Does that mean all this time I've thought there were, it was just my imagination?

He continues before I can ponder the matter further. "Then you understand why we must appear to mend fences—so it won't look suspicious, should they observe us working together on things?"

"Um, aren't we already working together?"

"On more than they think we are," Deran amends.

"Such as?"

When Deran laughs, the tension leaves his face, and I stop breathing. I'm more conscious than ever of our joined hands, our proximity.

"Easy, Tiger. You're trying to run before you can walk. We'll get to answering all your questions in due course. Let's start with the basics and work from there, alright?"

I huff out a sigh. "Why can't we just discuss things as they come up?"

There's that guarded look again. Deran runs a hand through his hair before catching himself and dropping the hand. Then he wriggles on the blanket, scooting around to face me, our knees touching. This would distract me, except he grips my biceps gently, looking into my eyes and holding my gaze with his.

"Look, I don't want you to feel like I'm hiding things. But there's so much you don't know. I've debated long and hard about telling you any of this. Part of me still feels you may be safer not knowing."

My shoulders hunch, and my fingers curl into fists. "I disagree."

Deran releases a pent-up breath, hands dropping away as he leans back. "Yes, I thought you'd feel that way, no matter how much I might try dissuade you. Hence the picnic. But," he cautions, tone serious, "we're doing this my way and in my timing. I don't want you freaking out."

His words chill me. For the first time, I truly grasp the immensity of what he's doing. The impossibility of it. If no one else was willing to share what they knew, what will it cost Deran?

"Will this make trouble for you?"

There's that mirthless laugh again. "What do you think?"

"Oh." I have no other words. I never thought Deran giving me answers would put him at risk. Now I'm not so sure I want to do this.

Deran understands my predicament. He takes my hands in his again. "I know what you're thinking—that you don't want to put me in danger. But, Chiara, no matter what you do or don't do, what you do or don't know, understand any danger is because *I* chose to put myself in that position. Not you."

I search his face, finding sincerity. Still, a part of me doesn't quite believe I'll be blameless should something happen to him. "Deran, I don't know. If it was just me—"

He cuts me off. "I know. Believe me, I know. But it *is* just you. I'm the only one who can make this decision, who can act on it. You're not holding a gun to my head."

I reel back, but don't escape his grip. "Don't say such things."

"I'm sorry, you're right. But I want you to understand, to be clear on this point before we move forward. Accept this is my decision and, if anything happens, it's on me, or you'll get no information."

Conflicted, I take a moment to process. If I agree and something happens to Deran, can I live with that? Can I really believe it was his choice?

Conversely, the selfish part of me screams for answers, desperate to sway my decision. Deran is the only one who's ever been prepared to answer my questions. Not even Sarissa would. I close my eyes, praying I'm not making a mistake. "Okay. Tell me."

38

Deran takes this to mean I understand and accept his terms. I only hope I know what I've agreed to. That this decision won't ever come back and bite me in the butt.

"Very well. To reiterate, you understand I brought you here, to this park, so we could speak away from HQ where they might record our discussions?"

"Yes. Is that why you sent a paper message—or because you think they monitor our comm links?"

Deran barks a surprised laugh. "You are paranoid, aren't you?" When I don't smile, he grimaces. "Chiara, our comm links have insane encryption. So, no, I don't think they're monitored, and yes, the paper message was so anyone watching us at CC HQ wouldn't know where or when we were meeting."

Somewhat relieved to discover not all my personal issues were aired for the world to hear, I still shudder at the possibility. The thought of Cygnus listening to my deepest secrets has me wanting reassurance. "To confirm, you left the note to avoid the cameras in CC HQ, not because you think they monitor our comm link conversations?"

"Yes." Deran eyes me as one would a skittish rabbit.

"Chill! I'm not about to run off screaming."

A smile quirks his lips. Lips I'd like to touch. With more than just my fingers. I blush at the unexpected thought. How can I be thinking of romance with such serious matters at stake?

Deran's smile widens, a gleam entering those fascinating eyes. "Now what's on your mind?"

My blush deepens. "You really don't want to know."

"Oh, I really do."

How do I tell him I was thinking about kissing him? I giggle nervously. "Honestly, please don't make me tell you."

He laughs, the sound rich. That he can laugh so freely at a time like this is astounding. His mirth is infectious, and soon, I'm laughing too. But our amusement dwindles, then dies, the pressure of my countless questions smothering the flames of our joy as effectively as carbon dioxide.

Deran sighs, looks skyward, then delivers his first blow. "I brought you here because it's far from the mindhunters."

Air leaves my body. Deran's last word sticks in my brain. My blood congeals at the mention of the name. Before I ask, I already know the answer. "That's what those 'upper level security' people are really called?"

"Yes. Although the name hardly does justice to their skills."

"Which are?" My words are a whisper, barely stirring the air between us, but he hears me.

"Chiara, they all have enhanced abilities. Some of them can even sift through people's thoughts, hunting out those who would subvert the conglomerate. Which is why you *must* understand your thoughts aren't safe. From now on, guard your mind. Your life depends on it."

I digest his words, a million questions clamoring for attention. "Tell me more about these mindhunters. And how I shield my thoughts. I've never heard of such a thing. Is that even possible?"

"I'll start with shielding your thoughts, since that's the easier question to answer."

"Hmm, are you sure you don't have that the wrong way around?"

"No, only because protecting your mind, as you pointed out, is an unknown. From my limited experience, it takes time and practice. However, we can't know we're succeeding until we find out we've done it incorrectly the hard way."

While Deran doesn't elaborate, his meaning is clear. If the mindhunters get you, you weren't doing it right. Lovely. "How do you *think* you shield your thoughts?"

"I can only tell you what's worked for me—so far."

"Which is?"

"Numbers. I count them, add them, multiply them. Whatever it takes, numbers only. No matter if someone asks a question or tackles me to the floor."

A giggle escapes. "Tackles you to the floor?"

"You never know what you might have to fortify yourself against." Deran's smile doesn't touch his eyes. "That did actually happen to me once, but it was an accident. The mindhunters were leaping for someone else and got me instead."

"You're kidding!"

"I wish."

"That couldn't have been fun."

"It wasn't. Have you seen the size of those people?"

Deran's pained expression provides hilarious mental images, and I chuckle. "They're impossible to miss. I take it 'people' means there are women in their ranks too?"

"Yes. Beware. They're meaner than the men."

"I'll remember that. You said you use numbers, so what I usually do to distract myself from myself should work."

Deran laughs. "That sounded weird, but I understand. What's your usual tactic?"

"Reciting chemical formulas, doing calculus in my head, that sort of thing."

Another rumble of laughter. "I should've known."

I grin, giving it a minute, but when he doesn't speak, I can't help myself. "So, are you going to tell me more about the mindhunters? Who they are?"

When Deran's face tenses again, I wish I'd left it alone. The morning is turning out to be a rollercoaster of emotional highs and lows. I admit, if this is a date, I wouldn't have expected these kinds of questions. Then again, how can we truly get to know one another if a wall of lies separates us before we even begin? A weary breath slips out.

Deran gives me a friendly nudge with his shoulder. "That was a gigantic sigh. I don't suppose you want to share the reason for it either?"

Recognizing I must share things of my own eventually, and that this is a safer topic than the last, I shake my head. "No, I'll tell you. I'd like to get to know you better. But you obviously have information I don't, so it's only right we deal with the lies I've been told first."

"You'd like to get to know me better? Seriously?"

His teasing tone has me giggling again. Then a loathsome blush colors my face for the… (ugh! I've lost count!) time today. "Yes." I lower my eyes to the blanket and run a finger down a line in the pattern.

Deran catches my hand, lifts my hand to his mouth, and kisses it. The gesture is so retro, so chivalrous, I'm stunned.

But the sweetness of the moment isn't lost on me. I glimpse the boy he must've been, and in an instant, my shyness disappears. I'm not the only one who's uncertain here.

While Deran appears to be a man of the world, nothing makes you quite as vulnerable as letting someone know you like them. Because they could turn around and dismiss you without further thought.

No, scratch that. I'm projecting. As I think it through, I realize he's more worried about moving too fast and me running away before we have a chance at a relationship than any uncertainty about his feelings for me. Little does he know—understanding his own mind just makes him more attractive.

"Do that again," I breathe, smiling when he does. His face transforms in his grin as he kisses my hand a second time. I allow myself to soak in the sensations his gesture invokes. Light and warmth and desire. That last one catches me off guard, and I inhale sharply.

"What?"

Deran's eyes are startled, unsure. I lift a finger of the hand he still holds near his mouth and run it down his jaw. "Nothing. I was just surprised."

Relief, then humor, flit across that handsome face. "Whew! I thought I'd missed a piece shaving this morning and scratched you with some stubble."

His comment is so unexpected, a laugh burbles out. Then we're both chuckling before the moment passes, and Deran sighs.

"Right, let's continue. Understand, I've never explained all this to anyone before, so stop me if you have questions. Also, it may come out a little jumbled with so much to tell, so don't get upset if I miss a few details."

I only hear him giving me permission to ask questions. "Please, please, tell me who the mindhunters are!"

"Yes, Miss Impatient. That's not a simple answer. Mindhunters have elected to elevate their standing in society."

"You mean increase their tier level?"

"Yes."

Disbelieving, I shake my head. "I've heard people can do that, but never seen it happen."

"Because it's a rare occurrence. However, should you elect to become a mindhunter, you're automatically elevated to tier eight. Or rather, what equates to tier eight, since mindhunters are only lower than tiers nine and ten."

"Tier *eight?*" My voice is high and squeaky. "I've never heard of anyone skipping tiers, let alone jumping to tier eight!"

"Well, it's not officially a tier, but because they have authority over any tier lower than nine or ten, most people agree that makes them an eight."

"Alrighty! An eight then." I blow out a breath, then almost hesitate before my next question. "What do they have to do to get there?"

Deran studies me, then nods. "You're not as oblivious as you seem."

"Pardon?"

"Apparently, you've worked out they have to sell their souls to achieve such a radical change in ranking."

"Common sense, really. So, do they?"

Deran shrugs. "I don't know. People who choose to become mind-hunters are subjected to a process—and there are plenty of rumors about the process's safety. Mostly because anyone who agrees to it is often never seen or heard from again by those they love."

I open my mouth to interrupt, but he raises a hand.

"Yes, there are also rumors these 'disappearances' happen because the mindhunters are transferred to other cities, but no one really knows what's true."

Questions swirl, and I pick the one rising to the top. "They're subjected to a process?"

Deran grins, wonder in his eyes. "How did you get there so fast?"

"Pardon?" This time, I really am confused.

"In all that information, all you heard was process. You know how many people overlook that?" I shake my head, but he doesn't notice. "Everyone thinks it's just some test or exam or training. If only they knew."

39

I sit up straighter. "Deran, are you just going to dangle the bait or tell me what it is?"

Deran regards me for a long time before he answers. "What I'm about to tell you is something I don't think anyone except the CC brass knows. Perhaps only Cygnus. And the people who perform the process."

I reach for his hand, needing contact, reassurance. Despite my apprehension, I want answers, no matter how heinous. "Carry on."

"Mindhunters have those special abilities because they have tech in their heads."

I draw a blank. "Don't we all have tech in our heads? I mean, with our comm links?"

"No, this is completely different. Our comm links are tiny capsules that only link peripherally. When people say becoming a mindhunter is a process, they don't understand it's actually a surgical procedure. They put you under and hack into your brain to implant an invasive piece of hardware."

My brain boggles, and I latch onto only one word. "Invasive?"

"How do you think normal people turn into those cold automatons you've encountered lately? No, those implants don't only give the mindhunters their abilities—they change them."

I sit in stunned silence. Finally, a question squeaks out. "Do you think some people are never seen again because it's such a barbaric procedure, it fails, and the people die?"

Deran closes his eyes for a moment before answering. His face is bleak. "I don't know, but surgeries don't always go as planned, so it's a possibility."

I frown. "You'd think with all the rumors, people wouldn't want to subject themselves to the risk."

"If they knew it was a surgery, more of them might. But as it is, it's just this mysterious 'process.' The only downside, as far as they're concerned, is the chance you may never see your loved ones again— which isn't a deterrent if you have none."

"That's depressing."

"I agree. But if you knew how some people lived, you'd understand."

My mind spins back to Sam and the other cleaners I inadvertently spotted that night when I got home so late. Despite my attempts at befriending them, I've never seen them since. "No, I understand how it might be attractive to some."

Deran cocks his head. "Care to explain?"

I do, and Deran's face is granite by the time I finish.

"Yes, you have an idea."

"Perhaps you can answer another question I have while we're on the subject." This is the perfect time to confirm a few things.

Deran cocks an eyebrow.

"How come there are people like Sam cleaning my building but bots cleaning my lab?"

"I think you can figure that one out." Deran's hand squeezes mine, encouraging, but his eyes search for something.

"What? What are you looking for?"

A quick shrug. "I'll tell you when I see it."

His words are an eerie reminder of that off-kilter meeting with Cygnus, where he had me so disoriented I even forgot his usual greeting. Suddenly desperate for an answer, I grip Deran's hand like a vise. "No, tell me now."

A long exhale. "You sure know how to ask the tough questions."

I wait, before realizing silence won't work on Deran. "Please?"

Gloriously muscled shoulders tensing and relaxing as he considers. Then bright gray eyes capturing my own. "Chiara, can I decide the best order you should learn things in?"

My own shoulders tense, spine going rigid. "Why?"

Deran thinks for a minute. "Math builds on itself, right?"

I nod, not sure I like where he's going.

"Well, the information you want, it's the same. If I rush on and tell you some things ahead of others, you won't understand."

My jaw clenches, but I get it. Doesn't mean I'm happy. "So hurry up and tell me things then."

Deran chuckles. "And we're back to Miss Impatient."

I scowl, snatching my hand free, and crossing my arms. "I don't like that name."

Deran only laughs harder. Infectious as his laugh is, I find my lips twitching. Although I don't want to succumb, I do, until I'm laughing with him again.

Unexpectedly, Deran's hand touches my face. "That's better."

About to reply, I stop, waiting for the drone as it buzzes noisily overhead. In an instant, several memories coalesce. "Oh!"

Deran grins. "What startling revelation just came to you?"

"I understand now. About the bots and Sam, I mean."

"Continue."

"Tiers. It has to do with tiers."

"What about them?"

"The higher your tier, the more money you earn. The more you earn, the more you can afford. That's why drones are so expensive! They're meant only for the higher tiers." I turn to him, eyes bright. "CC has cleaning bots because they can pay for them."

"They also keep their mouths shut."

Yes, confirmation! Then a mental image flashes of those cleaning bots with little tin mouths welded shut, and I giggle. "Indeed, they do."

"Do I even want to know what went through your mind just then?"

Still grinning, I shake my head. "No, it's not important." Then I sober. "But that's also why there are people like Sam. Because not everyone can afford drones or bots. And it gives people like him work when there would otherwise be none."

Eyes distant and unseeing, Deran stares at the nearby forest. "Now you understand. For some, the chance of the conglomerate's attention, of elevation to a higher tier with its perks, is irresistible. With all the money they can earn employing their newly acquired 'skills,' they can virtually write their own ticket."

"I suppose."

Hearing the wistfulness in my voice, Deran bumps his shoulder against mine. "But?"

"I can't help wondering if Sam would take the chance and become a mindhunter if they gave him the opportunity."

"An interesting question, but only one he could answer. Personally, even if they paid me all the money in the world, I still wouldn't choose to have that tech in my head. Who knows what they can do with it!"

His talk of the tech prompts another question. "You said the implant gives them their… abilities?"

"Yes. I don't know everything they can do, but as I've already told you, some mindhunters are capable of hearing your thoughts."

"Not all of them can do that?"

"No, it seems it's a gamble what abilities they get. Some can run as fast as a speeding car, others can force you to do things you don't want to, and some are extraordinarily strong. Some can even sense what you're feeling."

"They all only get one special ability?"

"No. A rare few have more. But these secondary abilities pale when compared to their dominant ability. Those with the strongest abilities end up leading the pack."

I snigger, finding the term odd. "The pack?"

But Deran shakes his head. "Don't laugh. I heard someone call them that, and I agree. They're like wolves. They hunt together, eat together, sleep together, live together. And you've seen firsthand how strange they are."

"You think they're more animal than human?"

"I do. And you know who's holding their leashes?"

I feel dead inside. "Cygnus."

This time, he only nods, and we sit in silence for a time. "Deran, you said you heard someone call them a pack. Who?"

"The medics inserting the device. They—"

"You *saw* them doing the surgery?"

Deran shifts, his gaze skating sideways before he physically moves away, ostensibly to retrieve the thermos again. But his eyes avoid mine as he studiously pours himself another mug of tea.

"If you don't want to tell me how you learned all this, that's fine. Just don't think about lying to me."

Deran's shoulders droop, and his hands still. When he finally meets my gaze, his eyes hold those familiar storm clouds. "I'm sorry. I guess I didn't consider how much of myself I'd be exposing telling you all this stuff. Also, now that these topics are coming up, I just don't think it's safe to let you know some details. I'm sorry." His gaze drops again.

I'm a little hurt he won't trust me with everything until reason kicks in. Would I tell a virtual stranger my deepest, darkest secrets? I think not. Yet here I am expecting him to. How ungrateful can I be?

"Deran." I wait for his eyes to meet mine again. When they don't, I repeat his name. "Deran!"

Uncertainty still billows through those clouds. "Yes?"

I scoot closer, until we face each other, our knees touching once more. Then I take his hands in mine, more accustomed to the spark every time we touch. "I understand if you can't tell me everything right now. I'm grateful you're letting me in on as much as you are. If I ask a question you aren't comfortable answering, just tell me. I'll accept it."

Deran searches my face before a tentative smile lights his face. "If you can live with that, I'd be grateful."

I squeeze his hands. "I can. For now."

His deep chuckle is music to my soul. I want to hold on to it, scared I'll chase it away again. No, that this horrid world we live in will pillage it again. I want to snuggle in close to him, to feel his powerful arms around me, supporting me, comforting me.

"You have that look on your face again."

I start. "What look?"

A wicked, wicked grin. "That one you wouldn't explain earlier."

Nervous giggles slip out as I wave my hands at him. "Shoo! You're still not getting an answer."

Deran laughs but doesn't press further. "Okay, if you can live with my vagaries, *for now*," he adds emphasis, "then accept I overheard a medic saying the strongest would lead the pack. I think he was referring to the person they were working on because he was showing signs of an 'abnormally high ability score.'"

"A score? You think they have a grading system to determine who's the most powerful?"

"That would be my guess."

I consider all he's told me. "So, why didn't they make a mindhunter my…" I falter, realizing I'm about to accuse him of being a spy for the conglomerate. Aware I still don't know if this is true or not (although I'm desperate to believe otherwise), I change where I was going with the sentence. "I mean, why didn't they have a mindhunter watching over me since my first day at CC?"

"That's easy. They're too volatile. Cygnus wouldn't want one of his animals attacking his best asset."

Several things about that sentence raise questions. "Their best asset?"

Deran smiles, shaking his head, a hint of incredulity on his face. "You still don't accept it, do you?"

"That I'm so important to them?"

"Yes. Do you know how powerful you've made Cygnus?"

Groaning, I cover my face with a hand. "Don't remind me. That's recently come to my attention."

"Oh?"

"Never mind. I should've seen it sooner. I don't know why I didn't."

Another strange look. "You haven't worked that one out yet either?"

I'm about to answer when a frisbee hurtles into our picnic basket with a loud *thwack!* I jump, as does Deran. Then he's on his feet, eyes scanning the area, body tense.

At the same moment, we spot the nearby kids. Deran pastes a grin onto his face as he lifts the frisbee and tosses it back to them with surprising accuracy. When he sits down again, he's nowhere near as relaxed as before. Instead, his eyes roam the nearby forest, his hands remaining clasped over his knees, his posture alert and ready for some unseen threat.

"Deran, what is it?" I whisper.

Rather than answer me, his hands explore the outside of the picnic basket, then the blanket. Then his gaze turns skyward, searching for something. Finally, his eyes meet mine.

"We've grown careless in the last few minutes, instead of remaining vigilant. There's no knowing when or how they can spy on you."

Ah! There it is. The reference I waited for earlier. Although oblique, it implies there could be cameras outside of CC HQ. That Deran didn't mention them directly concerns me. Does he think those kids and their frisbee were a threat? His actions would confirm this suspicion. Suddenly wary, I glance around, wondering who might be watching and why.

Deran reaches for the picnic basket again, the skin around his eyes still tight. "How about lunch? I have a few treats I think you'll enjoy."

His eyes hold mine the entire time he speaks, willing me to understand. I do. If we pretend this is nothing more than a meal and have a mundane conversation, perhaps whoever's lurking in the woods or out of sight will dismiss this meeting as inconsequential and leave.

I strive to keep my tone level, my fear bridled. "That sounds wonderful. I can't imagine what might outdo picalillies."

Throughout our meal, we keep our conversation light, bouncing from one frivolous topic to another: our team members' quirks, favorite things, places we enjoy. Nothing to incriminate either of us and, on the surface, just two colleagues exchanging small talk.

My fear keeps me from fully appreciating the delicious spread Deran has provided. From the way he surveys the food, I doubt he's finding it more appetizing.

As the minutes drag into an hour and then stretch to two and we natter on, we gradually relax. Deran suggests a walk to explore the park, and I agree, eager to stretch my legs. Mystified, I watch as he turns the music player off and pockets it.

Deran shrugs. "Don't want anyone messing with this while we're gone."

I understand what he doesn't say, but am too delighted by the hand he offers to dwell on such distressing matters. Happily accepting, we exit our leafy room, and I revel in the thought of some exercise. Only when I spot him peering into the shadows along the paths and up at the higher points do I realize this walk was more to confirm our privacy than for activity.

Satisfied when he finds nothing, Deran guides us back to our blanket, still undisturbed, a while later. Carefully setting the music player in place, Deran switches it back on, then notices my gaze.

"Yes. I don't know how I thought they'd hear us past this. I was having too much fun with you to think it through before. Those kids and their frisbee just put me on edge." He gives a sheepish grin. "My bad."

I grin, wondering if my expression is as alluring to him. "Never mind, we're probably both a bit jittery." Then I realize what else he said. "You were having fun—with me?"

Surprise streaks those incredible eyes. "You didn't think I would?"

With a shrug, I sigh. "I haven't exactly made a lot of friends here."

"Here?" Deran raises a hand. "No, sorry, I shouldn't ask. Also, I should tell you the things I planned to. Our time may be limited if my countermeasures, such as they are, truly are causing someone grief."

While continuing our earlier lighthearted conversation would've been blissful, I sense Deran's rising anxiety. I flip back to the last thing I remember having a question on. "You were about to explain why mindhunters are volatile?"

"Oh, yes! Were you to search for this on the 'net, which I wouldn't recommend, you wouldn't find it because the conglomerate destroys the reports as soon as they appear. But I know it's real because I was there when a mindhunter lost it. I mean went totally ballistic."

"What did he do?"

"Transformed from standing placidly in a corner of the store to attacking anything and everything in his path. It was insane, like a switch flipped. His rage was tangible. Scared me witless, considering their usual impassivity."

"Wow! That sounds scary. Who stopped him?"

Deran shrugs. "That's the second strange thing, right? I mean, one moment, he's full-on caveman. The next, he collapses in on himself. Again, like someone flipped his switch."

Horror batters me. "You mean—turned him off, like a machine?"

"Yeah. I think those implants have a killswitch built in, just in case something dangerous happens. Makes you wonder if they really know what they're doing messing with the brain if they have to resort to something so drastic."

"Agreed. What happened after he collapsed?"

Deran sighs, exhaustion stirring shadows into the silver of his eyes. "He died. Like that killswitch short-circuited his brain and executed him on the spot."

I gawk at Deran. "They killed him because the implant *they* put in him malfunctioned, and they had no other way to deal with it?"

Deran's smile is forlorn. "Isn't that what they do to people who no longer suit their needs?"

His tone hints at more than he's telling me, although I instinctively understand he's not ready to share. Yet. Struggling to find a less sensitive topic, I land on the obvious conclusion. "This is why you think they wouldn't assign me a mindhunter? Because the mindhunter could snap and accidentally kill me?"

"Not only that. I suspect they're afraid if they put a mindhunter over you, and you got attached, and then they were forced to terminate that person, you might object to working for them."

Deran eyes me as he speaks, watching for my reaction, but I don't know how to respond to his assessment. My situation with Sarissa has confused matters.

I thought she was my friend; then it turned out she wasn't. When she died, I didn't even behave the way an upset acquaintance would, let alone a onetime best friend. Perhaps my reaction to the mindhunter's death would've depended on whether I still thought them a friend at the time they died—was that it?

I shake my head, too weary to work it out, but Deran's explanation still niggles. After a half-hearted attempt at divining the reason, I realize I'm also too tired to crack the problem. Instead, I attempt a joke, hoping it will shatter the burden I'm abruptly carrying. "Perhaps. Or maybe they didn't want to risk assigning a mindhunter to me in case I turned their precious watchdog against them."

Deran moves so fast, I have no time to react. Without warning, I'm in his arms, his lips close to my ear, his breath brushing the hair at my temple. I don't know what sets my heart racing—the fright caused by his sudden movement or his proximity.

"Don't even joke about such things! They'll think you're part of the resistance."

Deran's tone is harsh, his grip on my arm fierce. So many thoughts and sensations bombard me, I can't think. Shellshocked. It's the only word that comes to mind right now. Deran's unexpected anger, his closeness, his far-too-tantalizing scents, and his last word all swamp me.

I go limp in his arms, and he draws back as rapidly as he drew me in, eyes wide and panicked. His hands run over me, like he's checking for… what?

"Deran?" My voice quavers, but it draws his eyes back to mine. "What are you looking for?"

Without a word, he crushes me to his chest again. I'm too startled to resist. Why would I want to? Haven't I longed to be here since I first laid eyes on him this morning?

I relax against him, my anxiety calmed by his steady heartbeat. A heartbeat almost as comforting as those muscular arms wrapped around me. Deran's face is in my hair, and a little thrill runs through me. Before I can act on it, he moves so his lips are near my ear again.

"I thought they'd killed you."

I stiffen, not understanding. Clearly, not the response Deran wanted because he tucks me in even closer, one hand rubbing my back in deliciously soothing circles.

Much as I want to groan and lean into the touch, encourage more of it, I need to understand. As gently as I can, I ease a hand between us, placing it on that solid chest and pushing until a small space forms.

"Deran, slow down." Then, realizing he may misinterpret the words, I shake my head vigorously. "No, no, not with us." I blush, realizing how that might've sounded too. I rush on, too frantic for answers to allow my discomfort to get in the way. "You thought *who* had killed me? And there's a resistance?"

For just a second, Deran draws me close to him again. Then he releases me, eyes haunted. I don't know him well enough yet to interpret where his motivations or actions come from. Yes, while much of his behavior these past few minutes would indicate he really does care for me, it still doesn't mean he's not a spy. *Ugh, the idea is even more repugnant now.*

Deran grunts. "Sorry, I warned you the information might come out all jumbled. I'm doing a superb job confusing you."

Before I can comment, Deran stands, then strides away from the blanket before striding back again. He paces back and forth, lips moving but the words drowned out by the loud music still pumping from his enhanced music player. When he makes some sort of peace with himself, he marches back to the blanket, face set.

Plopping down opposite me again, Deran leans forward until his lips brush my ear once more. "Yes, there is a resistance. People who disagree with CC and all it stands for. Anyone who's even suspected of collaborating with them disappears. Your guess is as good as mine about who orchestrates those disappearances, but I thought they might've been watching us, then killed you when you made that flippant remark."

Deran leans back, eyes finding mine. His mouth is set in that grim line again, and a small muscle tics along his jaw. It takes a moment, but then I realize he's angry—with me!

"Whoa! Dude! You're upset? Why?"

Deran's eyes smolder, dark smoke billowing above a fierce fire. "Why would you choose to put yourself in danger with a comment like that?"

Because I didn't know it was a dangerous comment, you idiot! That's what I want to say, but he has no way of knowing what I do or don't know. Besides, if I had known there was a resistance, let alone the consequences of being even remotely associated with it, I would never have said something so insouciant.

Deran must reach the same conclusion because suddenly, he deflates, and his eyes clear, the startling white light back in them again.

"Sorry, you were speaking out of honest ignorance. Forgive me?"

"Yes." The single word slips out before I realize how easily it did.

Huh, I don't even feel any lasting resentment. I don't want to delve too deeply into the reason after my last excursion revealed all too much of my dark side.

As if I hadn't interrupted, Deran leans closer, whispering again. "Since you mentioned it, I'm guessing the reason we've never heard of mindhunters joining the resistance is that killswitch. If it looks like their dogs might switch allegiances, they probably switch them off."

The thought is chilling, but I don't doubt Deran's right. "That begs the question: how do they know where the mindhunters are or what they're thinking? Do you think they built a tracking chip into the implant?"

"It wouldn't surprise me—and it would explain how they find their soldiers. But do you really think it's possible for them to know what the mindhunters are thinking?"

"I doubt the implant can read minds, but it may have sensors measuring things like eye dilation or body temperature or anger levels."

"Anger can be measured?"

"Sure. It's not that difficult. Anger increases heart rate, arterial tension, and testosterone production. Cortisol, the stress hormone, decreases. Then there's the stimulation in the left hemisphere of the brain. The implant could measure all these. Combined, they would show the mindhunter was getting worked up."

"Interesting. Do you think they could've built a warning system into the implant based on these sensors, alerting overseers to problems with a mindhunter so they can take care of it?"

I think about it before shaking my head, a little sickened by my conclusion. "No, that would be inefficient. It would be more expedient if the killswitch were just activated when those readings hit critical levels."

"Ugh, Chiara, really?" Deran shakes his own head, a mixture of disgust and anger on his face. "Sadly, that sounds about right. They wouldn't have to do their own dirty work."

"Hmm."

"Now what are you thinking?"

"These mindhunters can't be cheap to... make, right? So if they invest time and money creating these soldiers, do you think they'd simply let an implant decide if their expensive soldiers should be terminated?"

"I hadn't considered that. So, what? You're thinking I was correct? That there *is* an overseer who makes the final decision?"

"Possibly. I mean, the overseer would need a way of confirming the mindhunter was actually getting violent to harm enough people and make waves, right?"

"You mean, draw enough attention so CC couldn't cover it up?" I nod. "How would the overseers establish that?"

I shrug. "Perhaps the implant also connects to special contact lenses they give the mindhunters, sending video back to the overseers so they can see what the mindhunter does?"

Deran laughs. "Sure, and they add implants to their ears so they can hear them too."

About to laugh at his sarcastic retort, I clam up. Something on my face must hint at my insight because Deran stops laughing, his face apprehensive again. "What now?"

"Deran, they already have a way. And you said I was being paranoid!"

Deran's face drains of color. His hand goes up to the chip behind his ear. His voice is barely a whisper. "Our comm links?"

I nod, too scared to speak. How much have they already heard? If the conglomerate is listening in on people's conversations via their comm links, even Deran's nifty little invention couldn't stop it.

Furious at him for dismissing my earlier concerns out of hand, I wonder how much danger our discussion today has put us in. Either sensing my fury, or having regrets of his own, Deran takes my hand, waiting until my eyes meet his.

"Sorry," he mouths.

His eyes plead for me to understand, express his regret. But this time, I can't escape my anger. Does he not understand I have a family to protect?

I yank my hand free, rising. "I have to get home."

Deran recoils, but doesn't object.

"Thank you for the picnic." My words are stiff, and I can't bring myself to tell him how much I enjoyed our time together—until the last few minutes. Partly because I'm still seething. But mostly because I'm worried I've just given Cygnus another weapon to use against me.

I'm halfway back across the park before Deran catches up to me.

"Chiara! Wait!"

Torn between running from him and waiting, I falter. Then he's beside me, basket in hand, breathing hard. He must've put on some speed to pack everything away and catch up before I left the park. I cross my arms and wait.

"At least let me see you home."

Astatine! I don't want him worrying about me. I can't have another person's safety on my conscience. Before I can object, he's grasped my hand, a determined expression on his face.

I guess he won't take no for an answer and allow a resigned sigh. The small smile tweaking the corners of his lips tells me he knows he's won. I allow him to guide me out of the park, then onto the trundle.

We sit side by side, him still holding my hand, all the way back to my part of the city. When we arrive, Deran escorts me to the door of my apartment, offering to check inside before I enter. Somehow, I don't want him in my space. That would make today—and all I've realized I feel for him—too real.

I decline, thanking him for his concern, then slip inside my apartment and close the door before he can convince me otherwise. Regret fills me for shutting him out, for not speaking to him on the trundle on our way here, but I'm emotionally spent. I have nothing left to give.

Succumbing to the POMS, I crumple onto my new couch and give in to the tears. Tears of anger and frustration and fear. Tears that won't solve anything, but curiously, make me feel better all the same.

I don't know how much time passes before I stagger to my feet again, too tired for even my lovely spa shower. I collapse into bed, asleep as soon as my head hits the pillow.

When I wake the next morning, even though it's Sunday, I head into work. I need something to take my mind off… everything. And nothing does that effectively as drowning myself in science.

Besides, now that I know who mindhunters are and what they can do, I must finish the machine. I have to negotiate my family's release before I reveal something to those mindhunters condemning us all. If I haven't already done so.

Filled with trepidation, I enter CC HQ, half expecting I'll find mindhunters waiting for me after the things Deran shared yesterday. But the foyer is empty, except for the SerSents manning the front desk.

I hurry past, eager to reach the elevators so I can disappear from their sight—and minds—before they remember to apprehend me. At least, that's my thinking.

The sanctuary of my office is a relief, and I drop into my chair, taking a few moments to just breathe. Some time later, I'm deep into the problem of muon creation when my stomach growls. I inadvertently skipped breakfast this morning.

With a sigh, I stand and stretch, wondering what to do for food. The thought of vending machine fare is unappealing, and the cafeteria's closed today. Then I remember my new favorite place. It's a beautiful day out. Nothing like a bit of fresh air and sunshine on the way to *Little Italy*.

Almost skipping along the path, I grin, anticipating the appetizing morsels the restaurant offers. Upon arrival, I request a seat outside and am pleasantly surprised to find I have the intimate patio to myself. Not wanting to think overly much today, I order the Alfredo pasta I had last time, then watch the water trickling over the stones in the central water feature, keeping my mind carefully neutral until my food arrives.

The food doesn't disappoint, enough to distract me from anything except how delicious it is. I order dessert and I'm stuffing the last bite of the best cannoli I've ever tasted into my mouth when a couple are ushered into the courtyard. The dark-haired man leans across and whispers something into the woman's ear.

At that precise moment, a realization blindsides me. I want to spit the cannoli out. It suddenly tastes like ash. As it should. How can I be out here enjoying myself (or trying to) without once recognizing I'm not the only one affected by yesterday's events in the park?

As much as it hurts to understand, I was so caught up in myself and my own problems, I didn't acknowledge Deran is also in danger. Perhaps more than me. After all, he was the one divulging secrets no one else dared.

Further thoughts compound my guilt. Didn't I ask him to tell me? Accept risk could be associated with it? Then what did I do but criticize Deran the moment that danger became real. If I'd just left well enough alone, neither of us would be in this situation.

I cover my face with my hands, feeling worse than the most repugnant piece of muck in the filthiest corner of the pigpen. What have I done? I need to make this right. But how? I don't know where Deran lives. While I know his tier, that in itself doesn't help. Plenty of sectors house tier threes.

Restless, I pay my bill, then hurry back to CC HQ. Perhaps I'll find something in the workshop offering a clue about Deran's address. But can I go visit him, unannounced, after the abominable way I treated him yesterday?

Irrelevant. I must sort things out with Deran as soon as I can (no sense letting potential wounds fester), so I march directly to the workshop, bypassing my office. Intent on getting there, I don't notice Deran until I about knock him over. "Oh! Sorry!"

Deran's hand shoots out to catch me before I fall over my own feet, tangled as they suddenly are. "Steady on! Where are you off to in such a hurry?"

Now that he's standing right in front of me, words desert me. Why did I expect anything different? I search Deran's face, finding no light in those gray eyes. No hint of what he might feel on that handsome face.

I glance down, then notice I'm wringing my hands. Pulling them apart, I hide my hands behind my back. Then glance at the floor, gathering my scattered thoughts. I find them, pick up the pieces, and then look up again, somewhat relieved when my thoughts don't vanish again the moment I gaze into his eyes.

"Deran, I'm sorry about yesterday. I apologize for my behavior. You warned me, and I didn't listen. It's not your fault, but I treated you like it was. I'm ashamed of both the way I behaved and that I thought only of myself. Can you forgive me?"

Before I've finished my apology, I sense the change in him. Notice how those gray eyes soften, how the grim line of his jaw relaxes. Without meaning to, I step forward. Alarmed when I suddenly find myself so close to him, I mean to move away, but Deran's hands shoot up, gripping my arms and holding me in place.

With a wry smile, he leans closer and whispers, "Who knows what they can and can't hear, but I really hope they can't hear this. At this moment, I'd desperately like to kiss you."

Panic swells within me, and I want to run, but Deran holds me fast, not allowing me to slip even an inch further away. The smile becomes a grin as he leans even closer, whispering a second time.

"No need to stampede out of here. I said I'd *like* to kiss you. But this is neither the time nor place. I mean to take my time with you."

Curse the blush scalding my cheeks! Sure my face must be redder than a beet, I cover my flaming cheeks with my hands. "Stop it!"

His laugh is soft, sensuous. How does he do that? I really need space. Deran must realize it too, because he releases me, eyes sparkling with the devil's mischief when I dare peek at him.

"Fine, you've made your point. Satisfied?" It's all I can think of, and I feel marginally vindicated when he at least attempts to look more serious. Not that he succeeds. *Astatine!* That sexy grin undoes me again.

Turning so I don't have to look at him a second longer (and so I can retain at least a little dignity), I mutter an excuse about needing to get some work done, then dart away before I embarrass myself further.

Only when I'm back in my office and staring at my screen, do I realize I never asked him what he was doing here.

4 2

Aware I won't make progress on the prototype for the rest of the afternoon after that rather unsettling (thrilling? carnal?) run-in with Deran, I turn my attention to something else. Something I *can* solve. No, I won't admit I want to solve this problem just because I enjoyed what Deran said about kissing me—and I want him to say it again. *Just say it?*

I snort out a laugh. I'm toast, for sure. Time to focus on something else—my pesky little tech problem. I'm almost positive I'll find what I'm looking for in the basement. But which room? Or am I deceiving myself, hoping I'll find an old one there?

An hour later, I've answered my question—I was absolutely deceiving myself. Why I thought I'd find an old comm link in one of the basement rooms is beyond me, even with all the junk down there.

However, the trip was useful for another reason. This time, my presence didn't prompt the appearance of a SerSent. Have they been told I'm allowed to enter? If so, I might be in the clear for my midnight foray of over a week ago.

With my mind back on the comm link issue, I apply my intelligence to the problem instead of wild speculation. Pacing my office, I consider the best place I might find a comm device. No, I'm asking the wrong question. Where would someone go if they had a problem with their device?

This is the key I needed to unlock the answer. Over the next two hours, I rub the spot behind my ear where my comm link resides several times, increasing the frequency and the annoyance I express with each touch.

Eventually, when I think I've made it obvious my comm link is bothering me, I shut my PC down, grab my purse, and head out of the door.

I stop in at the lab's supply room, grabbing a few gel capsules about the right size. Nothing larger than a grain of rice. Despite creating the non-allergenic substance coating them, I've never seen a comm link device outside of a person's body, so I don't know what they look like. Best I cover as many bases as I can.

The emergency room is a long trundle ride away. Far from the on-call doctors at CC HQ who may have some sort of specialized equipment to disprove my claim. Not that the ER won't, but I'm hoping the chances are smaller.

When I exit the trundle, I stagger along, pretending my balance is now off. Then I ponder whether a faulty comm device would cause vertigo, like a blocked ear canal. I should've researched that. Too late now.

Belatedly, I comprehend it's also too late for me to have faked vertigo leaving CC HQ. Then just as quickly realize it's not a problem, but a solution. I've just given myself an explanation why I had the procedure done somewhere other than CC HQ.

I find a sympathetic listener in the ER intake nurse. After completing her health questionnaire, she ushers me into a small exam room. I expect her to leave, then to wait for someone else to come take care of the problem, but vital sign checks done, she washes her hands, then reaches into a cabinet up on the wall.

The pre-wrapped, sterile injector she extracts is nothing short of terrifying. Through the clear packaging, I can see it clearly. With two long barrels twisted one atop the other, one tipped with a giant needle, the other with some sort of suction system, it looks like some medieval torture device. Add to that a trigger-bearing, perpendicular stock at the end of the barrels as long as my forearm, and I question the wisdom of my decision. In an instant, my mouth is drier than century-old bones.

My alarm must be clear because Nursey (what am I supposed to call her if she doesn't wear a name tag?) pats my arm and croons. "There, there, nothing to worry about. I know this injector looks scary, but it'll take that nasty old comm link out and zip your new device in quick as can be. You'll be right as rain in a few seconds."

I swallow. I didn't actually mean for Nursey to replace my perfectly good comm link. All I wanted was an old one. A conundrum I scramble to escape. Desperate to delay her, I blurt, "What about the information on my old comm link? I can't lose it."

"Oh, no dear, don't worry. The information transfer happens simultaneously. That's why this injector's the size it is. See here?" Nursey points at the stock. "Software in there will take care of all that for you."

I stare at her for a moment, then squeak another question. "What happens to my old chip?"

Nursey gives me a funny look. "We discard it. It's medical waste."

Finally, thankfully, a solution presents itself. *Yes!* "Would it be possible for me to keep the old device? I know you said the information transfers across, but what if everything on the old device isn't erased? My comm link contains classified information, so I'd feel better if I can pass it on to the appropriate people at the conglomerate."

Another funny look from Nursey.

"I work at CC HQ."

"Then why didn't you just get this done there?"

At last, a question I'm prepared for. Although I expected the SerSents or mindhunters at CC HQ would be asking me. "Well, it was bothering me earlier at work, and—"

"You work on Sundays?"

"When I need to. Anyway, as I was saying, it was bothering me, so I left, thinking resting at home would help, but then I suddenly started feeling awful on the trundle. This ER was closer than going all the way back, so I chose the quicker solution."

Nursey (shouldn't she have at least introduced herself?) nods. "Wise choice. These things have gnarly side effects if you leave them in too long when they start glitching." When I don't answer, she puts on a bright smile. "Are we doing this?"

Mouth dry, but craving answers the chip can provide, I nod agreement, clamping my sweaty palms together.

"If you would just move your hair aside for me?"

Obligingly, I do. Nursey must worry I'm going to bolt because in deft movements, she dons gloves, cleans the area, opens the injector packet, and then presses the barrel against my neck without a warning.

Sharp pain explodes behind my right ear. I jerk away before wondering if I should've held still.

But Nursey is all smiles. "All done. I told you it was quick and easy."

I wait for the stabbing pains to subside, opening and closing my mouth a few times to ease the pain shooting down my jaw. "You didn't say it would be excruciating."

Nursey pats my knee. "Yes, I know, and I'm sorry for that. But would you have gone through with the procedure if I had?"

I have to give it to her. "No."

"Exactly. Then I would've had to sedate you, and it would've made the whole process far more complicated than it needed to be." Nursey opens a drawer, extracts a container, and hands it to me. "Now, let me see you take your nanites, and then you may leave. Tomorrow, you'll wake up, and you won't even know anything's changed."

Right. As long as I don't have some weird reaction. But considering I never had one the first time, it's unlikely. Besides, she tested me for all that on intake. When will I stop seeing danger lurking in every situation?

Obediently, I take the offered nanites (pre-programmed pills, not spray like Nanogo) and swallow them with the glass of water she hands me. "Thank you."

"You're most welcome. While you shouldn't experience any pain, fever, or other adverse reactions as noted on this pamphlet," she hands one to me, "if you do, please visit your nearest ER."

Turning back to the counter, Nursey picks up the discarded injector. When she sees me cringe, she smiles, before offering the stock end. "For you, as requested. I don't know how to remove the old device from the injector, but your employers should."

Gingerly, I take the injector, careful to keep my fingers far from the trigger. "Do you have a bag I can put this in?"

"Yes, hold on, let me fetch one."

I can't believe my luck. When Nursey exits, I leap up (ow!) and open the cabinet, grabbing a sterile injector in one movement, then stuffing it into my briefcase. I plop back onto the bed right on time.

Nursey returns with a self-sealing, opaque bag in hand. Smiling, she offers it to me. "Here you go."

"Thank you—again." I drop the injector into the bag, relieved not to have to hold it anymore, then seal the bag. "My employers will be glad to have this back." I wrinkle my nose, pretending disdain for the injector.

"No doubt." Nursey steps aside and holds the door open. "Take care now."

I guess I'm done. "Thanks, you too."

Leaving the ER as fast as the stabbing pains allow (mercifully already subsiding thanks to the nanites), I hurry back to the station and collapse onto a seat of the trundle. Seconds later, it's pulling away from the stop. I heave a sigh. I did it! Now to get home and find answers. Or rather, I will as soon as the nanites kill most of the pain.

43

Back home, I decide sleep is the best way of waiting out the healing hours. Thankful for the rest, I crawl under my covers, turning onto the side without my newly inserted comm link. I'm not even aware of falling asleep.

In the small hours of the morning, hunger wakes me. I reach up to check the time on my comm link, and only when the numbers pop up do I realize I'm pain free. *Good nanites!* Suddenly energized, I bounce out of bed and rush back to the living room.

The used injector is where I left it on the coffee table, the unused injector in its sterile pack still in my briefcase. I debate which one to use. If the injector allows an information exchange when the old device is removed and the new inserted, it's possible the unused device may not be activated until that scary trigger is pulled.

Since I need a device I know was functional, I open the bag with the used injector. I extract it carefully and lay it flat on the table, then study the horrendous tool from several angles, always keeping those dangerous barrels facing away from me.

Is it possible to extract my old comm link without destroying the injector? If so, I can hand it back "intact," then pretend ignorance should anyone question the missing comm link.

No, I shouldn't hand it back at all. That would only make them aware I switched out my comm link. Easier if I tell them I put the device in an incinerator on the way home, should they ask. That would take care of any residual information on the device, right?

They might incinerate medical waste at the hospital too. I don't let it bother me. Cygnus knows me well enough to be aware I don't always think on my feet. He should accept this was an oversight or lack of knowledge on my part.

Freed from the need to keep the injector intact, I return to my bedroom and collect my precision tools. Back at the table, I don eye protection, then start with the stock. Tiny pins in the four corners lock the two sides together. I tap on each pin in turn, surprised when removing them takes neither skill nor force.

The moment I free the last pin, the stock springs open. Circuit boards spill onto the table, along with something else. A flat black grain. My old comm link, black with dried blood.

I want to touch it, but fear disrupting unseen circuits. In times like these, I long for my lab equipment. My tiny handheld airpliers will have to do. With delicate movements, I lift the comm link and place it in the static-free bag I prepared for it.

Sudden fatigue washes over me, and I sink back onto my couch, but I must come up with a way to sneak this into the lab so I can use my fancy equipment to study it. Thankful again for no cameras in my personal lab due to the sensitive nature of my projects, I devise a plan, then rise and stretch my tired muscles.

What I need is my shower. Carefully, I pack the scattered injector pieces into another static-free bag, then stow it in my usual hiding place alongside Ferret. With a yawn threatening to dislocate my jaw, I stumble into the bathroom.

After my shower, I fall right back to sleep, the long day (and night) catching up with me. I wake late the next morning, groggy and wishing for more sleep. However, I'm all too aware of my body's inability to go back to sleep once I've woken after the sun's up. I drag myself out of bed.

Two cups of espresso, one at home and one on the way to the

trundle, do nothing to counter my exhaustion. I attribute my ongoing lethargy to my body still healing from the "surgery" yesterday. Then I rethink the word when I remember Deran's explanation about the brain implants the mindhunters are subjected to. My minor procedure was nothing like that.

Newly appreciative, I choose not to complain about a little lassitude. The morning drags, and since I'm not up to covert actions, my old comm link remains hidden where I deposited it last night.

It's early afternoon before I feel more like myself, the coffee finally kicking in or my body returning to normal. Either way, I have the energy to deal with my little private pursuit.

I message my team, letting them know I'll be in my lab and not to disturb me. Then I enter my personal workspace and shut the door on the world beyond. As soon as I'm sure I'm alone, I check for any cameras that might've mysteriously appeared since the last time I was in here—when I created the chards. It seems forever ago.

Gratified to find my personal lab still camera-free (I had to check!), I unpin the ornate brooch I put on this morning. A piece I've often worn previously, considering its source: Sarissa. She purchased it as a gift on one of our shopping excursions. My only reason for wearing the gaudy thing to work was to please her. But its design was perfect for today's purpose.

Tapping on the crisscrossing metal tubes bedazzled with fake gems, I grin when my old comm link slides out. Time for answers!

Two hours later, I'm dripping with sweat, but I've confirmed CC can't eavesdrop on a person via their comm link. While the comm link can transmit the wearer's location, it does nothing more sinister.

Or at least, nothing more sinister than possibly recording or monitoring any conversations we have, either through voice or text, when actively using our comm links. But definitely no circuits allowing the device to passively capture what's being said when the comm link isn't in use.

Deran and I lucked out with this reprieve. Peace returns, turning my legs a little wobbly now that I grasp how much trouble we could've been in.

In the future, Deran and I need only worry about our comm links when using them. However, that nasty tracking chip is another matter. Should I ever concoct a plan to escape CC and its insidious tentacles, I'll have to remove mine. At least my family don't have any.

I console myself with another incidental advantage of visiting the ER: knowing how to extract a comm link. Thankful I didn't smash the injector last night when retrieving my old device, I wonder if I'll be able to reverse-engineer it. Then I'd have a way to extract my new comm link, should I ever need to. Perhaps I'll luck out, and the injector will work regardless of a missing new unit.

Clearing my workbench so no sign remains of the work I've done, I head over to the workshop. The new prototype is taking shape, and this machine reaches nearly all the way to the ceiling.

But it's not the ceiling I'm looking at. With two of his team on either side of him, Deran has braced himself at the very top of the machine, supporting a large piece of metal while his team pin it in place.

He's stripped out of the long sleeves of his overalls, wearing only a t-shirt. Muscles bulge in his arms as he supports the heavy metal. I want to stand and gawk. No, drool. But the last time I did, he caught me. It would be mortifying should he tease me again, this time in front of his team.

Would he actually do that? I'm a little annoyed I don't know the answer. There are still so many things I haven't learned about him. Deep down, I can't help but sense some unseen clock ticking away, making me all too aware our time is running out.

Agitated, I turn to leave, deciding to come back later. Waiting around here like a lovesick puppy won't do. I don't want time to think. I need something to take my mind off Deran.

"Chiara!"

I jump, realizing this probably wasn't the first time Deran called my name. "Yes, sorry, here."

Deran's grin is quick, mischievous. "You mean physically here now as opposed to wherever you were a second ago?"

"What do you want, Deran?" My tone is sharper than I meant, and Deran's grin evaporates, those shutters I despise rolling over his eyes.

"Don't ask me. You came here. I expect you were the one with a question—or questions?"

"Yes, you're right. I'm sorry I was short with you." Deran nods but waits me out. "When you have a moment, could you come find me? I have something I need to discuss with you."

Interest sparks in those eyes before the shutters screen them again. "Sure. Give me about twenty minutes, yeah?"

I nod. "Thanks. See you later."

What am I going to do for twenty minutes? The question burns all the way back to the lab. But I needn't have worried. When I walk in, I spot countless projects I can dig into. Whether my team will appreciate or resent my interference is another story. I don't care. I need distraction, and their projects can provide it. After all, I am their supervisor as head of this lab.

Time shrinks, and I'm still in the midst of a problem when I sense Deran's proximity. I turn, finding him hovering in the aisle nearest the lab workbench.

Apologizing, I extract myself from the mini think-tank group I created, then smile at Deran as I approach. His face shows no inkling of what he might think or feel.

I make a show of checking the time. "I know it's early, but how about some dinner while we discuss the project? On me? I've found this lovely little Italian restaurant I can't get enough of. Even if you're not hungry, you will be once you smell their food."

Deran isn't stupid. He knows I want to talk, preferably somewhere else. He pretends to consider my proposal, then gestures toward his overalls. *Did he have to pull them back up over his arms and hide those muscles?* "If I'd known you'd be inviting me for dinner, I might've dressed up."

Laughing, I reply, "In that case, how about we meet downstairs in an hour? Will that give you enough time to make yourself pretty?"

His grin doesn't disappoint. I don't know I'll ever tire of seeing it. I'm so busy ogling him I almost miss his reply.

"Honey, I only need five. But let's say ninety minutes so we can also call it a day here at work and not have to come back after dinner."

Just like that, I'm adrift at sea again. I have no clue how to interpret his suggestion. Especially after he called me "honey." Yes, he was joking, but still...

I force myself to focus. Not needing to return (whatever the reason) is appealing. More so when I remember I have another project waiting for me at home. One far more interesting than sorting through my team's project questions.

"Sounds like a plan. Swing by and collect me on your way out?"

"Will do." Touching two fingers to his forehead in mock salute, Deran ambles back to the workshop. I watch every step until I realize he's walking slower than usual. Does he know I'm leering at his sexy rear end?

About to drag my gaze away, Deran turns, his grin pure evil as he gives a cocky wave. *Al-Li! I'm in so much trouble. I can't even gauge the depth of it.*

Snorting a laugh and shaking my head, I wave back, then try to remember what I was thinking about only minutes before. The knowing smiles on my team's faces heat my cheeks again. *Ugh! That man. What am I going to suffer through because of him?*

"Yes, yes, I know. But you all think he's sexy too, or you wouldn't have those goofy grins," I retort, some offense my best defense.

The general laughter dispels my discomfort. In minutes, we're sucked back into the problem we were dealing with before Deran arrived, no further discussions on the man required.

4 4

As the hostess ushers us toward a cozy booth in *Little Italy*, a gorgeous woman at a nearby table gives Deran the once-over. I want to gouge her eyes out, but I restrain the primitive urge and do something totally out of character. I place a hand on Deran's arm.

The woman's eyes narrow, then focus on me. I give her a sweet smile, pretending she's just another ordinary patron and no one of consequence. The irritation sparking in her eyes makes me grin all the more.

"Playing games, are you?"

Deran's words, so close to my ear, leaning down to whisper them as he did, have a ripple effect. First, shivering at his nearness, then flustered because he noticed what I was up to, and finally, alarm at his perceptiveness.

I hadn't even realized he was watching me. Then I remember the hand I placed on his arm. No doubt what tipped him off to my little charade. Opting in favor of the offensive again (I hate being embarrassed!), I lean close to him and whisper back, "And what if I am?"

Deran's exuberant laughter turns a few more heads our way, and I want to curl up inside and hide myself in Deran's arms. From the frying pan into the fire. I'm so relieved when we reach the booth, I sink down.

Too fast because I bump my hip on the way down. "Ow!" Although wincing at the painful contact, I don't moderate my descent, only taking time to rub the tender spot when I'm seated, the tall booth hiding me from all but the patrons at the table next to us.

When I cease the soothing rubbing and glance up, Deran's seated opposite me, a broad grin on his face. "What?"

"Are you naturally clumsy or just always in too much of a hurry?"

I sputter, fumbling for the right response. "Wow! Way to make a girl feel great!"

Chuckling, Deran takes my hand. "Sorry, but I won't sugarcoat my words. Besides, you're cute the way you're always bashing into things."

I want to be mad at him, but he has that sexy grin on his face, the one he always wears when teasing me, and I'm abruptly overcome by giggles. "I've never heard someone say it's cute before, but I'll take it."

We laugh; then I see that mischievous glint in his eyes again. *Now what?*

"You've had other men comment on your tendency to find random obstacles placing themselves in your way?"

I have to hand it to him. The way he said that made it sound so much better than me walking into things all the time. Then I get where he's really going with the question. *Huh, imagine that!* "Just friends."

"As in no boyfriends?"

I reach for my hair, searching for a stylus I hope might still be there. No such luck. Picking up and fiddling with my fork instead, I hope he'll leave it alone.

He doesn't. Merely sits and watches me, those gray eyes never leaving my face. When I know he'll wait me out, I huff. "No, no boyfriends." Does he look smug? Yes, my answer pleased him. What I can't figure out is why. "That doesn't bother you?"

"No."

"Care to elaborate?"

"Do I have to?"

His eyes are alight with amusement, the silver in his eyes playing off against the darker gray, mesmerizing. Before I lose myself, I drop my gaze, brain grasping for an explanation I'm having the toughest time finding.

Seconds pass before I find what I was searching for. *Oh! No!* I do *not* want him to explain. That could open the door to so many more discussions I don't think I'm ready for. Not true. So many conversations I'd rather have with him once I know he's not a spy for CC.

But how can I be sure I can trust him? The only way I know to test is as a scientist. To make observations, ask questions, and then form my hypothesis. Based on this, I can predict, then test, and rinse and repeat until it's possible to form a valid conclusion.

Armed with a plan, I smile, a little thrill tingling through me when his response is another lazy smile of his own. "No, no explanation needed. What you can tell me instead is more about yourself."

Not the answer he expected. Deran's eyes widen, then sharpen. "What do you want to know?"

"Whatever you'd like to tell me." I won't make this easy. Let's see what he feels comfortable sharing on his own.

"How about I'm a qualified mechanical engineer who has the best boss and an incredible project to work on?"

"Uh-huh. Tell me something I don't already know. And not the generic stuff we shared at the park."

Deran studies me for what feels like forever. His reply is quiet. "I had a sister."

Had a sister? I'm back in unfamiliar territory. I never know what to say in these situations. My palms sweat, and I go with the first thing that pops into my head. "I'm sorry you don't have her anymore."

While Deran nods, his eyes are distant, his mind on the past. Then he focuses on me again. "You're not going to ask how I have a sister?"

I'm confused. People have brothers and sisters. Is this a trick question? Or is he hinting at something else?

Deran sighs. "You don't know, do you?"

Really struggling here. "Know what?"

"Tell me, have you ever met people with siblings?"

"Of course I have."

"No, I mean in, say, the last five years?"

"That's a rather specific question."

"Humor me."

I shrug. "Sarissa is the only person I've known well enough in that time period to answer that question, but she had no siblings."

A growl from Deran. "Well, have you seen parents with more than one child?"

I sense Deran's frustration, but the cause is a mystery. Then I recall the boy and his parents I recently saw on the trundle, the family on their way to the park. I'd hoped they were meeting the boy's brothers and/or sisters there, so he wouldn't be alone, like I was that day on the trundle, without my family. But have I actually ever seen parents with multiple kids?

I allow my mental memory bank to run, the images flowing fast and furious. Minutes later, I blink. I can't find any instances. "People aren't allowed more than one child?"

Deran's expression is unfathomable. "You've never noticed before?"

"No. Why is this so important?"

There goes that hand again, burying itself in his dark hair, dragging it back so the spikes stand on end. Tired eyes gaze back at me, a world of weariness turning them slate gray. A dull shade with no hope, no depth, no life.

"Because it would give you a clue about my background."

In a flash, I'm incensed. Something lurks below the surface, but Deran isn't giving me answers. "Stop talking in riddles!"

Deran quirks an eyebrow. "Back to being impatient again?" He must realize he's skating on thin ice because he raises a placating hand. "Sorry. Back before Cygnus was the director, in extreme circumstances, people could have multiple children. We were one such family."

I think of my family. Do my siblings exist only because they were born before Cygnus took over? "Extreme circumstances? Such as?"

"Accommodations with other families who couldn't have, or didn't want, children."

Again, I sense more to this statement. Perhaps Deran isn't sharing because he doesn't feel safe? I realize I haven't yet explained about the comm links. But I need at least one more answer before I tell him. "Explain."

Sighing, Deran leans back in his seat. "Not much to say. If you could find another family who didn't want a child, your own could apply for a second."

"But?"

"You can imagine how many applications there were and how few were granted."

"Oh." Questions roil. "Was your sister older than you?"

"Yes." A single word, but Deran's voice cracks. An answer dredged from the depths where it's festered for a long time. A place sunk deep in his soul.

I puzzle the pieces together. If his sister was older, Deran was the child of "accommodation." Did this make him feel less somehow? Or more special? More importantly, was whatever happened to his sister related to this? Could he feel responsible for her death?

On and on the questions run, but I ask none because I don't know how without sounding callous. But he *has* given me something I didn't know about him. And not just a trivial piece of information. One clearly dear to his heart.

With fierce resolve, I set the questions aside. I can't ask him here. Or now. Too many things between us still need clarification before we get to that level of intimacy. Desperate to reach such a state sooner rather than later, I opt for the one thing that might get us there.

"Deran, I'm sorry about your sister, and I think you have a lot more to tell me about her, and… things. I want to hear—I want to get to know you. But you know the same as I do how much knowledge I have to gain before then."

A muscle twitches along Deran's jaw, and he bites out a reply. "You're being rather candid today."

Hurt, I blink, before remembering where he's coming from. I reach across the table, drawing the hand resting there into mine. He tenses, but I hold fast. "This is what I wanted to tell you earlier today. They can't hear us through our comm links."

Wide eyes meet mine before his gaze sweeps across the patrons nearest us, checking they aren't paying us undue attention. Then his gaze flicks back. "How do you know?"

Without embellishing, I explain.

"You had them take out your comm link just so you could test it?"

His bewildered expression makes me laugh. "It's not that bad. I know I made the process sound brutal, but it wasn't. I needed answers, so I found a way to get them."

Deran's grin is impish. "A woman on a mission. Remind me never to stand in your way."

"I'm sure I'll have occasion to remind you of that in the future."

Now he laughs, the sound soothing my soul. My heart aches for the hurt he so obviously still feels when speaking about his sister. Definitely more on her later. For now, all I want is to bask in the slice of sunshine his laughter brings.

My stomach growls, loud enough for Deran to hear, and I giggle, a little self-conscious. "Are you ready to order?"

"That depends. You said you like the food here. Why?"

I shrug. "It just tastes extraordinary! Every bite pure ecstasy." I expect a wicked grin, but his eyes gleam with unexpected curiosity.

"Have you ever wondered why the food here is so exceptional?"

"Because it's Italian?" I would laugh, but his eyes are suddenly guarded. "Deran?"

Between one blink and the next, Deran's face smooths, becomes unreadable. "Nothing, what color are you, anyway?"

Nervous about how he'll respond, I hesitate. "Blue?"

Deran's lips purse, and I glimpse something in those inscrutable eyes. Anger? Contempt? Resolve? Then it's gone, and his face relaxes into a smile. "Never mind. I believe you when you say the food here is superb. Shall we order?"

I want to ask more, but my stomach growls a second time. And I hate to spoil the lighter mood. "Yes, please! I'm ravenous!"

We take our time, him asking questions about the menu and me providing input on what I've tried so far and rating the options. In the end we settle on two of the day's specials, agreeing to share so we can both sample our choices.

Order placed, I lean back and study him. His face is more relaxed now. None of the earlier tension remains. I debate pressing him for more information on what I don't know, but I'm loathe to destroy the fragile peace.

Deran smiles. "Those questions you have are stamping themselves on your forehead."

I realize I'm frowning and rush to clear it away.

"No, don't. I like it when I can read your expression."

I nod. "Isn't that the truth? So many masks on so many people make you wonder who's really thinking what."

A chuckle. "You and your crazy sentences!"

Understanding I could've phrased my statement better, I smile. "But at least you understand me, right?"

"I do."

It's a wonder. Sarissa was the only other person who did, besides my family. Which reminds me. "How do you think my family got lucky so many times? I mean, I have two brothers *and* a sister. The odds of one family getting their applications approved so many times must be staggering."

Deran shrugs. "You misunderstand. My family isn't from here, which is why we had to apply. But can we talk about the prototype? I have some questions."

Two things jar. The way he brushed my question off and his reference to not being from here "explaining" the application. How aren't there others here (that I know of) with multiple children? Or does the restriction only apply to kids born after Cygnus became director?

I'm so confused! Making a mental note to follow up, I allow his not-so-subtle change of topic to lead us into easier discussions. Because one thing was undeniable in his answer: his desire to not discuss such serious subjects anymore.

"Sure. What questions do you have?"

As we discuss the project and eat our meal, the next hours pass peacefully. I can't say I regret the decision to take his hint because I can actually enjoy my food while discussing less contentious issues. Still, a part of me wants time with him to get those answers. I'll just have to find the opportunity.

4 5

Deran escorts me home after dinner, but doesn't offer to see me up to my apartment when we reach my building. Since our conversation remained disappointingly superficial for the rest of the evening, and with no meaningful conversation to foster intimacy, the likelihood of a goodnight kiss is off the table.

Filled with regret, I bid him goodnight and watch as he makes his way back to the trundle, my thoughts not too disturbed to enjoy the view as he does. When he finally disappears from sight, loneliness plagues me. I sigh. Deran's gone, and I can't change that now. Sleep. It's what I need, what I must have if I hope to save my family.

And Deran? A little voice prompts. But I shut it down, not wanting to go there or think about questions I don't have enough information to answer.

The pattern of insufficient information carries over into work the next day. I get into the lab early, determined to tackle the problem Deran raised concerning the catalyzation process. We aren't generating muons in the numbers I expected. But despite brainstorming the problem from several angles, I can't get a handle on it. There is simply no viable explanation for why the numbers don't add up. Frustrated, I check my formulas, only increasing my agitation when I prove my math correct.

The mindhunter who stalks into the lab just before lunch is a further hindrance. Besides upsetting my team to the point no one's getting any work done, I worry this mindhunter can fully read thoughts.

Unnerving, because I have so many things to hide: my desire to free myself and my family from the conglomerate's chains, the file I hacked, the conversations I've had with Deran.

While I know our comm links can't be used to spy on us, one of these creepy people could have super-hearing which bypassed Deran's augmented music player.

When the mindhunter leaves again, having spent less than fifteen minutes strolling the aisles, not even entering my office, I'm relieved. A reprieve I'm thankful for, but it does nothing to allay my fears.

Rattled, I call an impromptu team meeting in the cafeteria, almost smiling when I see how keen they are to escape the lab. Anywhere but here. I don't blame them.

Lunch is rowdier than usual. In fact, so rowdy, I urge my team outside. The fresh air, change of scenery, and ability to shed the excess adrenaline-fueled energy calms them (and me) so we venture back to the lab with renewed focus.

But the afternoon is as dismal as the morning in terms of progress. I've hit a wall with the interactions of lasers, plasma, drum and target. In desperate need of a break, I switch to the other project Cygnus assigned. The project I've yet to tell him I'm not qualified for, the one to help those with the unusual form of "dementia." I'm no expert, but I would disagree dementia is the correct term.

I'm just tapping the file with the trial results when several thoughts strike me simultaneously. This project made Deran angry enough to quit on the spot. While I meant to ask for an explanation when we went on our picnic, I forgot. We still haven't discussed it.

I rise, about to head to the workshop to ask, when I remember the cameras. Not only there, but all over HQ. Whatever resulted in such an adverse reaction is probably not something he'd want to talk about here.

I take my time getting to the workshop, picking my way through the benches in the lab as I think about how best to tackle the problem. By the time I reach the workshop, I have an answer. No rocket science required.

When I enter, Deran is nowhere in sight, and his team directs me to the machine's massive drum, meant to hold the electrons in their plasma, but now empty for troubleshooting. I use the ladder welded to the outside to go up and over, descending into the bowels of the drum.

Here, our modified lasers angle into the drum, and a vent funnels out directing the resulting GeV e-beam against a tungsten target. This beam hitting the target creates high-energy photons, whose own subsequent contact with the target results in the muon pairs we're after.

With his back to me and his headphones on, Deran doesn't hear my approach. When I place a hand on his shoulder, he startles so violently he drops his precision spanner.

"Don't you know you shouldn't sneak up on a man with tools in his hand?" Deran's grumble is out of character.

"Sorry, I didn't mean to give you a fright."

Deran shakes his head. "No, it's not you. Not really."

Stymied, I frown. "Deran, you're not making sense."

There goes that hand again. Not that the spikes need any help. They're already standing on end, and I resist the urge to touch them, although I'm desperate to know what they feel like. How are they always so spiky? I have to use tons of hairspray to even remotely duplicate a similar effect.

"Chiara! Are you listening?"

I realize I wasn't. "Sorry, I was distracted. Could you repeat that?"

"After our discussion last night, I started today by going through the explanations you gave me, trying to pinpoint the error."

I groan. "You're not alone. I've redone the calculations several times and still can't fathom why our results are off. Care to look at them with me again?"

A quick nod and Deran pulls a cube from his pocket.

"You carry that around with you?"

"Only when I'm working on a problem."

No smile, just a stern expression. This Deran is disconcerting. I want his smile back. With a flick of his wrist, Deran brings the holographic design to life.

He doesn't tarry. "I've checked our spectral beam combined fiber laser, and confirmed we are achieving the desired petawatts, as well as a pulse rate in your range of acceptable femtoseconds. So, the laser's not the problem."

"Alright, how about the injection point?"

"I've checked that too. Although it's a little more complicated, with us firing the laser into our specially-shaped drum at an angle instead of directly into the center of a cylinder like everyone else before us did."

I expand my fingers over the injection point on the holo to enlarge it. "So, we're firing the laser into the chamber, so it hits here," I point, "then using the drum's curvature to amplify the wakefield."

Deran scratches his head. "No, using a forty-five-degree angle as you specified, the laser hits here." Deran stabs a point lower down.

"That can't be right. If we use…" I begin listing the variables for the complex formula, only to have Deran interrupt after the third one.

"Wait! How did you get 1,432?"

I blink, the numbers so ingrained after my constant recalculations this morning, I have to think. "Based on the curvature of the drum at this point, a ten-degree angle, and—"

Clang!

The unexpected sound, harsh and resounding, makes me break off. I stare at Deran, never having seen him angry before. He's gripping the spanner he smashed against the metal wall of the drum so tightly, his knuckles are white.

"Deran?" The single word warbles out, too high pitched for him not to notice.

"Ugh, Chiara, I'm so sorry!"

Deran covers his face with his hand, then separates his fingers to peek out at me. At least he isn't angry anymore. "For what?"

A pained expression crosses Deran's face. "How mad would you be if I told you the problem was my fault?"

Not something I'd even considered. I keep my tone carefully neutral. "What do you mean?"

"The angle of beams was off. With the drum's curvature, I made adjustments based on the specs you gave me. Because I, *incorrectly*," Deran adds emphasis, "assumed you didn't take the curvature into account. I should've known you would've factored that in."

Huh, he's taking all the blame, laying none of it at my feet. Even though I should've thought to discuss this part of the design with him. But how was I to know we'd both assume the other wouldn't account for the curvature?

I'm so relieved we've solved the problem, it supersedes any anger I might otherwise have felt at this unnecessary delay. At last, we can move forward! I throw my arms around Deran, giving him a hug, then laughing at his surprise.

Deran tilts his head. "You're not mad?"

"No! I'm ecstatic we've solved this. We're nearly there!"

Now Deran laughs too, his relief finally coming through. What a glorious sound it is. Soon, we're bouncing around like firecrackers, shrieking with delight.

The ruckus we raise is enough for Silvan to peer at us over the edge from the outside. "Everything okay down there?"

His mystified expression only sends me into fresh fits of laughter, aware none of Deran's team has ever seen me acting less than professional before.

Deran answers for us both. "We've solved the problem."

The loud whoop from Silvan has me whooping too. Then Deran joins in, as Silvan explains to someone else outside, presumably on the floor.

From the multitude of hoots and hollers erupting, the entire team is assembled down there. Deran and I are still jumping about gleefully when I register the sudden silence.

Glancing up, I find fear on Silvan's face, note his rigid expression. *Ugh, now what?*

Deran notices it too because he stops jumping about, worry creasing his brow. "What's wrong?"

"Boss, you'd better come out here."

Silvan disappears back down the ladder. I glance at Deran but find him equally stumped. Instead of offering for me to go ahead of him as usual, he grabs the ladder before I can.

"I should go first and see what's wrong. Stay here."

I'm touched he wants to take care of me, but this is my workshop, my project. If anyone should deal with any trouble, it's me. Despite his reproachful backward glances, I follow him up.

We crest the rim, him first and me a second later. One glance at the workshop floor explains why he halted. A mindhunter lurks at the base of the drum, eyes roaming the immediate area, body poised for action.

"You the man in charge here?" The mindhunter addresses Deran, voice clipped, like grinding the words out takes enormous effort.

I don't care who this man is. I won't have him disrupting my work. "No, that would be me," I reply, voice cold. "Why are you here?"

I sense, rather than see, the shock in Deran and his team. I doubt anyone speaks to mi—these people this way. But I'm too angry to care. I won't have my work interrupted. It's too important. I *must* finish.

"My apologies, ma'am. I was just verifying there was no disturbance requiring my intervention."

Glucose is a monosaccharide with formula C6H12O6 or H–(C=O)–(CHOH)5–H. Its five hydroxyl (OH) groups are arranged in a precise pattern along its six-carbon back. "As you can see, no disturbance. Just a celebration at a breakthrough. Now please leave."

I'm almost shocked when the man does. *Photosynthesis: 6CO2 + 6H2O → C6H12O6 + 6O2.* I continue reciting formulas for at least five minutes after he departs. Then I turn to Deran. My words die on my lips when I see his expression and those of his team. "What?"

"I can't believe you told him to leave—and he did!" Leini, another team member, says, awe in her voice.

With a slow grin, I shake my head. "I can't believe it either."

Deran's team talk amongst themselves, and he steps closer, keeping his voice low. "Didn't I say you were special?"

I swat his arm. A deliciously muscular arm. The thought derails me before I remember what I was going to say. "Yeah, right. Only for as long as…" I leave the sentence unfinished, knowing Deran will understand the rest: *only for as long as I'm useful.*

Sighing at the thought, then remembering what made our unwelcome "guest" appear, I bounce from foot to foot. "Did we really solve the problem?"

"Yes! You had it right all along, or I did, depending how you look at it. Our problem lay in communication. Now we have that figured out, let's fix this first part. I'm hopeful we'll get the results we want."

"If not?"

"Then we work through every other part of your diagram and confirm we haven't miscommunicated on other things."

"Time to get to work then?"

Deran nods, and we begin by returning to the original sketch I gave him, me explaining my math, my reasoning behind the numbers. After working through the calculations together, Deran notes the adjustments required to the machinery supporting the tubes shooting the lasers into the drum.

Despite Deran's urging to go home and reassurances he'll call me as soon as the changes are complete, I stay in the workshop, too eager to be there when they finish to leave.

The engineering team work all the way through the night. I hadn't realized they would need to dismantle the drum and then build it up from scratch again, but I support them the best I can: passing tools, doing coffee runs, playing loud, thumping music. Anything to keep them going.

Because if this works, if I get the quantity of muons I want, I can free my family.

4 6

The sun, sneaking through the thin slits serving as windows in the workshop, rims the top of the machine with gold when Deran lopes up to me. He wipes his hands on a rag, a tired smile creasing his face.

"We're done."

I'm too excited to acknowledge my bone-deep weariness. "We can run a test?"

"Yes." Deran's laughter is more energizing than the cup of coffee I clutch in one hand.

"Let's do this then!" I turn, the coffee cup slipping from limp fingers and smashing onto the floor when I find the mind—man, security guy, right behind me.

I shriek and place a hand over my heart. "Don't you know better than to sneak up on people?"

Even though I'm already running formulas in my head again, I notice the way his eyes (face, body) show no emotion. I ramp up the difficulty of the formulas, then attack the Riemann hypothesis.

"Sorry, ma'am. I was ordered to be present for this test."

Questions rise and are quelled. My apprehension only increases when a second ULS (upper level security) man appears in the doorway. To my dismay, two more follow.

My voice shakes, but I get the question out, addressing the first man who snuck up on me. "Is there a problem here to need so much protection?"

"No, ma'am. Just want to be sure the area is secure."

Irritated and off my stride, I snap a response. "I would think being here in CC HQ, with all the safety measures required to enter the building, let alone my lab or this workshop, is security enough. We don't need you. Please leave."

"Sorry, ma'am. We can't do that."

Agitated, I put a mental clamp on my emotions. Like a rubbery eel, the clamp slithers off. I fasten it a second time, only thinking one thing: I want these ULSs gone. I don't want them here when I test the machine. They are too distracting. I don't have space to think. How am I supposed to test the machine properly if I can't think?

Are they here to… I concentrate on my math problem again, picking up pieces of the broken cup as I do. When I rise and start walking toward the exit, the same ULS blocks my way.

"I'll take that, ma'am."

Will you stop calling me that? "No, thank you, I'll take care of it."

Sidestepping him, I resume my walk toward the exit. My limbs are geared for flight, trembling with repressed adrenaline, but I maintain a measured pace. I exit the workshop, halfway back to the lab before I realize I have a shadow. Al-Li and Astatine!

Resigned, I stop at the next trash receptacle I encounter, dumping the broken pieces. Then, numb, I turn and traipse back, my shadow never leaving my side.

When I reenter the workshop, I witness the warning in Deran's eyes and acknowledge it with the barest hint of a nod. Nothing we can do except press on.

"Deran, are you and your team ready?"

"Yes. Everyone's in place."

I hear his unspoken words. *Ready to do this, so can we please get on with it so these people leave?*

With hands that won't stop trembling, I head for the control room, then take my place behind the viewing window separating this room from the rest of the workshop. I begin our pre-test checks.

Machines hum and come to life as we activate various parts of the machine. Colored lights blaze awake across the control panel once energy surges through them. Cursors blink on holoscreens, waiting for the information feeds to come through.

Then the checks are done. It's time. "Starting the lasers."

Deran and his team hush, watching as we repeat the process we've attempted so many times before. A process we've only ever failed at. My eyes never leave the information feed, scanning the data. As the numbers climb, I keep my growing glee in check.

When more than a minute passes, I observe the tentative jubilation Deran and his team display. At two minutes, grins have slipped onto some of their faces. By the time we reach five minutes, a cap we've never attained before, we're all bouncing in our chairs.

The numbers have exceeded my expectations. We're producing muons at an unprecedented rate. Unable to contain my excitement a second longer, I leap out of my chair and face Deran, knowing my smile is a higher wattage than the readings on some of my screens. "We did it!"

Instead of answering, Deran sweeps me into his arms, hugging me to him and lifting me off the ground as he swings me in circles. "We did!"

I laugh, his team joining in until we're one rambunctious mass, jumping and shouting and slapping each other's backs, pumping our fists in the air. Reality crashes down when Mr. Surly steps in front of me. (If he doesn't want to give me his name, I'll assign him one.)

"Was the test successful, Miss Baschet?"

His use of my name is ice water drenching me. More than a wake-up call. He's only using my name now when he's been calling me "ma'am" all along because—zeta of s equals one plus one divided by two to the power s plus...

"Miss Baschet?"

I blink, then remember his question. "Yes, the test was successful. Now will you and the others please leave?"

Almost fainting with relief when the man turns and marches away, I mentally return to Euler's product formula, multiplying both sides by the second term. This doesn't stop me from noticing the other ULSs following Mr. Surly, with not a single word exchanged between them.

I keep up my mental math, shivering, until Deran places a hand on my shoulder. "I think it's safe now."

Eyes wide and voice low, I turn to Deran. "Mr. Surly can read minds."

Deran raises an eyebrow. "Mr. Surly?"

"That—that—first one! The one I almost bumped into."

A smile quirks Deran's lips. "You gave them names?"

"It's what I do. Get over it and tell me I'm right. About what he could do."

Deran sighs. "You know I can't be sure. What makes you think you are?"

"I yelled at him to stop calling me 'ma'am' in my head. And what does he do? Next time he addresses me, it's 'Miss Baschet.'"

Silence follows my declaration. I can tell Deran's weighing my words, considering an answer.

"Based on your observation, you're more than likely right. But it would be dangerous to assume anything with those people."

I note how carefully Deran refers to them. No matter how low I keep my voice, there is still a remote chance either the cameras or some mindhunter with enhanced hearing could pick up on our conversation.

"Fine. But we know one thing for sure."

"What?"

"Word of this will get back to the director."

With a grim smile, Deran nods. "Since it will, we'd better make sure we're ready, should he decide to come down here and inspect things himself."

We turn. While we were talking, the rest of Deran's team has crept up on us. They've surrounded us in a loose circle. Intentional on their part? I want to ask Deran, but then he gives the faintest nod to his team.

Apparently, some unspoken agreement exists between them. Sudden curiosity burns, and I fidget again, searching for a stylus. Deran grins at me.

"What's up now?"

"Can we go get something to eat? Maybe pick up something for the team too? We've been here all night, and I just realized none of us have had any solid food for hours."

Laughter follows my comment. "You mean vending machine snacks aren't proper food?" But understanding glimmers in Deran's eyes. He turns to his team. "Chiara and I are doing a breakfast run. Who wants what?"

They negotiate a takeout place they can all agree on, and we place the order online since each of us is required to wand our arm over the order to match food (read: tray color) to people. Once the order has been placed, Deran addresses them again.

"Alright, Chiara and I will be back in about thirty minutes. Take some time to clean up or catch a power nap. We'll run more tests as soon as we finish eating." Fatigued smiles greet his words. Deran turns to me. "Shall we?"

"Yes! I'm ravenous!"

Neither of us speaks until we're well out of the building and far along the path to the mall. When Deran grasps my hand, then raises an eyebrow, I don't hesitate.

"Do you and your team have some sort of agreement to protect one another when you're trying to hide things from the cameras at HQ?"

Deran's grin erases some weariness from his face. "Chiara, I know you understand what you're asking, but you'll have to be a little more specific for my benefit."

I outline what I observed.

"Hmm, it seems we're not as discreet as I thought. We'll have to work on that."

"I knew it!" The thought of a team he can trust to this extent (and who trust him the same way) has me lapsing into silence.

"Not what you were expecting?"

The frown marring Deran's face has me rushing to explain. "No, no, I just wish… I wish I had friends I could trust as much and who would do the same for me."

Deran squeezes my hand. "Give it time. You've only been with the people in your lab a short while, right?"

"If you call two years a short time. That's when they made me head."

"In relative terms, it is a short time. Also, I'm sure you're aware your age counts against you."

I dip my head in agreement. Some in my lab I know I'll never call more than acquaintances. Many for whom the thought of accountability to someone so much younger than them will forever rankle.

Deran continues. "I've known the people in my team for years. We were at school together, graduated together, and have worked together ever since."

My mind goes to the people I was at school with. "At least you had friends."

Deran stops walking, turning me to face him, keeping his eyes on mine. "Chiara, accept that you're special. That's going to come with a few negatives, like small-minded individuals trying to diminish you. Don't let those negatives grow into monsters."

While I nod acceptance, I still yearn for the sort of friendships he has.

Nudging my chin up with a gentle hand, Deran's earnest eyes find mine again. "Give the relationships time. Until then, you have me."

Laughter bursts free, his expression so endearing I can't help it.

"That's better. Now let's collect our food."

By the time we pick up breakfast, return to the lab, and eat, nearly an hour has passed. I'm just rising to dust crumbs from my clothes, (thank you, workshop cleaning droids who never stop), ready to analyze the data, when the clomp of approaching boots sounds down the hallway.

My gaze flies to Deran. Boots like that belong to only one group of people—and there are a lot of them this time.

Seeing my panic, Deran uses subtle hand gestures to tell me to calm down. I notice him doing the same with his team. Telling them to stand down?

Before I can move, Cygnus sweeps into the workshop, entourage of min—minus men in tow. I stifle the giggle, wondering what they think of me calling them minus men. Then berate myself for thinking anything at all. Math formulas crowd my mind, and I pick one at random to work on as we all snap out the greeting Cygnus expects.

"Chiara! How lovely to see you!"

I dip my head in a small bow. "Thank you, Director. Likewise." No greeting for either Deran or his team.

"I hear you've had a breakthrough."

I give the minus men with Cygnus a withering stare, for all the good it will do since they're such automatons. "Yes, Director. But it's too early to draw any conclusions. We've only run the test once. I still have to analyze the data. Work out any wrinkles."

Cygnus walks right up to me, black eyes glittering, cold. "Come now, Chiara! We both know when you solve a problem, it's solved. Show me!"

"Director, I must object." I keep my family, and my plans for them and the machine, stashed in the very deepest recesses of my brain, the part not trying to solve the Hodge conjecture. Another tiny piece of my brain is given to the rest of my answer. "I haven't had time to vet our earlier results."

"Chiara, I hear your objections. But I want to see your work for myself."

Like you'd understand them. Al-Li! If $p>k$, then alpha must contain some dz, where z... "Director, if I could just have half a day to verify the results?" I glare at the minus men. Abruptly, I don't care. I have to speak my mind. "It was a little distracting having these upper-level security people here while we did the initial run. I'd just like to run more tests, be sure of my accomplishment, without them present and interfering."

"Nonsense. They're here for your safety."

"But—" I sense the others cringing as I attempt to defy Cygnus and then, too late, detect the malicious gleam lurking Cygnus's eyes. Was it there before? If so, why? I'm too addled to censor my thoughts.

"Run the machine, Chiara. Now!"

I dip my head a second time. "Yes, Director."

Trepidation filling me, I lead Cygnus to the control room. I don't know if we can replicate what happened earlier. While it's true the machine ran for longer than any of our previous tests, and the results were stellar at first blush, I have no confidence. Without analysis, I can't say for sure what produced the higher numbers.

But Cygnus has given his command. I have to go ahead with this— and pray the results will be equally remarkable the second time around.

47

To give Deran's team extra time to be sure all our pre-checks are accurate, I pace myself as I run through the safety routine required before starting the machine.

Then I can't delay any more. "Initiating the lasers."

I watch, holding my breath as numbers stream onto the screens again. For a few seconds, the test runs as before. Then I frown. Something's not right. The numbers are too low—and falling.

Cygnus realizes it too, only because the graph showing the differential between input and output veers violently into negative territory. Why didn't I think to turn the graphic off before we started?

I feel his eyes boring into me. I don't want to turn and face him.

"Miss Baschet!"

He only calls me that when I'm in serious trouble. With a deep breath, I turn to him. "Yes, Director?"

"You call this a success?"

"No, Director. These results are the opposite of what we achieved this—"

"No excuses, Miss Baschet. Either you succeed, or you don't. I suggest you attempt the former."

"If you would permit me to explain—"

"Fix it!"

Cygnus storms out of the control room. His minus men follow. Absolute silence is all that remains in the wake of his departure.

I can't move. As I gasp for air, I realize I can't breathe either, then can't seem to fill my lungs fast enough. Drowning, I bend forward, tucking my head between my knees.

A hand touches my shoulder, and without looking, I know it's Deran.

"How can I help?"

"I don't think you can."

Deran rubs gentle circles on my back, and I want to sob. As if the thought is permission, a tear leaks out. Then my nose is running. I sniffle, and a tissue appears.

With a sigh, I take the tissue, then slowly lift my head, blowing my nose and dabbing at my eyes. Why won't the tears stop? These are not the wrenching sobs of immediate anguish. No, they're the prelude to what's coming. Because I know something unthinkable is on the horizon.

The fury on Cygnus's face right before he left is proof. More terrifying was the triumph sparking in his eyes right before he snuffed it out.

I have no doubt he has something diabolical planned—I just don't know what, besides a punishment doled out to those I love, those I care about, rather than to me personally. Because why hurt his prize when he can torture me far more effectively through my family?

The sobs rise inside, but I stuff them back down. I have to fix this, have to find a solution before something atrocious happens. Resolve stiffens my spine. I finally turn to Deran, finding his face reflecting all the same mixed emotions I'm experiencing.

Deran's voice is soft. "What went wrong?"

"I don't know. But we have to fix it. Now."

There's no need to explain the ramifications of failing Cygnus to Deran. Or his team. They grasp the gravity of the situation too, if their bleak faces are any sign.

I inject enthusiasm into my voice, although I'm not sure I succeed when my voice comes out sounding like I've had one too many whiffs of helium. "Come on! We can do this! Let's break it down and find the problem."

Twitches on some faces as they try to hide their grins.

"Yes, you can all have some happy gas too if we can get this right." The distinction between nitrous oxide, more commonly known as happy gas, and helium will go over most of their heads so I don't bother explaining. But I think they get the gist of my meaning when laughter ripples through them.

"Right on!" Koni slaps Silvan's shoulder. "Let's get to it!"

Deran's team filters back into the workshop, but Deran places a hand on my arm, holding me back. "Are you going to explain your tears? I know they weren't purely a result of the failed test."

I run a hand under my right eye, wiping away the lingering moisture. My laugh is shaky. "Okay if I tell you later? I don't think I can deal with all that right now and fix the machine at the same time."

Deran's lips twist in displeasure. "Only if you promise to tell me and not let this slip past without confronting it."

"Deal." I turn before he can see the fresh tears spilling at the tenderness in his voice. His concern is a little overwhelming. How have I never noticed before that I haven't had a genuine connection like this with anyone outside of my family? Not even with Sarissa.

The discovery troubling, I shove it to the far reaches of my mind. It's getting crowded. Deran's right. I'll have to address those issues at some point. *But not right now.* Now, I need to focus on the machine. Get it fixed.

Despite the zeal with which we attack the problem, I can't shake the growing urgency within, the impending doom of the hammer dropping to strike a mortal blow.

When Hag Lady calls mid-afternoon, I'm deep into some calculations, stylus in hand, running formulas. I accept the call without checking who it is. Hag Lady's voice at the other end of the line stills me. "Chiara, the director has set up a meeting with your family."

My blood curdles. Hot water striking cold cream. Excitement over seeing my family clashing with that dread roiling in my gut. "When?"

"The SerSents are already on their way. Expect them any minute." Hag Lady ends the call. What did I expect? More information? A civil goodbye?

My stylus slips from numb fingers. I fumble for it, twisting it into my hair, trying to pull myself together. As if Deran has a sixth sense warning him something is up, I spot him through the window of the control room, striding toward me.

Before he makes it, the SerSents appear at the workshop entrance. Deran veers toward them mid-stride. Is he going to tell them I'm not here? Or just ask what they want? Only aware I don't want him getting into trouble on my behalf, I rush out of the control room.

"Deran! It's okay. They're here for me. They're taking me to see my family."

Deran halts, turning to face me. In this position, the SerSents can't see him mouthing words to me. "Are you sure about this?"

I shake my head. I'm not, but what choice do I have?

Deran's next question is audible. "Do you want me to come with you?"

While I desperately want to say yes, if Cygnus gets wind of it, my family, or Deran, will only be in more trouble. Because of me. "Thank you, I appreciate the offer. But I can't accept."

Deran must understand because instead of looking upset, his eyes flash. What rash idea is he concocting now?

The nearest SerSent has reached me. He grabs my arm and yanks me toward him. "Let's go."

I want to scream at him that there's no need to manhandle me. But the storm brewing in Deran's eyes deters me. If I say something, he may act on that anger of his. Again, causing more trouble than it's worth.

As the SerSents march me past, I try to reassure Deran. "I'll be okay. Don't worry."

Although Deran nods, his eyes are gray fire. Then I'm out of the workshop, being dragged down the corridor. When I'm shoved into the elevator, I turn so I can see the floor number they're taking me to.

I want to sink into a relieved puddle on the floor. It's the usual floor for visiting my family. The one requiring special access.

Not the level taking me on a circuitous route to the bowels of CC HQ. To the dungeons, which can only be reached using a special elevator leaving from the floor where Cygnus's office is located. Where I was confined to a cell, forced to watch my family starve. While I'm comforted, it's not *that* floor with its demons, the same mantra keeps running through my head: unscheduled, unscheduled, unscheduled.

The only time I get an unscheduled visit with my family is for punishment or reward. I know this meeting relates to the former. Imagining the punishment Cygnus has come up with this time, my heart quails within me.

When we reach the final corridor, the one with the door at the end that will open to my family, my legs can barely support me. The SerSents really are dragging me now, my feet not wanting to cooperate. If they're so eager, then let them handle my full weight. I slump against them.

The abrupt increase in their burden surprises the SerSents, and they almost drop me. Snappy growls and tightens his grip on my arm, hefting me up.

"Walk! Or we'll let you fall to the floor and pull you by your hair."

Stunned, I stutter back into a shuffle. The SerSents have never treated me this way before. This realization comes with the next: are they behaving so heinously because they know what I'll find on the other side of that door? And they're… what? Gearing themselves up for my reaction so they can beat me or subdue me, guilt-free?

Then I'm out of time for deliberations. We're at the final door. While Flinty holds me, Snappy wands his arm across the access panel. The door slides open. Without a chance to absorb what I'm seeing, I'm hurled inside. I stumble, regaining my balance, but the door hisses shut before I can twitch another muscle.

Not that I could. I remain rooted, fear freezing me in place, terror a vise squeezing my heart. My mother and brother and sister are crying, their wails tearing at my fragile control. Only one question comes to mind. "Where's Xanin?"

48

My mom is so caught up in her grief, she doesn't hear me the first time. Fearing the worst, I repeat the question more harshly. "Where's Xanin?"

Startled, my mother stops blubbering, then wails, her cry setting my siblings to squalling louder. "They took him!"

Took him? A strangled sob escapes my own lips. *He's not dead!* Struggling for a semblance of control, I grab my mother's arms, giving her a little shake. "Mom, get a grip. You're upsetting Tavi and Frankie." *And me.*

As my mom fights for calm, tries to stop the sobs gushing out of her, I take in her tear-stained face, red-rimmed eyes, bird's nest hair. Whatever happened to Xanin, it was a while ago.

Between shuddering gasps, my mom rasps an explanation. "Last night… we were sleeping… they broke the door down and grabbed him… six of them." Mom dissolves into a fresh jag of tears.

The jigsaw pieces she's provided fall around me, begging for order. "Last night?"

My mom just nods, too overwhelmed by grief to speak. My siblings have stopped crying, their eyes huge, watching me. *Can I please scream too?* They're expecting me to do something. To bring Xanin, their protector, back.

Carefully, I wrap an arm around each of them, tucking them in close, both to provide comfort and so I can no longer see their hopeful faces. I try to sort through the questions pummeling me. "Mom, why did they take Xanin?"

"I don't know." At least it wasn't a wail this time, but her tone conveys her confusion. "Xanin did nothing wrong. He was excelling in school—and his job."

Her reply gives rise to a fresh question best left for another time. They won't help me solve the current predicament. "Do you know where he is now?"

Mom only shakes her head, eyes frantic. "Chiara, why did they take him?"

I hear the accusation. Like I somehow had something to do with this. Then I recognize the bone-deep fear there, too. *She's thinking the same thing that happened to me is happening to Xanin.* One look at her face tells me she's worried Xanin won't be the last child they take from her either.

"Mom, *who* took Xanin?"

"The security people, you know, the ones who—"

Flinty and Snappy cut the rest of her sentence off as they barrel into the room, followed by four more SerSents.

"That's enough, Mrs. Baschet!" Snappy grabs my mom and propels her through the open door.

My mom beats her hands against Snappy's chest, shrieks at him to let her go. But her attempts are futile, her blows useless against the SerSent's armor. Before I can stop them, two other SerSents grab Tavi and Frankie, snatching them out of my arms.

Then they're tossing my squirming, bawling brother and sister over their shoulders as they hustle out of the door. I run after them, but I'm too late. When I'm less than an inch away, the door slams shut.

I stare at the door for a second before I beat it. "Let me out! Let me see my family!" I'm about to scream profanities, call them names, when I remember the camera.

Torn between expressing what I really feel and pretending I don't care, I realize it doesn't matter. Cygnus was no doubt watching this entire scene. He's already seen the anguish he's caused. No doubt relished it. What do I have to gain by not letting go?

Painful as it is, I can still scrape a small victory from the ashes heaped around me. I ban the cynical smile seeking release. If Cygnus was prepared to take my brother away on a failure, one I warned him was possible, he'll do *anything* to get this machine working. Does he realize how much he overplayed his hand?

Desperate for a problem I *can* solve, I ponder what's in it for him if I succeed. Why is *this* machine so important? Is he having troubles with his board? I haven't heard any rumblings. Then again, I rarely do. Whether by design or simply because I don't travel in high enough circles, it's irrelevant.

What is relevant is how much Cygnus wants this machine. Just how far will he go to get it? If I ask for Xanin back before I continue working, will he grant the request?

I weigh demanding his return now against the repercussions it might have for my mother and Tavi and Frankie, the exercise giving me a headache. Suddenly, the room is stifling. I want out!

I pound on the door again, then fall through and land on my hands and knees when it opens unexpectedly. I blink up at the SerSent staring down at me (where are Flinty and Snappy?) and aim for a glare. "Where have you taken my family? I demand to see them!"

The SerSent snorts, then touches his stun stick. "Are you going to come quietly, or do I need to encourage you?"

This time, my glare has all the heat it lacked the first time. It helps that I'm also no longer lying prone on the floor. I huff, shaking the dust off my lab coat as I wish I could shake the man off the planet. I tilt my head when he doesn't move. "Well? Are you leading the way?"

His hand twitches—I'll call him Switch—like he still wants to use his stun stick. But he must think better of it because his eyes slide up to the camera in the room, still visible through the open door.

Without another word, he spins and leads me back down the corridor. Now that I'm outside, my bravado fails me. Uncertain about where he's leading me, my mind tackles the problem of where they took Xanin and why.

The most obvious question is timing. Why take Xanin last night? Was the Director monitoring my progress through those hidden cameras and decided ahead of time I needed "motivation?" Or was the failed test merely a convenient excuse? Meaning if today's failure wasn't the reason he took Xanin, what was?

I find a viable answer in my mom's earlier accusation. Is Xanin's disappearance connected to mine—to the mysterious gene I read about in my file, a gene my brothers and sister and I share?

As I try to make the pieces fit, I scarcely notice where we're going until the SerSent dumps me in my office. I wouldn't have noticed that either, except he slams my door on his way out, making me jump and alerting me to where I am.

Thankful I wasn't led somewhere abysmal, my mind picks up the thread it was working on. If they took Xanin because of the gene, why now as opposed to any other time?

As though thinking of my mom and Tavi and Frankie generates the image, I see their faces again. How wan they all looked. Was it my imagination, or has Frankie gotten even thinner? And Tavi... *Astatine!* I replay the section, appalled I missed it the first time.

The purple skin of a bruise at least a few days old mars her lovely face. Meaning she had to have received the blow before they took Xanin. Did he try avenging her somehow, the reason they seized him?

My thoughts are corkscrewing out of control when my office door bangs open. I jump for a second time. Deran stands in the doorway, eyes obsidian storm clouds.

Face ashen, he crosses the space between us, drawing me into his arms. I feel so safe here, I want to stay, soak in the strength he offers. But I'm suddenly mad at him.

With an effort, I lean out of his arms and beat his chest. "Let me go! You're the reason he's gone!"

Deran doesn't release me, those arms steel bands binding me to him. "Who's gone?"

"My brother! They took him! Deran, they took him!" The gut-wrenching sobs I've been expecting come then. Deran crushes me to him.

My emotions tangle. I want him to comfort me. I want him to let me go. His carelessness caused my brother's abduction. No, I was the one who wanted the information. Went after it.

As if sensing my struggle, Deran leans in close, whispering so even the most sensitive microphone won't hear his words, let alone a mindhunter far from this lab. "Trust me. I'll help you get him back."

My reply is hissed, the best I can do at keeping the volume down, considering the rage flooding me. "And how are you going to do that? We don't even know who took him or where!"

Deran uses one hand to pretend to stroke my hair, when he's really pushing my head closer to his. His lips are fractions of an inch from my ear when he whispers a second time. "Like I said, trust me. There's so much you don't know, so much I still have to tell you."

But I'm done. I can't stand being in his arms one second longer. I need space to breathe, space to think, space to process. I knee his groin, a trick I learned a long time ago from Xanin.

With a guttural groan, Deran bends forward, releasing me. But I couldn't have done a decent enough job because his hand snakes out to grab my wrist as I turn to flee.

Deran's voice is gravel, but he scrapes the words out, barely loud enough for me to hear, yet still soft enough to be for our ears alone. "If you won't listen to me now, at least do me one favor?"

Sure my eyes are spitting fire at him, I try twisting free. His grip only tightens. Then he tugs me close enough to whisper directly into my ear again. "Whatever you do, stop eating the food the conglomerate provides."

His request is so startling, I stop struggling and stare. Did I hear right? What am I supposed to eat?

"Also, know I'll do everything in my power to make sure they don't do the same thing to your brother they did to my sister. And Sarissa."

My brain hitches, stuck on the words. Abruptly, there's no need to fight him anymore because he releases me, bending all the way over and breathing hard. Aware I'm free, I don't hesitate. I turn and bolt.

Sprinting past my gaping team, I tear out the lab, down the stairs, through the foyer and out of CC HQ. Questions driving me, I pressure my feet to keep up with my mind. Blind to where I'm going, I'm halfway to the trundle before I digest Deran's parting comment. What did he mean when he said he didn't want the same thing that happened to Sarissa (and his sister! *Astatine!*) happening to Xanin? Then there was his cryptic comment about the food. I almost regret kicking him now, hoping I haven't alienated my only potential ally.

But I'm sure of only one thing: Deran has the answers I need. And I plan to get them. One way or another, whether he's willing or not.

Visit Bronwyn's website for more of her books!
https://bronwynleroux.com/books/

ALSO BY BRONWYN LEROUX

Want more futuristic fantasy? Join Jaden and Kayla as they come face to face with a nightmare only they share... Pick up *Dawn of Dreams*, the first book in the *Destiny* series.

Feel like a little urban fantasy instead? Discover whether Forecaster wins her battle to regain the simplicity of the life she once cherished as Nylah. Get *Forecast of Shadows* now!

Other books by Bronwyn Leroux:

Breach (A *Destiny* companion novella)

Dawn of Dreams (*Destiny*, Book 1)

Dogs of Doom (*Destiny*, Book 2)

Doors of Destiny (*Destiny*, Book 3)

Duel of Death (*Destiny*, Book 4)

Forecast of Shadows

IF YOU ENJOYED THIS BOOK...

I would love it if you would please share it!

Reviews not only help other readers like you find great books to read, but they encourage authors like me. They provide both motivation to keep going, and insight into what else you might like me to write with you in mind!

You can leave a review at
https://bronwynleroux.com/Attrition1Review

Can't leave a review on Amazon?
Leave a review on Goodreads at
https://bronwynleroux.com/GR-review

GET A FREE BOOK!

I love interacting with my readers and getting to know them as people. I also understand my readers hate spam as much as I do. For this reason, I only send the occasional newsletter with details on new releases, special offers and other bits of news you may find noteworthy. If you are interested in writing your own book, you can opt in for the additional bonus of weekly writing tips.

Enjoy these wonderful benefits, including your above-mentioned welcome gift, by signing up at https://bronwynleroux.com/FreeBreach

ABOUT THE AUTHOR

Born near the famed gold mines of South Africa (where dwarves are sure to prowl), it was the perfect place for Bronwyn to begin her adventures. They took her to another province, her Prince Charming and finally, half a world away to the dark palace of San Francisco. While the majestic Golden Gate Bridge and its Bay views were spectacular, the magical pull of the Colorado Rockies was irresistible. Bronwyn's family set off to explore yet again. Finding a sanctuary at last, this is Bronwyn's perfect place to create alternative universes. Here, her mind can roam and explore and she can conjure up fantastical books for young adults.

facebook.com/AuthorBronwynLeroux
twitter.com/bronwyn_leroux
instagram.com/bronwyn.leroux